I0522514

They'd put him on a ship back to Columbia, so what the hell happened?

Jon immediately turned to Carlos. "All right, what the heck did you see, back there?"

"Jon, it wasn't the truck—it was the bus. I'm almost positive that I saw the kid who shot A.J. on that bus. He was sitting by the window, and he should be sitting back in Colombia. Pablo…Pablo Robles…is his name."

Silence was Jon's immediate reaction, but his mind was churning. *Why the hell won't the past stay in the past? Should I call the commander? No! Carlos could have been mistaken, yet he's usually quite accurate with his observations. A quick check may give us an answer.* "Let's call the bus terminal. With any luck, they'll know where the bus originated and where it's headed by the time and location when you spotted it. Did you happen to catch the company name?"

"Yes, it was Trailways."

"Great! We were headed southwest when we passed it, and it was somewhere between eleven forty-five to twelve a.m. Hopefully, we can get some solid information before we jump the gun."

The answers Jon received from the Trailways terminal were not what he wanted to hear but had almost anticipated. The bus originated out of Miami, Florida, made a number of stops on its route north, before the stop in Annapolis. It would then head southwest, continuing on to a small town in north-western West Virginia. Its run would terminate in Harrisburg, Pennsylvania.

Jon asked the final question that he had to, but didn't want to. "What's the name of the town in West Virginia?"

The ticket agent's answer not only set off alarm bells but angered him as well. "It's the town of Sheridan. Not much to see or do there, but we do a fair trade with the area residents."

Jon thanked the dispatcher for the information, put his phone away, looked at Carlos, and relayed the information he had just received. "It's not one-hundred percent, but it looks as if you may have spotted our boy. I knew we should have terminated him. I'd better give the commander a call."

Carlos, too, was angry. "Sheridan is just down the road from Dodsonville, where A.J. lived. We stayed at that Red Apple Rest Motel between the two towns when we checked out of the one in Dodsonville. That kid's definitely gonna be a problem, unless he's stopped."

El Tigre is dead. This is a confirmed fact, but the legacy of evil and violence that he has sown continues to sprout. When these erupt, they inevitably affect Jon Morton, and, by association, Carlos Montoto. Once again, Jon and Carlos are forced to abandon their peaceful refuge as commercial fishermen and return to the dark world of violence and death. As before, this return is attributed to El Tigre and his convoluted criminal mind. Jon's last involuntary return to the world of covert action came close to getting him killed. Now he is facing one known man, plus the addition of an unknown group of murderous criminals, all hunting El Tigre's money, and all headed toward rural Dodsonville, West Virginia. Can Jon and Carlos terminate these criminals in time to prevent a blood-bath?

KUDOS for *Blood Money*

In *Blood Money* by JJ Burke, we are reunited with Jon Morton and Carlos Montoto as they are once again drawn into the world of black ops, violence, and death. Even though the Colombian criminal and terrorist, El Tigre, is dead, Jon and Carlos still aren't free of him. Things El Tigre set in motion before his death are coming back to haunt them. Now a group of killers is converging on a small mountain village in West Virginia, and Jon and Carlos are the only ones who can identify at least one of them. Sent by their former commander to identify and stop the criminals, Jon and Carlos soon discover that what they thought would be a simple cleanup operation could be a deadly fight for their lives. Well written, intense, and fast paced, this story will have you biting your nails and turning pages as fast as you can. I thoroughly enjoyed it. ~ *Taylor Jones, The Review Team of Taylor Jones & Regan Murphy*

Blood Money by J. J. Burke is the story of two former black ops soldiers who just want to live the quiet life of commercial fishermen. Jon Morton and Carlos Montoto have long since retired from the service but the black ops missions they participated in just won't stay in the past. Criminals from groups they targeted while in the service are out for blood. Now that the leader of the main group is dead, rumors of money he paid an informant being stashed in a small town in West Virginia are spreading rapidly, drawing opportunists and cold-blooded killers into the area. Agents posing as INS are on the case, but only John and Carlos have seen at least one of the criminals, so they are the only ones who can identify him. Convinced by their former commander to go to West Virginia to point out the man to the other agents on the scene, Jon and Carlos get much more than they bargained for. Like the two before it, *The Lethal Fisherman* and *Scattered Pieces, Blood Money* is fast paced, intense, and compelling. Once you start, you'll find it very hard to stop reading. An excellent addition to the series. ~ *Regan Murphy, The Review Team of Taylor Jones & Regan Murphy*

BLOOD MONEY

J. J. BURKE

A Black Opal Books Publication

BLOOD
MONEY

PROLOGUE

The unknown shooter had been identified as A.J. and had been killed. The oddity was that he was not killed by Jon or Carlos, but by a young man named Pablo Robles. Pablo was unknown to either Jon or Carlos and was seeking to revenge the death of his father. His father had been killed in the raid on El Tigre's island headquarters. The young Colombian had also been hunting for two-million dollars that El Tigre was to have paid A.J. for the information that led him to Jon. El Tigre told Pablo it would be his when he killed A.J. Although the money was assumed to exist, no one living knew that to be factual, and, if it did exist, where it was hidden.

Jon and Carlos had taken Pablo Robles into custody and put him on *La Luna Media,* the freighter he first arrived on. He was now, unwillingly, headed back to Colombia on the same freighter—without the money he believed to be rightfully his. He had been strictly warned that if he returned to the US, and if caught, he would be put on trial for murder. The captain of the freighter had also been strictly warned that he would be tried as complicit, to ensure that Pablo did not get off the ship until their arrival in Colombia.

Jon and Carlos were driving back to North Carolina to meet with Rosita and Sheri. Both men were relaxed and looking forward to the reunion, now that the insidious threat was ended. Jon, however, had a nagging sensation and could not help but wondering if it was truly completely over.

CHAPTER 1

In Retrospect

Sheriff Gabriel Tanner was still at his desk. It was well after eight-thirty in the evening, but Gabe was oblivious of time as he painstakingly tried to sort out, and put together, the events of the past three weeks. The legal-size yellow pad on his desk was covered with names, dates, and events—many with question marks. Unfortunately, there were far too many questions and far too few answers. For someone in law enforcement, unanswered questions yielded nothing but problems, usually coupled with more questions.

Albert James Johnson, known to everyone in this small mountain town as A.J., had been buried alongside his parents, just three days ago. The events that led to his death presented some disturbing inequities. He could have let it go, and no one in this small mountain town would have questioned his decision, but Gabe had made up his mind. He intended to get this mess sorted out, and properly ordered. This file wasn't about to be closed, until he was completely satisfied. *Fust thing er ta check off whut ah know, fer a fact. Mizz Polk tole me thet she had give Zeke's gun ta th' Johnsons, efter Zeb were shot. Thet prob'ly 'splains how A.J. knew 'bout who th' gun b'longed ta.* He paused in his though process, at that point and took a long look at the rest of the items on his list. *They ain't but jest a few unanswered items. Problem er they're all th' big uns, 'n' all ah got er guesses 'n' mebbe's—no facts. Ah need sum solid answers.*

Ah'm near positive thet A.J.'s th' one whut put thet arrer through Zeke 'n' ah'm shore Zeke burnt A.J.'s folks house, 'n' thet's where ah'm stuck. Ah ain't got th' bow 'n' no proof thet A.J. er anyone else 'roun' these parts ever owned one. Zeke's dead so ah cain't question him, 'n' th' same fer A.J. Thet's two dead ends, fer shore. Them two guys whut come t' town, jest days afore we heerd thet A.J. got killed—jest know they wuz more 'n they let on t' be. T'other thing er how come ah found A.J.'s truck 'pon thet spur en th' woods? How'd he git t' town 'n' back t' th' base fer ta be shipped out? Shore as shit he didn't walk! Then ta top er all off, he left ever'thin' ta me en his will. Gabe stared at the yellow pad for a while longer then made the only logical decision that he could at the moment. *'Peers ta me thet sum, er all, a these questions might never git put ta bed. Reckin ah'll jest set this list aside, 'n' keep er tucked away fer when an answer shows, 'n' they allus do! Shore wish ah cud find me a deputy ta hire. Seems thet fer a right small town, they's right much work.*

CHAPTER 2

A New Day

Jon's days, when he was working, usually began as a carbon-copy of the day before. This was not the result of intentional planning, but just that it had become a smooth and comfortable procedure. Toilet first then wash, shave, brush his teeth, comb his hair, and finally dress. He would, on occasion, stop in the kitchen for a glass of orange juice, and then out the door for his solitary walk to the docks. His routine was purposely simple and repetitive—a direct opposite from his former, covert world. *Today there'll be a new and welcome change in my routine. I get to take delivery of my new fishing boat and finally get back to a peaceful existence.* He smiled visibly at the thought of this new custom-built boat. *Can't wait. Have to remember to thank Tony, with a bottle of good bourbon, for giving me that connection.* Today Jon went to the kitchen in a more relaxed state of mind. *I'll get the coffee started then relax until Sheri wakes up.* His thoughts went briefly to last night. *That was a fantastic dinner. Frank hasn't lost his touch, and the Blue Pelican looks as if it's going to be around for a long time. Coffee's ready.* He poured a mug full of black coffee and walked toward the screened porch then changed his mind. *I'll just sit here until she gets up. The lounge chair will do for now.*

Old habits, which were life-savers or learned lessons were hard to let go of, and he automatically started a mental review of the crazy hunt to track down and eliminate a turned opera-

tive. Could we have found him any quicker? Did we miss any of the clues or signs? The more I go over it, the more I'm convinced that we did everything possible under the circumstances. Now that it's over and, after all is said and done, the three of us, Ertugal, Carlos, and I are lucky to be alive. That might not have been the case if it weren't for the intrusion of the unknown factor, and a damn lucky one at that. Carlos's casual observation allowed us to save Ertugal's ass. That kid, Pablo, without knowing it probably saved me or Carlos or even both of us from a fatal bullet. That alone was worth just putting him back on that boat to Colombia instead of causing him to disappear. If that's the case then how come I still have that nagging feeling that we should have also terminated that kid. We had the perfect opportunity, regardless of what transpired. The termination of the kid would have closed all the doors, leaving the field clean.

ᙒᘓᙒᘓ

He was abruptly brought back to the present. "Good morning, hon. Have you been up long? You must have been deep in thought for me to be able to walk right up to you without your noticing."

"I was doing a mental review of the new boat." *She doesn't need to know the truth in this instance.* He stole a glance at the clock. "Just shy of one hour till I have to go. Coffee's ready. I need a refill, and I'll get yours while I'm at it. Why don't you get comfortable on the porch, and I'll be right there?" *Let's see if I can push my luck.* "That is, unless you'd like to get comfortable in the bedroom?"

"Funny boy—coffee and the porch sound perfect, right now." She started for the porch door.

He was on the porch a minute later. "Here's your coffee and something else." He leaned over and kissed her long and firmly on the lips.

"That's a perfect starter. By the way, what time do we have to leave?"

"If we leave here by six-thirty, that should allow ample

time. I'll drop you with Rosita, and Carlos and I will continue to the dock."

"What time do you think you'll be back?"

"Barring any problems, we should be back in time for lunch. We're going to take her out for a shake-down run."

Sheri changed the subject abruptly and unexpectedly. "Jon, is it finally all over? No more return visits to that horrible military experience of yours. Can you—we—finally look forward to a normal life? I'm asking because I can't enjoy a relationship where I have to be in constant fear that something else is lurking in the shadows of your past."

I should have expected this, and I guess I can't blame her. "Yes, it's over and done with. This last mess has put the past behind me, and we can look forward to a future of normal lives." *I sure hope that's true, and I'm not just saying this for the moment. Sadly only time will tell.*

"Fantastic! Let's get dressed."

CHAPTER 3

Suerte

The *Luna Media* was rocking and pitching violently. She had gotten caught in a sudden squall that was sweeping across the southeastern Atlantic Ocean, off the coast of Georgia. Pablo Robles struggled to maintain his balance while climbing the ships ladder that led to the deck. A cold, clammy film of sweat coated his arms, neck, and forehead. His interior "room" in the ship's lower recesses was not much bigger than a closet, and like a closet was lacking a window. The ship's irregular, storm-tossed motion together with an ever-present aroma of diesel fuel had given him a severe case of motion sickness.

He threw open the door, lurched onto the deck, ignored the driving rain, and barely succeeded in stumbling to the rail. He was able to get his head over the rail an instant before beginning to vomit violently. This bout of regurgitation lasted for several minutes. When his stomach finally stopped churning, he stepped back, wiped his mouth on his sleeve, and retreated to a nearby bulkhead.

With his back planted against the steel wall, he slid to a sitting position on the deck, oblivious of the coarse, rusted areas on the steel wall. He looked out at the tossing wind whipped sea, and the visual effect of the waves going one way and the ship pitching and rolling, in various opposing directions, started another wave of nausea. This time Pablo couldn't make it to the rail. With a spasmodic lurch, he rolled to his side, in a futile attempt to rise. He managed to get to his knees, but no further, as violent retching took control leaving him helpless.

One half-hour later the squall was finally spent, and Pablo's resolve returned instantly, to replace his seasickness. *I must get the captain to take me back to Virginia, when he returns.* With that burning thought driving him, he headed for the bridge and the captain.

Pablo climbed the three ladders to the bridge and walked in. The captain was at the helm and didn't turn at the sound of his entry. "*Señor Capitán! Señor Capitán*! I must know—how soon do you return to *Los Estados Unidos*? I must get back and soon, very soon."

The captain was aghast at this rash request. "Didn't you hear a word when they told you that if you returned, you would be tried for murder? Worse still, if I bring you on my ship, I will be held as an accomplice and loose my captain's license. That is one thing I will never let happen. If you arc crazy enough to return, you're on your own." He paused to check his compass bearings then continued. "Now get th' hell out of here and leave me alone. I have to set a course for the port of Miami."

Pablo immediately changed his demeanor. "Miami? Where is this place?"

Not thinking along the same devious lines, the captain responded simply. "Florida—Miami is in southern Florida. I have to take on a shipment of farm machinery." He didn't, however, miss the slight smile that appeared briefly on Pablo's lips. "Don't get any fuckin' ideas about sneaking ashore. I will have a man stationed at the gangway, to ensure that you remain on board."

All traces of Pablo's smile of excited anticipation quickly vanished.

⌘⌘⌘

The sun had reappeared as two tugboats met the *Luna Media*, at the harbor channel entry, and expertly maneuvered her to the pre-designated pier for loading. Hawsers were tied off,

the gangway was lowered, and the captain went ashore to receive his copies of the shipping manifests and export documents. On board, members of the crew were preparing the on-
deck cargo area to receive the shipment. Pablo watched all of
this with a sinking sense of despair. He paced the deck, staying
away from the cargo area, his eyes darting repeatedly from the
dock to the gangway and inevitably, to the man standing
guard. When he met the guard's eyes, the man's visage went
from blank to a sardonic grin that read, *Just try it—I dare you.*
Pablo wasn't a fool. This man was, easily, twice his size and
from his looks, would truly relish the task of "keeping" him on
the ship.

❧❧❧

The shipment of new cargo was being hoisted aboard by
immense dockside cranes. The large wooden crates with black
stencils—denoting their contents, weight, and place of origin
—were stacked on deck, in the now readied on-deck cargo
area. The deck crew was busy with the loading and securing of
the crated cargo. Pablo purposely stayed well out of their way.
He walked casually along the dockside rail, but not closely
enough to arouse any suspicion. His eyes were constantly
searching, in a guarded manor, seeking some avenue of escape. As if seeing them for the first time, Pablo's gaze fell upon the hawsers, running from on deck cleats to dockside cap-
stans.

These heavy ropes were nearly two inches in diameter. *I
could, easily, slide down one of these, to the dock. It would be
no different than the lianas and vines, near my village, that I
used to swing on.* He started to, quickly, and without being
obvious look for the one that would offer the best opportunity.
It didn't take long for him to find his target. *That one, at the
rear of the ship, is furthest from the loading area. It will be a
longer slide but no matter. It is also the most distant point
from the gangway. That's my answer!*

Closer inspection of the tail of one of the hawsers showed a
glaring flaw in his plan. *There's no way I can slide on this*

rough, twisted cord. He would either have to find something that would slide on such a coarse surface or he would have to hang under the hawser, wrapping his legs around it and pulling himself along with a hand over hand progression. *That's much too long distance for me to try that type of escape, fifteen meters more or less.* It was at this time that his very empty stomach began to ache for food. His thoughts went from escape to his belly. *Perhaps I can go to the cook and pay him for a plate of food or even a simple sandwich.* His planning temporarily put aside, Pablo abandoned his inspection of the hawsers and went below, heading for the galley.

When he arrived at the galley, it was immediately evident, even prior to his entry. The air in that room held a mixed assortment of latent aromas from the residue of the last prepared meal, bacon being the primary one. The cook was nowhere to be seen. Pablo called out, "*Cocinero*! Where are you?"

After two repetitions, each louder than the former, an answer came from somewhere behind the kitchen equipment. "*Aqui*! You little pain in the ass. What do you want?"

Pablo wasn't intimidated by the strong response of the cook. "I'm hungry. Why else would I be here?" At first, there was no response to his statement, which prompted Pablo to start in the direction the cook's voice had come from.

He had barely gone ten feet when the response came. "I've got a hell of a mess here, to clean up. I don't have time to take care of your small problem."

Pablo continued walking towards the voice. He began to pick up a strange scraping sound, as he drew closer. *The sound is coming from that room with the light on.* It was the storeroom, and there was the cook, using a floor squeegee to gather a thick white substance which had spread over a substantial area of the floor.

Pablo saw an opportunity for free food. "What is that stuff? Perhaps I can help you clean it up."

The cook may not have cared one bit about this young man's hunger, but the offer to help was not only a surprise but very welcome. "It's lard. When that storm hit, a twelve kilo pail toppled from the shelf and split like a ripe melon." He paused, waving his arm about in a sweeping motion. "This is the result. It sticks to everything and is slippery as a skinned papaya." The cook had been scraping the slippery cooking grease into low piles then, using a dust pan, shoveling the lard into a large, black, garbage bag. This got rid of the bulk, but still left the floor dangerously slippery.

Pablo recalled his mother cleaning a greasy skillet with sand and a small amount of added salt. He saw an opportunity to benefit from the cook's dilemma. "I know how to clean the balance of this lard from the floor."

The cook paused in his efforts and looked at Pablo, skeptically. "Tell me, my smart young man, how would you do this?"

Without a moment's hesitation, Pablo responded, "Scrub the grease with a mixture of sand and some salt. I know that this works as I have seen it used."

The cook paused in his cleaning and thought about this for a moment, a perplexed look on his face. Suddenly, he brightened as if a problem had been solved. "Wait here for me. We have a drum of sand in the engine room, in case of an oil spill. I'll be right back." With that, he ran out of the kitchen.

Pablo stood without moving, for a moment, his eyes surveying the storeroom. His gaze fell upon the box of large, plastic garbage bags with a caution label indicating that each bag had a maximum capacity of thirty kilos. He paused, calculating the possibilities. *If a bag can hold that much weight, surely it would be much stronger in layers. That's my way ashore.*

Quickly, he pulled two bags from the box, pulled up his shirt, and wrapped them, tightly around his waist, at the same time, glancing nervously, toward the doorway. He then tucked his shirt back into his pants, securing and hiding the bags. With his prize secured, Pablo began to work on the remaining few areas of lard, collecting it in the same manner as the cook had.

Not more than five minutes had gone by, and the cook returned. "I have a bucket of sand. I'll get a box of salt then you can show me how we will clean this floor."

❦

A mixture of sand and salt was spread liberally over the lard coated area of floor and, with a coarse-bristle floor broom, the mixture was brushed back and forth to absorb the lard. The residue was then collected in piles and scooped up. Not only was the floor completely devoid of that dangerously slippery lard, it was actually cleaner than before the accident. Pablo's reward was a generous ham and cheese sandwich, with mayonnaise and lettuce, accompanied by a cold soda. They parted amicably, the cook immensely pleased with the clean-up and, Pablo, his hunger now satiated, and with what he was sure would be his means of escape to shore.

CHAPTER 4

Escape

Pablo again ventured back on deck and was met with a baleful look as he approached the gangway. It was quite evident that the "guard," appointed by the captain, was still hoping for a confrontation. "You don't think you're good enough to get by me, do you, *perito*?" The man was defiant and definitely challenging.

Pablo's reply caught him by surprise. "I have no wish to go ashore. I just want to know how soon we are leaving. I miss my home and my mother who, by now, must surely believe that I'm dead."

Caught totally by surprise, the burly man answered truthfully. "We sail this evening with the tide, sometime between seven-thirty and eight."

Pablo thanked the man in a deferent manner. "*Muchas gracias, señor.*" He then turned and headed for the stairway that led to the belly of the ship and the small cubicle, which was his room. The burly guard was left alone and more than a little disappointed.

Cramped quarters were forgotten as Pablo began to prepare for his escape. The two, plastic garbage bags were laid out flat one on top of the other. He then cut a square from his bed sheet, approximately the same size as the bags and laid it on top of them. He rolled the three layers tightly together, the sheet section becoming the inner layer. The thick, black roll was then tightly bound, at each end, using strips cut from the same bed sheet. Pablo was getting excited. *That should work perfectly!* He went to the door, opened it, then casually looked out. *Good! No one is in the passageway!* He turned and quickly retrieved the plastic roll, tossing one end over the top of the door. One more check to make sure there were no witnesses and, with each hand, he grabbed an end, above the binding. Holding tightly, he let his full weight drop. The sheet-strip binding held, and his weight was easily supported. A big smile appeared on Pablo's face. *Muy Bueno! Now to wait for just the perfect moment.*

∽∾∽

Dusk was upon them, and night was fast approaching, the sun just slipping below the western horizon. The gangway had been lifted, and preparations were underway to leave port when Pablo made his way on deck. His shirt was hanging out to act as cover for his plastic "slide." Still, it took his using one hand to prevent it from slipping into view as he made his way aft.

Darkness was quickly enveloping the port. The oncoming night afforded him the cover he sought as he moved close to his chosen hawser. *Too bad the gangway is gone. That ape of a guard is also gone, but no matter, I have my escape.* A quick, last look to ensure that no one was watching then he climbed over the rail and down onto that heavy rope. By now darkness had fallen. Pablo draped his makeshift plastic slide over the hawser, reaching under with his left hand to grab the loose end of his slide, just above the knot. Then, with his right hand gripping the other end in the same manner, he allowed his body to ease off his perch. He was now hanging beneath the hawser. He used his feet to push away from the ship. Slowly at first, he began to slide toward the quay. He was elated. *It works!* He began to slide at a more rapid rate as momentum took over. *Just a minute or two, and I'll be on my way to collect my money.* Suddenly, looming out of the dark was a large, circular object. It surrounded the line blocking his escape route. He was sliding rapidly toward this looming obstruction, which, without doubt, was about to abort his escape. His slide hit the disc, and he was jerked to a stop. *What is this and why is it here?* In his excitement at having discovered a way off the ship, Pablo had not fully surveyed the hawsers along their entire length. At a point, approximately two-thirds the distance from the ship to the quay was a large metal disc, three feet in diameter, and slightly conical. He did not know that this was a rat guard, commonly used when large commercial vessels tied up. These conical metal discs were utilized to prevent the despised rodents from using the docking hawsers as an avenue on board.

Unprepared for this obstacle, Pablo hung, swinging helplessly, trying desperately to come up with a way around this blockade. There were only two options. The first and least desirable was to just let go, fall into the harbor and swim to some point at which he could climb out. He had very limited swimming experience. His limited aquatic abilities coupled with the roughly twenty-foot drop into the unknown, night-blackened waters below, caused a sickening fear to well up in his stomach. He did not consider this as a prime possibility. The second and most appealing option would be to swing and try to get his legs over the hawser, on the quay side of the rat guard.

I am sure I can do this. Just like swinging from vine to vine when I played in the jungle. He started to swing his legs, and, just as he did, a deep rumbling sound reverberated from within the ship. *They've started the engines!* Anxiety was now coupled with fear as the driving force. *I must get to the shore now, or I'll be discovered.* He swung his legs with renewed vigor, building the arc that would bring his legs high enough to wrap around the hawser on the quay side of the rat guard.

Pablo was being driven by his quest for the riches promised him as a reward, by the now dead El Tigre, for the killing of A.J. That had been an unexpected bonus, which had been coupled with his desire for personal revenge. However, in his desperate gamble to get ashore, he had, due to a lack of knowledge and experience, overlooked an important fact. The rough texture of the hawser was like a file against his plastic bag slide. By the time Pablo encountered the rat guard, the makeshift bag slide had been cut more than half-way through. The interior wrap of cheap, flimsy cotton sheet was also frayed and cut. His accelerated swinging created a sawing motion, which increased the abrasive cutting action. Without warning, the weakened plastic slide parted, plunging him into the dark waters below.

"Aayieee!" His cry of fear, cut short by his sudden, painful, contact with the oily harbor water, went unheard onboard the ship. Pablo hit the water flat on his back. The impact drove the air from his lungs, and at the same time, stunned him. His first gasp for air brought in more foul water than air—some swallowed, and some finding its way into his lungs. The second did the same, and panic was rapidly taking hold. He began thrashing at the water, forgetting to swim or even to float. He was screaming, when not choking. *"Ayuda me! Ayuda me, por favor!"*

Drowning was not far from a looming reality.

Suddenly, a large object materialized in the water next to him, and a voice in Spanish cut through his panic. "Calm down, *hombre*, calm down! I have you. Try to relax and let me help."

It was almost impossible to relax when you were in a state of panic, and Pablo was completely out of control. Suddenly, he felt himself being pulled bodily out of the water. Coughing and sputtering, he began to breathe, and, with oxygen in his lungs, the terror of drowning dissipated. This allowed him to take a calmer note of his new surroundings. He twisted around, trying to get oriented and found three dark faces, above him, staring down.

One of the faces spoke. "Looks like he'll live. Let's get out of here. We don't know who may have heard his screams."

Pablo managed to mutter, to no one in particular. *"Gracias! Muchas gracias."*

That brought a faceless response. "Hey! Cholo! Find out who this guy is and how he got in the water."

With that, there was the roar of an engine and the definite sensation of rapid acceleration. Pablo was in a small but powerful boat. He tried to sit up and see what was around him or where he was headed.

The man he believed to be Cholo told him, in no uncertain terms, "Stay down, or you could die!"

Completely disoriented, Pablo was not in the mood to question or complain. He did as he was told. His driving force was simple. *All these men have to do is get me on land. I can take care of the rest!* He couldn't have any idea how far from reality his last thought would prove to be.

CHAPTER 5

The New "Adventure"

Jon, accompanied by Carlos, Bjorn, and Sven stood on the pier at the head of slip thirteen and watched as the boat was expertly berthed by the ferrying crew. The name on the stern stood out in bold black letters, *Adventure II*. He had told Carlos of his choice with a simple comment. "I think it's appropriate."

Bjorn and Sven had been told that the old boat had been stolen and was lost at sea, along with the thieves. When this one became available, it was too good a deal to pass up. The Swedes would never be informed of the actual events surrounding the loss of the original *Adventure*. Jon glanced momentarily at his crew. All three men were grinning broadly, as if the boat was theirs personally.

The ferrying crew came ashore, handed Jon their three sets of keys, and walked up the pier to the waiting car, which was their ride back to the boatworks. Jon couldn't resist. "Well, what are you waiting for? Get on board!" None of them required a second invitation. *My plan is simple, but necessary. First, we'll do an onboard inspection at the dock. The next step will be to take the boat out for a shakedown run for two or three hours. This will allow each of us to get a "feel" of the vessel, and hopefully would point out any inadequacies before we actually went after fish.* The new boat was ten feet longer than the original *Adventure*, and just over one foot wider in the beam.

After a slow walk around the deck, the Swedes disappeared below, calling back to Carlos. "Ve haf to check der galley."

Carlos just grinned and shook his head. *They sure do love their food.* He then headed for the wheel house where he and Jon would go over the instrumentation and layout. After about half an hour, Bjorn and Sven returned to the wheel house, brimming with enthusiasm about the amenities of the new galley.

Sven couldn't hold back. "Det er also a freezer og two microvave ovens. Der stove haf eight burners og tvin ovens. Ve vill eat godt here." Addressing Jon specifically, he added. "Here er der basic shopping list. Ve vill add as ve go."

Jon took the list, without a glance. He knew that it would be only items that were needed. The list went into his shirt pocket. "Okay! Now let's take this boat for a ride and see how she handles."

Like a well-oiled machine, they each moved to the tasks required to cast off and sail. As they eased out of their slip, Jon looked at the Hatteras, still tied up in the adjacent slip. *I wonder if Sheri and her mom have decided what to do with her.*

Three plus hours later, the *Adventure II* returned to port and eased into slip number thirteen. There had been no disappointments. The drug dealer who had been the original buyer of this custom-built fishing boat had thought of amenities that would have never crossed Jon's mind, no less that of an average commercial fisherman. Twin 850 horsepower diesel engines with extended range fuel tanks, long range radar and an on-board generator, which could tap the fuel supply and power all electric items. Nothing was sub-standard and all systems operated to perfection. The only thing left would be their personal requirements. Jon had placed orders for those self-inflating life vests which, he had learned, could be life savers, in spite of having had to deflate his last one, to save his own life. Those had been delivered, much earlier today. Jon had arranged ahead of time for Red to accept the delivery. *After my last experience, I definitely won't sail without them.*

A thin man, with shoulder-length hair and a gangly physique was patiently waiting at the dock, when they tied up.

The clothes he wore were those of a tradesman, and the small canvas satchel in his left hand had seen better days. He was leaning against a piling and never moved or said a word, just waited. Jon gave no indication that he was aware of the man and addressed his crew. "It's Thursday and now that you've seen the boat, think about anything we might need on board that you didn't notice. If you have a doubt, write it down. If you're sure and have the cash, buy it and get a receipt. If it can be had at the suppliers we use, put it on my account. We'll sail Monday and go for Mahi and Spanish mackerel. Have a good weekend."

The Swedes waved as they left, Bjorn calling back. "Til Mondag."

Carlos and Jon each gave a short wave of acknowledgement. Carlos turned to his friend. "Guess we'd better get back to the house. The girls are waiting."

A broad grin spread across Jon's face. It had almost become reflexive, when he thought of Sheri. "In just one minute. One more detail I need to take care of." With that, Jon called to the man on the pier. "August, come on aboard." The man moved, at a casual pace towards the boat and Jon noted the look on Carlos' face, a combination of question and perplexity. He then remembered that he hadn't mentioned this to anyone, including Carlos. He needed to fill Carlos in. "This man is one of the best custom cabinet makers around, and I want some special work done on board. This is personal, and you're the only other person who will know about it." Carlos's face told Jon that he was even more confused now than before. "I'll make it quick and simple. After my showdown with El Tigre and while I was recovering, I started thinking about having a weapon or two, completely concealed, on board. It might have made the difference then and in today's world, with the drug dealers and modern pirates—you just never know. There's also the fact that we don't know, for sure, that another bad memory won't come home to roost." Carlos knew better than to protest. There were too many times in the past when Jon's inner sense of imminent or possible danger had proved correct.

Jon let it go at that and turned to greet the carpenter. "August Cavendish, I'm Jon Morton, pleased to meet you."

Cavendish, true to his northern Maine heritage, was less effusive. "Likewise."

With nothing else offered, Jon proceeded to outline his requirements. "I need you to build three small and totally concealed compartments—I'll show you where. They need to have a release that won't allow them to be opened by an accidental bump or push, will need to be water tight, and lined with "egg-crate" foam. I'll give you the approximate dimensions." No response or questions from August, so Jon proceeded. "Follow me, and I'll show you the locations." Jon led, and the cabinet maker followed. So far, he hadn't uttered a single word other than his one-word greeting. They went from the main cabin to the wheel house and then below to the galley. In each area, Jon indicated the specific location, which he believed would be best for the purpose. Carlos remained on deck since he reasoned that he'd only be in the way and Jon would fill him in afterward.

～∽✺∽～

Back on deck, Jon felt it was about time to evoke some form of response from August, and came right to the point. "Can you do it? If so, when can you start, and how long will it take?"

A two-minute pause and August answered in a clipped response. "Yep! Can do. Best I don't get in th' way of yer business. Weekends are best. Prob'ly one fer each. That do?"

The time frame wasn't critical, and the fact that August was willing to work on weekends was ideal. "That will work out just fine. When can you start? Do you need a deposit? I'll pay you in cash, so you don't have to bill me."

After another long pause, coupled with no facial expression or physical animation, August responded. "Don't need a deposit. If it suits you, I can start this weekend."

That was perfect for Jon. He reached out to shake August's hand, sealing the deal. "Here's a set of cabin keys. You can get started right away since we don't plan to sail until Monday."

Jon never asked the price and August never offered. What he was seeking had to be very good and required a first class craftsman. The price for this "insurance" was unimportant. August turned, gave a slight nod to Carlos, stepped onto the gunwale, then to the pier and walked off in the same, unhurried, manner.

Jon watched as the cabinetmaker departed. He had to tell Carlos. "I'd hate to be stuck on a desert island with him. I'd probably go nuts trying to have a simple conversation. Let's go home."

CHAPTER 6

A Dangerous Friendship

Pablo had, through no fault of his own, stepped into a human hornet's nest. For the moment, and due to his simplistic mind-set, he was totally unaware of what his fall into the harbor had gotten him involved in. The boat that he was on, along with its' three man crew, was speeding through the harbor waters, without running lights or any other form of illumination. If he knew anything about boating regulations, Pablo would have recognized this as a sure sign of trouble.

Cholo moved close to him and leaned over, putting his face close to Pablo's. Even in the poor light of night, Pablo could see the heavily pock-marked complexion of an obviously Hispanic man. Even more defining was the ragged scar, which ran from the far left edge of Cholo's upper lip, straight up his cheek, across his left eye and disappeared at his hairline. The disfigurement did not seem to affect the eye that it bisected with almost surgical precision. He whispered, in Spanish, with an intense urgency. "What is your name and how did you get in the water?"

Pablo saw no reason for anything other than the truth. "*Mi nombre es Pablo*. I was trying to get off that ship *La Luna Media*. I fell from the rope that tied the ship to the pier, into the water."

Cholo wasn't ignorant and pursued the obvious point. "You are an illegal." It was more a statement than a question. "Either you were being deported or you had hidden onboard and were sneaking into the United States. Which is it?"

The hard and direct manner of Cholo's questioning was making Pablo uneasy, but he was still open and truthful. "I am illegal, yes. I came into this country to take care of a personal debt of honor, but got caught and was being sent home to Colombia."

Cholo would not let this simple answer suffice. "What was this 'debt of honor' and if you were caught why would you return?"

Pablo was not about to divulge the existence of two-million in cash to total strangers, and so the truth was put aside. "Maybe three or four years ago, an anglo shot and killed my father in Cali. I found out where he now lives and went to kill him. I was almost successful but got caught. I will not go home without knowing that my father is avenged."

His interrogator thought about this for a minute and was, almost, at a point of acceptance when he recognized a possible flaw in the story. "When did you get caught?"

Pablo didn't know enough about the immigration system and this time, answered truthfully. "Three days ago."

Cholo, without pause, simply answered. "*Bueno*." Then carefully balancing in the speeding craft, he inched his way forward to enlighten his companions. After relaying the information he continued, outlining his thoughts. "If this kid was caught three days ago, by INS or the law, he'd be sitting in a lock-up, awaiting deportation hearings. Whoever nailed him wants him out of the country, quietly. There's more to this than he's letting on. Perhaps something we could profit from."

The man at the wheel thought about what Cholo said, as he expertly maneuvered the small speedboat, then gave a simple yet brutal directive. "Press him and if you get nothing else, cut his throat and toss him overboard. If you get valuable information and still see no more use for the kid, do the same." He turned his full attention back to piloting the craft across the harbor.

⌘

Pablo had, by now, fully recovered from his near drowning experience and was starting to think about the best way to return to West Virginia and his fortune. When Cholo sat down beside him, he jumped, slightly, having been startled out of his state of mental planning. The smile that started to form on his lips turned to a gasp, as he was grabbed by the collar and a very large and nasty looking knife was pressed, tightly, against his neck, the blade angled downward from behind and under his ear to his trachea. This man was no stranger to violent death, and he held his weapon in the perfect position. One downward slash would severe Pablo's carotid artery, then his jugular, and, finally, his trachea. Once a person had received this mortal wound, death was just moments away, with no opportunity for a reprieve.

Whimpering with fear, Pablo wasn't even aware that in his terrified state his bladder had convulsed, causing him to urinate in his pants. "What do you want from me?" was all he managed to whisper, not daring to move a muscle for fear that the cold steel, pressed tight against his skin, would slip.

Cholo answered the question with a sneering reply. "I want the truth! You lied to me, and I don't like lies. Now, since you were not put in jail, whoever put you on that ship was either a criminal or a member of an "off the record" government operation. Either way, if you want to go back, so badly, there has to be something worth the risk, and since we saved your life, we want part of it." The knife was pressed more tightly against Pablo's neck, causing a slight break in his skin. A thin crimson line welled up to define the superficial wound. "Now, little man, what is it?"

The intense fear that gripped this young Colombian was unlike anything he had ever known. He was shivering, uncontrollably. One thing he was sure of, he had to offer something substantial and very believable, or he would die here on this boat. Personal resolve and the desperate need to survive took over, and Pablo began his desperate bid for life. "I'm sorry that I didn't tell you everything. After all, you did save my life!" A slight easing of the blade's pressure, on his neck, convinced Pablo that he was headed, more or less, in the right direction. He then began to tell how the man he was seeking had, also, been part of the force that had destroyed El Tigre's camp. "El Tigre promised me a huge reward, more than two-hundred thousand dollars, held by that Anglo. That money is now sitting in Dodsonville, West Virginia, in a shed on the Anglo's land."

At the mention of El Tigre, there was an immediate change in Cholo's demeanor. "El Tigre? You know El Tigre?"

The knife had immediately disappeared, at the mention of that name and Cholo was working his way forward, to speak with the other two men.

Suddenly, all conversation halted as the loud and unmistakable sound of powerful boat engines swept over them. At the same time, their small craft was bathed in bright white light. "Ahoy, in the power boat, cut your engines at once and prepare for inspection! This is the United States Coast Guard!" The message was then repeated in Spanish. Instead of obeying the command, the man at the controls brought the boat up to full speed and began a zigzag course, across the water, in a wild attempt to elude the Coast Guard vessel. Cholo, crouched down between the two forward seats, and clinging tenaciously to them in order to avoid being thrown overboard, posed a direct question. "What should I do with the kid?"

Without warning, there was a staccato burst of gunfire, and the water in front of their craft erupted. These criminals had thirty kilos of high grade cocaine on board. That cargo was worth more than they were willing to loose without a fight. The cocaine had been lowered to them from a stern porthole, in the *Media Luna*, just moments before Pablo hit the water. The only reason these drug runners had pulled him out was to use as a possible bargaining chip, if needed. The opportunity had just materialized, and the man at the controls gave an immediate response. "Throw him overboard—alive! They value life and will slow down to pull him out. Then we'll be rid of the bastards."

Cholo didn't hesitate. Another warning of "Heave to," followed by a second burst of gunfire, caused him to stay as low in the boat as possible, as he made his way rapidly back to

Pablo. There was no evidence of a knife, so Pablo smiled broadly, thinking he had achieved a strong position just by mentioning El Tigre. He started to question what was happening, but never got the opportunity to find out. Without a word, Cholo pulled Pablo roughly to his feet and, with a violent shove, sent him, flailing wildly and screaming in terror, over the side. A new wave of fear, coupled with near panic, gripped Pablo as first he spun in the boat's wake, went under, resurfaced, then struggled to employ his poor swimming abilities. *I have no idea where, or how far away, the shore is.*

CHAPTER 7

Questions

It was already late on Sunday morning, and Jon was driving back to Carlos's house when his cell phone rang. He answered it reflexively. "Jon Morton." He wasn't prepared for the voice on the other end.

"Bet you didn't think you'd hear my voice, again, so soon!"

"Commander, what's up? Give me a second to pull over." The opening question was also a reflex response. *One thing I know with certainty is that Ertugal didn't just call to say hello.* Whatever it is, Jon sensed an uneasy feeling start to churn in his gut. *Why th' hell can't the past leave me in peace and stay in the past?*

"Jon! That kid that we put on that freighter, to Colombia… Pablo something. As you know, our standard procedure in this type of operation is to take prints a DNA sample and a photo, for future reference if needed. Coast Guard requested a general 'wants and warrants,' which we tap into, and guess what? They picked our boy up in Biscayne Bay—alive! Says he fell overboard when the freighter was docked in Miami—probably bullshit—and was picked up by three men in a small power boat. They threatened his life, but when the Coast Guard showed up and told them to heave to, they shoved him overboard and ran for it. Based on what he told the Coast Guard and the description the kid gave them of one of the men, this Pablo kid got picked up by some members of a serious drug running operation. It's being run by some men that the guard was hoping to put permanently out of business. The guys in the boat evidently are just mules but could have been a direct lead. Unfortunately, with this little diversion, they got away. Right now, our boy Pablo is in a detention cell, in Miami."

Ertugal finally paused long enough for Jon to get a word in. "Commander, if you want my opinion, for what it's worth, he probably jumped ship in Miami, with the intent of returning to West Virginia to find the supposed two-million, which he considers to be rightfully his. I have a feeling that no matter what, at some point in time, he's going to make a try for it. That being said, you might get a picture of him sent to the sheriff in Dodsonville. Advise him that this guy's an illegal and to apprehend and hold him if he shows up. I think for our peace of mind, you should have that kid sent back to Colombia or have him 'disappear,' and quick. In fact, if you can, as an option—pull some strings, get the Guard to chase down that freighter and put him back on board."

Ertugal was silent for a moment, then responded. "Sounds like the best idea, all around. I'll get it done." With that, the line went dead.

Jon eased his phone back into his pocket and sat there for a minute, engrossed in thought, mulling over the conversation that had just transpired. *I knew we should have terminated that kid when we had the chance.* The loud backfire from a passing vehicle jolted him. Instinctively Jon ducked then recovered, and looked up in time to see an antiquated VW Bus with obviously deteriorated mufflers, as it drove by. The appearance of that vehicle, coupled with that explosive backfire, catapulted Jon back into the unwanted realism of another buried, deadly memory…

ೲೲ

The US Aircraft Carrier Nimitz was cruising less than 100 miles off the coast of east Africa. Her exact bearing was ninety-two miles, due east of Mogadishu, Somalia. Ignoring a country's nautical boundary was not customary procedure, but neither was their mission. The carrier was operating under maximum secured conditions. All deck guns were armed and manned, all non-essential personnel were below decks, and the entire above-deck area was under blackout rule. The ship was functioning as the floating base for a pair of covert operations teams. The first four-man team had, just a few hours prior, been inserted into Somalia on a special mission. Now, if all went well, the ship would receive a call for extraction within the next hour. Then, as the commander had bluntly stated, "We'll get-the-hell out of here."

Team number two was relaxing in the operations room. They were anything but relaxed and were in full battle gear. Jon Morton, team leader, addressed his men. "I'm hoping that team one has a smooth op, but in that hot bed I have my doubts. Somalia is a failed state, and it's strictly a matter of survival of the fittest. The fittest, in this specific instance, means the most ruthless. Team one's been on site for almost three hours and—" He never finished his sentence.

The intercom came to life with a moment's static, then the commander's voice. "Jon you and your men on deck, now."

The team was on its feet and moving before the last word finished.

As the team left the deck elevator, a midshipman was waiting to direct them to the flight deck position where a Blackhawk helicopter was readied, rotors already on and idling. No conversation was needed. The four men scrambled aboard, the rotors became a whirling blur, and the chopper immediately left the deck, turned sharply to the west, and headed toward land. They were headed directly for Mogadishu, flying barely fifty-feet above the ocean's surface when pilot gave them a brief update. "Your boys ran into more than planned for and are dealing with heavy resistance. Insert will be approximately five clicks from our LZ. Ground transport is waiting. Here's the cab fare, plus." He handed Jon a one-hundred dollar bill and five twenties. "The hundred's for the driver." He quipped lightly. "Don't go drinking with the balance."

The pilot set the Blackhawk down in a vacant field. Instantly the side-door gunner leaned out with a small infra-red light.

He flashed a recognition signal toward a cluster of small buildings. A pair of headlights returned the signal, and in less than a minute a time-worn Volkswagon Mini-bus was spotted driving toward the helicopter. The pilot offered one last statement as the men exited the chopper. "Good luck. Don't spare the ammo and bring 'em all home."

The Blackhawk lifted off and disappeared into the night sky.

The '59 Volkswagen Mini-Bus eased to a squeaking stop at the cobbled intersection. The clay brick walls of the Old City, the rebel stronghold, were clearly visible across the street. Their vehicle was a relic of times past with faded paint, some rust and balding tires. On the exterior of the bus, on both sides, someone had painted, in Arabic, the word for taxi. The driver turned to Jon. "You here—go there." He pointed to the entry gate in the wall. "Good, you go now. My money now. You out—fast."

Jon turned to the three men in his team. "Show time. Let's go." He then turned back to the driver and handed him one-hundred dollars, US. The man grinned, bobbed his head as a "thank you," and watched Jon open the passenger door and start to exit. Suddenly, Jon whirled about and trained his pistol on the driver. "Cell phone. Give me your cell phone, now, or you die."

The driver was shaking his head side-to-side and mimicking the side-to-side action with his right hand, indicating that he was not about to give up his phone.

Jon pressed his point by jamming the barrel of his gun hard against the man's forehead. He reiterated his demand. "Cellphone—*Now!*"

The driver, shaking visibly, gave up his phone. Jon handed the man another twenty dollars with a simple statement. "Buy a new phone." The team climbed out. The driver made a rapid U-turn and sped off.

They moved quickly into the entryway of a dilapidated building to review their tactical procedure. Kevin hesitated for a moment but had to ask. "Jon, why'd you take the man's phone? Intel' said he could be trusted."

"Trust in this arena translates to dollars. That man could make one call and collect a hefty bit of cash for turning us in to the rebels. We want to go home in one piece." Jon dropped the confiscated phone to the ground and shattered it with a single blow from the butt of his tactical rifle. "Now, let's get our brothers out."

They rushed forward, quickly crossing the street and through the gateway.

The sharp crack of small arms' fire, overshadowed by the staccato bursts of automatic weapons' fire, grew louder as the team approached. Jon's team moved with extreme caution, each member covering for the others, all eyes searching for the enemy. Their rifles were held in ready combat position, able to spit death in an instant. As they worked their way forward, they made use of the many doorways, alleys, and abandoned vehicles for cover and protection. Two crippled trucks were on the road ahead, both burning fiercely. A body was visible in the cab of one truck, and two more bodies lay in the street. *Not ours!* A wounded fighter was desperately trying to crawl to shelter. He would manage to drag himself a few feet then pause, and scream either Arabic or perhaps a Somali dialect, obviously for help. When he screamed, he would raise one arm in a supplicating manner. A burst from an unseen automatic weapon caused the wounded fighter's body to shudder and twitch as the rounds slammed into him. The arm dropped. He was still—no more screams. Bullets were a brutal but simple fix.

The air reeked of burning rubber, which turned the atmosphere thick with a heavy, black pallor. The unmistakable stench of burning human flesh as well as cordite could also be detected. Team one had been inserted to terminate the rebel army's leader, Ngikamo. When they had burst into his headquarters, centrally located in the Old City, they found only a mother and her infant. She screamed a loud warning before one of the team shot her, and now they were cut off, surrounded, and outgunned, as well as outnumbered.

Team Two had only one option: Pinpoint the location of the first team then call for an air strike by Blackhawk helicopters. They continued their stealthy, forward progress. Suddenly, a burst of automatic weapons' fire impacted the wall just above their heads, the rounds splintering the clay bricks. "We've been spotted." Before they had a chance to seek a more secure cover, a second burst, and one man went down, hit in the shoulder and bleeding profusely. "Shit! He needs a medic. Get a tight wrap on that to slow the bleeding." Jon scanned the surrounding buildings and pointed. "Kevin, roof top!"

"Got it, boss." A head and rifle were visible over the parapet on the roof across the street. Kevin swung his rifle on target, sighted, and squeezed off a shot. The head disappeared in a spray of blood. "That problem's solved, boss."

Another multi-round burst pockmarked the same wall barely two feet from Kevin. The situation was deteriorating, rapidly. They had quickly gone from an offensive action to a defensive one. Jon turned to his team. "We can't wait any longer. We've got to get air support, and now. Call it in!"

The radio man made the call. "Falcon two calling mother. Falcon two calling mother. Position compromised and failing. One wounded. Team one positioned fifty meters south—heavy enemy fire—must evac. Requesting big birds, and fast. Do you copy?"

A static filled reply came back, within seconds. "Copy Falcon two. Four birds on the way. Prepare teams for evac. Do you copy?"

"Copy and wilco, mother."

Four Blackhawk helicopters arrived within eighteen minutes. The choppers unleashed a devastating barrage of missiles, as well as murderous fire from their on-board fifty-caliber machine guns. Two of the 'copters broke away and came in for the evacuation, one for each team, while the other two hovered above, maintaining a withering cover fire.

∽✀∾

Jon shook his head and took a deep breath. His pulse slowed. *That mission was seven years ago.* The nerve wracking memory faded and was instantly replaced by the reality of the present. *Something tells me that we haven't seen the last of that kid, and when he does reappear, it won't be pretty.* With that ominous thought, he pulled back on the road and switched his thoughts to a brighter subject—the impending luncheon with Carlos and Rosita—his two closest friends—Sheri, and another two couples. What had begun a short while ago, as a quick trip home for a few extra bottles of wine, suddenly had a cloud of concern hanging over it. *With any luck, this'll all add up to nothing—I hope.* With less than one mile to go, Jon made one last decision about the information, just received. *Better tell Carlos when the opportunity arises.*

ᴄᴙᴄᴙ

Sheri was waiting on the front lawn when he pulled into the driveway at Carlos's house. As soon as Jon got out of his car, she met him with that wonderful smile that made him feel like a king. "Traffic? I thought you'd be here ten minutes ago."

She was aware of the basics of what had, so recently, happened, and he saw no reason to cover up the phone call from Ertugal. "A courtesy call from the commander, just wanting to fill me in on the final aspects of that mess we just cleaned up."

Sheri was just a little skeptical. "Are you sure that's all it was?"

I'm not one bit surprised by her response. After all, two life-threatening incidents so close together would make almost any civilian doubtful. Jon answered as strongly as he could, considering that the seeds of doubt had just been sown by that call from the commander.

"Of course I'm sure!" *She doesn't need to hear about that flashback. They seem to be less often, now.* "Now, let's get inside. It's not polite of me to keep everyone waiting any longer."

Both Carlos and Rosita looked at Jon when they entered. The looks on their faces mirroring the same question Sheri had posed, as to "What took so long?"

He'd fill Carlos in when the opportunity presented itself

and let Carlos handle his wife. "Carlos! Where'd you put the cooler? I need to get this wine on ice."

CHAPTER 8

Smoldering

Inspector Alejandro Cantrell was punctual in his personal life, his work-life was anything but. He was as proud of his accomplishments in the war against the drug cartels as was the city of Cali.

When the headquarters of the Noche del Gato criminal gang was blown into oblivion by what had to have been a foreign led commando-type raid, Cantrell jumped on the opportunity. He immediately began to start cleaning up the rest of the local crime elements. His hand-picked team had arrested or killed eighteen drug dealers, murderers, and pornography dealers. It was becoming safe to walk the streets again. He had every reason to be proud. He was also ambitious, and, at the age of thirty-one, had set his mental sights set on the presidency of Colombia.

His morning routine was punctual, and exact. Exact to the point that an observer could set a clock by his schedule. Promptly awake at four, he would wash and dress. As he prepared to face the day, the special and very beautiful woman he lived with would prepare their morning coffee. She was an exquisite example of Spanish femininity. A woman blessed with raven hair, skin the color of cream, and a body that even other women were envious of. She was the picture of female perfection! Four-thirty and Cantrell walked into the kitchen, a cup of black coffee already poured and waiting. Elena met him midway between the entry way and his coffee. They embraced, and he slid his hands down inside the rear of the pants of her man-tailored, satin pajamas. He cupped her firm buttocks and held her tightly against him for a prolonged kiss. No more than that. They broke away from each other, and he completed the journey to his coffee. Two swallows of the rich blend and the cup went back on the table, to be finished upon his return. A short two-note whistle and an Australian Collie bounded into the room. "*Hola, Diablo*, let's go!"

The dog raced to the front door, with Alejandro following. When at the door, Alejandro snapped on the dog's leash, unlocked the door, and stepped outside.

Two police officers were waiting, automatic rifles at the ready. "*Buenos días, Señor Inspector.*"

He responded in kind. "*Buenos días,* Pedro, Jorge."

The officers fell in step alongside, as he made his way through the streets. A short distance behind, an unmarked police car followed. It did not take much to realize that this man had made many enemies in the criminal world, and although the streets were substantially safer now, a man of his notoriety still required the utmost of caution.

His morning walk with Diablo was approximately five kilometers, and except for the bodyguards, he enjoyed this time with his dog. The walk took about thirty to forty-five minutes, depending upon Diablo's needs and curiosities. The officers would joke, at times that this duty was "keeping them in shape." They left when he reentered his home, with a wave and two words, "*Hasta luego.*"

Both officers knew he would be at his desk in, exactly, one hour.

This day went surprisingly easily for Alejandro. There had been two overnight homicides. One was the result of a knife fight in a neighborhood bar. The other death was a known drug addict, who "forgot" to pay for his weeks' supply of cocaine. Everything else in his day was basic. Inspector Cantrell left for home at four-thirty p.m., exiting through the private, guarded, garage in his armored car. He was looking forward to a martini and a relaxing evening with Elena. The drive home would be circuitous, as the route he took to and from his office was never the same. Caution had to be the primary method of survival when you were in direct opposition to the strong, scheming, and murderous, criminal elements of Colombia.

Alejandro drew his H&K nine-millimeter pistol, snapped the safety to "off," and placed it in his lap before pressing the remote control to open his garage. This was a time of high vulnerability, and he took no chances. Experience had taught him that it only took one small lapse in vigilance to wind up in the morgue. The previous police inspector had stopped for a pack of cigarettes, on his way home. The small vendor's stall was barely ten feet from his stopped car. As he turned to take the few steps back to his vehicle, a motorcycle carrying two riders slowed, and the rider on the rear opened up with an automatic rifle. The bike then fled at a very high rate of speed. The medical examiner removed nine bullets from the inspector's body and four from that of the vendor, an innocent bystander. The assassination, according to witnesses, took less than thirty seconds. The killers were never apprehended.

Bright metal-halide lights, activated when the garage door remote was pressed, illuminated both the driveway and surrounding landscape—no lights came on in the garage. This set-up would make it extremely unlikely that a hidden gunman could take an accurate shot. The car and passengers would be almost invisible in their dark surroundings once the vehicle headlights had been turned off and those blinding spotlights would prevent any shooter from finding a target. The only other possibility would be a hand grenade or an RPG. When those ultra-bright lights came on, Alejandro didn't hesitate for a moment. He turned off his car lights and drove rapidly into the garage, pushing the remote control as he entered to start the door closing. Without a pause, he jumped from his car, checked the rapidly narrowing space between the garage door and the concrete floor to ensure that no one slipped in. He rushed through the door, into the house. The door to the house was steel, and the wall in which it was fitted was reinforced concrete, as was the ceiling above. The garage door had already closed and, when it did, the halide illumination turned off automatically. The steel entry door slammed shut behind him. It wasn't perfect, but it was the best the limited resources of his department could manage. His pistol, safety re-engaged, went back in its holster.

"Elena! Estoy a casa!" When he didn't get her usual, bubbly, response, he was about to call again then paused. *Perhaps she's in the bathroom.* With that thought in mind, he directed his steps to the kitchen, the refrigerator now his target. *Elena always has the pitcher of martinis chilled and ready.*

He pulled open the refrigerator door—a horror-induced scream erupted, unchecked from his lips. "Aaaaiieeee—No, no, noooo!"

Alejandro backed away in numbed shock from the open refrigerator, his knees going weak. He stumbled away, his stomach heaving. Beautiful Elena's head had been placed on the top shelf. It was propped against the pitcher of chilled martinis, sightless eyes staring, an envelope stuffed between those perfect, now dead, lips. A pool of her blood had collected and was beginning to coagulate on the shelf below. Inspector Alejandro Cantrell, hardened officer, accustomed to all forms of gruesome death, collapsed in tears on the cold tile floor. He didn't even have the mental strength, at this moment, to consider that the killer might still be in his home. He just lay there on the floor and sobbed.

An insistent banging on the front door and the faint sound of his name being called brought Alejandro back to reality. He drew his gun and walked with deadly purpose to the front door and stood to one side. *"Quien es?"* he demanded.

The response was immediate and easily recognized. *"Es Alonzo!* When you didn't follow protocol and call in, we were dispatched."

Cantrell's gun arm went limp as he recognized the voice. His pistol now dangled in his fingers, and with his left hand he unlocked and opened the door. Alonzo and three additional police walked in, Alonzo returning his pistol to its holster, the others returning their automatic rifles to rest, slung over their shoulders. Inspector Cantrell pointed, his hand shaking, toward the kitchen. He mumbled softly. "They've killed her! They've killed my Elena."

Instantly the newly arrived police team reacted, brought their weapons to a ready position and started with cautious, shuffling steps, for the kitchen. Alejandro was rapidly returning to the extreme caution procedures, which had seen him through many violent encounters with the drug cartels.

He drew his pistol and in a lowered voice, he advised the four men. "I didn't check the house." That statement caused the men to split into two groups and begin a room to room search, with the utmost of caution, considering the possibility that the perpetrator might possibly still be in the house. Alejandro returned to the kitchen and slumped into a chair, pistol in his lap. The most important person in his life had been taken from him, despite his attempts at the most stringent of precautions.

Time stood still for the chief inspector and, when the four police returned to the kitchen, an hour or a minute could have passed. It mattered not a bit.

Alonzo, being senior, spoke softly. "We located her body, in the bedroom. It's best that you remain here."

Alejandro nodded, almost imperceptibly, and pointed to the refrigerator. One of the policemen, nearest the refrigerator, pulled open the door and stepped back, with a startled gasp. Alonzo took a quick look then indicated, with an abbreviated hand wave, that the door should be closed to hide the macabre sight, and again addressed Alejandro. "I have contacted the medical examiner and the forensics team. They will be here, shortly."

An awareness that something was missing suddenly broke through Alejandro's pain. "My dog! Where is Diablo! *Diablo—Diablo, venga aqui!*" No response from his dog brought a numbed response from him. "That's strange. Perhaps he was locked in another room. I should go look for him."

As he started to rise, Corporal Lopez walked over, a sorrowful expression on his face. "*Señor* Inspector. We found Diablo, also—also in the bedroom." He paused, seeking an easy way out. There was none. "He was hacked into pieces, actually dismembered—" Lopez paused, summoning his resolve. "—maybe disabled first?"

Cantrell dropped back into the chair, buried his face in his hands, and again, wept bitterly.

ഇഇ

The coroner's report came back just four days later. Corporal Lopez, considered to be the most sympathetic man on the force, was given the distasteful job of delivering a copy of it to Inspector Cantrell. The corporal was not pleased about this duty. Cantrell had remained at home all that week, despite pleas from friends that he live, at least temporarily, elsewhere. He answered the door after Lopez, wisely, called to advise that he was there.

"I have the coroner's report, *Señor* Inspector." He offered the manila envelope. "Do you wish me to remain?"

Alejandro responded with the answer the Corporal was praying for. "That won't be necessary, Corporal. I will call headquarters if I have any questions. *Muchas gracias*." With that, Lopez made his way hastily back to his patrol car and drove off. Alejandro Cantrell locked his door, went into his den, opened the manila envelope, and began to read, going straight to the findings. As he read, the words seared into his memory and both his fury and anger mounted.

The cause of death was decapitation. My examination indicates that the victim was initially shocked with a Taser, which was indicated by two small burn marks found on her abdomen. We must, from that point, make an assumption, which appears quite evident. When the victim was incapacitated by electric shock, a dose of the chemical Rohypnol was administered orally, (see toxicology findings). This served to remove all control from the victim, even when the effects of the electric shock had worn off. At that point, the victim was sodomized, raped, and subsequently, decapitated.

He read the report one more time to be sure that he hadn't missed anything. He hadn't. Alejandro leaned back in his chair, staring at the ceiling. One basic thought summed up the totality of his current feelings. *I will hunt these animals down and slaughter them like the pigs they are!*

It was time to get started. Elena's killer or killers would pay and not in a court of law. As Alejandro leaned forward, to get up, he spotted a smaller manila envelope, on the floor. *It must have fallen out when I opened the large one.* Quickly, he reached down to retrieve the envelope, opened the clasp, and withdrew a note wrapped around an even smaller envelope.

The message in the note said simply, *This is a copy of the note we found with Elena.*

He had a vague recollection of seeing something white in the mouth of his fiancé's head when he had opened the refrigerator. He tore the small envelope open, unfolded the sheet of paper, and read a short but chilling message.

You have pushed me too far, Alejandro. Now it is my turn to push you.

There was no signature—none was needed. This had to be the work of Cholo. His task force had been decimating Cholo's criminal organization, which had been rapidly filling the vacancy left by the destruction of El Tigre and his Noche del Gato guerillas. Inspector Cantrell had conducted or orchestrated raids, confiscation of drugs, cash, and weapons, as well as the imprisonment of all those not killed in the raids. It had been noted that not many went to prison. Alejandro was shaking with anger. He ran to his front door and pulled it open, with no thought for his personal safety, and screamed into the night. "I'll get you, Cholo and, when I do, you will pay in ways that will make you wish you'd never heard my name!"

～◌～

Morning came, and Inspector Cantrell dismissed the guard in front of his house. Next, he called in to headquarters and requested a one-month leave of absence, for mourning and mental cleansing. His second call was to the mortician. "Domingo, please, I beg of you don't let her parents see her this way. Do your utmost to prevent them this horror. I would ask that you recommend cremation, but I doubt they will allow that. At least, advise a closed casket."

"I will do everything in my power," Domingo assured him, "both for you and for them, Alejandro."

৩৩৩

Padre Hidalgo Ignacio was a close friend of Elena's family and also of Alejandro. They were regular attendees at his church. For this reason, the services, both in the Church of *Sangre de Christo*, and at graveside, were heartfelt and touching. It was as if the armed guards in attendance did not exist. When Alejandro came to him with personal thanks, after the burial, he was given a personal blessing by the padre and then was shocked to hear the priest utter these words. "God damn these villains who are destroying lives and our country. May they journey quickly to hell and burn there, for all eternity!"

Inspector Alejandro Cantrell started his leave of absence, that day.

CHAPTER 9

Retribution

Barely more than a trail, the narrow dirt road was rarely traveled. This was readily quite evident. Based upon the encroaching tree and bush limbs, as well as the numerous sprouts of weeds, some almost two-feet high, a vehicle had not traveled this path in at least six months. The frequent rains and high humidity in Cali afforded the Land Rover and its driver a dust-free passage. Alejandro handled the wheel casually as would any driver on familiar territory. The road, in reality, was simply an extremely long cul-de-sac, a private drive. At the termination of its eight-kilometer length was a pristine lake and a small cabin. Alejandro's ideal and long, but infrequently used, get-a-way. Rough-sawn clapboard siding sheathed the exterior. The roof was likewise simple, plain, corrugated metal. This was the type of small structure that would draw little attention. That was exactly his plan when Alejandro had it constructed eight years ago.

The true quality of the construction was known only to him and the builder. Beneath the wood siding, there was a double layer of cement board, installed over cement-filled concrete block. Rock-wool insulation, as well as another layer of cement board, covered the interior walls. Each course of concrete block was tied together with ladder wire, embedded in the mortar, and topped with a rebar-imbedded bond-beam. The interior walls were finished with a covering of fire-code sheet rock. This created a structure that was not only highly fire resistant but could easily withstand small arms and rifle fire,as well as the explosive force of hand grenades.

The interior living space was simple and basic. The entire area was just one large room, encompassing a small kitchen, a bedroom area, and a sitting area. This arrangement was serviced by a single bathroom. Water was supplied by a well that had been dug prior to construction. Waste was piped to to a small septic system. Having the well and waste systems in place, prior to the construction of his cabin, ensured the secret of construction. A practical home, unusually secure and designed for simplistic living. A closet and a small dresser were in the bedroom area and a pantry for staples and pots in the kitchen area. The floor was a monolithic pour of concrete, six-inches thick and reinforced with rebar. Under the corrugated metal roof was a four inch layer of compressed "rock-wool," a non-flammable insulation, sandwiched from below by a heavier, thicker layer of structural corrugated metal. One small window, twelve inches square, in each of the four sides was glazed with one-half-inch-thick bullet-proof glass. These windows were installed in a manner similar to a ship's portholes, hinged to open toward the interior. Both the hinges and latching devices were of a type that would withstand high-impact contact. The primary purpose of the windows was to allow for some daylight, secondarily to allow the inhabitant to be able to safely check the exterior and, if need be, to open them and fire a weapon.

This simple but unusually well-constructed, cabin would now become his headquarters, for Inspector Alejandro Cantrell was about to step outside of the law, which he so vigorously defended, and in a way that would not be forgotten in Cali for years to come.

ↄ∕ↄↄ

Elena's funeral was on a Sunday. The following Tuesday, at seven-thirty a.m., a call came in at police headquarters. The caller made a simple statement. "You need to send your men to Eight-Nineteen *Calle de Cerros*. There's trouble!"

That was all that the caller said, and the line went dead. Two cars, carrying a total of eight heavily armed and highly trained special police, arrived at the scene within ten minutes of the call. The address was well known to these officers, for it was the home of *Enrique Patos*, known to be either the number two or three man in Cholo's crime family. The street was quiet, and there was no sign of "trouble." It was then that one of the officers noticed that the front door was slightly ajar. Weapons at the ready, they approached the door. The police protectively hugged the front of the building, two at either side of the door.

The lead officer used the tip of his automatic rifle to push it open and called, *"Enrique—Enrique Patos—es la policia!"* No response.

Another call was made, repeating the first and after a short period of silence, there came a moan and a cry, from within the darkened house. *"Ayuda me!* Help me!"

Cautiously, the men moved in. They had been trained to expect this to be a ploy, and that it could very easily be an ambush. However, in this man's home, it was highly unlikely. The entry hall held the first sign of trouble. The body of Enrique's personal bodyguard lay on the floor. A quick inspection showed that he had been shot in the forehead, at very close range, with a small caliber gun. Now on high alert, the team went room by room, each covering the other and finding nothing more. Another loud moan led them to a partially closed door.

"Enrique, where are you?"

A moan from within was the only response. Positioned at either side of the door, they did a three count, flung open the door, and rushed the room, flashlights searching the darkness.

Enrique was found, in his bed, bleeding from numerous gunshot wounds. Whoever shot him did not intend for him to die, at least not quickly. The gunman or men had used a twenty-two caliber pistol, firing hollow-point bullets, and had shot Enrique once, in each ankle, knee, and elbow—six shots, effectively damaging or destroying those joints. This man, if he lived, would be severely crippled for the rest of his life.

While waiting for the ambulance and unable to question the victim, one officer remarked, casually. "Someone was most pissed off, at him."

∞

Questioning, the next day, at the hospital offered little to go on. "He wore a hood and said nothing. He showed me a note that said 'sit.' When I sat on the bed, he walked up to me and shot me in the left knee, then before I knew it, in the right one. From there, both ankles then both elbows. He never said a word, just turned and left. Where was Paco, when I needed him most?"

Alonzo, who was leading the questioning, had no love for this man and no compunctions about not easing his response. "He was dead in the hallway, not ten feet from your room's door."

The look on Enrique's face of sheer horror and disbelief, to Alonzo, was worth his statement.

∞

The next three weeks brought numerous, similar, incidents. All were directed against known members or affiliates of Cholo's mob. It was being openly said, around police headquarters, that some vigilante or vigilantes, were doing a great job in cleaning up the filth and instilling the same fear within the criminal element as these criminals had instilled in the public. The current total stood at eleven severely wounded, with crippling effects, and four homicides. Even more thrilling news was the word on the street that Cholo had fled, either to Mexico or *Los Estados Unidos*. The police and detectives couldn't wait to see the look on Inspector Cantrell's face when he was told the news.

∞

When Inspector Cantrell walked into headquarters on the

following Monday morning, he was greeted with many "welcome backs" and well wishes. The first order of business was to get caught up on what had transpired during his absence.

Alejandro called Alonzo to his office and after a few social pleasantries, got down to business. "So, *mi amigo*, what has happened during the past month?"

What Alejandro didn't know was that Alonzo secretly suspected him of the past month's mayhem against Cali's widespread criminal infestation. Alonzo had not informed anyone else on the force of his suspicions. Alejandro, however, was no fool and was reasonably sure that his absence, at the same time as the "vigilante" shootings, might raise some suspicion. He had saved his "Ace card" for just such a purpose. Alonzo began with the usual retinue of day-to-day events then got down to the shootings, all the time watching for some flicker of recognition. There was none.

Instead, Alejandro countered. "What has been done to find this person or persons who have committed these shootings? Have you any suspects? Have you started a file and collected evidence and photographs?"

Cantrell was on this, as he would be with any other case, and Alonzo's secret suspicion was fast fading. Alonzo answered as best he could. "We have files on each of the incidents, including photos. We have been unable, in any of these shootings, to find a single witness and other than casings from twenty-two caliber center-fire bullets, have no other evidence, not even a single fingerprint. Even the casings were clean. Whoever is responsible for this is very good."

Alejandro was silent for a short period then gave Alonzo an order. "I want all of these files on my desk for review. There may be a pattern that will lead us to a solution."

Alonzo jumped up. "Right away, Inspector!" he said and rushed out of the office. At this moment, Alonzo was in serious doubt about his suspicions.

Alejandro Cantrell, on the other hand, was smiling inwardly. His thoughts were quite different. *Yes, it's true that a good offense is most definitely a great defense.*

ↄ⌀ↄↄ

A week had gone by since Alejandro had returned to the office, and there had been no new vigilante shootings. Alonzo's suspicions were returning. The mail arrived that day, at police headquarters, and this morning there was a letter addressed to Inspector Cantrell, the envelope marked *Private & Personal*. It was delivered to his desk. The typed note in the envelope was simple and direct.

There is still more garbage on our streets than you and your men can handle. My methods will change.

Alejandro called Alonzo to his desk. "Take this to the lab and have it thoroughly checked."

At the end of the day, the answer was as he knew it would be. Everyday paper, printed on an old typewriter, no watermarks, and no fingerprints. The envelope offered the same degree of nothing.

Alonzo read the report and looked at his boss. "Guess we'll find out what this means, soon enough."

ↄ⌀ↄↄ

Two days later, an informant advised one of the police on the street that two of Cholo's lieutenants had been seen the night before returning to the house they were known to be using for a part-time headquarters. Four squad cars, Alejandro in the lead, all filled with heavily armed officers drove quickly, without lights or sirens, to the house. The officers spilled from the vehicles and surrounded the home.

Alejandro commanded a bullhorn. "Paco, Guillermo, this is the police! We have you surrounded. Come out now, no weapons, hands raised, and you'll live to grow old. You have one minute to reply. The clock is ticking."

With twenty seconds left, a voice from within the house called out. "We're coming out! We have no guns. *Por favor*, don't shoot!"

Alejandro responded. "You have my word. We will not shoot. When you get outside, lie flat on the ground, face down, with arms and legs spread wide, hands open!"

Slowly, the front door opened, and the two men stood, hesitating for a moment, then took their first tentative steps out, one closely behind the other. Suddenly, a concussive and momentarily blinding explosion erupted under the two men, decimating the front of the building. The police dove for any cover available. It was over in an instant, and in the doorway, where an instant earlier two men had stood, there now were two mounds of mangled, bloodied, human flesh. Alejandro raised his bullhorn. "All officers back away from the building immediately. No one goes near or in until after the bomb squad has given us clearance." He turned and grabbed a passing sergeant by the arm. "Take four men and scour the buildings facing the front of this house. The bomb may well have been visually activated. Maybe we'll get lucky."

Suddenly, the squad was getting showered with small pellets, as the steel bearings, which were blown skyward and were not caught or slowed by either the building or the two targeted men, started to rain back down, making ticking sounds when they hit pavement or vehicles and no sound when they contacted a person or grass. It was over in a moment. As to getting lucky at finding the bomber—they didn't!

When the officers had recovered their composure and looked at the scene, the entire entry to the building was blown away, one side was on fire, and a fine, wet, red film, intermixed with small pieces of flesh, bone, and organs covered what was left of the front of the structure. The two men who had stood in the doorway were, between the explosive force and the steel bearings, reduced to bits and shreds of human flesh and bone. What was left offered no indication of race, gender, age, or, even with certainty, how many people had been the victims. An officer ran up with a hand-held fire extinguisher to stop the possible spread of the fire.

⟡⟡⟡

That afternoon, the bomb squad's report was in Inspector Cantrell's hands. He didn't have to read it because it was his bomb. A section of L-shaped steel lintel with steel plates welded to close both ends, creating a V-shaped trough, had been placed beneath the simple wooden porch of that house, close to the door. He had worked quickly in the dead of night, and since he knew the timing of the patrols, was able to avoid any recognition.

In the trough, they found the fragments of a remotely activated detonator. Based upon chemical residue and the degree of damage, the lab calculated there had to have been almost one kilo of PETN. The plastic explosive was covered with an estimated two or three kilos of steel ball bearings, six millimeters in diameter. The explosion drove the bearings up, in a flared V-shaped pattern, similar in nature to an over size shotgun blast.

The radio detonator in his pocket would be disassembled and find its way into a few sewers on his way home.

Alonzo, after this double murder, was having terrible guilt feelings about having suspected his boss of the earlier shootings. Alejandro, on the other hand, had other feelings. *Too bad that son-of-a-bitch Cholo got out of the country. He'll be back, and, when he returns—it's payback time.*

CHAPTER 10

Bad Chemistry

Pablo was both furious and frustrated beyond belief. He had been so close in his effort to return and continue the quest for "his" money. Then his life turned into one piece of bad luck after another. The only good thing that happened was that Cholo didn't kill him. Now, he was back where he started, on board *La Luna Media*, out in the ocean and headed directly away from where he so desperately needed to be. *I have to get back, and soon. In my fear, I gave that Cholo bastard too much information. I have to beat him to my money!* Pablo was fast loosing any traces of innocence and starting to think along the same lines as the element he was dealing with. *The captain! It is obvious that he takes bribes and who knows what else? Maybe there is a way I can get him to turn around. We're not that far from shore.*

Pablo knew nothing about maritime trade or regulations. He wrongly assumed that this vessel was just like the small fishing boats in the coastal villages of Colombia, which could come and go as they pleased. Once again he sought out the captain. "I have an idea that would benefit both of us. I will give you three hundred dollars to take me back to Miami, very good for you and for me, too."

"Are you out of your fuckin' mind? I can't just turn this ship around on a whim. Get the hell out of my sight, and I don't want to see you again till we make port in Cartagena.

Pablo was beaten and, as far as he could see, his fortune

was lost. The captain, however, was both devious and greedy, and three hundred US dollars was not to be sneezed at. *I could take his money and throw him to the sharks, but if word got out or the body was discovered, it would come back to bite me.* He pondered the idea for a while and finally came up with a scheme that was plausible, and would benefit him in two ways. *We pass many fishing boats, from the US. Perhaps, I can convince one that we found this boy hiding aboard, and he must be returned to Miami. Then I can get the money for this service and get rid of this annoying flea. It's sure worth a try because this fuckin' kid has become more trouble than I could ever have imagined.* He began to scan the radar screen.

❦

Cholo and his two companions were, at the same time, sitting in a motel room on the north bound side of US Highway 1, in Kendall, Florida, just a short distance southwest of Miami. "From what that kid told me, there has to be at least one-hundred-fifty thousand in cash sitting in a shed in West Virginia. Some meaningless little town called Dodsonville." He wasn't about to disclose what he knew, or thought he knew, to be the true dollar amount. His plan was to use these two to help locate the money then kill them, take the money, and return to Colombia. His rational was simple. *I need to run my own organization again, not be a mule for others. There's too little money in that, and, as to these two recent, but very temporary partners, I'll continue to play the willing accomplice and use these idiots to accomplish my goal.* Cholo had arrived at the dollar amount, based on what they had received for just the pick-up and delivery of the cocaine shipment from *La Luna Media,* then tripled the amount to sweeten the deal. The three started to devise a plan to locate and get away with the money. They agreed it would be as Cholo said, much less risky than avoiding the Coast Guard and the DEA.

The two original partners were at the same time plotting to kill Cholo. Their thought process was almost similar to his. Jorge presented it simply. "Once we locate the money, we dispose of this bastard then go back to operating with just the two of us." He reasoned that it had been foolish to take on a third man, even though the man had proven to be experienced. Pepe agreed wholeheartedly.

☙❧

Sheriff Gabriel Tanner was at his desk at seven a.m. when he had a sudden and very shocking thought. *Ah jest bet thet th' two strangers whut come t' town lookin' fer A.J. were part a sum special, mebbe even secret, unit thet A.J. were in. He musta left wi' them, which would 'splain how he got back t' th' base.* That thought held water for about fifteen minutes. A knock on his door and Sally walked in, carrying two shopping bags. "Mornin', Sally. Startin' late t'day?"

She came right to the point. "Mornin', Gabe. Ah tole 'em ah'd be a bit late t'day fer a pers'nal errund." She took a deep breath, paused for a moment and continued. "Last time A.J. were in town, he stayed t' mah place fer a couple a days." She stopped, waiting for a possible response. Gabe knew better and just waited. Sally continued as if there hadn't been a break. "Leastways, he jest up 'n' disappeared 'n' even lef' his b'longin's. Next ah knowed, he were dead. Been workin' a lot a doubles lately, so's this be th' fust chance ah had t' bring his stuff by. Didn't know whut else t' do wi' it 'n' didn't wan' ta jest trash it." It was Sally's revelation that almost completely dispelled Gabe's earlier thought and started to give him an uneasy feeling in his gut. Suddenly, the road to the solutions he was seeking, which seemed to be getting straight and simple, had taken a dangerous turn. *Ah got me a nasty feeling thet ah'm a teeterin' on th' edge a someplace whar ah don't b'long.* His feelings must have showed on his face because he suddenly heard Sally's voice, again.

"Ya okay, Gabe? Ya all uv a sudden 'peer a mite stressed."

Gabe recovered and quickly covered up. "Ah'm good—jest r'membered a mess ah got ta git ta, er all."

Her smile indicated her understanding, and having accomplished what she came for, Sally rose to leave. "Thet's got er,

Gabe. Got ta git a goin' ta work. Cain't miss too much. Reck-en ah'll see ya cum lunch."

Gabe rose when she did and, after her parting words, dropped back in his chair. *This un's startin' ta stink 'n' 'peers ta be headin' en a real bad d'rection. Ah wunda if'n eny a A.J.'s things'll offer a clue? Fer shore he jest wouldn't a left all a his clothes ta Sally's place. Come ta think on er, ah'd best give A.J.'s pick-up a real tight goin' over.*

CHAPTER 11

The Quest

Cholo listened carefully as Jorge and Pepe planned their trip to West Virginia. He was listening for the one odd word or statement, which would indicate that a trap was being set for him. He heard nothing to cause alarm.

Jorge, obviously the leader and planner laid out the trip on a map spread out in front of them on the coffee table. "We'll steal a car, an older one, from a used car lot then take the plates off a car from a different state. We'll drive north on US One 'til—"

Cholo broke in. "Why not I-Ninety-Five, that looks like a major road, be a much faster route."

Jorge, obviously annoyed at being questioned, responded curtly. "Yes, that would be faster, but you need to shut up, listen, and go along with what I say. The authorities monitor that road, looking for people just like us, and, if we're spotted, it's too far between exits to make a run for it. Now just shut your damn mouth and listen! I know what I'm doing."

Cholo was furious. No one ever dared to speak to him in that manner in Cali. If they did, they had signed their death warrant. He kept his fury bottled inside, biding his time, but, in his mind, he planned his retribution. *We'll see how big his speech is when I cut his lousy tongue out and watch him drown in his own blood.*

⌀⌀

Just a few miles east, a commercial shrimp trawler was preparing to dock in Miami. On board sat Pablo Robles, nauseous from the combined smell of live shrimp and diesel fumes, coupled with the wave created motion of the trawler. That wonderful ham sandwich, which he had enjoyed, just a few hours ago, had been regurgitated with his latest bout of seasickness. The ocean was not for him. The captain of the trawler was a Cuban and, luckily for Pablo, sympathetic. "When we tie up, just walk away, and I'll forget we ever saw you. You may not be so lucky, next time. That freighter captain could have called the Coast Guard. Get a job, save your money, and return home in a more secure manner."

Pablo was more than grateful, and, for the sake of appearances, he agreed completely with the trawler captain. "*Muchas gracias Señor Capitán*. I will do as you say."

The truth was far from evident in this short conversation, and Pablo's spoken words and unspoken intent were as different as ice and steam.

⁕

In Dodsonville, West Virginia, Sheriff Tanner was casually tossing the wanted fugitive faxes, which he received on an almost daily basis and were usually of no value, into the trash. That job completed, he started back to his desk when something was triggered in his subconscious that caused him to pause. *Ah b'lieve thet ah recognized one a them boys.* He did an about face and retrieved the faxes. Thumbing through them he spotted the one that had jogged a memory. *Well, ah'll be a three-legged chicken. Thet shore as shootin' er thet Latino kid whut were in town round th' time wi' all thet mess wi' A.J. Ah'd best hang on ta this un. Fer shore, this puzzle's gettin' more complicated, 'n' smellin worse by th' day.*

CHAPTER 12

Closure

The afternoon had been wonderfully relaxed and low key. The two other couples at Carlos and Rosita's home were easy to be with, and talk too. That suited Jon perfectly as he rarely made time to socialize outside of his immediate close and very limited circle of friends. It was early evening when the small party broke up. The two other couples left and Rosita, along with Sheri, started to do a quick clean up.

Jon seized this opportunity and pulled Carlos aside. "I need to fill you in on why I was a little late, getting back."

When he was finished, Carlos sat without responding for almost two minutes. When he did, it was with a tinge of hope, but lacking conviction. "Jon, maybe this will blow over quickly. The kid is untrained, and probably will get picked up and deported or jailed before he ever reaches West Virginia." The moment after he made that statement, Carlos became serious. "If he gets picked up and found to be illegal, that could possibly open a can of worms for us and maybe the commander."

His friend smiled, slightly. "My thoughts exactly, Carlos—maybe I should give the commander a quick call and have him withdraw that wanted bulletin. I need to speak to him, anyway."

Jon's last remark left Carlos puzzled. *The turned operative had been killed and the killer, although now back in the country, was an untrained kid who had gotten lucky—no problem*

*there. So what else would make Jon need to speak to the com-
mander?*

Carlos's curiosity got the better of him. "I can see your
point about withdrawing the wanted status on the kid—makes
good sense. But you sound as if there's something else on your
mind. Do you mind sharing it?"

Carlos must have had a serious look on his face when he
asked that question because Jon broke into a broad grin. "Relax *mi amigo*! It's not that serious. I'd like the opportunity to
meet, and personally thank, the crew of that rescue chopper—
especially that fellow Hunting Eagle. From what you've told
me, I'd be just a memory right now if it weren't for his unique
abilities. Carlos was silent and momentarily pensive. Just the
thought of how close he had come to loosing his closest friend,
no—more like a brother—robbed him of speech.

Jon picked up on it immediately and moved on. "Come on
let's give Ertugal a call while the girls are cleaning up. That
way we'll avoid their suspicious looks."

That last comment brought Carlos to life. He knew exactly
what Jon meant, especially since Rosita had the nose of a
bloodhound when he tried to hide something. "Let's go!"

Both men stood and headed, instinctively, for the porch.
Out there, they couldn't be overheard from within the house
and would not be accidentally intruded upon. Jon was already
going through the dialing sequence, for the commander, on his
cell phone.

"Jon! How th' hell are you, and to what do I owe the unexpected pleasure? Please tell me that you're finally coming
back."

Jon was slowly shaking his head. *That man just doesn't
give up.* "No, sir. I'm still content with the simple life—
although lately, it hasn't been that simple. Tell you why I
called. I think that you should withdraw that wanted notice on
Pablo Robles. If anyone with any intelligence collars him, it
could open a big can of worms. It would be better to have one
or two undercovers hang out in that town in West Virginia
where A.J. was from. They could pick Mr. Pablo up quietly

'cause unless I miss my guess, he'll be headed there for the money that he believes is rightfully his."

There was silence for a moment, on the other end of the conversation while Ertugal ruminated over what Jon had just said. It didn't take long. The commander could assess a situation faster than most men could spell their names. "Good thinking, Jon! I'll get right on it. You haven't lost your edge, or your field savvy. Thanks for the call."

Jon broke in quickly. "Hang on, Commander. I have a personal question." *That man just can't wait to get off the phone.* Jon had stopped him just in time. "Commander, the air/sea rescue team that picked me up—are they available any time in the next two weeks? I'd like to thank them personally, and since I'm a brother, it wouldn't be a breach of protocol." Jon waited while his request was considered—it took perhaps all of ten seconds.

"Can do. I'll get back with you as soon as I verify that they're not shipping out." The phone went dead.

Carlos waited while Jon put his phone away, and when his friend appeared lost in thought, broke in. "Well, are you going to keep it a secret or fill me in? What did the commander say?"

It was as if Carlos's words jarred Jon back to the present. "Sorry, just sorting out a few things. Ertugal had no problem with my request and will call back as soon as he verifies the team's availability. We might as well go back inside. There wasn't that much clean-up, and the way the two of them go at it they should be about finished."

The words were barely out of Jon's mouth when his cell phone rang. "That was fast, Commander."

"Jon, the team will be in Annapolis, Maryland, all next week. I'll fax you some of their contact numbers." The phone went dead. Ertugal had said all that he had to say.

This time, Jon didn't wait for Carlos to ask. "He said that the rescue team would be in Annapolis all next week. I know of a great hotel in the downtown area, right on the bay. Why don't you and Rosita pack a bag and join us, as my guest, for three or four days? It would be fun to get away together. What do you say, partner?"

Carlos started to protest, "Jon you're always doing things for Rosita and me or buying things for us, and yet you never let us do anything for you."

Jon was ready for him and had the perfect answer. "Consider it a thank you for the time I spent here recuperating and enjoying Rosita's fantastic cooking—it's the least I can do." He knew he had a good argument, but added one small but critical after-thought. "Of course, that is if Sheri is willing."

They had been walking as they talked and now were in the living room. Almost on cue, Rosita and Sheri entered the room, catching them in the middle of their give and take. Rosita took one look at her husband and knew something was going on. "Okay! What are the two of you scheming about now?" She stood poised, hands on her hips, as if waiting to hear something outrageous.

Carlos and Jon both started to respond, simultaneously, but Jon won out. Quickly he told them about his call to Commander Ertugal, and how he had wanted to thank the rescue team. "The commander told me that they would be in Annapolis all next week, and so I came up with an idea. If it suits Sheri, how would you and Carlos like to join us in Annapolis, as my guest, for three or four days? I can thank my rescuers, you can meet them, and we can enjoy some of the wonderful restaurants as well as a great hotel." He paused for a moment, letting the request register. *I can see from Sheri's expression that she's more than willing.* "Rosita, *por favor*. It's the least I can do to thank you and Carlos for letting me recuperate in your home."

Rosita, true to her Spanish nature, was not about to accept this generosity without some small objection. "You are always doing nice and generous things for us, and as to your stay here to recuperate that is insignificant. You would always be welcome in our home for any period of time. However, we will accept your most generous offer because it will do Carlos good to see more than just this island and the ocean."

Once Rosita confirmed her acceptance, Carlos developed a broad grin, and Sheri was likewise thrilled.

Jon now had to put all the travel pieces in place. First, a call to the two Swedes to advise them that they were not sailing on Monday, in order that some small details that had been overlooked during the construction of the boat could be corrected. The second call was to August Cavendish to advise the cabinet maker that the boat would be available all next week. The last call would be to the Annapolis Marriott to reserve two double rooms. Those calls took less than ten minutes.

As he hung up the phone, from the last call, Jon looked up with a smile. "We're all set! Let's get ourselves packed. We leave in the morning." A momentary pause and a quizzical expression on his face caused Sheri to start to question, but he cut her short. "I need to make one more call. We need a bigger car!" He reserved a luxury SUV, and they were set.

CHAPTER 13

Money Run

Jorge presented his plan, which was very explicit. "We steal an older Ford or a Chevy, nothing fancy. That way we won't stand out. Try to get one that has a license plate that doesn't say Florida. This car that we've been using is a beat up Datsun, just about ready for the scrap heap, and if we have to run for it, we won't stand a chance. I'm going to store this car at that long term open-air storage unit, in case a need for it comes up in the future. I'll drop both of you at the liquor store, the one that's only three blocks away. Pick me up when you have the car. It's dark now, and that will make you harder to spot or identify."

The plan was fairly simple, and the three of them climbed into the Datsun. Jorge drove quickly to the liquor store, dropping Cholo and Pepe half a block enough away so that it wouldn't be obvious to anyone that the liquor store was their intended destination—then he was gone.

The two men hid in the bushes alongside the parking area and waited. An assortment of pickup and work trucks came and went. The store was obviously a stopping point for laborers and craftsmen at the end of the day. Most would leave their vehicle motors running and hurry in to the store. They would emerge in just a few minutes with whatever their usual liquid sedative was to help ease the pain of another rough day. Perhaps a pint of vodka, a pint of bourbon, maybe tequila, or a cheap wine. It was the poor man's catharsis. Alcohol was a cheap way to forget today, get through the night, and be ready for tomorrow.

After the rush of working class traffic, there was a lull, then a new assortment of cars began to arrive. These drivers would turn off their engines and almost always lock their vehicle. It would take these patrons a little longer in the store and, by the size of the bags they carried out, it was evident that they had purchased fifths or two-liter bottles. Cholo was getting anxious. This was taking longer than he was comfortable with. *If we had gone to a shopping center, we would have a fuckin' car, already.* Another lull then suddenly a BMW sedan pulled in at a high rate of speed and screeched to a stop in front of the entrance. The driver jumped from his vehicle, wearing a ski mask, pulled a gun, left his car motor running, and ran into the store. Cholo saw the perfect opportunity. *Grab this car. A hold-up man isn't about to run to the police without taking the time to set up an alibi.* He grabbed Pepe by the arm. "Let's go!" Pepe hesitated. *"Ahora pronto, tu culo!"*

Pepe was not overly quick, mentally, but he knew that the man with the gun would not let them get away with his escape car. *"El tienes una pistola!"*

Cholo was adamant. *"Ahora, pronto.* We'll be gone before he comes out."

With that statement, he started to run for the car. Pepe, in fear of being left behind, was right on his heels. Cholo climbed into the driver's seat. Suddenly, from within the store, three shots fired in short succession. Pepe wasn't waiting and dove into the back seat, staying down low on the floor, praying not to get shot. It took a moment for Cholo to figure out the controls, and that was a moment too long.

The robber was out and running for his car. "Hey!" he screamed at Cholo. "Get th' fuck outa my car!" He started to point the gun at Cholo.

Cholo was not intimidated but acted reflexively. He pulled the razor-sharp knife from his belt, and, in one fluid motion, drove it out of the open window and up under the man's chin. The power of his thrust drove the knife through the soft underside of the man's lower jaw, up through his tongue then his soft palette, and into his brain. The thief was dead on his feet. A hard jerk pulled the knife free, even before the man's legs collapsed. Cholo put the car in reverse and drove calmly away. As they rounded the corner, the sounds of approaching police sirens reached them.

Pepe was still lying prone, except now up on the back seat, when they picked Jorge up.

❧

Both the police and crime scene unit were completely confused. They had a dead shop owner with three thirty-eight caliber slugs in his chest and, in the parking lot, the obvious killer and robber. The murder weapon was on the ground near the body and six-hundred and eighteen dollars, from the register, was in his pocket. That part was simple—any schoolboy could have put it together. That's where simple ended. The hard question was who killed this robber and why?

The answers came the next day as the tapes from the store and parking lot security cameras were played. The tape from the camera inside of the liquor store was straightforward. Robber brandishes a gun and demands the money; store owner starts to protest; robber, impatient, shoots store owner and rifles the register; robber turns and runs. The tape from the parking lot security camera told a bizarre story of unbelievable chance. The black BMW drove rapidly into the lot. The driver exited, wearing a ski mask, left the motor running, and ran into the store. In less than a minute, two men ran up to the car and jumped in. From their actions on the tape, it was evident that their intent was to steal the car. For some unexplained reason, they did not drive off, immediately. That's when the robber reappeared and aimed his gun at the driver. The knife attack was so fast that they had to rerun the tape at a slower speed to identify it.

One of the detectives watching the tape, crudely and explicitly, vocalized what they all were thinking. "Jeez! That guy knew exactly where to stab and did it as if it was second nature. This guy's so fuckin' fast with a knife, he'd beat a gun."

An "all points" bulletin was immediately issued for a black 1996 BMW 328i with Florida license plates and two male Hispanic occupants.

જ્જ

When they picked Jorge up, he was enraged, and he directed his fury at Cholo who was driving. "You fuckin' idiot! What didn't you understand? I said a Ford or a Chevy, not some high profile import that will make us stick out like a pig among chickens. Now what, asshole? Do you want to spend the next twenty-years in a federal prison?

Cholo controlled his reaction. This was not the time to vent his anger. He needed these two mules to help carry out his plan to locate the money that Pablo had spoken of. "The only vehicles that came to the liquor store, for the first forty-five minutes, were pickup trucks. We were running out of time, and when this car pulled in and the driver ran in to rob the store, leaving the motor running, we grabbed it. Besides, he probably stole it for the robbery. We can just pull in at the next shopping center and trade this for the car of your choice, but at least we can get moving."

He never mentioned the fact that he had killed the driver of the car and Pepe, who had been cowering on the floor in the rear, hadn't seen or heard a thing.

One hour later, they were headed north on US Highway 1, in a tired-looking, blue, Ford Fairlane, its Florida plates switched with the Georgia plates from another car. The BMW was left, all doors locked, in the shopping center where they had stolen the Ford.

Jorge was now driving and Pepe, now more at ease, was in front with him.

Cholo sat quietly in the rear, finished a cigarette then crushed it out on the car floor. Mentally he was contemplating, *What a pleasure it will be to kill these two peros.* A smile spread across his pockmarked face as he thought about that and the rebuilding of his criminal network.

ɔɔɛɔ

At the same time, less than eight miles away, Pablo Robles finally had some good luck, having recently made what he considered to be a perfect deal. Pablo had accidentally encountered a Guatemalan man in the bus depot. The man was trying to get to Annapolis, Maryland, to visit family, but came up short of funds. He would now be forced to wait a week until he earned a little more money for the bus ticket. The man was also reasonably comfortable with English.

The deal was simple. "You make sure that I don't make a mistake traveling to West Virginia, and I will buy the balance of your ticket to Maryland."

The man was thrilled, and the deal was struck. The Guatemalan collected a duffel bag and a jacket from a short-term locker, and the two men boarded a Trailways bus headed north. It was two forty-five p.m. Pablo was elated. *Now I'll get the money that is rightfully mine.*

ɔɔɛɔ

Approximately eleven-hundred miles north, a rented Cadillac Escalade with two relaxed and happy couples turned onto Compromise Street and pulled up in front of the Annapolis Marriott. The valet service had the luggage out and on a rolling carrier in a minute.

Jon took the ticket for the car and handed the parking attendant a five. Carlos stretched lazily and decided he would have a little fun at Jon's expense. "You ought to buy a car like that. I feel as if we drove here on my couch." He knew how conservative Jon was in his personal life, and the look of disbelief on his face confirmed it. Immediately after his comment, a broad grin lit up Calos's face, followed by Jon's matching grin. Carlos pretended that he didn't see the scowl of disapproval on Rosita's face.

CHAPTER 14

Annapolis

Que bonita!" Those were Rosita's first words when the bellhop opened the door to their room. "Jon must be crazy to be spending this much money."

Carlos was less effusive until he walked to the window. "Wow! Take a look at this view and all of those yachts." He knew his wife's nature, and the next words out of his mouth made that evident. "Don't say a word to Jon about the expense or money. He knows what he is doing and does just what he wants to—okay?"

It wasn't often, but this time Rosita acquiesced. "Okay, I'll say nothing, but it still must be way too expensive."

A last minute cancellation allowed Jon to take everyone to dinner at the Café Normandie, which usually required reservations days in advance. The restaurant was renowned for superior food and service, and it didn't let any of them down.

After dinner, the valet service brought their car to the entrance, and as Jon started to drive, he offered a suggestion. "I'd like to meet with the 'copter rescue team tomorrow, if that's okay with all of you. I'll give the captain a call when we get back to the hotel and see if that works. Speaking of the hotel, they have a great lounge. Why don't we have a nightcap and if tomorrow is good for the meeting, we'll meet at seven a.m. for breakfast and take it from there?"

The lounge was just what the name implied, furnished with comfortable leather upholstered seats, oak tables, paneled walls and soft lighting. It was the ideal setting, in which one could relax, and enjoy a drink, not just "have" one. They found a comfortable table in a corner. A waiter came over almost immediately. "Good evening, folks. Do you require menus or is it just for cocktails? If it's just cocktails may I take your order?"

Jon responded casually. "I believe that it'll be just drinks." He turned, slightly, toward the others. "Ladies?"

Sheri requested a "Madras," on the rocks. The name of the drink piqued Rosita's interest, and, after the contents were explained by the waiter, she opted for the same. "It's about time that I learned about some new choices."

Carlos ordered a Dos Equis beer, and Jon, after a moments' thought requested a Martel Cordon Bleu Cognac.

This surprised Carlos, and he had to comment. "I didn't think you drank anything but Laphroaig or an occasional glass of wine or beer."

Jon gave him a friendly slap on the back. "*Mi amigo*, I do have other tastes—just rarely have the time for them. Now, let me call and see if I can set up that meeting." Jon got up to head outside. "I shouldn't be more than a couple of minutes." He turned and left.

The waiter returned with their drinks, and, at the same time placed a small bowl of mixed nuts and mini-pretzels in the center of the table. "If you need anything else, just signal or catch my eye." With everyone satisfied, he left and turned his attention to a newly arrived couple.

Not even five minutes had passed, and Jon reappeared. "Just got off the phone with Captain Harrison. He'll have the whole team assembled at the north end of the Naval Academy Parade Field at ten a.m. in the morning. He said it would be a pleasure to meet with us under these more pleasant circumstances." Jon slid into his chair, swirled the cognac for about a minute, holding the bowl of the snifter in his palm for warming, then took a slow, appreciative sip. "Now that's what I call good!"

They made small talk for a while, ordered a second round of drinks, and it seemed that, in no time, it was eleven o'clock.

Rosita gave a secretive look to Carlos and said to no one in particular. "Why don't we call it a night?"

Sheri caught the tone of that "look" and immediately seconded the motion. "Sounds like a good idea. That way we can all be fresh for tomorrow."

Neither of the men needed any coaxing, Jon caught the waiter's attention, signed for the drinks, and they left for their rooms.

CHAPTER 15

Hunting Eagle

It didn't matter that he was away from home and work. It didn't matter that the meeting he had set up was at ten a.m. Jon was up at forty-thirty a.m., wide awake and mentally cursing his inner clock that refused to let him sleep. He slipped out of bed, careful to not wake Sheri, pulled a terry wrap around his waist, and walked toward the balcony. He didn't open the covering blackout drape, instead simply stepped behind it.

The sliding door opened with just a whisper of noise, and he stepped outside then settled into a comfortable chair. The view of the harbor, at this hour, was limited to areas along the dock that were illuminated and the few vessels that had running lights on. The scene triggered a mental recall of his final encounter with El Tigre and a reflexively automatic attempt to second guess the past. His past had him forever reworking an incident to see if he could have improved on the procedure, or how the overall "op" had played out. As a Monday morning quarterback, he now could exercise that luxury, but that event was definitely in the past.

Why bother? El Tigre is dead, and the smart thing to do is move on. I wonder how long it will take for that Pablo kid to get picked up and sent back home? Sure hope it's before a new round of trouble. His thought process switched to Sheri. *The longer our relationship continues, the deeper my involvement, both mentally and physically, is becoming.*

His mind was, quite often now, considering a move to permanence.

The soft hiss of the sliding door as it opened brought Jon to an instant alert state. *Damn! Still have the old reflexes.* He relaxed. "Good morning, Sheri. Hope you slept well.

She smiled seductively. "After that wonderful 'sleeping pill,' I sure did. How about you?"

"Couldn't make it past four-thirty. But our bedtime activity sure helped me to fall asleep, quickly. How about getting a good start to the day?"

Sheri hit him, playfully, on the shoulder. "My idea of a good start, at least today, would be a good breakfast. Do you think that Rosita and Carlos are up?"

"I'd be willing to bet on it. When it comes to sleep, he and I are poured from the same mold—four to five hours, and that's it. Why don't you ring their room and ask them to meet us in the lobby at seven? We can either have breakfast here or in town."

৩৩৩

Rosita insisted that they have breakfast in the hotel. "I saw that it's included with the rooms, which means that you've already paid for it, so why spend money that you don't have to?"

Her logic was irrefutable, and they truly enjoyed their breakfast in the hotel café. Both the food and service were excellent. Jon had to compliment Rosita. "You had the right idea, both from a cost-consciousness aspect and the immediate convenience of not having to drive or find parking."

"*Gracias,* Jon."

৩৩৩

The morning sky was a soft shade of cornflower blue, dotted with a light scattering of snow white cumulus clouds, when they arrived at the Naval Academy. Jon questioned an upper classman who directed them to the parade field. As Jon was parking, a drill instructor was marching a dozen cadets across the field.

Carlos watched, silently then turned to Jon. "Hey, *amigo,* seems like a hundred years ago that we were doing that in the Marines."

Jon watched for a moment then started to walk toward the north end of the field. He offered a response over his shoulder. "Don't miss a bit of it."

He kept walking. Sheri caught up and fell into step with him. They reached the appointed meeting area with no sign of the rescue team.

Jon glanced at his watch. "We're ten minutes early."

The words were barely out of his mouth when five men, dressed in civilian clothes, entered the field through a wrought iron gate at the opposite end of the field.

The two groups began to walk toward each other, Jon leading one and the other led by a tall, lanky man.

The tall man spoke first when the distance between them was comfortable. "Would you be Jon Morton?" He received an affirmative nod. "I'm Captain Harrison, but Doug will do just fine."

When they had closed the distance between them, Doug offered his hand to Jon. They shook hands then embraced in a tight hug, the kind that only occurred between true friends.

When they stepped apart, Doug quipped lightly. "I've got to tell you, Jon, you look a hell of a lot better than you did at our first meeting."

Jon smiled broadly as he responded. "Ya think so?" The two men faced each other silently, for a few moments. Jon broke the silence. "How about introducing me to your crew?"

Doug turned toward the four men standing just behind him and began the introductions, pointing to each of the men as he offered their names. "This is Kevin, Sean, Grady, and Hal."

As each man was indicated, he would step forward, shake hands with Jon, and would also hug with a strong intensity.

Sheri noted this and added it to her list of unanswered questions. *Jon said that he wanted to meet the rescue team, and yet they act as if they're almost like brothers.* She had no idea how accurate her observation was. She also noted that no last names were offered and no rank, other than Doug's, was mentioned.

The team then offered general and relaxed greetings to Carlos, who, as Kevin stated, said, "We've met before."

He then went through the same hand shake and hug greeting, as had Jon. He then introduced Rosita.

Jon then introduced Sheri. Both women received just a casual "hello" or a simple "pleased to meet you."

"Doug, do you mind if I take a few minutes of Hal's time?" Jon asked. "Based on what Carlos has told me, I understand that he was critical in your getting to me in time."

"No problem, Jon. That's entirely up to him. We managed to get a couple of days off, so it's Hal's choice."

Both men looked to Hal for his answer.

"Glad to do it, Jon. I have the rest of the morning free."

With Hal's acceptance, the rest of the team turned to go.

"Thanks, again, for taking the time to meet with me, Doug."

Doug responded to Jon's statement with a just a few words. "There's always time for a brother."

Sheri didn't miss that remark. The four men turned and walked off, leaving Hal with the two couples.

"Hal, let's all go sit in the bleachers for a few minutes."

A nod of agreement and they all turned to walk the short distance to the seating. Once seated, Jon turned to Hal and presented the question that had elevated his personal curiosity. "Carlos tells me that you spotted the scattered floating wreckage of my boat in low visibility weather conditions—rain, wind, and high seas. He also said that when you spotted it, it was located about six-hundred yards out, and he couldn't even make it out with high-power binoculars. You probably saved my life, but could you explain how that's possible?"

Hal was quiet for a minute or so then responded. "I will answer your question by telling you a story that has been passed down from a time when this land was the homeland of many great tribes, long before the coming of the white man. It began with a great Sioux, Lone Bear. Are you willing to listen?"

He had all of their attention, now.

Jon answered quickly, with conviction. "Absolutely! Go ahead."

CHAPTER 16

Lone Bear

Hal left his seat and moved to the grass area in front of them. He sat cross-legged on the grass, faced Jon, then paused and closed his eyes. He was summoning up a story that had its beginning in the ancestral times of the Sioux.

"This was the time long before the white man came, with his thunder-sticks that brought death, his diseases, and his greed," he began. "Life was good, and the Sioux were one with the land. They could not know of, or defend against, the scourge that was soon to come. You will now hear a tale of a great chief and the origin of my special name."

ᕼᗝᕼ

Lone Bear pushed back the deerskin cover and emerged into the dawn of a new day. The early morning air still held the chill of winter, but on this fifth day of the new moon, the rising sun gave a promise of warmth. The season of new growth had begun, and the signs of a good hunt were evident.

He looked back, with a feeling of pride, at his teepee. Inside, his wife slept peacefully under a warm bear's skin. She was big with child and soon would bring forth their first one—hopefully, a man-child. He took a deep breath of the crisp, clean early spring air, and was glad for this day. The aroma of the camp fires mingled with the new smells of tree buds, young grass, strong-running streams, and the calls of returning birds. Yes, today would be good for the hunt. The time of deep snows, and the winds with cold teeth biting, had been hard, and game was scarce, but the snows had melted, and the cutting winds had turned to mild breezes, carrying a touch of warmth from the now strengthening sun. The many scents of the earth were returning, telling of renewed life.

He would hunt alone, today, as would most of the warriors. It was too early for the herds of buffalo to return, and lone hunters fared best against deer. All kills were shared, but the hunter who brought down the game was given first selection of the choice parts.

The deerskin flap, once again, covered the teepee entry. Lone Bear slipped his quiver of flint-tipped arrows across his back, picked up his bow, and moved out of the clearing. He was headed north, toward the fields that got the earliest growth of ferns and wildflowers. The deer knew this and would be seeking the fresh new growth. The smell of the air was good. It gave promise of an early spring. He moved easily through the trees—not cautious, but not making unnecessary noise. Lone Bear was in his natural element. He was a natural part of the world in which he lived. Soon the stream of sweet waters came into sight. He would stop and drink before crossing. The area of the hunt would not be reached until the sun had risen above the trees. If the Great Spirit was on his side today, the deer would have come to feed.

Ice outcroppings still clung to the rocks and shoreline of the stream. The water was cold, and he drank thirstily then filled the deer bladder that served as a canteen. The stream had not yet begun to swell with runoff from the melting snows, allowing for an easy crossing, on the exposed rocks. As he stepped from rock to rock, a movement in the water caught his eye. It was a large brook trout. Lone Bear made a mental note to return soon with his fish spear.

Once across the stream, he began to jog toward his objective, which was the valley at the base of the mountains, beyond the wooded area he had just entered. One hour at a well-paced trot, and the valley lay ahead. He stopped at the last outcropping of trees and surveyed the verdant arena. Slowly his piercing gaze traversed the landscape. Suddenly, his gaze froze. At least ten large deer were grazing in the field. All were does, and six of them were with new young. Lone Bear watched carefully, observing the movements of the deer to be certain that, when his arrow flew, it would not seek a new mother.

The wind was coming from the east as he began to close the distance. He circled to the west. The deer were too far for his bow, and it would not do for them to catch his scent. He crouched low, seeking small bushes for cover. Slowly he closed the distance, freezing in place, when he met the gaze of a watchful doe, then proceeding forward again when the gaze changed direction. The distance was closing steadily, and he dropped to his belly. There was very little cover now, and he would need all of his skill to outwit this wary game.

A movement in the sky overhead caught his attention. It was a golden eagle, also hunting the valley. Suddenly, the eagle circled. It had spotted a target. The great bird dove from the heavens at amazing speed, headed for a location just beyond the deer that Lone Bear was hunting. The raptor disappeared behind the deer and, in just a moment, rose, its powerful wings taking it skyward. In its talons was a rabbit. It was then that the bird emitted its shrill cry of victory. That piercing cry spooked the deer, and they ran from the imagined danger. Because the eagle had been beyond the deer when they spooked, their flight had them running straight toward Lone Bear. Quickly, he fitted an arrow to the buffalo sinew bowstring and drew his bow taut. The deer were almost upon him when he rose and released his arrow. His aim was true, and the stricken deer ran on, almost one-hundred feet farther, before dropping. The arrow that had pierced its lungs caused them to fill with blood, killing the animal. Lone Bear held his bow high, looked skyward, and he too gave a cry of victory. "Kii ah Yiii Wah! *The Great Spirit has been kind. He guided my arrow and gave me a sign. My child will be called Hunting Eagle.*"

ↂↄ

"Now you have heard the history of my name. It has survived many generations, many battles, even the power and cruelty of the white man. The name has only been given to a first born son, and, with the name, has come the gift, which the Great Spirit gave to the hunting eagle—the true skills of a superior hunter and the distance-piercing vision of the eagle."

The four listeners sat silently, absorbing the power of the story told by this young Sioux. They could not help but wonder as to the special powers this name seemed to carry. Two of them had, just recently, been witness to his skills. One had been saved from death by them, and the other had scoffed at the sighting announced by Hunting Eagle, when he himself saw nothing, only to be awed, in the end, by the truth of the sighting and the fact that this skill had saved his closest friend from a watery grave. Hunting Eagle was a man neither would ever forget.

"Hal is easier, for most, than my true given name and is more-or-less a contraction," Hal continued then beckoned. "Jon, come, sit here in front of me."

Perplexed, Jon did as Hal requested and also sat cross-legged. Hal then raised his arms and looked to the sky. He began a slow chant, in Sioux, which lasted about two minutes. He then lowered his arms and looked at Jon. "I have asked that the Great Spirit protect you, for you are a brave and honest warrior." He stood up, and Jon did likewise. "I must go now. It was good for us to meet."

With that, he turned and walked, without pausing, back across the field in the direction from which he had originally come.

Jon remained where he stood, his mind trying to wrap itself around the possibility that some things, which he had been sure were just folk legend, actually might be true. He was deep in thought when a voice broke in.

It was Carlos. "Hey, *amigo,* you okay?"

"Sorry! Yeah, I was just trying to make sense of this Indian thing. The whole thing seems like a fiction story yet we're both here to attest to the reality of it. Absolutely amazing!"

"Por seguro, Jon. You can imagine how I felt on that

chopper when he said he saw the wreckage and, even with high-power binoculars, all I could see was water. What was that chanting about, before he left? Seemed pretty intense."

"I guess it was in Sioux. Hal was asking the Great Spirit to protect me. How about that? Let's collect the girls and walk around in town for a while. There are a number of unique shops, and that should keep them occupied long enough for us to avoid too many questions." Jon turned toward the two women, who were now engrossed in an animated conversation, and hollered, "Sheri, Rosita, come on. We thought we'd go into town and look at some of the interesting shops."

Both women lit up at the prospect of some shopping. They paused in their conversation, and both began to smile.

Sheri tucked the meeting with the rescue team away for future questions and conversation. "That's a great idea!" she called. "We're coming."

In what seemed like just moments, they were back in the car.

CHAPTER 17

Smoke

Traffic had been steadily increasing, as they neared town. There was now almost a continuous stream of cars, trucks, and an occasional bus on Baltimore Annapolis Boulevard. Jon spotted a break in the oncoming traffic and pulled rapidly out to pass the few cars and one bus, all of which were being slowed by a heavily loaded flatbed trailer. Jon accelerated and, as he passed the slow moving traffic, Carlos gave an exclamation of surprise. "What th—"

Jon pulled back in lane, but his friend's remark had not gone unnoticed. "What got your attention, back there Carlos? I caught a glimpse of your face, and it looked as if you'd seen a ghost or something just as shocking."

Carlos wanted to spit out just what it was that shocked him, but he didn't want either of the women to know. He covered it with a fabrication. "Just saw some outlandish graffiti on the side of that truck you passed. It was really foul, and not worth repeating."

Jon knew his friend well enough to recognize a cover-up and also knew that as soon as the opportunity presented itself, he would be informed.

They drove slowly down Main Street until Jon spotted a parking space. As luck would have it, it was right in front of a fashionable women's boutique.

Sheri saw the perfect opening for a remark to Jon, "You parked in the perfect place for us to start. Oh! Also, I was glad to see that you drove in the right direction on this one way street." This was a not-so-subtle reference to an incident early on in their relationship.

Jon just grinned at her comment. "Carlos and I will wait out here. Call if you need us."

With that, Rosita and Sheri quickly left the car, turned, and hurried into the store.

Jon immediately turned to Carlos. "All right, what the heck did you see, back there?"

"Jon, it wasn't the truck—it was the bus. I'm almost positive that I saw the kid who shot A.J. on that bus. He was sitting by the window, and he should be sitting back in Colombia. Pablo…Pablo Robles…is his name."

Silence was Jon's immediate reaction, but his mind was churning. *Why the hell won't the past stay in the past? Should I call the commander? No! Carlos could have been mistaken, yet he's usually quite accurate with his observations. A quick check may give us an answer.* "Let's call the bus terminal. With any luck, they'll know where the bus originated and where it's headed by the time and location when you spotted it. Did you happen to catch the company name?"

"Yes, it was Trailways."

"Great! We were headed southwest when we passed it, and it was somewhere between eleven forty-five to twelve a.m. Hopefully, we can get some solid information before we jump the gun."

The answers Jon received from the Trailways terminal were not what he wanted to hear, but what he had almost anticipated. The bus originated out of Miami, Florida, made a number of stops on its route north, before the stop in Annapolis. It would then head southwest, continuing on to a small town in northwestern West Virginia. Its run would terminate in Harrisburg, Pennsylvania.

Jon asked the final question that he had to, but didn't want to. "What's the name of the town in West Virginia?"

The ticket agent's answer not only set off alarm bells but angered him as well. "It's the town of Sheridan. Not much to see or do there, but we do a fair trade with the area residents."

Jon thanked the dispatcher for the information, put his phone away, looked at Carlos, and relayed the information he had just received. "It's not one-hundred percent, but it looks as if you may have spotted our boy. I knew we should have terminated him. I'd better give the commander a call."

Carlos, too, was angry. "Sheridan is just down the road from Dodsonville, where A.J. lived. We stayed at that Red Apple Rest Motel between the two towns when we checked out of the one in Dodsonville. That kid's definitely gonna be a problem, unless he's stopped."

Jon was about to call Ertugal when Rosita and Sheri exited the store, each with a shopping bag and radiant grins of satisfaction on their faces.

Sheri was bubbling. "Jon, they had some of the nicest clothing I've seen in a long time. I got two adorable blouses, and Rosita picked up a stunning jacket." The look on Carlos's face told Sheri that he was sure that they couldn't afford it, so she quickly added. "When she saw the jacket, I insisted that she try it on. It was perfect, and I insisted that I buy it for her as a thank you for the wonderful hospitality she has shown to Mom and me."

The happy look on Rosita's face told Carlos he should let the matter drop. He changed the subject. "It's almost one o'clock, and I could use some lunch. What about it?"

Everyone responded positively, and Jon figured that, when they got to the restaurant, he'd go to the men's room then call the commander.

Carlos then added a thought. "I saw a sign, just a little way up the street, for a delicatessen. What about that?"

Sheri and Rosita responded almost simultaneously. "Sounds like a great idea."

Then looked at each other and laughed.

Jon didn't need pretense. "The deli it is."

⌘

The Trailways bus pulled into the Annapolis terminal, and Pablo's travel companion turned to him. "*El terminal segundo que viene es tuyo. Nombre es Sheridan. Entiendes?"* A positive nod from Pablo, and he continued. "Thank you, very much, for the purchase of my ticket. *Vaya con Dios, Pablo."*

Pablo responded simply. *"Y gracias, tambien."*

His mind was already in Dodsonville, mulling over where the money most likely would be and how he would get it and get back to Colombia.

CHAPTER 18

Journey of Trouble

The temperature gauge needle, on the dash panel of the blue Ford, was showing well into the red zone. Heavy gray smoke was billowing from under the hood as well as from beneath the engine compartment. The vehicle they had stolen was not going to take them much further. *"Puta madre!"* Jorge was furious. Pepe recoiled from his partner's angry outburst.

Cholo, on the other hand, was completely relaxed. They had driven as far as Jacksonville, Florida, and since they were on Route 1, there was no shortage of shopping centers with enormous parking areas. "We can just pull into one of these centers and get another car. Besides, if the owner of this wreck went to the police, they are already looking for it, so this may be a stroke of luck."

Jorge wasn't about to acknowledge that Cholo was right on both points and said nothing but drove into the first shopping center that they came to. He pulled into the parking place with the poorest lighting and turned off the engine. "I hope this heavy smoke doesn't attract the damned police."

They all got out of the car, and Jorge opened the hood in an attempt to let the over-heated engine cool down and allow the smoke to dissipate. They had just begun to consider where to search for their next transportation when a young man in an extended-cab Chevy truck pulled up. "Y'all got a problem? Maybe I can get ya goin'. I'm an auto mechanic. Le'me give it a look." With that, he walked over to the Ford, leaned forward, and peered under the hood. It didn't take him long to spot the problem. "You've got a busted radiator hose."

Cholo knew exactly what that meant but played dumb. He had quickly assessed the vehicle that this Good Samaritan had driven up in. "Show me, please. I'm not sure what that means."

The young mechanic was more than happy to exhibit his expertise and comply. "Come over here. I'll point out the problem and explain what that means." With that, he turned to face the car's engine compartment.

Jorge was beginning to understand where this was headed but just watched and waited as Cholo walked over to the mechanic. Cholo couldn't have been nicer. "Thank you and please forgive my lack of understanding. Now—what is a busted radiator hose?"

"It's right here." The mechanic leaned in to the engine area, pointing with his right hand at a hose that was now useless, coolant still draining from the evident rupture.

As he leaned in, Cholo took a step back, took a quick look around, and pulled his knife from under his shirt.

"This is the—" Those were the mechanic's last words as Cholo rammed his knife into the young man's back, straight to his heart.

With a sharp tug, Cholo withdrew his knife and wiped it on the shirt of the corpse, now bent over from the waist and lying on the overheated engine, the exposed flesh starting to singe where it came in contact with the extremely hot engine block. Cholo's next action was to remove all of the contents of the mechanic's pockets, quickly transferring them to his own.

"Quick, give me a hand and let's sit him in the driver's seat of the Ford."

Jorge moved quickly to help, since Pepe was numbed into inaction. "You didn't have to kill him, Cholo."

"He could identify us. Besides, we now have a worthy vehicle. When the car is found and the occupant has no ID, that will delay any search for us. It will probably be morning before that happens, and we should be hundreds of kilometers from here by then."

Jorge couldn't dispute a thing Cholo said, but a note of personal caution arose in his mind. *This one kills too quickly and too easily. I'd better keep a very close watch on him.*

Once the body was in the driver's seat, Cholo adjusted the seat to a reclined position and closed the young mechanic's eyes. "If someone is curious, he will appear to be asleep. Now, Jorge, I think we should leave."

The silver, extended-cab pickup truck eased slowly out of the shopping center parking area and into the northbound lane on US Route 1.

CHAPTER 19

Growing Concerns

The deli was crowded, every seat occupied, but the food being served looked extremely appetizing and had an aroma that was more than enticing. That combination was enough for the hungry foursome to opt to wait the approximate fifteen minutes it would take to get a table. During the wait, Jon excused himself and went to the men's room. He went through the usual dialing sequence and recognition code to reach Commander Ertugal. After two rings, the phone was answered. "Jon! How are you and why the call?"

"I'm fine, Commander. There may be a problem brewing. Remember the kid we put on the boat to Colombia—the one who shot A.J.?" Jon was positive that the commander knew exactly who he was referring to and didn't wait for a response. "We're ninety-nine percent sure that we spotted him on a Trailways bus in Annapolis and did a quick check. One of the stops that bus will make is Sheridan, West Virginia. Sheridan is ten or fifteen miles from Dodsonville, the town where A.J. lived. Unless we missed on the identity, he must have somehow jumped ship and is going after that money. Did you place any assets in Dodsonville?"

"Yes—a man and woman field team, posing as a married couple. They're good and, if they spot the target, you can be sure they'll neutralize him. I'll keep you posted." With that comment, the phone went dead.

Jon stood for a minute without moving, mentally reviewing

what the commander had just said, a gnawing concern starting to brew in his gut. *This team may be good but if the commander can afford to send them off on a non-critical mission— unless I miss my guess—they can't be on the top of the qualified field list. In a small country town, that's not good.* He slipped his phone back into his pocket, left the men's room, put a smile on his face, and headed toward their table.

As he approached the table, Jon could see the question forming in Carlos's eyes. The answer would have to wait until they could find a moment alone. He apologized as he took his seat. "Sorry for the delay. There was a waiting line in the men's room." Quickly changing the subject, he continued. "Have all of you decided what you're having? I know exactly what I want."

The conversation was light and varied, during lunch. Their meal finished, Jon paid the check, and Sheri offered a suggestion. "Why don't we walk around a bit more? I saw a few more shops that I'd love to take a look at. There is also what I believe to be an intriguing jewelry store almost directly across the street. The name, alone, is intriguing, La Belle Cezanne, how about it?"

Carlos gave one of those non-committal shrugs, Rosita was smiling broadly, obviously in favor, and Jon saw this as an opportunity to talk privately with Carlos. He answered for the three of them. "That's fine, Sheri, only Carlos and I may not follow you into every store."

They left the deli, and the two women made a bee-line across the street to the jewelry store. As soon as the shop's door closed behind them, Jon began to fill Carlos in on his conversation with the commander.

Carlos was in complete agreement with Jon's thoughts about the field team that the commander had dispatched. "Unless they've had undercover experience and know the ways of rural small town life, they'll stick out like a whale in a backyard swimming pool. Also, that sheriff we met isn't stupid. Jon, I don't like this, one bit. It looks as if unless someone gets lucky, we may get pulled back into this mess for a final clean-up."

"That's exactly what I'm afraid of. We're the only two with first hand experience on this whole operation and the only ones who have had direct visual and personal contact with this Pablo kid, possibly excepting that waitress, Sally. We can only hope that the field team gets lucky." He paused then changed the subject. "Let's catch up with the girls before they get into too much trouble."

The four of them spent the balance of the day perusing the various shops. Sheri was effusive about the quality of the items in the jewelry store and how they rivaled some of the finest European salons. She was particularly descriptive when she brought up the diamonds and the ring settings. Jon made a mental note but offered no response. The day was waning so they spent about half an hour at Ego Alley, a short inlet off the bay, which jutted into the center of town. Owners of fancy or high dollar boats would use this waterway to parade their luxuries around, showing off their floating pride and/or their ability to spend big money.

Sheri glanced at her watch. It was ten minutes after five. She said aloud to the group, "I'm running low on energy. Why don't we find someplace where we can sit and have a relaxing drink?"

The response was unanimous and, since they were not familiar with the area, opted to return to their hotel for, as Carlos put it, "The bar there is more than adequate, and the atmosphere is totally relaxed."

❧❧❧

Four-hundred fifty miles west, southwest of Annapolis, a Trailways bus slowed as it entered a small West Virginia town.

"Sheridan—we're comin' into Sheridan. Any passengers for Sheridan don't forget to check for your personal belongings. I have a message for *Señor* Pablo."

Pablo's head came up when his name was announced, his attention captured.

"Your friend told me to alert you that this is your stop."

The driver read from a scrap of paper. *"Pablo, este es su terminal."*

The bus came to a stop in front of a general store. Pablo stood, stretched, and walked to the front of the bus, pausing for a moment at the driver's seat. He offered a quick acknowledgement to the driver. *"Gracias, señor."*

Then he went quickly down the three steps to exit on the street.

CHAPTER 20

Morning Mayhem

Seven a.m. and Deputy Sheriff Julio Sanchez was thirty minutes into his shift, making his rounds in Jacksonville, just north of the center of town. The sun was up, and there was a slight breeze coming from the east. It was already eighty-four degrees, and the promise of sweltering heat coupled with high humidity could not be ignored. He would stop for coffee at La Mesa Grande. *For some reason this morning, I'm surprisingly hungry. I think I'll add one of those juevos y chorizo breakfast burritos.* As he drove into the shopping center that was home to his favorite restaurant, he noticed an older Ford Fairlane parked out in the center of the parking area, its blue finish faded by sun and time. Nothing special about it, and he pointed his cruiser toward *La Mesa.*

A large *café Cubano* and a breakfast burrito in hand, Julio walked back to his car, called in to report, and took a slow, appreciative sip of his coffee. *Man, this is about as good as it gets when it comes to coffee.* Both of his parents were from Cuba, but he was too young to have lived there for any length of time, other than his infancy. For some unknown reason, his thought processes drew him back to that Ford. *It was parked much too far from the shops for this hour. Could be someone sleeping off a drunk or maybe stolen. Better check it out.* He pulled out of his parking space, took another sip of his coffee, and drove, without rushing, toward the Ford's location.

In less than one minute, it became evident that he should

make a closer check. *Still there.* Coffee went into the cup holder, and Julio got serious. One of the most important things he had learned in courses on terrorism and drug enforcement was that he should always expect the unexpected, for as his trainers had constantly reiterated, "The casual investigator is the dead investigator."

When within fifty feet of the vehicle, he drove in a slow circle around it, looking for anything out of place. He then drove to within fifteen feet of the Ford, turned his cruiser to face away from the subject, and called his position and intent into his dispatch. With his car in park, he climbed out, leaving his door open and the engine running. He snapped the containment strap off his holster, in case he had to bring his weapon quickly into play. When within five feet of the vehicle, he began a slow investigative walk around the car. *Windows all closed. No sign of forced entry. A lot of moisture condensation on the windows. Something in the car is creating that.* On his second trip around the car, he examined the immediate perimeter. That was when he spotted it. Just below the driver's door was a small, red spot no more than one-inch in diameter. *Puta madre! That looks like blood.* His Sig-Sauer came out of its holster.

He called dispatch. "Need backup at the Sun-Palm Mall, main parking lot near section marker C-Six, that's Charlie six, Blue Ford Fairlane, Georgia plate number LR three-one-nine C-Charlie. Vehicle is locked and has a probable blood spot beneath driver's door." He backed away and waited.

In less than three minutes, an unmarked gray Dodge sedan drove up and stopped near his cruiser. Detective Alison Peters got out and walked over, all the while keeping an eye on the Ford. "What've you got, Julio?"

He filled her in, briefly.

"All right—let's take a look." She brought her Glock to bear on the front left door of the car and began a cautious approach. "Julio. Check the passenger door—slowly."

Julio could feel his pulse elevating. He leaned forward, peering intensely into the vehicle. Through the condensation, he could make out the hazy form of someone in the driver's seat with the seat reclined. *No one in the rear.* "I can just make out one person in the driver's seat. No evidence of movement." He tried the door. "Passenger door is locked."

Alison responded immediately. "Come around and cover me." As soon as Julio was in position, she tried the driver's door. "Locked! Do you have a "slap-bar"?

"I do!"

"Get it." He was back at the Ford quickly, slap-bar in hand. Alison started by rapping on the window with the business end of her pistol. The sharp sound of metal on glass should wake even the soundest of sleepers.

They were interrupted by a radio call. "Julio. The plates on your suspect vehicle do not match the car—probably stolen. Over."

Alison overheard the audible call. "Tell dispatch that I'm on the scene, and we'll call back in five minutes."

Julio relayed the message.

Alison nodded. "Okay, let's pop the door."

Julio slid the bar down between the window and the metal door casing, located the locking slide, and pushed. A soft click could be heard as the lock released.

He quickly withdrew the bar, laying it on the roof of the Ford, and looked at Detective Peters. She had her gun leveled at the passenger's door and gave him a slight nod. Julio gripped the door handle, pressed the release, and pulled, stepping back and away as he did so. "Whew! What a stink."

If you'd ever smelled death, you never forgot that odor. Detective Peters had experienced that smell on more than one occasion. "No need to go farther, Julio. He's beyond help." She pulled out her cell phone and made the call. "This is Peters at the Sun-Palm Mall. We've got a possible homicide here. I need a CSI team and the ME. We'll keep the scene secured."

Julio's breakfast and coffee were cold, by the time he got to them. He ate part of the burrito, took a few sips of the coffee, and the rest went into the trash.

This would not be the last time a meal, while on duty, would go unfinished.

☙❧

Four days later, the police had their answers. Dental records had identified the victim. The Ford was traced by the vehicle identification numbers. Intense efforts by the CSI team found that the Ford had been driven by and probably stolen by the same men who had killed the robber of the liquor store then stole his stolen BMW. They didn't have an answer as to "why," but the trail was headed north, which meant that the perpetrators might be in Georgia or even farther, by now. An all points bulletin was issued for the dead mechanic's pickup truck, coupled with the statement that the two suspects were to be considered armed and extremely dangerous.

CHAPTER 21

Thoughts and Plans

Sheriff Tanner started his day as usual, breakfast at Ethyl's. Sally came bouncing over, in her usual friendly manner. "Mornin', Gabe. Yer usual?"

Gabe thought for a moment. His mind was not on his breakfast. "Ah reckin. Say, Sally, kin ya take a sec ta talk? Got sumpin bin playin' on mah brain."

"Gimme two shakes ta git yer order en, 'n' take Sarah her hot cakes. If'n ah kin, thet'll be th' time."

That was fine with Gabe. He wasn't in a hurry, just seeking answers to some nagging questions. There had been just too many odd happenings over the past couple of months and the one thing that would put it all to rest would be some solid answers. So far there hadn't been many. Gabe took a slow, thoughtful sip of his coffee, his mind turning over the facts and seeking any possibilities.

Sally returned in barely three minutes. "Whut cha want ta talk en, Gabe?"

"Ya mentioned thet th' last time A.J. were in town, he stayed ta yer place." No objection so Gabe continued. "Did he say aught 'bout his plans er intents? Whut ah'm gittin at er this. Fust, we got A.J., live 'n' well, next we know, few days later, he's dead. Ah'm tryin' ta git a handle 'pon whut went en twixt one 'n' t'other."

Sally sat quietly, thinking hard and trying to remember more than just the great sex. A couple of minutes went by before she offered a tentative response. "Gabe, ah cain't recall nuthin, but small talk. Mebe a word er two 'bout his folks 'n' headin' back ta th' base, but thet's 'bout it. Hope thet'll he'p."

"Thank ya, Sally." Gabe knew it was a wild shot before he asked, but in his business, wild shot or not, you took it and hoped for a hit. This was another dead end. He turned to the balance of his breakfast as Sally hurried off to take care of a recently arrived customer. *Ah shore wish ah cud be done wi' this mess.*

ℭ⋑ℭ⋑

Inspector Alejandro Cantrell was sitting quietly at his desk. It had been more than three months since he had received word that Cholo had fled to Mexico or the United States. During that period, he and his men had cleaned up a lot of the scum that were part of Cholo's gang. That was good, but not good enough. Cantrell had blood on his mind—Cholo's! He knew that Cholo would return to Colombia, and, when he did, the inspector would put aside his uniform and badge then seek his personal revenge. He was positive that this deranged criminal couldn't stay away and that he thought he was smarter than the law. *The law—maybe yes, but not when I step outside of the law. Then he's mine.* It was then that Alejandro started to, once again, think like the superior lawman that had advanced his career to this point. *Cholo would not go to Mexico. The cartels trust no outsiders and would destroy him. He would go to Los Estados Unidos. There he could disappear. I think a bulletin to their FBI is in order. Too bad I don't have a decent picture to go with it—just this poor long distance profile shot. If he starts to get heat in the States, he will be forced to return here.*

ℭ⋑ℭ⋑

Jon and his three companions were driving south on I-95, headed home. Once they crossed into North Carolina, they would exit on to I-40 east. They would follow it straight to

Wilmington, continuing through town and over the Snow's Cut Bridge, then on to Kure Beach. It had been a good week for the four of them. Other than their meeting with the air/sea rescue team that had saved Jon's life, they did nothing but relax, shop, and enjoy fine dining, as well as enjoying each other's company.

Carlos had been lazily gazing out of the window while the two women in the back seemed to find an endless array of items for conversation. Suddenly Carlos sat up and turned toward Jon. "*Amigo,* what do you make of Hal's Sioux prayer, on your behalf?"

Jon had never had any formal religious training and never thought much about religion except that when in the service he was always amazed at how many overseas ops they became involved in, which had a fanatical religious aspect. "To tell you the truth, I never gave it much thought. I can't say for sure that I do or don't believe in some higher power. Either way, if one exists or doesn't, the thought was sincere, and that's what counts—" He glanced at a road sign as they passed. "Great! Just a couple of miles more till we pick up I-Forty." *I sure hope that Ertugal's team can head that kid off before he does something crazy.*

മാന

Sheridan was by no means a large town, but compared to Dodsonville, it was a city. Pablo Robles watched the bus as it drove away, then his thoughts turned to his quest. *Now to get to Dodsonville and my money, but how? I could walk or hitch a ride, but that leaves me stranded.* He was walking in the general direction of his goal without a specific plan when he spotted a small roadside store with a sign that stated *Consignment Shop.* Pablo had no idea what that meant but saw a wide array of used items, many with sale stickers on them. He slowed his pace and, after a few yards, spotted what could be his transportation. The bicycle was an old Schwinn that had seen better days. It had chipped paint, patches of rust, and some gouges in the frame. The seat cover was worn, but the tires looked good and, best of all, there was a set of cargo baskets mounted one on each side of the rear wheel. He encountered one problem. *There is no visible price sticker.*

An elderly man came quickly out of the shop and headed straight to him. He wasn't about to let some "Mex" kid steal the bike.

Pablo caught him off guard, pointing to the bike. *"Cuanto es?* No…" He paused, searching for the words. "How much?"

The answer of twenty-five dollars had him turning away and leaving, but he was convinced to wait by the shop owner. A negotiated price, using hand signs, of ten dollars was agreed upon. For another two dollars, a used sleeping bag was added. *A few more things and I'll be all set.* His lack of worldly experience blinded him to the complexity of the search he had naively become engaged in. Greed was his sole motivation.

CHAPTER 22

Cold Trail

Cholo was far from the ordinary criminal. He was devious, cunning, a cold-blooded killer, and possessed of a most sinister and compounding element. He was highly intelligent—overall, a very dangerous combination.

The trio had by now crossed into Georgia, and being confident of their vehicle had picked up I-95, northbound. Cholo, all this time, was planning two schemes. The most pressing was how to reach their goal without being discovered by the authorities.

Almost equally as important was how he would return with the money, to Colombia. *I may be forced to suffer the discomfort of one of those ocean freighters.* He had worked out the first plan. The second would fall into place once the money was located.

It was time to act. "Jorge, we need to pull into the next town and get rid of this vehicle."

Jorge was not at all pleased at being told what to do, and he let him know it. "Mind your own fuckin' business. I'm running this show, and I say what we do or don't do." He did not even question why Cholo said this—just reacted.

Cholo swallowed his outrage and replied, as calmly as he could, "It has been more than six hours since we left Jacksonville. By now, it is almost a sure thing that the body has been discovered, and it won't take long for him to be identified and found to be the owner of this truck. If we pull into a town and find a small used car dealership, we can sell or trade this truck for another car. Then we'll have a 'cold' vehicle."

Jorge said nothing for more than two minutes. The man made perfect sense, and Jorge was reluctant to admit it. "We need to pull off and get some food. If we see a used car place, we can try your idea. Maybe it'll work."

Pepe added a meaningless comment. "Good idea! I have to piss so bad my back teeth are floating."

That useless statement helped ease Jorge's submission.

An upcoming highway exit sign read *Route 204 Savannah*. Jorge moved to reestablish his command. "We'll take this exit. Savannah is a good size town, so no one will pay attention to our arrival." He pulled off at the exit ramp and followed Route 204 to downtown Savannah. As they came into the town area, they passed a used car dealership that appeared perfect. The sign out front read: *Mercado de Auto, Compra aqui, Vende aqui y Pague aqui.* From the condition of the signage as well as the inventory on the lot it, was immediately evident that this was not the most savory operation. Jorge jumped at the chance to reaffirm his leadership. "This might just be the place to try your crazy idea. First, let's get some food." He slowed as they drove by the car lot. Cholo took the moment to do a fast survey of the vehicles on display. He didn't miss the three cars that still had license plates on them.

Less than one-half mile farther and a sign advertised a local cafeteria. There was plenty of parking in the lot, and the sign in the window, *Se habla Español*, was an indication that they would encounter no racial bias.

Forty-five minutes later, bellies full and basic physical needs satisfied, they were back in the truck. Cholo had, unobserved, used the public phone near the restroom to call a number that only took messages. "Headed for Dodsonville, meet in Sheridan."

By now, Cholo had already formulated a plan of action. "We need to get an adjustable wrench and both types of screwdrivers from the toolbox in the truck bed. I saw three cars with license plates still on them. He probably has them for consignment sale. When we pull in, Pepe can slip out and steal the plates from one of the cars, hopefully, not Georgia plates. When we trade the truck for a car, we let them transfer the truck plates to the car. After we leave, we can stop, get rid of the truck plates, and put the new ones on. We will be completely 'clean.'" At that point, he decided to soften the effect of his stated plan, on Jorge. "I've done this before, and I know that it works." *If this pero refuses the plan, I'll kill them both, now, and go for the money on my own.*

Jorge was silent for a while, thinking over what Cholo had just presented. When he responded, it was not what Cholo had anticipated. "You know, that would put us in the clear. I think we should try it."

⌘⌘

Hector Alvarez was seated at his cluttered desk in the small single-wide trailer that served as an office for his used car business. He catered, primarily, to the immigrant trade for car sales, but his main and unrecorded income was derived from acting as an intermediary between car thieves and "chop shops." When an extended cab Chevy pickup, in near new condition, pulled slowly onto his lot, he brightened. *I can move that one quickly and for real good money.* He rose and walked out onto the lot, a welcoming smile on his face, to greet this new customer.

His loose hanging and very colorful sports shirt hid the Walther PPK tucked in his belt. His was a 7.65 millimeter, which had fascinated him when he first saw it in an early James Bond movie. He also had a Glock nine-millimeter in his desk. *You can't be too careful, these days.* Mentally, he was already preparing his negotiating strategy. One quick look at the occupants of the truck, and he began with a greeting. *"Hola, mis amigos.* How may I be of service?"

Cholo walked casually over, offering his hand. Jorge followed closely behind. "I have found new employment and no longer require this truck, which is too expensive to run. I need to get a regular car."

Jorge said nothing.

Hector warmed up and started with his standard reply. "Do you have anything particular in mind?" He waited, his smile never fading.

Cholo pretended to think for a moment. He had noticed the way the drape of Hector's shirt had "broken" when he shook hands. He knew there was a hidden gun but didn't care. Guns were as everyday an item to him as coffee. "I have a family," he lied, "and therefore need a good size car, a four-door would be best. Hopefully, you have something that won't suck my wallet dry at the gas pump."

Hector, too, pretended to think for a moment. Thought wasn't at all necessary—Hector knew his inventory like a mother knows her child. "I have two that would be perfect—a 1995 Chevy Impala and a 2001 Buick Regal. They're both at the front of the lot." He started in the direction of the cars he mentioned, Cholo and Jorge following.

While the sales talk had begun, Pepe, who had been left on the sidewalk before they drove in, managed to remove a Louisiana license plate with current dating. He slid the plate under his shirt, walked off the lot, and sat under a nearby tree, to wait.

Cholo liked the Chevy best. It was older and therefore, would be less noticeable, and it had an eight-cylinder engine, in case they needed power and speed. He turned to Jorge. "Well, Paco, what do you think? Do you agree that I would be better off with the Chevy?"

Jorge fell right into step. "Absolutely, besides, the Buick will make you appear too old."

Now they had to be sure that it was in good working order. Cholo turned to Hector. "Can I take a short test drive?"

Hector was agreeable. "But of course! Let me make a copy of your driver's license, leave me the keys to your truck, and you can go."

Cholo handed over the license of the mechanic he had slain just a few hours ago, asked Jorge for the keys, and as soon as the license copy was made, he had the keys to the Chevy. Ten minutes later, he and Jorge were back on the lot. Hector was waiting. He had looked at the license copy and had confirmed his initial thoughts, *stolen.*

Cholo offered his satisfaction. "This car will be perfect!"

The negotiations didn't take long. It was agreed that they would make the exchange of the truck for the Impala and one-thousand dollars in cash. Cholo signed the papers, using the mechanic's name, Antonio Graziano. Hector took the license plate from the pickup truck, attaching it to the Impala. Cholo and Jorge climbed in, thanked Hector, and drove off the lot. They stopped and picked up Pepe who couldn't wait to tell them what a great job he had done. Half a mile down the road and they pulled over to let Pepe switch the plates.

Hector was thrilled. He had paid only six-hundred dollars for the Impala, having purchased it from a man who was desperate. Hector knew that his contacts would pay at least four-thousand or possibly more, for the two-year old extended cab truck. That meant a minimum of twenty-four hundred dollars profit after allowing for the thousand as part of the deal. *Not bad for less than one hour's work.* He knew that the truck was "hot," but so what? It would be gone before morning. He sat down at his desk, opened the bottom draw, and removed a bottle of cheap Tequila, pouring an overly generous amount into a convenient week-old, stained, and overly used plastic cup. He then lit a cigarette, glanced briefly at, then ignored, the overflowing ashtray, its contents spilling onto his desk. He picked up his phone and dialed a "favorite."

The phone rang twice, and a female voice answered. "Name it!"

Hector responded simply. "A 2011 Chevy, pickup, extended cab, six cylinder, loaded, and in A-One condition."

The female voice was brief in response. "Be ready in fifteen minutes. We'll go five big."

Hector was ecstatic. His profit had just increased by one-thousand dollars. The Chevy would be gone in less than one-half hour and, in all likelihood, on its way to South America within a few days. He downed the tequila in two large gulps. The broad smile on his face was now an outward indication of his inner satisfaction.

⌀⌀⌀

They were again driving north on I-95, and Jorge acted as if the whole idea had been his. "We're 'clean' now and no longer have to keep looking over our shoulders for the cops."

Cholo said nothing.

⌀⌀⌀

The police in Florida had hit a wall. They were able to trace the Chevy pickup as far as a gas station in southeastern Georgia, and that's where the trail ended.

As one detective put it, "It's as if they fell off the earth."

The chief knew this wasn't good. A vague idea of the perpetrators, two Hispanic males, was all they had to go on, and one thing could almost certainly be counted on. Another body would almost and, without much doubt, mark the spot where they resurfaced.

CHAPTER 23

Ghosts

Gabe shuffled through the stack of papers on his desk until he found what he was looking for, the wanted bulletin for Pablo Robles. He had stapled to it the notice that came through, on the very next day, stating "Request Cancelled." *Thet shore er odd. Don't say why she's cancelled. Nary word 'bout captured er killed er eny reason. Ah cain't put ma finger on er, but fer shore this puzzle's getting' more pieces ever' day. Ah'll bet me a month's pay thet when th' pieces come t'gether, A.J. 'n' them two strangers whut come t' town'll be dead en th' middle a th' answer.* Sheriff Gabe was frustrated with the puzzle of events he was trying desperately to piece together. *She's like one a them go-'round carni' rides where ya set'pon a wood horse 'n' go 'round en circles 'n' try ta grab thet brass ring. Seems lahk no matter how fur ya stretch, she's all a time jest outa reach.*

༄༅

It was early evening when the four of them crossed the Snow's Cut Bridge, which would take them first to Carolina Beach. The road then continued on to Kure Beach. Carlos realized the time and offered a suggestion. "Instead of going home and cooking, why don't we stop at Stavros's diner and grab a bite? My treat."

Sheri was all for it. "Great idea! That way Rosita and I

won't have to jump into the kitchen, the minute we get home."
Rosita's expression mirrored what Sheri had just expressed.

Jon knew better than to comment. He also knew that he had
to let Carlos pay for the meal, to satisfy his machismo. He
made a left turn and drove toward the harbor and Stavros's
diner. With no active safety concerns, he parked in the public
area, half a block away. They had just gotten out of the car and
started to walk when his cell phone rang. He glanced at the
number. *Oh shit! It's the commander.* He felt a slight wave of
tension begin in his gut and fought it down. "I need to take this
call. It'll just take a moment, and I'll catch up with you. He
slowed then stopped, letting the trio of friends get well ahead
before he responded. "Commander, to what do I owe the hon-
or of this call?" He was being a little flip to offset his concerns.

Ertugal came right to the point. "As you know, we have a
domestic surveillance group. I have a pretty sharp lady—yes, a
lady—running that show. She has put together some recent
data and has come up with a theory that just may involve your
boy Pablo."

Jon knew the commander well enough not to interrupt.

"We received a notice from the FBI, which had been sent
to them from an Inspector Alejandro Cantrell, Chief of Police,
in Cali, Colombia. Seems that he believes that a high-ranking
gangster, who goes by the name of Cholo, had been moving in
to fill the space vacated by the death of El Tigre. Cantrell had
been decimating his operation, and he believes that this Cholo
took off for the US until things cool down. Oh, yes, I forgot to
mention, this guy prefers a knife to a gun. Next, we have local
news from Florida about a couple of knife killings and auto
thefts that ran a short trail north into Georgia and has dead
ended. The report says that the perpetrators are a couple of
Hispanics, but the killings were expert—one perfectly placed
stab wound each. Based on what we have, she believes that
there is the possibility that Cholo and Pablo have, somehow,
joined forces and may be heading to West Virginia to try for
that supposed two-million. Right now, it's just theory, but

there is enough base evidence to suggest the possibility. I'll keep you informed." With that, the line went dead.

Jon stood for a moment, holding his now silent phone, while a wave of speculative thoughts paraded through his mind. Almost subconsciously he returned the instrument to his pocket. *I sure as hell hope that lady's wrong, 'cause if she's right, there's going to be a very bad scenario in a little town that sure as shit can't handle it.* He picked up the pace to catch up with his friends. As he closed the gap with Carlos and the ladies, one more thought, which had become hauntingly repetitive, surfaced. *Why can't the past and its ghosts stay dead and leave me in peace?* He now had to face the trio and the obvious question as to what the call was about.

∽∾∽

Pablo was starting to deal with a combination of emotions. There was the excitement of getting that huge amount of money. That was coupled with the tension of how to accomplish that and not get caught. The third was a bit of bravado. *My father would be proud of me now. I have avenged his death and soon will make my life and that of my mother, one of ease and comfort.* The last thought brought a happy smile to his face, but at the same time tears of sorrow trickled down his cheeks. He had one more thought. This one was of a more sinister nature. *I need to find a way to get a gun—just in case.*

CHAPTER 24

Strange Faces

Sally was taking a short cigarette break, after a hectic lunch rush. She was seated on the wooden bench out front, looking at nothing in particular, when an unfamiliar vehicle caught her attention. *Thet shore er a fancy lookin' car fer these parts.* The car was a new GMC Yukon. Ertugal's field team had arrived and at the same time had made their first monumental blunder. They had driven into town with a vehicle that made them stand out, without any doubt, as foreign to this part of the country.

They drove through the town to the far west end then turned at the gas station and slowly drove back. The woman passenger uttered the obvious, indicating Ethyl's. "That looks like it's the only place to eat in this backwater."

The car slowed then stopped just a few feet from Sally's perch. The passenger side window opened, and a woman called out. "How's the food in there?"

The team had just made their second error, and this one was even bigger. A rude, big-city approach was not taken kindly to, in the country. Sally didn't respond, and the approach got worse. "Hey, miss, on the bench, didn't you hear me? Is the food any good in there?" The woman wasn't ready for the response she got.

Sally stood slowly, straightened her apron, then turned to go back into Ethyl's. Without even looking back at the car, she answered loudly, "Onliest way y'll find out be on yer own."

The door closed behind her. Sally started for the waitress station to refill the ketchup bottles. *Thet girl fer shore ain't had a decent upbringin'.*

The male driver of the Yukon turned to his passenger. "We might as well try it. I didn't see any place else to eat. Anne, we'd better soften our approach with these people. I think that you definitely pissed that waitress off."

He pulled into one of the diagonal parking spots. Gary slipped off his sports jacket and put on a lightweight nylon jacket—not that it was cool, but he needed to cover his shoulder holster. He locked the car, and they walked toward Ethyl's.

Sally looked up as they walked in. *Guess they're goin' ta give er a try.* She adopted her service manner. "Set whar ya please. Be wi' ya en jest a sec."

The pair picked a table in the center of the room and got as comfortable as they could. They stood out like a pair of sharks among goldfish. They were obviously overdressed for the area and appeared to be slightly uneasy.

Sally walked over in her usual bouncy manner. "Brought ya sum menus 'n' water 'n' ah'll give ya a minute ta take a look. Special t'day be roast pork w' collards 'n' black eye peas." She turned to leave but was stopped by Anne.

"Excuse me, miss. I want to apologize for my behavior when we first drove up." She made an off-hand excuse. "We had a rough ride, and my nerves are shot."

Sally decided that this was the perfect time to set her straight. "No harm done, 'cept ya cain't come at folk roun' here so hard. It'll do ya more harm than good. 'Pology accepted." Sally walked off, feeling good about herself. She waited about five minutes then returned and took their order.

Each of them went for a cheeseburger, fries, and a coke. Neither was willing to try anything that appeared unfamiliar to their city palettes.

When Sally returned with their order, the male half of the team decided to try civility. "My names Gary and this is my wife Anne. We took some time off and decided to see some of the country."

He reached across the table to Sally, to shake her hand. His somewhat awkward movement caused his parka to open just enough for her to catch a glimpse of the gun. She shook his hand, giving no indication of what she saw.

He continued, feeling more secure. "Is there a hotel or motel in town or nearby in case we decide to stay for a few days?"

Sally told them about Parker's High Mountain Inn and where it was located. Before she could offer any other possibilities, he stopped her, saying that the inn sounded ideal. She turned and walked back behind the counter, picked up the phone, and dialed Gabe. "Sheriff—Sally here—over ta Ethyl's. Couple a out-a-towners, man 'n' a woman jest cum en, dressed all proper like, 'ceptin' he's got a gun hid 'neath his jacket. Ah jest served 'em so's ah reckin they'll be a bit— thought ya should know."

Gabe wasn't happy about this call. *Th' last time a couple a strangers come ta town, someone died, 'n' ah got left a mess ta figure out.* His response didn't mirror his inner feelings. "Thanks, Sally. B'lieve ah'll drop by 'n' introduce m'self."

The walk across the narrow main street, from Gabe's office to Ethyl's wasn't more than one-hundred feet. With the uneasy feeling that had started to churn in his gut, it felt more like ten-times the distance, to Gabe. *Hope ah'm wrong, but mah instincts er a tellin' me thet this ain't a goin' ta turn out well. B'lieve ah'd best take a peek at thet car they cum en. Yukon— ah reckin thet's en Alaska. Back roads here'd tear this over-fancy car raht up. Cain't see much—got them damn blacked out winders.* He turned from the vehicle and started for Ethyl's. When he walked in, the object of his visit stood out in a glaringly evident manner. He let his presence be known with a greeting to Sally. "Afternoon, Sally. Kin ah git a cup-a?"

Gabe walked straight to the table at which the couple was seated. "Afternoon, folks. Name's Sheriff Gabriel Tanner. Welcome to Dodsonville. Mind if'n ah set fer a bit?"

With that, he reached out to shake both of their hands. He didn't miss the brief exposure of the concealed pistol when Gary offered his hand. With no objection, he pulled out a chair, at the same time Sally arrived with his coffee.

The man spoke first. "Good afternoon, Sheriff. My names Gary Davis and this is my wife, Anne. We've been driving around some of the towns, looking for a good place to buy a vacation cabin." Gary had sorely misjudged the man he was speaking to, basing his opinion completely on the country manner of speech used by this local sheriff.

Gabe's mind went into high gear. *Car's spotless 'n' these two er dressed fer a Sunday go-ta-meetin', not drivin' back roads 'n' small towns.* "Had eny luck?"

Anne responded. "Not yet, Sheriff, but we thought we might stay for a few nights and look around here. This sure is beautiful country."

"Shore is, 'n' peaceful too. Yep!'n' thet's th' way we lahk ta keep er." *Ah've yet ta see city folk come out here fer other 'n a quick stop. They cain't give up their fancy luxuries. Time ta quit dancin' 'n' git ta business.* "Whut say we quit dancin' 'n' give th' truth a shot. First off, ya got a permit fer thet pistol tucked 'neath yer jacket? Secondly, whut's th' true reason fer yer visit?" Gabe hadn't yet touched his cup of coffee.

The look of dazed surprise on both of their faces told Gabe that he had nailed them down. Now the couple had two choices—the truth or another story. Gabe followed his statement by unholstering his pistol and placing it on the table. "Ah'm out a patience, so ya best git started." After a slight pause, while he waited for the couple across the table to regain their composure, he offered an incentive. "If'n ah'm not happy wi' whut ya got ta say fer yerselves, y'all er goin' ta be mah guest 'til this gits sorted out."

Gary and Anne had blank looks on their faces, like two deer in the headlights. They had just found out, and quickly, that country doesn't mean stupid. Their only way out would be the truth, or at least a substantial part of the truth.

Gary looked around, furtively, then leaned across the table toward Gabe. He kept his hands in his lap. *Wouldn't do to have this sheriff think I'm going for his gun or mine.* "Sheriff, what I am about to tell you is completely confidential." No response from Gabe, so he continued. "We work with the Immigration and Naturalization Agency to try and locate illegal aliens who are considered to pose a real or potential threat." Again there was no response from Gabe. "We have reason to believe that one such person, of Hispanic origin, may be headed for your town, but we don't know why." Gary paused, expecting some kind of question or reaction from this country sheriff. He eased back in his chair and waited.

Gabe took a slow sip of his coffee. His mind rapidly assessing what this man had just divulged and quickly tied it to the memory of that rapidly withdrawn wanted bulletin. "Kin ya show me sum ID—er credentials ta back yer story?"

Gary reached into his jacket and Anne, her large handbag.

"Real slow like. Wouldn't do fer ya ta do enythin' foolish."

Both of them slowly withdrew IDs that indicated them to be agents of the Immigration & Naturalization Agency.

Gabe pushed their credentials back across the table then returned his sidearm to its holster. He took a slow breath and asked the one question that came to mind. "D' ya know th' name a this Hispanic feller?"

Anne responded. "We have a name but don't know if it's actual or assumed. It's Pablo Robles. We also have a recent photo."

She reached into her handbag and withdrew a brown manila envelope. From the envelope, she pulled a photo and passed it to the sheriff. One quick glance was enough, and he pushed the picture back. She quickly slid it back in the envelope and the envelope back into her handbag.

Gabe sat silently for a moment. *Ah knew when Sally called, thet this ud be no good.* "How long ya plan t' be en town, 'n'd' ya have a place ta stay? 'N' one more thing. If'n ya don' want ta have ever' soul in town a gawkin at ya, change yer clothes 'n' get sumpin more fittin' ta drive." He decided not to mention the wanted notice. There weren't enough cards on the table for Gabe to comfortably play his full hand.

Something dark had begun gnawing at this back-country sheriff, and it wouldn't go away. *Ah got me a real bad feelin' thet these two, lookin' fer thet Mex kid whut were en town, er all tied in wi' A.J.'s death. More 'n likely also them two army fellas, if'n they wuz army, whut come lookin fer A.J. jest afore he were killed. Worse still er a raht powerful feelin' thet when th' answers show, she'll be sore bad.*

Gabe stood and excused himself. "Got ta git back ta m' desk. Seems paper work jest don't let up. Reckin ah'll see ya 'round fer th' next few days." As he turned to leave, Gary's cell phone started to emit a chirping sound.

"Excuse me, Sheriff. I've got to take this call." He waited for two more "rings" as the sheriff walked toward the door then answered. "Yes, Commander." Less than thirty seconds into the call, Gary motioned to Anne and, by pointing, got her to stop Gabe before he got out of the door.

Anne didn't hesitate. "Sheriff, Sheriff Tanner—could you wait just a moment?"

Gary turned his attention to the caller. "Hold on, Commander." Gabe was already headed back to their table. "Sheriff, do you have a fax machine in your office?" When he received an affirmative response, Gary followed with another question. "May I have the number, and may I have something sent to your office?" Another positive response and he spoke into the phone, relaying the availability of a fax machine and the number as Gabe offered it. As soon as the number had been given, Gary shut his cell phone. "Would it be all right if we head over to your office now, Sheriff? Fax should be there when we get there."

"Ah'm set. Ah'll git Sally so's ya kin pay yer check." He raised his arm and waved at Sally who came quickly over. "They'r a wantin' ta pay their check."

Sally pulled out her pad, did a quick count, and handed Gary the check. She looked at Gabe with a question in her eye. "Ah'll jest put yourn ta breakfast, Gabe." He just gave a positive nod as a response.

Gary looked at the total—eight dollars, thirty seven cents. "Wow! We need to eat here more often." He handed Sally fifteen dollars. "Keep it! Let's go, Sheriff."

Gabe started for the door, and the couple fell into step with him. His thoughts were anything but peaceful. *This mess er gettin' worse 'n' 'less ah miss ma guess, this be jest th' top a th' manure pile. Wunda if they's really wi' I 'n' N. Guess time 'll tell.*

th' manure pile. Wunda if they's really wi' I 'n' N. Guess time 'll tell.

CHAPTER 25

Entangled

Jon caught up with the three of them within minutes, and Carlos couldn't help asking. "What was that about, or is it private?" It was immediately evident that all three of them were curious.

He knew that a lie wouldn't work, but neither would the entire truth. He sought a mid-point answer. "It was the commander. He just wanted to update me on our run-in with that turned Marine. As far as he is concerned, that file can finally be closed." *God, I wish that were true.* "Now, let's get some dinner."

⌘⌘

Cholo and his two traveling companions had made it through Georgia and also South Carolina, without a single incident. They crossed the border into North Carolina on I-95 and got off on Highway 130, heading northeast to the town of Rowland. Their objective was simple, some food, and a motel to spend the night. Simple didn't last for a long time.

⌘⌘

Deputy Irene Bailey was patrolling on Highway 130, south of town. She was near the end of her shift, and her thoughts were of home, and a day off. When the Chevy Impala passed her, going the opposite way toward town, neither the vehicle nor its occupants raised any concern. It was a chance brief glance in her rearview mirror that caught her attention. *No license plate!* She was now wide awake and made the call. "Check wants and warrants on a 1995 Chevrolet Impala, gray. No plates on the vehicle. Three occupants—possibly Hispanic." She made a U-turn and began to follow the vehicle, at a distance.

The call came back after a longer-than-usual pause. "Not enough info. Give approximate location for intended stop. Back-up will be dispatched."

"Will stop subject vehicle at Bracey Cemetery Road— over." Deputy Bailey pressed down on the accelerator and activated the on-board video camera. She was fast closing the gap. With two-hundred yards between her vehicle and the Impala, she turned on the blue lights.

Pepe was driving and caught the reflection of the flashing blue lights in the rear-view mirror. He started to panic, "Jorge, the police are behind us! What should I do?"

"Ignore them. You're not speeding. They may just need to pass us. Stay to the right." Pepe followed Jorge's instructions to perfection. Cholo slid down low in the back seat.

Deputy Bailey saw no indication that her lights were observed or, if so, they were being ignored. She pulled behind the Chevy to within one car-length and after one-eighth mile, turned on the siren.

All color drained from Pepe's face. Timidly he asked aloud, "What do I do?"

Jorge, sitting up front gave instructions. "Pull over and stop. Do not get out of the car and say nothing—absolutely nothing."

Cholo immediately saw the possibility of big trouble. "Tell the police that I'm sick with bad stomach cramps." With that, he doubled over on the rear seat.

The car came to a stop, and the deputy got out, unsnapped the guard strap that secured her pistol, and walked toward the driver's window. "License and registration, please." Pepe stared straight ahead and said nothing. She backed up one step and repeated her request. "License and registration, please." She darted occasional glances toward the male figure doubled over in the rear seat.

Jorge leaned across Pepe and started his ploy. "I'm very sorry, miss. He is new to this country and doesn't speak any English. I thought I would start to teach him to drive so when the time comes he can apply for a license. Why did you stop us?"

"You are driving a car without license plates, and I need to see your driver's license, the vehicle registration, and your friend's learner's permit."

Jorge was getting nervous. This wasn't going well. The deputy had her hand on her pistol grip. "Okay, just a moment." He made a show of searching and after a moment responded, "Son-of-a-bitch! We left everything on the table at home. If you can wait, we will go back and get everything you need."

Irene Bailey wasn't new to this game. Her pistol came out. "Out of the car! Now! All of you." *Where the hell is my back-up?* "Hands on the car roof, legs spread." She didn't miss the fact that Pepe responded immediately. Jorge and Pepe got out and assumed the position. "You—in the back—out, now." Cholo didn't move but stayed doubled over. Irene pulled open the rear door and stepped away. "I said out—now!" Still no reaction, just a low moan. She questioned the two standing against the car. "What's wrong with him?"

Jorge answered as instructed. "He is very sick with stomach cramps." He tried a hopeful ruse. "We were looking for some doctor or medical assistance."

Deputy Bailey was unrelenting, the story ignored. "I'm sorry you don't feel well, but you have to get out of the car, or you'll be headed for jail."

Cholo moaned loudly. "If I stand, I'm sure I'll shit myself."

Bailey softened a little. "I'm very sorry, but this is the law, and you must comply."

Cholo moaned again. "I don't think I can move, miss."

"Move slowly and, if you need, I'll help you to stand up." Cholo started to inch toward the open door. All the time he remained doubled over, hands clutching his belly.

He reached the door and stuck out one hand with a plea. "Please give me a hand, miss."

Irene Bailey was known among fellow officers as a good deputy with a tendency to be a little too compassionate. She reached for the proffered hand and, without warning, was grabbed with a vise-like grip then pulled with a violent wrench toward this supposedly sick man. Caught totally by surprise and with no time to react, she never saw the knife that drove through her trachea then slashed through her neck, back to her spine. The deadly knife attack severed her windpipe then cut through muscles, veins, and arteries, unleashing a shower of blood. The pistol dropped from her grip. Pepe quickly retrieved it, planning to keep it for himself.

Cholo moved with lightning speed. He was out of the car before she dropped to the ground. He dragged her back to her patrol car, shoved her body in, hit the door lock, and almost slammed the door when he spotted the camera. *'Puta madre!"* An anger-fueled yank tore it from the dashboard and exposed a cable that would run to the recorder. A quick search revealed the trunk release.

He hit the release, slammed the car door, and ran to the trunk. The recorder was running when he tore it loose. "Pepe throw that gun in the trunk. We damn sure don't need that with us."

Pepe hesitated, not wanting to loose his new weapon. "Now, asshole. That gun's registered to this cop and can tie us to her."

Reluctantly Pepe obeyed. Cholo then slammed the trunk closed. He went to the rear of the Chevy to put the camera and recorder in the trunk. He didn't miss the license plate holder, hanging open on the rear of the Chevy. With the camera and recorder in his possession, he yelled at the others. "Get th' fuck in th' car! We've got ta get out of here, and fast." They didn't need a second invitation.

They continued to town, turned right on East Main, following the signs toward I-95 north. Cholo was beyond outrage. "What th' hell did you do with the fuckin' plate, you dumb bastard?"

Pepe was intimidated by the intensity of Cholo's angry demand and answered at once. "I put it in place and snapped the holder on."

"What about the damn screws?" Cholo's immediate and vitriolic follow-up question zeroed in on the problem.

"I didn't think they were needed with that frame." Pepe had wrongly assumed that the plate holder was all that was needed. Who knew how long ago they had lost the license plate? Now they were back in a very precarious position.

"We need to dump this car, *pronto*." Cholo was furious at the level of stupidity. *I should kill both of them right now and go on my own.* He choked back his reaction and continued driving. He drove under the I-95 overpass, without attempting to get on. Jorge started to say something but Cholo was ahead of him. "We need another car. We can't get on the main highway in a car with no license plate, and we don't know if that cop called in about us."

The opportunity presented itself just a mile farther down the road. An old house stood a little way off the road. In the driveway, parked in front of a wood garage, was a silver Buick Regal. The house shades were drawn, and there appeared to be several days' mail in the roadside mailbox. Cholo stopped, backed up, and drove down the driveway, stopping after he had passed the Buick. "This looks perfect. See if that garage is empty." He slid out of the car and started toward the house. "Keep the motor running. I'm going to check the house."

With that, he mounted the steps to the rear door and looked through the glass. There on the kitchen table were what appeared to be car keys, lying on a note or letter. He tried the door. *Locked!* He then tried the porch window. The old wood framed window opened stiffly when he applied upward pressure. Quickly climbing in, he went straight to the table. *Yes! Car keys. Hope they're for that Buick.* He glanced at the note. *Charles, I'll be out of town for two weeks. I left the keys in case you need to borrow my car.*

Cholo smiled broadly and turned back to exit the way he came in. He hesitated and went to the kitchen sink to wash the blood from his face and hands then went to find the bedroom.

Once the bedroom was located, he opened the closet, selected a shirt and pants, then changed. His had been heavily bloodied. *Now to get out of here.* He grabbed a handful of paper towels from a dispenser by the sink and moved rapidly to the open window. He climbed out, pulling it shut and wiping the frame, once he was out. He was not a haphazard criminal and knew how easily simple errors could trap you.

"Is the garage empty?" A positive response and he gave an order. "Put our car in the garage and close the door afterward. Wait!" He increased his pace and, upon reaching the Chevy, threw his bloody clothes in to the back seat, then removed the camera and recorder. "Okay, now."

The incriminating vehicle was safely out of sight, and the Buick Regal, with three occupants, was heading north on East Main. The sign up ahead read I-*95 north, right one-quarter mile*. There was an arrow, indicating a right turn.

Cholo was emphatic. "We need to destroy this recording equipment and quickly."

CHAPTER 26

Back!

Mary Ann DeAngelo was excited and filled with a typical young woman's anticipation of going to what should be a fantastic party. The music on her car radio was blaring, and she was singing along, perhaps driving a little too fast. She crested a low hill and, up ahead, was a sheriff's car, blue lights flashing. Nervously, she tapped the brake pedal, reduced her speed, and turned down the radio as she approached. She passed the patrol car well below the posted speed, glancing timidly at it as she went by. *That's strange. I don't see anyone, and there's no wreck and no other car.* She continued by then took a nervous look in her rear-view mirror. *That's really odd. I'm sure that's a deputy's hat lying on the side of the road. Weird, wonder how that happened? Maybe he's hurt or sick. I really should check.*

She drove onto the shoulder and stopped then put on her four-way flashers and slowly backed up, stopping a couple of car-lengths in front of the sheriff's car. Mary Ann turned off her engine and got out. "Hello! Sheriff or Deputy—are you okay?"

No response. All she heard was the car engine and the faint ticking sound that the flashing blue lights made. The sun had just gone below the hills and daylight was fading quickly. Timidly she walked closer, her focus on the sheriff's vehicle, and called out again, only louder. "Sheriff—Deputy?"

Still no response. Slowly she approached the driver's side

of the car then looked in. Her mouth opened to scream, but her scream strangled in her throat. The world started to spin, and everything went black.

ᴄᴏᴄᴏ

Deputy Aaron Thomas was speeding, blue lights flashing. He had been delayed by a fist fight between two drivers and was trying to make up time for the back-up call. The pulsating blue glow was visible to him as he approached the low rising hill. He wasn't that late, but he was still annoyed with himself. His car crested the hill at eighty-six miles an hour, lifting slightly as it topped the rise. There was Irene's patrol car, blue lights flashing. *Oh shit! That sure looks like a body lying in the road.*

He slammed on the brakes. His car screeched to a skidding, angled stop, leaving dark, broad, black ribbons of scorched rubber on the pavement. Aaron wasn't overly brave and had never been in a situation like this. He drew his gun, snapping off the safety as it came out of the holster. He stepped rapidly out of his cruiser then started a slow to advance in a very cautious combat-style approach, step by nervous step. Carefully, he scanned the area, gun aimed where his eyes focused.

It was only then, in the failing daylight, that he realized that the body on the ground was wearing a rather short dress and heels. *That's not Irene!* He stopped, snapped on his radio, and called for back-up. "I'm advancing on foot to Irene's patrol car, and there's a female on the ground that's definitely not her. No sign of Irene. Don't have a handle on it yet, but I know I need assistance—quickly."

A positive response came, warning him to be extremely careful, and with a click, he was off the air. *First thing is to see about the body.* As he cautiously approached the inert figure, his mind was running at full speed, all a rush of typical crime scene questions. *Who is the girl? Where is Irene? Is there anyone in that car up ahead? Could they be armed?* As in any new law-enforcement scenario, the questions were endless and came quickly. The answers usually took more time.

He had reached the girl. *No signs of blood or injury. I guess that's good.*

Aaron leaned over, putting one hand on the girl's shoulder, giving her a gentle pat. "Miss—are you okay?" No response, so he tried another slightly firmer pat. "Miss—can you hear me? I'm a deputy sheriff."

Suddenly, Mary Ann rolled onto her back and sat bolt upright, emitting that shrill scream of terror that had bottled up inside her when she fainted. Startled, he jumped back reflexively. She stared straight at Aaron for almost ten seconds then pointed numbly at Irene's patrol car, arm trembling and unable to speak. It was then that he noticed that the front of her dress was covered with blood.

"Miss—are you hurt?"

She shook her head to indicate that she was not. It was at this moment that Aaron became aware of the blood patches and the trail of splatters leading to the driver's door in Irene's vehicle. He had been too focused on the girl to notice them. Fear began to well up in his gut.

Oh, my God! Oh, God! He started for the car. His feet felt as if they were mired in mud, and it took a monumental effort to place one in front of the other. The distance was only about half-a-dozen steps, but, to Aaron, it felt as if it were hundreds. His concern about the car parked a short distance up the road, and the possibilities involved with it, had been obliterated by the splashes of blood. Moisture had fogged the windows by now, but Aaron could make out the figure inside. He could feel his heart pounding violently in his chest as he reached for the door handle. *Locked!* Momentarily frozen he tried to reason out his next move. *The slap-bar—that's it!*

"Stay right here, miss." He turned and raced back to his car. The warbling sound of an approaching siren came to his ears as he grabbed the slap-bar and turned back toward his objective. Aaron wasn't waiting.

By now, Mary Ann had regained enough composure to get to her feet and back away to a respectably safe distance to wait. She was trembling visibly but felt more secure now that the deputy was here. One look at her clothes, and she knew that this was one party she'd have to miss. *I can't wait to get home, get undressed, and take a long hot shower. Oh God, look at my dress. As much as I love it, it's definitely going in the trash.* Her gaze turned to the road as her ears followed the approaching siren. She could tell by the sound that it was very close. Then there it was. The state police car came over the hill, slowed, then headed straight for the two sheriff's cars and Deputy Thomas.

Trooper Alex Kwan was out of his car as soon as it came to a stop. He didn't waste any time. "What have we got, Deputy?"

Aaron was relieved to have the presence of the state police. They would have a better approach to this mess—whatever it was. "I received a standard call for back-up. Arrived and found that—" He pointed at Mary Ann. "—young lady unconscious near the patrol car. When she came around, I discovered the front of her dress was covered in blood. She's uninjured. Found Irene's car locked, and I could just make out a person in the car. I was just about to pop the lock when you arrived."

Again Kwan wasted no time or words. "Let's do it!"

Aaron slipped the flat metal bar down between the door frame and the window, maneuvering it until he felt the lock bar. A stiff push and an audible click indicated that the doorlock had released. He stepped back and glanced questioningly at the trooper.

Trooper Kwan didn't hesitate. "Cover me!" He reached forward, grabbed the door handle, and pulled it open. The smell of death boiled out, momentarily polluting the clean country air. The car seat where she was seated, and most of Irene's uniform, were blood drenched. "Good Lord! She's been damn near decapitated."

Aaron hadn't missed seeing that, and, when Alex turned, he found the deputy on his knees, white as a sheet and taking deep breaths in an attempt to remain in control. Irene's head was twisted and tilted at a crazy angle. The exposed bloodied neck muscles, blood vessels, and the pink tinged froth, created by the last breath that escaped the severed gray-white rings of esophageal cartilage, still ringing the severed tube—it was the most ghastly thing this deputy had ever seen. "Who th' hell would do something that crazy?"

The state trooper was a veteran and had served two tours in Vietnam. He had been witness to many forms of death and had become hardened to the experience. "Some sick bastard, that's who. Did you get any info from the girl?"

The girl had been completely forgotten in light of what Aaron had just witnessed. That question jarred him back to reality, and he quickly got back on his feet. "No, I didn't. Everything happened so fast that I didn't even get her name."

"Well, let's get started." With that statement, the trooper turned and called to Mary Ann. "Miss, would you please come over to my car?" He started toward his patrol car, Deputy Thomas right alongside. A backward glance indicated that Mary Ann hadn't budged an inch. "Miss—right now, please."

His more emphatic second request provided the catalyst to jar her from her numbed inactivity. She started, with plodding steps, toward his car. She took a wide path, however, looking away from and avoiding the scene of death as much as possible. By the time she arrived at Kwan's car, the trooper had already called in his initial report, as well as a request for a crime scene investigation unit and the medial examiner.

The short interview with Mary Ann proved fruitless but eliminated her as a suspect.

"I was on my way to a party at a friend's house when I saw the deputy's car with the lights flashing. I wouldn't've stopped, but I saw her hat lying in the road. I called out but got no answer, so I walked to the car. The motor was running. I never looked at the ground 'cause if I'd a seen the blood, I probably would've run off. When I got to the car and looked in…" Her voice trailed off as she fought for control, "…well, when I saw that, I guess I fainted. Never saw anything so frightening and horrible before, and I hope to God that I never do again." She paused for a moment, as if mentally lost. Then she brightened. "Can I go home now?" She looked at the officer, hopefully.

"Sorry, miss. You'll have to wait for the CSI team. They may have additional questions."

Mary Ann was running out of the ability to control her emotions, and silent tears began to course down her cheeks.

The "all-points-bulletin" was hand delivered to the chief of police, in Jacksonville. He read it twice, slowly. *Son-of-a-bitch! It must be them. I knew they'd show again. At least, thankfully, it's in another jurisdiction, but I guess I'll get dragged in, somehow.*

CHAPTER 27

A Special Request

Two short knocks resonated on the solid wood door. The soft buzzing sound indicated the release of an electric lock. A woman dressed in fatigues entered, and quickly covered the five steps to the desk and the man seated at it. He gave no indication of her presence, continuing with whatever the task at hand was. The woman stopped directly in front of the desk, and without introduction, stated her mission. "You requested info on any unusual situations on the East Coast, involving Hispanics. We just picked this one up."

Ertugal looked up and reached across the desk for the offered paperwork. "Thank you, Trina." She turned and left, without another word. Commander Ertugal began to read the report. Within three minutes, he picked up a phone and dialed. "Looks as if they're headed your way. We know it's at least two males, for sure. They've killed once in Florida, once in Georgia, and now in southeastern North Carolina. All three killings were by knife. The last one was a female sheriff's deputy. When identities are confirmed, termination is mandatory. I'll email all pertinent data." He ended the call and thought for a moment. *Should I make the other call now or hold off?*

Gary Davis put his cell phone away and turned to Anne. "That was the commander—sounds like trouble is definitely headed our way."

Ertugal, after a moments pause and rapid review of the situation, decided to make the call now. He speed dialed while looking through the large, and recently installed, bullet-proof picture window. It was early evening, and a crescent moon had just appeared. *Weather sure has been nice. Too bad life isn't. I must be getting tired—used to make all my decisions reflexively. Now I think about some of them first.*

☙❧

Carlos looked around and signaled for the check. The waitress was new but attentive and came hurrying over. Stavros was, as always, true to his word. The check only listed three dinners. Carlos observed the missing items and commented aloud. "She missed one meal. There are only three on the check." He looked around for the waitress.

Jon stopped him. "The check's correct. The first time I brought Sheri in here, Stavros commented that she could not pay for anything in his restaurant. He must have been serious 'cause he's still not charging for her meals."

Carlos gave one of his all-encompassing shrugs, added a tip based on four meals, and left the payment on the table. The four of them rose to leave. Carlos caught the waitress's eye and pointed to the payment on the table.

They had barely stepped into the cool night air when Jon's cell phone rang. Sheri, this time, made an annoyed comment about the interruption. "You should turn that damn thing off after six, and have a little peace in the evening."

Jon looked at the display. It was the commander. *Two calls, in the same afternoon. That can't be good.* "I probably should. It's been a habit for years and, other than personal use, you're right, I should turn it off." He looked thoughtfully at the phone again then responded. A faint note of annoyance crept into his tone. "Yes, sir. Now what?"

Ertugal didn't miss the tone of Jon's response but couldn't avoid this call. *I know he's retired, but he may also be my best link to put this mess to bed.* "Jon, I hate to disturb your evening, but I need to fill you in. You have to believe me when I tell you that I'm doing this only because you may be the only key to the solution. If you weren't, you wouldn't hear from me." He paused, hoping his diplomatic approach would make the rest of the call go easier. By the time Ertugal had finished updating Jon on the recent events, one thing had become glaringly evident. Jon and Carlos, unless a combination of luck blended with a small miracle occurred, would be drawn back into another conflict, which very possibly could prove deadly.

Jon was seething with inner anger. Not at the commander, but at the ongoing string of events that kept resurrecting his past. An extremely violent past he wanted desperately to be put completely behind him, and with any luck completely forgotten. *Got to tell Carlos and how th' hell am I going to tell Sheri? Sure hope that team of Ertugal's knows their job.* Without conscious thought, something else had automatically begun. Jon already knew this West Virginia arena and was reflexively starting to, mentally, plan a battlefield strategy.

CHAPTER 28

The Search

*T*he more I think about it, the more I am convinced that I need to get a gun. How do I do this? I know little English and don't know where guns are sold or how much they cost. I need to find this out, and quickly. He was pedaling toward Dodsonville and trying to figure out an answer to his driving need for a gun. As he rounded a bend in the road, he heard the melodic strains of guitar music drifting in the wind. The music became louder as he progressed. When he had gotten closer to the source, Pablo realized that the music was coming from down a narrow dirt trail that was just ahead on the left. His curiosity was peaked, and he decided to seek out the musician. *I know that is a Mexican melody. Perhaps there are some Mexicans or South Americans down that road. If I'm lucky, they will know where I can get a gun.* The trail was extensively eroded and too rutted for bike travel, so he hid his bike in some bushes and continued on foot.

Pablo had walked about one-hundred yards, the rich aroma of the pine grove enveloping him, when he heard voices. *Español! They speak my language. I'm in luck.* His sudden euphoria turned, almost instantly, to caution. The recent memory of three other men who also spoke Spanish had destroyed his naivety. *I have to be careful—trust no one and give no information.* He put a smile on his face and, although ready to run in an instant, walked forward. He came upon two men seated in a small clearing. *"Hola! Buenos tarde, mis amigos."* The two men turned quickly at this sudden and unexpected interruption. From their reaction, it was evident that they didn't belong there and didn't expect, or care to deal with, an intruder.

Both men had jumped to their feet and appeared ready to fight or, if necessary, run. The bigger man spoke first. "We're not your friends and don't know who in hell you are—so why don't you get th' fuck out a here?"

Pablo wasn't frightened by this rather coarse and negative response. Rather he was oddly pleased. *They obviously are like me—illegal. That's good.* He altered his approach. "Please forgive my intrusion, but when I heard the music, I thought of safety. I accidentally became involved with some very dangerous men who are running from the law. I got away from them just in time. They wanted to kill me just because I had been with them. Now I fear for my life and want nothing more than to get safely back to my country." He paused, waiting to see the effect of his manufactured statement. The big man turned toward his partner and whispered something then turned back to face Pablo. There was a softening to his countenance. *I figured correctly*

"What country are you from and how did you get here?"

Pablo brightened. "I am from Colombia, a small village west of Cali. I hid on a freighter to get to this country to find work. Instead, I have found nothing but trouble and wish to get back home."

The big man wasn't easily swayed. "This is a long way from the ocean. Again, how did you get here?

Pablo was quickly becoming a glib liar and story teller. "The criminals I spoke of forced me to work with them to transport drugs. When I escaped, I had no idea where I was or how to get back to a seaport."

That last statement did the trick. The big man offered his name. "I'm Guillermo, and my friend is Salvador. We're from Mexico. Would you care for something to drink?"

Pablo had connected. First names and hospitality, in the Spanish culture, indicated a positive sign of acceptance. "A little water would be most welcome. Thank you." He paused for a moment then figured he would test their intentions. "Perhaps you could offer some advice. I speak very little English and these men that I am running from are extremely dangerous. Do you perhaps know of a place where I might buy a pistol to protect myself?" Without knowing it, Pablo had just crossed a line from which he could not retreat.

Guillermo's voice turned hard. "Who told you that we might be a source for guns? Who are you working for? The truth, *perito*, or you may not see tomorrow." He began to advance on Pablo in a very menacing manner, Salvador close behind.

Pablo raised his hands, palms out. *"Por favor, Señor Guillermo*, I work for no one. I just need to protect myself until I can get back home to Colombia." He had started to back away from the advancing man but stopped and reiterated his position in a pleading voice. "Please, I am by myself and in fear for my life. I am just seeking a way to protect myself until I can find a way home." Pablo dropped to his knees, holding his hands out in a supplicating pose.

The two men stopped. Salvador called to Pablo. "Come over here and keep your hands where we can see them."

Pablo stumbled to his feet and walked quickly toward Salvador, his hands extended in front of him. As he passed Guillermo, the man grabbed him, encircling his torso in a vise-like grip. Salvador then gave him a thorough pat-down search, from head to toe, quickly and very professionally. "He's clean."

A perplexed look was followed by a question from Pablo. "What is this 'clean'? I don't think I'm dirty."

His response brought laughter from the two men, but it also brought something better—trust. Salvador managed to stop laughing. "Turn him loose—he's okay. Come get your water, Pablo."

With that, he turned and beckoned Pablo to follow him to the rear of a van. He unlocked the rear doors and pulled one open, which revealed several coolers. He opened the nearest and reached into the cooler for a bottle of water then slammed the door shut, relocking both of them.

Pablo took the offered bottle of water, thankfully. *"Muchas gracias, Señor Salvador."*

He settled on to a nearby log, unscrewed the bottle-cap, and drank thirstily, finishing half of the pint bottle before stopping.

Guillermoo had, by now, seated himself next to Pablo. "Guns are very expensive. Have you ever used a gun before? Have you ever shot someone?"

It didn't take Pablo but a second to realize that the whole truth would not do in this situation. "I never had to purchase a gun, so I know nothing of the price, but I have used a gun before. I shot a man in Colombia when I worked for a famous guerilla known as El Tigre."

The reaction of both men when the name El Tigre was mentioned was almost one of awe.

"You worked for El Tigre?" Salvadore blurted out. The tone of the man's response was indicative of the fact that they had not only heard of El Tigre, but the Colombian criminal was even held in high esteem. Pablo had suddenly become a minor celebrity. "Do you have a place to sleep, tonight?"

Pablo was not oblivious to what had just happened and realized that he had just exchanged a position of disadvantage for one of advantage. "I thought I would stay in the next town." He was wise enough to not mention the name of the town, which would indicate that the story he told earlier was a lie. He was also now positive that these two men were, in some manner or other, on the wrong side of the law.

Guillermo was quick to make an offer. "We have a large tent, back in the woods. There is ample room for another, and we have enough rice and beans for you to join us for dinner. It is almost dark, and you would do better to stay with us since you know little English. What do you say?"

The offer was enticing, but now that Pablo felt that he had bargaining power, he hesitated before answering. "I appreciate your most generous offer, but I still must be on the lookout for those men. If I leave now, I might find an unlocked house that will have a pistol I can steal. That is—unless you have a better idea for me." He had put out the bait. Now it was a matter of the answer he received.

Guillermo looked at his partner and received an almost imperceptible but positive nod. He turned back to face Pablo. "I believe we can help you with the pistol, now that we see you are most trustworthy. Come with me to the van."

He rose and started toward the van. Pablo jumped to his feet and followed closely. When they reached the van, Guillermo unlocked and reopened the rear doors reaching past the first cooler to the one just behind it. Once opened, the inside of the cooler revealed what appeared to be cloth wrapped packages, somewhat similar in size. The cloth wrapping appeared to Pablo to be oil impregnated. The distinctive odor of gun oil, once he was closer, confirmed the fact.

Guillermo looked pensively into the cooler then sorted through several of the packages, selecting one in particular. Quickly removing the cloth, he exposed a small black pistol. "This one is small enough to conceal without too much difficulty, but has enough punch to do the job." He gave a sly smile then continued. "It's a Taurus Millennium—nine millimeter with a twelve round mag. What do you think?"

Pablo was in a tight spot. His extremely limited experience with handguns didn't allow him to confirm or deny the weapon. He tried a slight sidestep. "The pistol that I am used to is quite different—bigger. It is called Luger and has a longer barrel."

Guillermo gave a nod of recognition and understanding. He reached for the Taurus and gave a quick demonstration—showing Pablo how to load, insert, and eject the magazine; the safety; and how to chamber the first round. "So you see—quite simple and definitely easier to conceal than a Luger."

"Yes, I see that now. I think this will be perfect. How much is it? Do you have bullets and perhaps an extra magazine?" He hoped that he sounded convincing.

Guillermo was obviously unaware that El Tigre's body was lying on the ocean floor, feeding crabs, under eighty-plus feet of water. "I have both, and, as you are with El Tigre, I will charge you only one-hundred dollars for everything—gun, extra mag, and two twenty-five-round boxes of hollow point bullets." He emphasized the quality of the offered deal. "You won't get a better deal anywhere without stealing it all."

Pablo knew enough to know that he had a very good deal. "Sounds good—I'll take it."

That would still leave him with about three hundred dollars to cover his time until he retrieved the money. Once he had the cash, expenses wouldn't matter. He reached between the waistband of his pants and his body, pulling a plastic bag out of his underwear. From the bag, he removed a hundred-dollar bill and offered it to Guillermo. In return, he received all that was promised. He immediately set to the task of loading both mags then snapping one into the pistol. That done, he pulled the slide, chambering the first round, and snapped the safety to on.

Guillermo offered a tip. "Let me show you something. Give me the pistol." There was evident hesitation from Pablo. "Don't worry, *amigo*. I just want to teach you a little something." The gun was handed back to Guillermo, and he ejected the mag. He then inserted the last round from the opened box of bullets into the magazine then reinserted it into the pistol. "Now you have thirteen shots to start and one less box to carry."

Pablo had just learned something new about magazine-loaded guns.

"Now, let's get some dinner."

Pablo smiled softly. He was feeling very confident, due to the false sense of power he felt with his new pistol. He was now eager to proceed, completely unaware of the manifold problems he would be facing. *Finally, things are starting to go in my favor. Este noche, arroz con frijoles y mañana—quien sabes?*

❧❧❧

When the moment presented itself, Salvador whispered softly to Guillermo. "Has he called, yet?"

The other man looked up before responding, to confirm that Pablo was not within listening range, and responded with a quick whisper, "No, not yet."

CHAPTER 29

Back To Business

When the two men pulled into the driveway at Carlos and Rosita's, it was just after seven p.m. Jon was already planning the following day's schedule.

"Carlos, why don't I pick you up in the morning? We'll check the boat and call Bjorn and Sven to meet us at the dock. After our final shake-down, if we think we're set, plan to make our first fishing run on Tuesday."

Carlos was aware that Jon had not made reference to August, the cabinet maker. He knew enough not to mention it. "That sounds good to me. What time do you want to get started?

"Not too early, because we have to return the car—that is unless you want to follow me, and we'll drop it off tonight."

After a moment's thought, Carlos answered. "Why don't we take it back tonight? That way we can devote all of tomorrow to getting back up to full readiness for fishing."

Jon had to rib his friend. "My thoughts exactly. I just thought this long weekend might have tired you out, and you'd want to hit the sack, early." He turned to Sheri. "We'll just be about an hour. I'm sure you and Rosita can find a way to kill a little time."

Sheri just smiled, glanced at Rosita, and answered coyly. "I think we can trust the two of you for an hour—but just one hour." She laughed lightly then added, "Go on. The sooner you go, the sooner you'll be back."

Jon needed no convincing. "Let's go, Carlos. You can follow me to the rental agency."

As soon as Carlos had opened the garage, Jon backed out of the driveway and started off. One quick glance in the rearview mirror to confirm that Carlos was following, and he pulled out his cell phone, punched the favorites list and hit a number. The phone rang five times and was starting the sixth when it was answered.

"Eh, hello. August here." Then silence.

Jon didn't wait. "August, Jon Morton calling—owner of the *Adventure Two*. How's the project coming, and do you need any money, yet?"

The reply couldn't have been more simplistic. "Job's finished. Comes to six hundred forty-seven dollars and eighteen cents."

"How about meeting me at the boat, tomorrow morning…say seven-thirty. That is unless you're booked."

August was less than conversational. "Mornin's fine." The phone went dead.

By now they were over the bridge and about ten minutes from the rental agency. Jon was still thinking about the clipped and almost cryptic method of communication used by August. *Bet that man doesn't have more than two hundred words in his whole vocabulary.*

The car was parked in the return area, and the keys deposited in the slot in the side of the building, marked for key return. Jon climbed in with Carlos, and they started for home.

"We have an appointment with August, at the boat, seven-thirty tomorrow morning." Jon spotted the quizzical look on his friend's face. "He's the cabinet maker that met us at the boat." It was evident by the change in his expression that Carlos had not put the name and the person together. "Can you drive Sheri and me to my place or can I borrow your pick-up? I forgot that we had the rental delivery, and my car's parked in my garage."

Carlos didn't hesitate. "Take the pick-up. Then you can swing by in the morning and pick me up. You always walk to the dock, anyway so that'll work out perfectly." There was a relaxed silence for a couple of minutes, then Carlos brought up an existing topic. "How's it going with you and Sheri? Rosita thinks you make a great couple and that she would be good for you. I hate to say this, but I think she's right."

Jon didn't respond for more than five minutes, and Carlos was starting to think that he should have kept that thought to himself.

Suddenly, Jon answered. "To tell you the truth, she's the best thing that's happened to me since Tina's death. I do agree with both of you, and I can't believe how happy I am when I'm with her. I just need a little more time to be sure that I'm not fooling myself about my feelings. Please don't pass this along *amigo*. One more thing, don't walk into the house with that smug grin on your face. Rosita can read you like a book."

Ten more minutes and they were pulling into Carlos's driveway. Ten minutes more had Jon and Sheri on the way to Jon's house.

"Jon, when we get to your place, I'd love a glass of that Soave. That is if you still have some.

"That's an easy request. I still have a few bottles and at least two are in the chiller." He glanced at her and saw the impish grin.

"There you go again, trying to ply me with wine. I said a glass, not go on a bender."

All he could do was chuckle at her reply. *This lady brings nothing but joy to my life, and I may soon ask her to make that permanent. Just wait until I see which way this latest mess is going to blow.*

CHAPTER 30

Plans

Gary was starting to have some second thoughts, as well as gnawing concerns, about an impending confrontation with possibly two or more Hispanics.

His concerns were compounded by the fact that the suspects were not photo identified, and they were on an unspecified time table.

He had been ruminating over this for two days and finally broached the subject to his partner. "Anne, I don't know how you feel about this assignment, but I think our next best move is to fill the sheriff in. It's his town, and although he appears pretty sharp, this is probably beyond his experience or expertise. However, I'm sure he knows the town and the surrounding country like the back of his hand. That's something we may definitely need."

Anne thought for a minute about what her partner had just proposed, before responding. "You're probably right, but we had better run this idea by the commander before we make a move."

Gary just gave an affirmative nod, took out his cell phone and made the call. Once the checks and blocks had been satisfied, the commander's phone rang. Ertugal answered in his typically brusque manner. "What's up, Gary? Have the targets been identified?"

"Not yet. We believe that it would be a sound plan to fill the local sheriff in on what's going down. He's pretty sharp and, in this rural jurisdiction, might offer some valuable assistance."

The commander didn't even pause. "Idea's good, but no reference is to be made to the prior operation. All he needs to know is that there are two and possibly more Hispanic males headed his way. Tell him that they're related to drug smuggling and considered dangerous. Your next call is only for a confirmation of target and/or completion." The line went dead.

Gary returned his cell phone to his pocket then, without a moment's pause, filled Anne in. "Commander says it's a go, but no mention of the prior history. Let's go find Sheriff Tanner."

೧೨೧

Gabe was at his desk when they walked into his office. He wasn't in a good mood because he had just received the fax from the commander's office for the two agents. Along with that came a fax from the FBI about an international fugitive from Colombia who was a gang leader and known killer.

He glanced up when he heard the office door open. "Well, ya'll er jest en time fer th' trouble party. Got a fax fum yer boss about th fella yer huntin' 'n' one fum th' FBI, 'bout a real bad fugitive, Colombian. They's also an all points fum Florida bout two Hispanic's whut have been involved en a killin'. This follered by more bulletins fum Georgia 'n' South C'lina thet appear ta be bout th' same boys. 'Peers those boys have been on a killin' spree 'n' they're headed north. If'n all a this mess er related, y'all er dealin' with two—mebbe as many as four, er more, Hispanics thet don't care none 'bout killin'. Whut's come ta light so far er two dead civilians 'n' a dead deputy sheriff—female. Now, whut makes ya'll so shore they're headed this a way? Ah want me straight answers, 'n' ah want 'em now."

Gary glanced at Anne. This country sheriff already knew more about what was going on than they did, and that put them in a weak position. He stalled for a little time. "Mind if we sit? This may take a little time."

They took Gabe's glance at the chairs as an affirmative response, each of them pulling one up to face the desk.

Thirty-four minutes later, the explanations and cross referencing of data was complete, and Sheriff Gabriel Tanner was faced with a possibility that he never could have foreseen when he took this office. *Somewhere en er 'round mah town there cud possibly be hid a real large amount a money. Thet en itself er near unthinkable, but ta add a heap ta th' problem there cud be few as one er as many as four er more Hispanic drug dealers chasin' efter this mebbe pile a money. Based 'pon th' notices thet've come en th' past couple a days, these boys take killin' as lightly as orderin' a burger. How th' hell do ah prepare fer a mess like this un? It cud happen er not 'n' if'n she does, how kin ah keep mah citizens safe?* He gave a hard look at the two agents across the desk from him and looked for a hole in their story. "Tell me ag'in. How'd ya say this supposed money got here?"

Anne reiterated. "To the best of our knowledge, if it exists, it was being transported by drug dealers and for some reason that we're not aware of, had to be temporarily hidden."

Gabe sat pensively for a few minutes before saying anything. When he did comment, his response was a total surprise to Gary and Anne. "Reckin thet th' fust thing ta do er put up mah radar." He could see the amazed looks on their faces and with barely a pause went on to explain. "Got five folk en town whut ah kin trust complete. Owner a th' gas station, th' coroner, Amos, owner a Parker's High Mountain Inn, 'n' Sally, th' waitress over ta Ethyl's. 'tween em they got a handle on th' comin's 'n' goin's a ever' soul en this town. Ah'll tell em ta let me know if'n they spot eny new Hispanics en town. If'n ah tell 'em she's ta be kep' quiet, they'll do 'er. More'n likely they'll come fum th' d'rection a Sheridan. So it be best ta keep a sharp eye ta thet end a town. Guess thet'll fall ta th' three a us. 'Tween us ah believe we kin keep 'er covered. One thing more, ah'd like fer ya ta do yer best ta avoid eny shootin' en town. Too easy fer th' wrong people ta git shot."

Anne and Gary sat silently. They were both more than a little impressed and had just gained a very high degree of respect for this sheriff. Gabe had covered all of the immediate bases, and better than they could. This country sheriff was not only a lot smarter than they had initially assumed but was also a reasonable tactician.

Gabe broke the silence. "Jest r'membered. Ah got one more piece a th' radar—th' stone trio." The bewildered looks of the couple facing him caused him to explain. "Got three ol' boys whut set on th' bench, front a Ethyl's, ever' day, five a.m. 'til noon. Cain't nothin' go by thet they don't spot, 'n' they know ever' soul en this town. They's tight as th' bark on a tree 'n' honest as th' bible. Best er they won't have more 'n three words wi' but a handful a locals." He rose abruptly. "Guess ah better git th' word out. Best ah do 'er alone. Strangers make these folk kind a wary." He then noticed that blank stare that translated as, "What should we do?" He solved that one easily. "Y'all jest git out thar 'n' be whut ya look like—a couple a tourists whut got lost. Mebbe grab a camera er binoculars ta make er look fer real."

Gary had one strong concern with the sheriff's immediate plan. "How do you know these people won't let someone else in on it or tell you something incorrect just to look good?"

Gabe paused before answering. "Shore kin tell yer big city. These folk er mount'in folk. They ain't got much, but they're hard workin', close mouthed, 'n' honest as th'rain. Don't make no stories 'n' don't carry no stories,'n' thet's th' simple fact. Eny other questions?"

Gary's silence was response enough. The truth was on the table, and nothing would change that.

CHAPTER 31

Closing In

Jorge was reading a road map, trying to keep them on target. "There, up ahead—get off at exit fourteen and take Highway seventy-four northwest. That will take us to the city of Charlotte. From there we take Highway seventy-seven north to Virginia and on to West Virginia."

Cholo was driving at just five miles above the speed limit, being careful to avoid any unnecessary lane changes. He wanted to remain as inconspicuous as possible. They had driven about forty miles when a sign indicated that they were approaching an exit for Laurinburg. "We need to get off here— get some food and find a place to stay for the night. It's getting late, and with less traffic, we'll be more noticeable."

By now, even though he didn't like him, Jorge had come to realize that Cholo had a survivor's thought process. "Sounds okay to me. How about you, Pepe?" All he got in response was an affirmative shake of his partner's head. "Okay! Let's do it."

Cholo was pleased that there was no argument about his decision. *At last, I'm getting a little of the respect that I deserve. This will make later easier, they'll be less guarded. Now I'll have a chance to make my phone call without their worthless questions.* Turn signal on, he eased off the exit to the stop sign then made a right turn toward town. "First let's find a place to eat. Then we can locate a motel." With no negative reaction, he was beginning to feel that he had gained some recognition and control. As he drove, he watched, hoping to locate a small electronics or hardware store. None appeared, but a neon sign ahead advertised *Pop's Diner, Home Cooking 24/7*. There were just three cars in the lot when he drove in. *That's good. The fewer people that see us, the better.*

Forty minutes later, hunger satiated, Cholo asked the waitress for the check. He still had the mechanics credit card, and it would be safer to try it here than in a motel. The check arrived and, without pause, he added a very generous tip, sliding the check and credit card to the waitress. *Now we'll see.*

The waitress was back in just a few moments. "Here you are, Mr. Graziano. Just sign at the bottom and thank you, very much." She watched as Cholo signed Antonio Graziano, smiled broadly and reiterated, "Thank you, again." She turned away and the three men departed.

Cholo had an idea. "Oh, miss," he called to the waitress.

She turned and started back. "Yes, sir. Is something wrong?"

"No, not at all. We're from out of the area and traveling through. Is there a nice but not too expensive motel nearby? We just need a place for one night."

She thought for a few seconds. "Why, yes. There's Wayne's Family Inn about half-a-mile up the road, toward town. Nice and clean and you won't be paying for things like a swimming pool or gym…you know, things like that."

"Thank you very much. That sounds like just what we need." He looked around casually, to see where Jorge and Pepe were. They were waiting at the door. "There is one more thing, please. My cell phone has stopped working. Is there also a place where I can buy one of those inexpensive ones, in case I need to make a call?"

She didn't stop to think, this time. "My cousin owns the State-Line Hardware Store, almost across the road from the motel. I know he has what you're looking for, and he stays open until ten at night, so you should be able to get there with plenty of time."

"Great! Thank you, for your help." *It's about time a few things started to go my way.* He started for the door and his two unlikely companions. As soon as they were outside, he told them about the motel. He never mentioned the hardware store. "Let's go, I'm damn tired from this drive."

Check in went smoothly, and Antonio Graziano's credit card was readily accepted. The desk clerk confirmed, "One single room and one double-room."

A wake-up call for both, at five a.m. was requested. The hardware store was readily visible across the road. They parted ways, Cholo headed to his room and the other two to theirs. As soon as he was sure that they were in their room, Cholo ran across the road to the hardware store and asked to buy a cheap cell phone and buy sixty hours of calling time.

It was nearly closing time, but Donald was more than willing to help. It was an easy sale and for cash. His cousin had called and said that a Mr. Graziano would be in, to purchase a cell phone.

Once back in his room, Cholo dialed a number that he had memorized. The phone at the other end rang three times before being answered. *"Hola. Quien es?"*

"Hola, El Cuchillo." A prearranged code name, one that had started to be associated with Cholo in Colombia was used—The Blade. "Do you have my order, exactly as requested?"

"We have everything you requested. Do you have the agreed payment and when will you take delivery?"

Cholo was more than pleased. He had heard of this organization and, after sneaking out of Colombia to await a cool down of the law enforcement sweep, had made contact. His informant had said that this group was one-hundred percent reliable and very discreet. When this lead for a cash windfall in West Virginia had materialized, he called and was given the phone number of the area representative, placed his order, and was advised of the purchase price.

Guillermo and Salvador were not small-time freelance dealers. They were part of a world-wide network of agents working for a German firm, Precision Metal Parts, AG, generally referred to by clients as PMP. There were twenty-three sales agents in the United States, South and Central America, none with a specific territory of operation. As technical as the name sounded, the real business of this firm was the international sale of armaments, legal and illegal, but all unregistered. The agents could arrange for the sale of a single weapon or with advance notice and guarantee of payment, could equip a small army.

Cholo thought for a few seconds. "I'll take delivery within the next two days. I'll call to let you know when I'm in your location and we'll arrange for the exchange."

"Two days is your limit. We have to meet with a group in New Jersey in four days so, if you're not here, the deal's off, and your validity is cancelled." Guillermo ended the call.

I'll be there, don't you worry. This is my ace, and perhaps they may be a solid link for my future in Colombia.

ల఩ల

The phone rang at eight a.m. in the police headquarters at Jacksonville, Florida. When the call was answered, it was directed, immediately, to the chief. It was the Fraud Division of Visa. The woman's voice on the other end was not stressed or excited—to her, it was just another call. "Chief, I'm calling as a courtesy of the FBI. Antonio Graziano's Visa card was used, twice, last night in Rowland, North Carolina. Have a good day." The phone call was terminated after his "thank you."

Son-of-a-gun, the feds had it figured right when they said that the card should be left active. Thankfully, it's now in their hands. I hope they catch the bastards and with luck get the opportunity to finish them in the street. The only type of trial killers like those deserve is an ounce of well-placed lead.

ల఩ల

A double knock resonated on Ertugal's door. One firm, the other soft betrayed to him who the person was on the other side. He pressed the release for the lock. "Come in, Trina. What's up?"

"You asked me to stay on top of that Hispanic thing. This

fax just arrived from the feds." She handed Ertugal the single printed sheet, turned, and left without another word, pulling the door shut behind her.

The commander picked up the sheet and saw the point of concern. A credit card, from one of the murder victims, had been used, twice, in North Carolina.

This mess is starting to escalate in a very strange way. I would like to think that these events are unrelated, but my gut says big trouble is on the horizon. We just might be in for more than planned for in West Virginia.

CHAPTER 32

Jon woke with an unusual aura of peace and contentment. He rolled onto his side to look at Sheri, still in a deep sleep. Last night they had finished the bottle of Soave, sat in the sauna for half an hour then showered, together. This was capped by a deeply intense and extended session of love making. They had drifted off to sleep, wrapped in each other's arms. *That was just a perfect evening, and one that I know I'd like to repeat again and again. This lady is everything and more that I could wish for.* His thoughts wandered from Sheri to his new boat then suddenly were rudely interrupted by the possibility of once more being drawn, unwillingly, into a possibly violent confrontation. He looked at the bedside clock. *Five a.m., about an hour too early to call the commander. I'll give him a call later, on my way to meet Carlos. Might as well get up and get started.*

Jon was dressed and enjoying his first cup of coffee when he heard her footsteps. "Good morning hon. I didn't want to wake you. I've got the coffee ready." He met her as she was headed for the kitchen, took her in his arms and planted a long, firm kiss on her lips.

"Good morning. Now that's better than any coffee, but I still want some."

He turned back to the porch. "Bring it out here. It's a beautiful morning, and I have to be out of here by six, forty-five to pick Carlos up." The question in her eyes made him continue.

"Remember? I was having a mechanic check a few things on the new boat before we get out on the ocean." The honest truth, at this point, would not do anything but create questions and doubts. "I spoke with him, and he got it all done while we were in Annapolis. Just have to go over what was done and pay him. Why don't you take my car and meet us at Rosita's when we finish. We meet him at seven-thirty, and I doubt we'll be more than an hour at most."

"Sounds like a plan. By the way—do you know of a good yacht broker, around here? Mom asked me to put the Hatteras on the market. She'll never use it, and I could never set foot on board again, with the bad memories it holds." By now Sheri knew enough of the details about her dad's death, and the fact that most of the events leading to that death took place on or in conjunction with that boat.

Jon was pensive for a moment. "Can't say that I do, but Tony will be able to steer us in the right direction. Now, I need to go." He stood, kissed her lightly, and was off. "See you in an hour or so."

Carlos was outside waiting when Jon drove up. His usual beaming smile when he saw Jon was evident, even at a distance. Jon stopped in the driveway, and Carlos jumped in on the passenger side. "*Buenos días, jefe!* You might as well keep driving." He was silent for a minute or two then had to make a point. "I have to tell you, Jon. Since you're with Sheri, you have a more relaxed look on your face. That lady is definitely good for you."

Jon had given up on asking Carlos not to call him *jefe*. He just didn't think of himself as a boss, rather as a partner. "You're definitely right about Sheri." He caught himself and paused. *If I tell all of my thoughts and feelings to Carlos, Rosita will pry it out of him in no time flat.* "I guess time will tell where this is going, *amigo*."

Jon parked the pickup in the lot to the south of both the pier and Stavros' diner. He handed Carlos the keys and asked, "How about getting some coffee? We're a little early, and we can take the coffee with us and meet August at the *Adventure*."

"Sounds good to me, and that will let give that liquid fire time to start cooling down."

The temperature of Stavros's coffee had become legend in this area, so there was no need for Jon to comment on the obvious. They altered their direction and walked to the diner.

With two large cups of coffee in hand, they headed for the *Adventure II*. It was ten after seven and Jon had forgotten to call the commander. "Carlos, I hate to do this but I need to call Ertugal. I'm hoping that there have been some positive occurrences and that we won't be drawn into another crisis." Carlos's silent nod was the go-ahead. The dialing sequence completed the phone rang twice then went dead. "He must be involved with something and will call back when he's free." Past experience had shown this to be the commander's working pattern.

As they stepped on to the pier Carlos spotted the lanky man sitting on the stern of the *Adventure II*. "I think your man beat us here."

They were within twenty feet of the *Adventure II* when Jon called out, "Morning, August."

The only reply was a slight nod of the man's head. He then slowly stood, by first stretching his legs to the pier then pushing himself off the stern. Once on the pier, he turned to meet the two approaching men. By now they were face to face and Jon reached out to shake the man's hand then right to business. "Well, let's see what you've done." Jon gave a short jump to the transom, Carlos right behind. They were followed by August.

Jon went straight to the wheelhouse and then to the controls. As he approached he was visually searching the first location, which he had indicated to August. He saw nothing that would indicate that anything had been done, but wasn't sure if the trim in the area was original or new. August walked up and finally spoke. "This un's th' fust." He placed his hand on the location indicated and gave three firm pushes. A panel, completely obscured, popped out about one-half inch then opened outward like a pull-down shelf. The exposed interior was lined with "egg-crate" foam rubber. "Panel's on a memory release catch. Needs three pushes, all within one minute. Wait too long and you'll need to start over after a one minute delay."

The exposed cavity was big enough to house a full size pistol and at least three additional magazines.

Jon was more than impressed, evident by the look on his face. "This is perfect—even better than I had imagined it would be. Let's see the other two." They went next to the main cabin, near the head of the bed, and then to the galley. In each location, the results were the same. You couldn't tell that anything was concealed behind the target locations and each compartment worked in the same manner. The three men returned to the stern deck. "August, they're all perfect—couldn't be better." Jon reached into his pocket.

A comment by the cabinet maker caused Jon to pause. "Had ta re-route a couple of wires in th' galley. Tested everything they might control—no problem."

Jon continued. "You said the job came to six-hundred, forty-seven dollars and eighteen cents. This should cover it." Jon handed August seven one-hundred dollar bills. "No change required. I appreciate first-quality workmanship. Besides, you never know if I might need to call on you again."

August Cavendish slowly folded the bills and stuffed them in an old and badly worn leather wallet. He reached out to shake Jon's hand and return the set of keys. "Much obliged. You have my number."

With that, he stepped up on the transom and down to the pier. He turned west and, at what appeared to be his fixed speed, walked slowly back in the direction of the access ramp.

The two of them watched him for almost a minute before Carlos had to comment. "I don't think that man has more than two speeds in his transmission—stop and slow. But, on the other hand, his workmanship is amazing. No one would know there's anything there except for what is visible."

"That was my plan and what I hoped he could accomplish. I'll put a Glock nine in each of the compartments, loaded and with a round chambered, of course, each with three additional loaded mags. You're the only one to know about this. If we ever have another run-in, either from our past or something new, I want to be ready. Now, as long as we're here, let's do a quick check to see if there's anything that we need. Knowing Sven and Bjorn, there'll be nothing missing in the galley."

In fifteen minutes, they had completed a quick walk-through and compiled a short list of incidental items. "That's got it. Now let's give your wife a call and head over there. If I know Rosita, she has a sumptuous breakfast already in the works."

Carlos had that look of joyful anticipation on his face when he replied. "You bet. That woman can sure cook, and don't think I don't appreciate it. As long as I'm driving, why don't you call the Swedes and give them a heads up? That is, if we're going out tomorrow."

Jon smiled. "Can't wait to get back to work, huh? Word is the Spanish mackerel are running, and there are still tuna to be had, as well as Mahi. We might as well break the boat in, and earn a buck or two." Jon caught Bjorn and told him they would sail tomorrow, at five a.m. It was now eight fifteen a.m. "I'm going to call your place and tell the girls that we'll be there at nine. That way, we can stop now and pick up the few things we need. That will be one less thing for tomorrow."

They had finished with their few purchases and were almost at Carlos's house, when Jon's cell phone rang. He looked at the display. It was an out of area number. *I don't recognize that number, but since my number is unregistered, it either has to be a wrong number or someone that I must have given the number to.* He decided to answer it but in a noncommittal way. "Hello...Yes, of course, I do. How are you and why the call?...That's great. Let me know when you're set up. Thanks for the call, speak to you soon." Jon put his phone back in his pocket and was quiet until Carlos couldn't hold out any longer.

"Who was that, *amigo*?"

"Carlos, your curiosity will get you in trouble, one day. That was the accountant that I met in the barber shop when we had the first trouble with Sheri's dad. Name's Arthur Silverstein, said he finally cut the cord with the corporate world and is going to open an office in town. I had told him to give me a call if he decided to make the move. That's all that the call was about."

Carlos's inquisitive nature was satisfied, and they drove the next half-mile in silence. As they pulled into the driveway, Jon caught himself smiling. *Seems to happen whenever I think about her or get ready to see her.*

໑ຈ໑ຈ

Pablo was awakened abruptly at four a.m. by a strong case of nervous jitters. He had embarked on this quest driven by personal greed.

Now that he was nearing the town, and, in all likelihood, the place where the money was hidden, reality reared its ugly head.

Is it safe for me to go into town or have they been told about me? What size suitcase will I require to carry two million dollars, and how heavy will it be? Will I be able to locate the money and not get caught? How do I get it safely home to Colombia?

These were just a few of the questions and problems that he had not considered, but which now were very real. Something else had him deeply concerned, and he didn't know whether or not it involved him.

Guillermo had received a phone call last night, and believing Pablo to be asleep, spoke openly. One statement that was made kept playing on Pablo's mind. "We have everything you requested. Do you have the agreed payment and when will you take delivery?"

Could this be about me? It doesn't sound like it is, but quién sabes? At that point, he began to think strongly about his survival. *Should I leave now, before they get up? Then I have to think about food and a place to sleep until I get my money and leave.* Pablo tossed his mental dilemmas around for almost an hour then arrived at what he believed to be his best choice. *I will have breakfast here then depart and set up a camp outside of town. Perhaps near where that dog that I shot had his shed. That must be where the money is.*

☙❧

Sheriff Tanner had set up his "radar." None of them were told about the others in his system, and each was told to report only, and directly, to him. He had turned the two government agents into just what they looked like—out of place tourists. That was the best he could do for now. As a precautionary move, he put both his shotgun and 30.30 deer rifle in the gun rack his Jeep. He still had one underlying concern. Gabe was the kind of lawman who wasn't afraid of a confrontation. He had complete faith in his abilities. The concern that gnawed at him was a bigger one. *Ah fer shore cain't have mah town turn enta a shootin' gallery. Too many good folk cud git hurt er killed.*

☙❧

Jon was angry—very angry. He had begun to think of his phone as an enemy. *It seems, lately, that every time it rings, it's a major problem.* His gut told him that this Pablo kid was going to become a bigger problem than anyone thought he could ever be. This was now coupled with another unknown. *Who are these others? Are they headed for the same destination or are they an independent problem. We know the one on the international wants and warrants notice is involved with Colombian drug gangs and is a cold-blooded killer. The other two have also been involved in killings. Could all of this be related? I don't have enough pieces yet to put this new puzzle together. At this moment my primary concern is this Pablo. Unless this kid can be removed quietly, he could open a major can of worms.* The realization that at one time all of this would have been more like a source of annoyance, rather than a source of anger, was the fact that Sheri had become an extremely important part of his life. *Will she tolerate another break that takes me back on the firing line? I sure hope so, but hope to hell that I won't have to find out. With a little luck, the two operatives Ertugal placed can efficiently handle this situation.* This was a position Jon had never been in, before. With no emotional ties to anyone outside of his team, he had never encountered a mental struggle when it came to dealing with a conflict.

Carlos was worried, primarily about Jon and his relationship with Sheri. Rosita had told him that everything she had seen indicated they would be perfect for each other, in the long run. She also had observed that Sheri had reservations about Jon's past and the fact that it had a way of becoming part of the very real present. *If we have to go to West Virginia will that be the straw that destroys their relationship?* So far neither his wife nor Sheri had any indication that another fragment from their covert past might, at any moment, rear its ugly head.

෧෧෧

Cholo was faced with a few looming concerns. He would soon be faced with what to do about Jorge and Pepe. Pepe did not represent a big worry for him. *He is like clay, easily molded, and without a backbone. Un hombre sin cohones. He lives in fear. Jorge, on the other hand, has a reasonable amount of nerve and intelligence. For now he is useful and serving my purpose. The time will come when he thinks he is in control and will, most assuredly, try to take me out. If that Pablo kid didn't drown when I threw him in the bay, and the authorities didn't deport him, he'll also be a problem. I saw right through his story. There must be a lot more money hidden than he divulged and I don't plan to share it with anyone.*

෧෧෧

Commander Hamid Yusef Ertugal was no stranger to conflict. In fact, he had been deeply involved in conflict from his pre-teen years as a Turkish resistance fighter in World War II. His next move was into counterintelligence then on to America's Delta Force in their Elite Operations sector. His final position was as commander of an off-the-record black ops force. He had seen almost every form of killing and torture that mankind could inflict on its own. *I've got an operation going in North Africa, one in Albania, and one in Macao. Now I have this possible mess in, of all places, West Virginia, and this one, unless cleaned up quickly and quietly, could have ugly repercussions. I sure wish they had a better picture of this Colombian gangster. The one we have is as good as worthless.* This would be the first time he would have a cargo plane ready for a covert clean-up operation within the continental USA. A body or bodies would be stripped of all clothing, jewelry, and even identifiable tattoos. These items would be incinerated in an ultra-high temperature furnace. The corpse would then be placed in a large, sisal-mesh net bag with an added two-hundred pounds of anchoring stone, flown out to an ocean area having depths of one-thousand or more feet, far from commercial shipping lanes, and dumped. This method of disposal was quiet, effective, and left no traces. By the time the sisal mesh deteriorated, the body or bodies would be nothing but detached bones, which currents and sand would disperse and cover.

CHAPTER 33

Simplicity

Ve er here!" Bjorn's booming Swedish accent announced the arrival of the two brothers, who rounded out the trim boat crew of four. Both of the brothers had their usual happy grins and appeared anxious to get back to work.

Carlos made a quiet remark to Jon. "They look extra happy, today. I bet it's because they're looking forward to getting into the new galley."

Jon couldn't sidestep that comment. "This time, Carlos, I think you may have hit the nail on the head." A glance to the east told him that they'd better set out soon. The sun was almost one-quarter above the horizon, in a clear blue morning sky. He yelled so all could hear. "It's getting late, and I know we've all gotten a bit lazy due to the lay-off, but let's get out there, or we'll miss a day's fishing."

Within five minutes, Carlos, Bjorn, and Sven had checked their requirements and announced that they were ready to go. Sven cast off the fore line, and Bjorn was about to release the aft when Stavros appeared. "Hey! You maybe vant lunch, yes?" He handed Bjorn Jon's cooler and yelled to Jon, "Cook, yes, mind-reader no. One day maybe you eat bait for lunch." Then he grinned, broadly.

Jon hadn't even mentioned to Stavros that they were going out, today. "Sorry, old friend. I forgot to let you know that we were back on schedule. Thanks." *How th' hell does he do it?*

The *Adventure II* eased out of her slip and turned toward the mouth of the harbor. Jon could feel an aura of calm come over him as the powerful engines drove his new boat forward. *I had almost forgotten how good this escape feels. Sure puts everything into a simple perspective.* Jon opened two of the windscreens, enjoying the rush of the cool, salty air on his face. He then took his first sip of Stavros' super-hot coffee from the large Styrofoam cup. Stavros hadn't forgotten their routine and handed Jon the cup of his infamous brew, before he walked out to the *Adventure II.*

Sudden activity on the ship-to-shore radio interrupted his reverie. "*Albatross* calling *Adventure Two*—*Albatross* calling *Adventure Two*—come in, Jon."

Jon picked up the mic and responded. "This is the *Adventure Two, Albatross*. What's up Mike? Over." He released the send button and waited.

"*Adventure*, we're running nets for Spanish, and the catch is good. There's also a lot of tuna activity out here. We're not set up for that, but if you are. The catch should be good. Over."

"What's your location, Mike? Over."

"Jon we're just south of latitude fifty, longitude seventy-seven, eight minutes, and headed due south. Over and out."

"Got it, *Albatross*. Thanks, Mike. Have a good run. *Adventure Two,* over and out." Jon put the mic back in its cradle, set the auto pilot, and walked to the wheelhouse door. He spotted Sven on deck and called to him. "Sven, the *Albatross* just called and said there is still a heavy tuna presence. I'm making a slight change in course to intersect the coordinates he gave me. Tell the others to prepare."

Sven just offered a wave of acknowledgement and was off to find Bjorn and Carlos.

Within minutes, tuna rigs were on deck, and Carlos was on his way to the wheelhouse. Once in the wheelhouse, Carlos picked up a pair of marine binoculars. "I'm going up on the flying bridge. Better visibility from there."

Jon just gave a positive nod, and Carlos turned and left.

Both friends were now alone, each enjoying the peace of

the open ocean, and each lost in his own thoughts. Neither of them had enjoyed this special and personal peace for quite a few weeks, and each, in his own way, was relishing the moment. Carlos would occasionally scan the ocean, more out of habit than anticipation. They were still a good half-hour from the area in which the tuna were spotted. Carlos picked up the binoculars for another scan and, as he swept the area, spotted something that caught his attention. *Oh no—not again.* He picked up the mic and buzzed Jon. "Hey, *amigo*, look to the far right. The way those gulls are acting there's something unusual in the water."

Jon was shaken out of his peaceful reverie, and, like Carlos, his first thought was the same. *Not again.* He picked up his binoculars and looked in the direction Carlos had indicated. Sure enough, a large gathering of gulls was circling, wheeling, and diving to the surface, only to rise and repeat their actions. Jon's response was a typical reaction. "Let's see what we've got. It's not too far off." He spun the wheel and pressed the twin power levers forward to increase their speed. Bjorn and Sven were immediately aware of the change and worked their way forward to see what the reason for the change in direction and speed was.

Carlos had stayed zeroed in on the location and again called to Jon. "Got a few sharks hitting whatever it is."

This was almost an exact replay of the incident that precipitated the return of El Tigre, and neither man could shake that thought. Bjorn and Sven also remembered that incident.

Bjorn yelled to Carlos. "Hope ve don't haf another floater."

Jon slowed as they neared the location, straining to see what the cause of the activity was. Carlos, being higher up had a better line of sight. Suddenly his tension vanished, and a broad grin split his countenance. "Jon—it's a dead whale. Looks like a Minke, and the sharks are having a feast."

With that announcement, the whole crew relaxed. Jon, especially, breathed a sigh of relief. That other event, coupled with his close call with death, was still too fresh in his mind, and the only good thing to come out of it was Sheri. He eased the boat to within twenty feet of the whale, so they could all get a closer look. The sharks were makos. From their boat's location, coupled with what was visible, there appeared to be at least six. They were big, between twelve and fourteen feet. The sharks would swim at high speed, slamming into the whale's corpse, jaws gaped wide at the last moment. Then with a violent twisting, wrenching shake would tear out spade sized chunks of blubber. They watched the violent feeding orgy for a few minutes. Jon then spun the wheel reorienting the *Adventure* to their original course and speed.

Carlos climbed slowly down from the flying bridge and entered the wheelhouse. He and Jon stared blankly at each other for a moment. Jon broke the silence. "What are the odds of that? What are the Goddamned odds?"

Carlos had no response—just offered a non-committal shrug, turned slowly and headed for the deck.

They were approaching the area in which they planned to fish, and Jon turned on the electronic fish finder. A large moving mass showed on the screen. *Wow! That looks like a huge school of Spanish. It's tuna first 'cause they bring more money at market. Then if they run out or we have no luck, we'll go for the mackerel.* He eased off on the running speed and began to look for signs of feeding tuna.

Twenty minutes and there's still no sign of tuna. Jon was about to tell the crew to prepare the nets for mackerel when Bjorn yelled to him. "I tink ve haf fish—to der port side."

Jon eased the wheel to the left. Wheeling gulls and an area of choppy water were positive indications. A moment later and tuna were breaking the surface "Looks good. Get ready for some action." In two minutes, he had the boat in with the tuna, set the cruise control for speed and direction, and headed for the deck and the action. By the time his feet hit the deck, tuna were also hitting the deck. Jon opened the aft holding bin, to receive the catch. His next move was to grab a fishing pole and join the fray.

The fishing lasted for almost forty-five minutes before the tuna disappeared. The crew pushed the last of the boated tuna into the refrigerated holding bin then shoveled in ice. The down-time, since they were last out, was evident to all, especially Jon, and he knew he had lost some physical stamina. "What say we break for lunch a little earlier, then we can push it for the rest of the day."

Each of them broke out his cooler then found a convenient spot to sit and enjoy lunch. Jon played his usual mental game, before opening his cooler, trying to guess what Stavros had packed for him. He was today, as he had been most times in the past, wrong. Fifteen minutes later, and lunch was just a pleasant memory.

Jon stood, stretched, and made a general request. "What d' ya say we chase down some more tuna? The day is still young." Without waiting for an answer, he started for the wheelhouse. He knew what the answer was, and it didn't require verbalizing. His question was more rhetorical than direct.

They encountered two more small schools of tuna before that game disappeared. A decision was made to go after Spanish mackerel, and Jon turned on the fish-finder. The nets were deployed and, by four p.m., they had boated almost six-hundred fifty pounds of mackerel. These were dumped directly from the nets into a holding bin, accomplished by a release mechanism that opened a trap in the pocket of the nets. Just the few fish that slipped aside had to be manually tossed into the bin. The nets were stowed, the fish were iced, and the *Adventure II* was pointed toward home. Bjorn then surprised them with the first meal prepared in the new galley—stuffed cabbage. He had managed all of the preparation while on the way to the fishing grounds and slow cooked the meal while they fished. Jon called Tony, at Anthony's Fish Processing, to advise that they were bringing in a mixed catch—tuna and Spanish mackerel. He was about to sign off when he remembered what Sheri had asked. "By the way, Tony, do you happen to know the name of a good yacht broker? Sheri and her mom want to sell the Hatteras—too many bad memories."

Tony responded positively and said that he would email the names and numbers. Jon signed off then devoted himself to steering the *Adventure II* home and enjoying the savory dinner.

Jon left the windscreens open, enjoying the mild weather and the occasional coolness of the fine salt spray, kicked up by the *Adventure II* and carried in by the breeze, as the boat cut its way through the light swells. They were headed due east back to Kure Beach. They would off-load at Tony's first then back to their home slip. The sun had slipped below the horizon, and a breathtaking North Carolina sunset was splashed across the western sky. Various shades of blue, turquoise, gold, pink, vivid crimson, and purple splashed in a random, constantly changing, pattern that no artist's brush could reproduce. *This is true peace. Let's just hope it stays that way.* Somewhere, deep in his heart, he knew this might very well prove to be a futile wish.

CHAPTER 34

Homecoming

The taxi slowed then made a left turn into the driveway at 2761 East Main Street, in Rowland, North Carolina. Marvin had returned home. It was immediately evident that his car was missing. *Guess Charles must have needed to borrow it.* He paid the driver, took his single suitcase, and walked to the porch. The comfort of home swept over him when Marvin turned the key in the front door, walked in, and set his suitcase down. The first task, when he arrived home, was to go to the electric panel and flip the water heater breaker to "on." He had learned to turn it off when he went out of town after an electrician had told him that the water heater was the biggest electricity user in his house. He was also told that it didn't take very long to bring the water back up to temperature.

The savings were definitely worth it. Marvin had, through bitter experience, learned to save money wherever he could. He had destroyed both of his two marriages. The first was to a wealthy woman, and when he lost his job, instead of cutting back, he continued to spend lavishly until she couldn't take it anymore. The second disaster was due to his characteristic need to control everything and everyone. Wife number two was too strong willed for his control, and his second marriage ended explosively. During the period of those two marriages, he also managed to alienate his children, family, and most of his friends. One lonely night while drinking heavily and wallowing in a combination of self-pity and personal loathing, he removed a forty caliber Kimber semi-automatic pistol from his night table, put the barrel in his mouth, and pulled the trigger. This was the one time he had forgotten to have a round loaded in the chamber, but the sharp snap of the firing pin had an un-believably profound and catalytic effect on him. The next day he made a single phone call, packed a few belongings, and drove straight south from New York to a little known Buddhist Monastery in Bolivia, North Carolina. Once there, he went into seclusion for a full year. During that year, he had almost daily counseling from an eighty-year-old monk. Marvin must have wanted to change desperately, because he did.

He now had a simple job, working at a local bank in the small town of Rowland, North Carolina. His house was unpre-tentious, and his life style was almost monastic. This late af-ternoon, after arriving home from his annual two week visit to the monastery, he decided to celebrate his overall feeling of well-being. He rarely drank alcoholic beverages anymore, but this would be one of the few exceptions. He took a glass from the cabinet near the stove, put some ice in it, and went to the sink. It took a bit of a stretch to reach the cabinet high above the sink, and Marvin went up on his tip-toes. That was when his right foot slipped, and he almost went down. *What could be on the floor that's so slippery?* He was a meticulous house-keeper. He stepped back and looked down. There was a smeared reddish stain where his foot had slipped and, near it, several red drops. *That looks like blood. I hope Charles didn't get hurt.* His drink forgotten, Marvin rushed to the phone and punched in Charles's number. Three rings, four rings, five rings—he was about to hang up when the phone was an-swered.

Charles had a newer phone system, one that displayed the incoming call number. "Hi, Marvin. Welcome home. Hope—"

Marvin cut off the friendly welcome with a tense question. "Charles, first tell me. Are you okay? Are you hurt?"

The response from one of his very few friends could not come fast enough.

"Why, yes, I'm okay and, no, I'm not hurt. What makes you ask an odd question like that?"

Marvin was feeling just a little foolish but explained himself. "I just got home and decided to have a drink. When I was at the sink, my foot slipped on something, and when I looked down, I saw what looked like blood. My first thought was that when you came and got my car, you had gotten cut or injured and—" He never finished what he was about to say.

"Marvin, I didn't need to borrow your car and never even stopped by."

Marvin's heart started to race. "My car's gone—I've been robbed and, maybe when they were in the house, someone was hurt. I've got to get off and call the police."

Charles agreed. "Don't touch anything. I think that after you make the call you should wait outside. I'll come right over."

The sheriff arrived within four minutes of Marvin's phone call and confirmed that it was blood. Three minutes later, a crime scene investigation unit pulled into the driveway. Charles arrived a minute later and parked on the street. The investigators went over Marvin's house carefully and dusted for finger prints at the doors, ground level windows, the sink, and the table on which the car keys had been left.

The sheriff knew how often people got confused and disoriented when their personal dwelling and property had been violated. "Are you sure that you didn't possibly put your car in the garage and forgot that you did it?"

Marvin got annoyed at his question. "I'm not stupid, and I'm not senile. I left my car in the driveway in case Charles needed to borrow it. I left the keys on that table." He pointed to the small table where the note still remained. "If you think I'm nuts, why don't you just haul your butt out to the garage and check for yourself?"

Responses of that nature were everyday to the sheriff. "Marvin—relax, I'm not inferring anything. It's just when situations such as this occur, we have to look at all possibilities." He called to one of the deputies. "Carl, take a walk over and look in the garage." The somewhat overweight deputy stopped what he was doing and looked at the sheriff questioningly. The question on the man's face was evident. "Now, Carl. I want to eliminate that possibility, right now."

The portly deputy left, obviously not thrilled about what, to him, was an unnecessary and overly long walk.

Charles had been standing off to one side and watched the deputy as he walked to the garage, opened the side door, and walked in. In less than a minute, the deputy came charging out of the garage door. He turned toward the house and began to run as fast as he could, back toward the house.

Charles caught the sheriff's attention. "Here comes your deputy, Sheriff, and it looks like the devil's chasing him.

Sheriff Dooley looked up quickly and turned toward the garage. "For Carl to be running like that, there must be something wrong."

Carl reached the porch and, between gasps for air, managed to spit out what he had found. "There's a car in th' garage— not Marvin's—looks like bloody clothes—layin' in the back seat—car's locked." He was leaning over, hands on his knees, and stopped talking after his clipped report, his efforts now restricted to catching his breath. Carl had definitely gotten everyone's attention, and they all started for the garage.

The sheriff stopped Marvin and Charles. "We may have more than we bargained for, and I don't need the two of you in the way." Surprisingly, the two men listened and went no farther. The sheriff called back into the house. "I need CSI out at the garage—now!"

Twenty-four hours later, they had the disturbing facts. The blood on the floor and on the shirt were typed and found to be RH Negative. That was the same type as Irene's blood type, the deputy who had been brutally murdered just the evening before. The blood type was too uncommon for this to be a co-incidence. The fingerprints in the house and garage were-Marvin's and some unknown. The killers had definitely been there and were now driving Marvin's Buick, but where to and for what insane reason?

CHAPTER 35

Covering Tracks

Cholo was awakened abruptly by a bright flash of light, then three seconds later, the booming crash of thunder. An average person might be upset by now having to travel by car in a thunderstorm. Cholo was far from average. *This will offer good cover. With less people on the street, there'll be fewer witnesses to our leaving and travel direction.* He looked at the clock. It was four-fifteen a.m. The wake-up call had been placed for five. He didn't wait but dressed rapidly. He wanted to be on the road early. He also didn't like the idea of spending too much time in one location. He lived his criminal life with a simple logic that had proven its worth. "A moving target is harder to hit."

The night clerk at the front desk looked up when he heard the door. "Good morning, sir. How may I help you?"

"We're checking out of rooms eleven and eighteen. There should be no additional charges, and I'd like to keep the payment on my credit card."

The clerk did a fast review of the rooms. "That's correct. No additional charges." He ran the credit card. "Here are your receipts. Thank you, Mr. Graziano, and please come back and see us."

Cholo didn't bother to respond, just turned and left. He was in the car waiting outside of room eighteen when Jorge and Pepe stepped out. "Get in. Let's get some breakfast then hit the road." His mind was way ahead of their short-sighted thinking.

That note on the table with the car keys said the owner would be away for two weeks, but there was no date on it. That means we could be safe for two weeks with this car or he could be home now and know his car was stolen. We need to change cars. Too bad, at least this one's comfortable.

Jorge saw a low key way to start to reassert his authority. "Let's go back to that diner we went to last night. Food was decent and not high priced."

Cholo said nothing; just nodded in agreement. *Let this idiot think he's in charge. Just a little while longer and then the vultures will have two more bodies to feast on.*

There were only a handful of customers in the diner when they came in. Bad weather had a way of dramatically reducing client flow. They opted for a corner booth in the rear. The waitress was pleasant enough, and they ordered simple items to avoid possible cooking time delays. When they had entered, Cholo noticed the small customer service area offering assorted candies, tourist guides, postcards, and road maps, for sale. "I'll be right back. We need a map." He quickly located a map of both North Carolina and Virginia, paid cash, and returned to the table. When the waitress returned with their order, he sought her assistance. "Miss, is there an airport nearby?"

She responded readily. "D'pends whut ya call an airport. Couple a small private ones not far off, but if yer lookin' fer a good one, that'll be the Charlotte-Douglas International Airport, up by Charlotte."

Cholo couldn't have been more polite. "We're not from this area so would you mind pointing it out on this map?" The waitress quickly indicated the location, marked on the map by the figure of an airplane. "How long do you think it would take to drive there, from here?"

She was in her element now. "That's easy—took mah cousin, last week. Dependin' 'pon traffic, b'tween two 'n' three hours. More coffee?"

Jorge and Pepe said nothing during this exchange, but as soon as she left, Jorge demanded in a harsh whisper. "What the hell was that about, and why an airport?"

He didn't get the immediate answer that he anticipated. Instead, Cholo let him dangle for a while and took several long and slow sips of his coffee before answering. "I'll tell you when we're outside. This place has too many ears." He returned with purposeful slowness to his coffee, enjoying Jorge's frustrated silence. "I have to use the bathroom. Then we can go." Without another word, he rose from the table and started in the direction of the men's room.

Jorge was furious. *Who does this son-of-a-bitch think he is?* He jumped up. Pepe was about to follow but was told, "Wait here. I'll be right back." With that, Jorge made haste to catch up with Cholo. His intent was to set him straight about who was in charge.

One small sink, a fouled urinal, a stained toilet, and an overflowing waste can. There was nothing spectacular, just an ordinary public bathroom. Yet when Jorge entered, he found Cholo standing in the center of this small chamber of porcelain and ceramic tile, slowly surveying his surroundings. This odd scene put an instant check on his animosity, but not his attitude. "What th' fuck are you doing, now?"

Cholo didn't respond to the crude question. He was now standing in front of the urinal, his knife in hand. While Jorge watched in angry frustration, he could see the thin cut that Cholo was making in the caulking between the back of the urinal and the tile wall. It was as if Jorge wasn't even in the room. Cholo withdrew Anthony Graziano's credit card from his pocket and carefully pressed it into the cut he had just created. The card slipped all the way in to the plumbing cavity, becoming completely hidden. Firm pressure, with his thumb, along the cut in the caulk, and it was almost completely sealed. He had just solved what had become to him, and evidently only him, a major problem.

"I'll tell you what I'm doing." Cholo buried his anger at being addressed in this manner by an ignorant mule. "I'm staying alive." The lack of understanding was immediately evident by the look on Jorge's face. "By now, this card should have been canceled." Once again a blank look. "Its owner is dead and, without any doubt, has been discovered. This card is being used to track us. *Entiendes?* We have to get out of here and fast. We also need to get rid of the car." This time, he didn't wait for understanding but went on and told Jorge about the note by the car keys. "So you see, we may have almost two weeks, or we may be out of time already. The airport is a place to get a car and leave this one. Maybe when it is found, the police will assume we have flown away. This will buy us valuable time."

Jorge suddenly realized that Cholo was far above his simple criminal mind-set. *This man is not the fool I thought he was. He is a deep thinker and a planner with tomorrow always in mind.* A new-found respect was formed, but also a new fear. *He could be planning to kill us when we locate the money. I have to be more careful than ever if I want to come out of this venture alive. Can't warn Pepe. He could easily betray my concerns.* The realization became most evident when Jorge thought about Cholo's disposal of the credit card. *I would have tossed it in the trash or on the street or, even better—would have sold it. What Cholo did was to make the card disappear—no links, no traces—cunning and careful.*

A right turn, out of the parking lot, and Route 501 north was just a half-mile up the road. Cholo had picked the travel route when the waitress had pointed out the location of the airport. They would then get on Highway 74, headed northwest. That would take them directly to Charlotte. Road signs would then lead them to the airport, which was located to the west of the city.

⋐⋑⋐⋑

Two hours and they were at the outskirts of Charlotte. They made a quick stop at a large home improvement center where Cholo purchased a twenty-four-inch length of one-eighth-inch-thick, flat aluminum bar stock. That stop took barely fifteen minutes. From there they drove straight to the airport. Cholo spotted what he was looking for, the long-term parking lot. He drove up to the entry, pressed the ticket request button and, when the bar lifted, drove in. "Now we wait until the right car comes in." That took less than eight minutes.

The two-tone green sedan was an Oldsmobile, and the driver pulled it into row C, space 237, and parked. A man and woman got out of the car and removed two suitcases and a small duffle from the trunk.

Cholo was ready with an explanation. "That's the car for us. The two of them are going away for at least a week, based on their luggage. That means we have at least that much time."

While they watched, the man returned to the driver's side, slipped the parking ticket above the visor, locked the doors, and the couple started toward the terminal.

Cholo had them wait for ten minutes before making a move. "Wait here and wipe down the car. Then collect all of our things and be ready to move." He walked casually toward the Olds, the bar of aluminum held close against his arm for concealment. Upon reaching the car, he looked around to insure that the car's owners had, indeed, departed the area and that no one nearby was watching. Quickly, he slipped the length of aluminum down between the door frame and the window, made contact with the locking mechanism, and with a hard push, released the door lock. He gave a beckoning wave to Jorge and Pepe to get them moving then reached under the dashboard and hot-wired the car. The minute they were in, he put the car in drive, spotted the exit sign, and followed the arrows to the payment booth and exit.

The attendant looked at the time stamped on the ticket. "You should have parked in the short-term lot. Would've saved ya some money. That'll be two dollars. Need a receipt?"

Cholo handed over the money and offered a simple response. "Guess I'll know better next time. No receipt."

Highway 77 was just a short distance from the exit and, in just minutes, they were headed north toward Virginia.

CHAPTER 36

Grasping Straws

This particular morning, Gabe's office felt as if it were closing in on him. *Ah'm all caught up here 'n' nothin' doin' en town. 'Bout time ah see if'n A.J.'s truck has sumpin ta offer.* Gabe locked the office door and walked across the street to Ethyl's. Instead of his usual table, he went straight to the counter. Out of habit coupled with his training, he scanned the dining area as he walked. It was six-ten a.m. and other than two regulars at the counter and four at one table, the place was empty.

Sally spotted Gabe as she returned from serving the foursome. "Mornin', Gabe. Ain't ya stayin'?"

"Not t'day. Goin' up ta th' Johnson lot fer a bit. Jest a large black coffee ta take 'long."

By now the whole town knew that A.J. had left the land to Gabe. The only reason he told Sally where he was headed was so that, if he were needed, she would know where he was. The restaurant was the hub of the town's information, and if his office was closed, the locals would automatically check with whoever was on duty at Ethyl's.

Sally poured the coffee, snapped on the lid, and handed it to him. "Best take yer slicker wi' ya. Got us a fair storm headed this a way. Weatherman says she might be a rough un. Ya plannin' ta build on er?"

"Don't rightly know jest yet. Figured ah'd walk 'round a bit 'n' see if'n thet he'ps. Shouldn't be out a town more 'n a hour, mebbe th' most hour 'n' a half." The true purpose of his short trip had no need to be divulged.

He turned and started for the door, pausing to offer a wave of recognition, in response to a "Mornin', Gabe," from the foursome at the table.

His Jeep was parked in front of his office. He had the one reserved parking spot in town. Gabe took a quick glance skyward then climbed in, pulled the sip tab on the coffee lid and placed the cup in the cup holder. *Fum th' look a th' sky, storm's not too fur off. Best git a movin' raht now.* It took less than two minutes to drive through the small town. The road he was now on was, as were most outside of town, hard dirt. He took the left fork, when the road split, and slowed for the poor road conditions. *'Peers Zeke figger'd jest th' raht spot fer his ambush. Johnson would a had ta slow ta a near crawl, 'pon this stretch.* When your mind's tied up in thought, it's easy to loose track of time, and, before he knew it, he was at the Johnsons'. The chimney still stood, and the burned remnants of the home had been mellowed by the weather. The truck was right where he had parked it, untouched.

Gabe walked slowly around the old pick-up, seeking any indication of something that was out of place or did not fit right. Then he checked the wheel wells. From there he went to the truck bed then lifted the hood and checked the engine compartment. *Jest th' usual.* The cab was next. Before he got in, he checked behind and under the seats. *Clean.* Next, the floor and under the mats. He was drawing a blank and rapidly beginning to think that this was another zero on his check list. *Glove compartment's last.* He popped it open. *Let's see whut we've got here. Coupons fer pizza? Guess A.J. had gotten a likin' fer thet. Tire gauge, a ice scraper, 'n' whut's this?* Gabe had been removing the items as he found them and placed them on the seat alongside of him. The last item in the back corner of the compartment made his heart gain a beat or two. It was a large, conical cork. *Jest th' thing ta stopper a jug a 'shine.* Around the middle of the cork, about half way between the narrow and wide ends was a definite impression from the mouth of a jug or large bottle. Slowly he brought the narrow end to his nose. The aroma was faint but instantly recognized. *Son-of-a-bitch, squeezin's. A.J. must a come 'pon er around th' house 'n' figgered 'twas Zeke's. Prob'ly dropped when he burnt th' place. Don't much matter now seein' as both a them's dead. Jury'd call this circumstantial, but she shore puts er all en place.*

The reality of the weather brought him back to the moment. The wind had picked up, and it had begun to rain. It was the first crash of thunder that brought his mind off his find and back to the moment. *Gonna be a bad un. Best git back ta town.* He stuffed the cork in his jacket pocket closed the pick-up doors, jumped back in his Jeep, started the motor and aimed his vehicle toward town. In that short time, the weather had become severe.

Lightning, thunder, high winds, and near torrential rain do not make driving on a narrow dirt road edged with ancient oak and maple trees, an easy task. Sheriff Tanner was doing fifteen miles an hour coming down the hill when a bolt of lightning hit the upper trunk of a one hundred-fifty year old oak tree, snapping off the top twenty-feet. The tree section dropped from fifty feet above, lower branches offering little slowing resistance, to crash onto the cab of the Jeep. The thin canvas roof with its tubular steel frame was no match for close to six-hundred pounds of oak. Gabe never knew what hit him.

ⱸⱯⱸⱯ

Gary and Anne decided they would have an early lunch, and as they approached Ethyl's Anne had a thought. "Why don't we stop at the sheriff's office and see if there's any kind of an update? We haven't seen him in two days."

Gary didn't respond. He just parked in front of Gabe's office, instead of across the street at Ethyl's.

Gary reached the door and tried it. Anne had remained in the car to avoid the weather. He had turned to face Anne and yelled for her to hear. *"Door's locked."* He started back to the car and spotted another thing as he was getting in. "Man this is a hell of a storm. Sheriff's Jeep is gone. Let's get some lunch.

In a town this small someone in the restaurant is bound to know where he is and when he'll be back." He backed the car out and swung the wheel to do a one-eighty degree turn, and park in front of Ethyl's. "Might as well get as close as possible."

They both rushed to the door, and once in went directly to a table that they had chosen as their preference. Sally started over as they sat down. "Mornin'. Whut'll ya have? Late breakfast er early lunch?"

Anne smiled gently as she answered. "We decided to get an early lunch, before the crowd rolls in."

Sally glanced toward the front windows. "Don't 'peer they's gonna be much uv a rush t'day. Weather took keer a thet. Whut'll ya have? Special t'day er roast pork, mashed taters, 'n' collards. B'lieve it's ready."

Gary answered first. "I'll have the special and a black coffee, cream on the side."

Anne, surprisingly, requested the same. They were both now on much better terms with Sally then when they first encountered her. Sally had turned on her heels and was about to rush off to get their order in when Anne stopped her. "Sally, do you happen to know where Sheriff Tanner is?"

Sally stopped dead in her tracks then looked at the clock on the wall. It was eleven-forty a.m. Gabe had left Ethyl's at six-twenty a.m. and said he'd be an hour and a half, at most. That was nearly five and one-half hours ago. Sally turned back to their table. "Gabe was en this mornin', 'round 'bout six-twenty, 'n' said he'd be back en most a hour 'n' a half. She's goin' on five 'n' a half hours now, 'n' thet ain't lahk Gabe." She paused and turned to the restaurant in general. She raised her voice. "*Anyone seen Gabe since six-twenty this morning?*" All responses were negative. She turned back to the table. "Gabe said he were goin' up ta th' Johnson property 'n' didn't 'spect ta be more 'n a hour 'n' a half. He could a met wi' sum trouble."

Gary stood, and Anne followed immediately. "Tell us how to get there, and we'll take a drive out to check."

Sally couldn't help grinning. "Wi thet car a yourn, ya'll be lucky ta make it ta th' junction. Gimme a sec." She turned away and called to a bearded, long-haired man in overalls, who had just walked in. "Amos, ya busy?" A slight negative shake of the shaggy head indicated no. She went on. "Kin ya carry these folk ta th' Johnson site raht now? They'll pay yer gas." She hadn't asked but made her own decision that that would be the least these two could do.

Amos looked at Gary and Anne and after a moment gave his answer. "City folk, huh? Reckin ah best do er so's they don't kill theirselves. This weather, they'd stan' less chance 'n a grasshopper en a trout stream. Let's git a move on."

Sally offered one bit of advice as they stood to leave. "Amos'll git ya there, thet's fer shore. Jest r'member ta hang on."

Anne and Gary followed Amos out and a few feet up the sidewalk. His vehicle turned out to be a converted army five-ton truck, with a large tool bin behind the cab. Mounted above the rear bumper was a winch with half-inch cable on the spool. Amos lifted one arm, slightly and with his forefinger, pointed at the door. Anne climbed in first, and Gary followed. Amos climbed in and slammed the driver's door shut. He offered advice and a suggestion. "Best ya hang on good 'n' don't be a jawin' all th' way."

Anne turned to Gary as soon as he was in. There was a distasteful odor, like something rotten and sour, in the cab of the truck. She wrinkled her nose to indicate her displeasure. Gary gave a slight nod to indicate that he, too, was aware of it.

The ride was a bone-shaking, nerve-wracking one. Amos drove as if tomorrow didn't matter for him or his two passengers, but, amazingly, he stayed on the road. They turned left at the split, and Amos slowed just a bit. Gary whispered to Anne. "Must be worse than no road at all, if he's slowed down a bit."

Amos ended any chance of a response from Anne. "Ah tole ya no jawin'. Ah cain't pay good 'tention ta mah drivin' when there's folk a jabberin'."

That ended any conversation.

They crested the hill, and Amos resumed his speed. They rounded a corner and, without warning, he slammed the brakes, threw the gear shift into neutral, and yanked the emergency brake. Gary's first instinct was to reach for his gun, then he saw the reason for the gut-wrenching stop. Directly in front of them was Gabe's Jeep. The windshield was lying on the hood, and the front end of the vehicle was crumpled against the trunk of a large oak. What looked every bit like a small tree was lying diagonally across the cab. Amos was already out and starting for the Jeep by the time Gary and Anne realized the gravity of the situation and followed.

"Gabe's en er 'n' 'live. 'Peers he's unconscious 'n' hurt bad. Clothes er bloodied some, but th' rain washed th' blood off'n him so's ah cain't rightly tell whut kinda injuries there be. Got ta git him back ta town 'n' prob'ly ta th' hospital."

As soon as he made that statement, he turned and jogged back to the truck. He climbed up on the bed, opened the toolbox, and pulled out a large chainsaw and a length of rope. He jumped down, collected the two items, and returned to the crippled Jeep. "Got ta cut away some a this limb top a Gabe, so's we kin lift th' rest off'n him."

Anne had had some first aid training and was shocked at what this man proposed. "We can't move him. That's a decision for trained medical personnel. If we move him, we might injure him worse."

Amos turned on her so abruptly that she stumbled back. "Lady, this man's been here, hurt bad, mebbe four hour. Time we would git ta town 'n' git, he'p likely be least six hour more. Fum what ah kin see, Gabe'd be dead by then so stop jawin' 'n' do whut ah say. Ya'll got one a them fancy pocket phones?" Both of them responded positively. "Call this number." He gave them a number from memory. "Thet be ta Ethyl's. More 'n likely, Sally'll answer. Tell her whut we got 'n' tell her we're bringin' him in. She'll know whut ta do." He turned to Gary. "Let her do th' callin. Grab th' rope 'n' do jest whut ah say."

The sudden realization that this man made perfect sense caused Gary to realize that he needed to listen carefully to every direction he would receive. This was not the world he was used to. This was backwoods mountain country, and he was with people who had been dealing with their own problems for generations. Gary watched as Amos threw the end of the rope over a low branch above the Jeep. He then looked carefully, gauging the distance between the limb lying across Gabe and the Jeep floor. Amos fired up the chain saw, stepped off the road, and walked up to a tree that was about eight inches in diameter at the trunk base. He called Gary over and directed, "Ya push here, hard's ya kin—when ah say push."

He started to cut, just about a foot below Gary's hands. Gary had never been that close to the working end of a chain-saw, and he was more than a little nervous. He had his eyes fixed on that saw, the chain a spinning blur, spitting sawdust, and as far as he was concerned, *too damn close to my hands.*

The command came. *"Push!"* Gary did as he was told. *"Harder!"*

Gary was giving it all that he had. Suddenly, the tree gave and toppled, and Gary almost went with it. Amos didn't even seem to notice. He started to cut again. This time he used the saw like a router, creating a U-shaped indent in the exposed stump end. Again he cut. This time about two feet below the first cut. When his chosen length was freed, he directed Gary. "Grab thet hunk 'n' bring er."

Gary was shocked at how heavy that piece of tree was, but he managed. Amos took it and placed it, standing, on the floor of the Jeep. He looked at it for a moment then pulled it out, started up the saw, and cut about two inches off the flush end. "Thet's got er," he declared then angled the beveled end under the limb that was lying across Gabe.

Once that was in place, he pushed the flat end to try and bring it vertical. The limb across Gabe was too heavy to allow that, so Amos chose another tactic. Back to the tool box and, when he returned, he was holding a twenty-pound sledge hammer. Both Gary and Anne were aghast at this but were ignored. Three gentle blows at the base, and the quickly fash-ioned wood brace had been securely placed. Amos then tied the end of the rope around the tree limb, about a foot from where the brace had been placed. "Ahm gonna cut er 'tween the brace 'n' th' rope. Ya'll pull on th' rope wi' all ya got.

When th' cut goes through, she'll swing away fum th' jeep, so mind whar ya be. Ready?"

Anne looked at Gary as if she was in shock. Numbly, she nodded her head yes, and Gary yelled to Amos, "Ready, go for it."

The saw started and, in a few moments, the limb parted. The cut end swung quickly around, barely missing Anne.

Amos didn't have time for such a meaningless event. "Git er untied."

Gary followed orders. The moment he finished, the next order came.

"Thar's a loggin' chain en th' tool box. She's 'bout ten foot long 'n' wi' a hook ta both ends. Git er 'n' bring er."

Gary found the chain with relative ease. Carrying it was a different story. "This thing's heavy as hell. How do you do this without help?"

Amos was merciless. "Ain't near thet bad. Git er over here 'n' hurry."

As soon as Gary reached him, Amos took the chain from him, with seemingly little effort.

"Watch whut ah do wi' er 'n' watch kerful 'cause yer a goin' ta do th' same ta th' other side a Gabe." Amos then looped the chain around the cut end of the limb and slid the hook over one of the links, securing the limb. "Now g'wan over at th' other side a Gabe 'n' do th' same wi' th' other end a th' chain. 'Bout two foot out fum Gabe," Amos then told him. "Jest hold th' chain up, so she don' drop, 'n' wait."

Gary didn't even have time to question the action and Amos was headed back to his truck.

Anne took this brief interlude to inform Gary that she had spoken to Sally who had simply said, "Ah'll take keer a ever'thin'." She looked in the direction of the truck and asked, "What's he doing now?"

Within five minutes, on this one-lane dirt road, with no shoulders or side clearance, Amos had turned his truck around and was backing it toward them. He flipped a switch and four large lights, mounted on the roof of the cab, came to life. The lights, mounted facing the rear for just this purpose, illuminated the scene like daylight. He came to within ten feet of the front of the Jeep and stopped, left the motor running, pulled the brake, and got out. He quickly went to the rear of his truck and released the winch cable. It was then that Gary got his next order.

"See thet big branch 'bout ten foot up?" Amos didn't wait for an answer. "Throw th' rope over her."

Gary did as he was told, but it took him three attempts, while Amos shook his head in disbelief. With the rope over the branch, Amos collected the end on his side of the branch and tied it to the hook at the end of the winch cable. "Ahm gonna let cable out 'n' ya'll pull er up 'n' over."

Again, Gary did as told. The rope was untied from the cable, and Amos positioned the hook in the center of the logging chain. He then put the winch in reverse and slowly took up the slack until the cable was taught. He then took up a little more until the weight was off Gabe, but not enough for the brace under the cut end to slip. Once sure that everything was secure, he took the chain saw, went to the other side of the huge branch, and, after first cutting a V notch on the underside, cut through the branch about one-foot beyond the logging chain. The large, cut-off branch section dropped with a resounding crash, leaving the piece lying on Gabe stable and neatly suspended.

Gary turned to Anne. "Bet he never went past the sixth grade, but he's as good as any engineer I ever encountered. If I were in trouble, I'd like to have him on the rescue team."

"Quit a jawin'. We got a life ta tend ta. Both a ya git over here."

They didn't hesitate a bit. By now, Amos had tied the rope to the left end of the suspended log, just behind the end of the logging chain. He took a quick survey of the surrounding trees and started off toward the one of his choice. "C'mon, foller me close." They were right on his heels. He ran the rope around the tree and back in the direction of the jeep. "Both a ya grab a holt a th' rope 'n' listen close. Ahm gonna lift thet log off'n Gabe 'n' up 'bout five foot. When ah say pull, ya pull lahk y'all er a tryin' ta close th' gates a hell afor' th' devil gits out. Don't ya stop fer a sec, til ah say ya kin. Ready?"

Anne's level of respect had by now multiplied greatly, and she answered as if talking to a superior officer. "Yes, sir. We're ready. You just say when."

Amos turned and retreated to the winch controls. He, Gary, and Anne were all completely soaked, but from the moment Gabe had been discovered, were totally oblivious of the storm.

"Ahm gonna lift er now. Don't pull yet, but don' 'low nary slack, neither."

The section of branch began to slowly rise. It immediately became evident that Anne and Gary were on the working end of what now was a guy line. The branch came to a stop, and Amos walked over to survey the position.

"Got ta git 'bout two foot more."

Again the branch began to elevate. Six inches—one foot— sixteen inches—two feet. The branch stopped moving.

Amos took one last look, walked back to the winch and gave the command. "*Pull! Pull!* Gabe's 'pendin' 'pon ya."

They both put all they had into it. Gary actually put both feet on the tree, bracing himself, and was pulling hand over hand, with Anne right behind. Anne noticed a result in their work. "We're gaining rope," she panted.

"Quit jawin' 'n' pull. Put yer energy en yer hands, not yer mouth." Amos didn't let up for a second.

In spite of the weather, Anne and Gary were perspiring, freely. The task was grueling, sometimes just a few inches, sometimes more than a foot gained. Then, abruptly, they came to a dead stop. They couldn't gain an inch. They felt as if they were trying to pull a mountain. Anne yelled over her shoulder. "Amos, we've hit a snag or something. We can't get another inch. What should we do?"

There was silence for a moment then the answer came. "Le' go a th' rope. She's done."

Gary wasn't at all sure that he had heard correctly and continued to strain against the unmovable rope. "Did you say let go of the rope?"

"Yep. We got er done."

They both let go of the rope and simultaneously stepped back, as if anticipating that all they had gained would fly in reverse. The rope lay at their feet and didn't move. They turned to face Amos, and the realization of what he had contrived was instantly evident. They were pulling the section of branch away from the Jeep, as Amos reversed the winch. The branch section lay on the ground almost three feet from the Jeep and Gabe. They both, almost in chorus, started to congratulate Amos and got the same response as they had earlier. "Quit jawin' 'n' git over here. Ain't time fer idle talk. We got ta git Gabe ta town. Untie mah rope 'n' ah'll git th' chain."

Again they followed orders. Since both of them had military backgrounds, following orders was part of their being. Once the chain was off the branch section, Amos put the winch in forward and reclaimed the cable.

Amos was a man on a mission and wasn't about to let up until he accomplished what he had set out to do. "Lady, coil up mah rope 'n' put er back en mah box." He pointed at Gary. "He'p me push th' Jeep back fum th' tree." Amos made sure that the gear shift was in neutral. "Now ya push 'n' push hard."

Luck was with them. The ground behind the Jeep was nearly level, and, as they applied muscle, it began to roll back from the tree that it had come to rest against. One foot, then three then five and after about seven feet they came against a rise and were forced to stop.

Amos looked at the distance gained. "Thet'll do 'er. Make sure she don' roll back."

Gary was left standing in front of the Jeep, and Amos quickly returned to his truck. In no time, the truck was backing toward the Jeep. He came to within two feet of the front end, applied his brakes, and jumped out.

Anne took this moment to check on Gabe. "He appears to be in shock. His breathing is kind of short and shallow. He needs medical attention and soon."

Amos looked at her, and the expression on his face was one of incredulity. "Thet's whut we're doin', lady. Git on up en th' truck. We're movin' en 'bout five minute th' most."

While he dealt with Anne, he ran the logging chain through the tow ring on the front of the jeep, locked the hook on a link, then did the same at the rear of his truck. A look around and he took the chain saw to a nearby sapling, quickly cutting it off to a length of about five feet, trimming off all of the small branches.

He then turned to Gary. "Gabe's got his seatbelt on 'n' thet's best 'cause we fer shore best not move him. Git up en th' seat next ta him 'n' take this." He handed Gary the trimmed length of sapling. "Ah'm gonna tow th' jeep. Ah'll take 'er easy as ah kin. If'n ya see yer gainin' 'pon me, use th' end a thet ta mash th' brake." He never asked if Gary could do it—just told him. He saw the hint of concern in Gary's eyes. "Cain't be choicey here. Needs doin' 'n' yer th' onliest one ta do 'er. Ah don' b'lieve yer lady kin. Now git en 'n' let's be a goin'."

Gary climbed into the passenger seat of the Jeep, fastened his seatbelt, and took the length of sapling. He steeled himself for what he was sure would be a very rough ride.

Amos put the truck in gear and eased up on the clutch. The slack came out of the logging chain, and they were moving. It didn't take long for both Anne and Gary to realize that he was driving with a lot more thought to Gabe than he had for his two passengers on the way out. Amos was still covering all possibilities. "Lady, git yer pocket phone 'n' call back ta Sally. She gits on, ya ask whar we need ta go."

Anne immediately pulled out her phone and punched the redial for the last number. Sally answered after two rings. Obviously, she was staying close to the phone. "Ethyl's, Sally here."

"Sally, this is Anne, with Amos. He wants to know where we should go. I guess you know what he means."

"Tell him th' hayin' field off'n th' main road ta th' east side a town. He'p's waitin."

Anne repeated the message to Amos who gave a grunt of agreement. Anne translated the gutteral response. "Amos said okay. We're on the road, but he's driving a bit more cautiously now."

Word of trouble clearly spread quickly in rural communities, because when they reached town, there must have been twenty to thirty people on the main street, none of them giving any regard to the weather, waiting and watching. Sheriff Gabriel Tanner was highly respected and loved. The evidence was there. Amos didn't slow down for the people. He continued through town, headed in the direction of Sheridan. Suddenly, the pulsating glow of flashing lights pierced the dark of the storm. The source of the lights was a medical helicopter awaiting their arrival. Four EMS crew wasted no time in getting vitals on Gabe, hanging an IV, and placing him on a stretcher. Within ten minutes, at most, the helicopter with Gabe on board lifted off. Sally, who was waiting at the field, rushed to give Amos a hug.

Gary and Anne stood off to the side. They were, at this moment, insignificant outsiders. They were soaked, cut, and bruised and both were experiencing stress let-down. Gary looked at his hands. They were badly blistered, and some of the blisters had torn open. Anne's weren't as bad, but she wasn't happy about their condition. Gary voiced his immediate feelings, aloud to Anne. "I sure as hell could use a stiff drink, right now."

One of the locals in the crowd had heard that these two city folk helped Amos with Gabe's rescue and hollered out to the crowd. "These folk cud stan' fer a drink 'bout now. Eny here got some 'shine?"

Momentary silence then a man stepped forward. It was Nate, from the hardware store. "B'lieve ah kin be uv he'p 'bout now. Git on over ta mah truck." They followed him and stopped by his Ford pick-up. Nate opened the passenger side door, reached in, and pulled out a jug. With a quick, practiced twisting motion, he pulled the cork. "Take a pull a this. It'll git ya raht fer shore, 'n' don' worry none. This be first-class squeezin's."

Gary took the offered jug, sniffed the contents, and raised it to his lips. He took two good swallows and eased the jug back down, offering it to Anne. She followed suit, starting with one swallow. She did not often drink hard liquor and almost choked on the first pull of this powerful moonshine. She paused, however, surprised at how smooth this illegal liquor was, then took another long swallow. The effects of the one-sixty proof alcohol were starting to get to Gary. "Man that went down a lot smoother than I would have expected, but now I feel as if there's a fire in my gut—in a good way." He reached for the jug, now in Nate's hands.

Before letting go, Nate offered some advice. "Best be kerful. She got more kick 'n yer store bought likker 'n' if'n ya ain't used ta er, she'll put ya down." Gary hesitated for a moment then took the jug and took one more swallow of the liquid fire. Anne followed Gary, reached for the jug, and took another healthy swallow.

By now, Sally had come over to where they stood. "Shore be a good thing thet ya'll were lookin' fer Gabe. EMTs said he's got a busted collar bone 'n' a broke arm 'n' mebbe some internal bleedin', but he'll be fine now. Also said if'n Gabe'd been out a few more hours, he might a died, 'tween th' weather 'n' injuries. Ya'll hungry? Restaurant's shet now but ah reckin we can rustle up sumpin'."

Anne looked at Gary, and he shook his head to indicate that at this moment food held no interest. She answered for both of them. "Right now we both need a hat—no—hot, yes hot shower and some sleep, but we appreciate your offer. Besides, I think that drink we had issh shtarting to get to me, and, and I think Gary too. We'll just have a bigg breaffast in th' mornin'."

The slurred voices of the two agents were more than evident to Sally. "Best ya don' drive ta th' hotel. Ah'll git someone ta carry ya." With that, she turned and hollered to the crowd. "These folk be needin' a ride ta Parker's."

Amos stepped quickly forward. "Ah'll do er. They done raht good fer city folk. Least ah kin do."

CHAPTER 37

Confusion

Anne awoke in a groggy and confused state of mind, not sure of where she was, what day it was, or even why she was here. The one thing that she did know was that her bladder was aching for relief. She started to rise and felt as if she was pinned down. She glanced down toward her chest. *Holy shit! Who is*—She looked to her left. *It's Gary. My God, he's naked—shit! I'm naked. Did we—*

She carefully lifted Gary's arm, slid out of bed, and rushed to the bathroom. To the left, on the floor lay two piles of soggy clothes, hers and Gary's. She closed the door behind her, heading straight for the toilet, sat, and let go. She finished and wiped then had a thought, held on to the paper in her hand, and turned on the light. She peered into the bowl of urine, searching. She found what she was hoping she wouldn't. *Damn it! That's semen. I don't remember having sex, but we must have. Maybe he won't remember, and I can let this go. Good thing I'm on the pill.*

She dropped the toilet paper into the bowl and flushed then wrapped a bath towel around her and left the bathroom to collect some clothes. Gary hadn't budged. Anne retrieved the clothing she needed then returned to the bathroom to dress. This activity brought immediate attention to the pain in her blistered hands, as well as to the aching muscles in her arms, neck, and shoulders. *Got to get something for these blisters.* She finished dressing and stepped back into the bedroom. She glanced at Gary. *Just stay asleep a little bit longer.* Quickly, she went to the other bed, pulled back the covers and rumpled the bedding to make it look slept in, then over to the one chair near the window to sit and wait for Gary to awaken.

Gary awoke fifteen minutes later and sat up on the edge of the bed. *Damn it! I must have climbed in naked. Hope I didn't piss Anne off.* He looked for her and saw that she was sitting in the chair, looking out of the window. He went the opposite way—to the bathroom. His movement brought an immediate realization of the physical strain he had been under, yesterday. Gary ached all over and his palms hurt like hell. *I haven't felt this shitty since early basic training.* He, too, wrapped a towel around him after the pent up stream of urine finally came to an end, and went back into the room to collect his clothes. Then, like Anne, he returned to the bathroom. Once dressed, he came back in the room. "Good morning, Anne. Sleep okay? I know I did. That was some potent shit in that jug. I can't remember a thing after Amos said 'We're here.' How about you?"

Anne nervously figured that she was off the hook, and offered a response in the most casual manner she could summon. "Me too. I might want to take some of that stuff home with us for nights when I can't sleep. I'm starving. Let's go get some breakfast."

They walked, hunched over in the driving rain, to Ethyl's. When they arrived a quick check indicated that their unlocked car was untouched, contents intact. His off-hand comment said it all. "Sure not like the city." He held the door, and they walked in, straight to the table they had adopted.

CHAPTER 38

Complications

Sally saw them enter and hurried over. "Mornin' folks. Coffee 'n' a menu? If'n ya want, ya kin hang yer rain coats ta th' wall yonder." She pointed to her rear, indicating a row of coat hanger pegs on the far wall.

Anne answered immediately. "Good morning Sally. Coffee, definitely and yes menus too, thank you. We'll just drape our raincoats over this chair." Her dealings with Sally had done a complete one-eighty, since their first rough encounter.

Sally turned and hurried off. "Back en jest two shakes."

Gary had noticed something different about Anne, this morning. He couldn't pin it down, but she was acting strangely. *Might just be the result of yesterday. I'll let it go for a bit, but if it continues, I'll ask.*

Sally reappeared with their coffee and menus. "Ah'll give ya'll time ta decide. Th' town folk shore 'preciate whut ya done, ta he'p rescue Gabe. Amos said ya done real fine. Ethyl's be payin fer yer breakfast t'day. Kinda a thank ya uv sorts. Hospital called ta say th' same whut the EMT folk offered. Gabe's got a broke arm 'n' colla' bone, lota cuts 'n' scrapes 'n' also a minor 'cussion. Th' lady whut called also said 'twas good ya'll got ta him 'n' brought him ta town. If'n he were out en th' weather fer th' night, things cud a been a fair bit worse." Sally paused for a breath. She wasn't prone to long, one-sided conversations. "Well, here ah been, jest a jawin' away. D' ya know whut ya wantin' er should ah give ya a mite more time?"

Gary had decided on breakfast while Sally was giving her speech. "I'll have blueberry pancakes, a couple of eggs over easy, ham and home fries. Oh, also, add a couple of those fantastic biscuits."

Anne hadn't made her decision when Gary ordered but liked what she heard. "I'll have the same, Sally, only no eggs. I would also like a glass of orange juice and, when you have a moment, some more coffee, please."

Sally was off in an instant, headed for the grill man to get their order in. The two of them sat in silence for a few minutes, both lost in thought. Gary broke the silence, and when he spoke, Anne gave a slight jump, as if startled. He made a mental note of that and started. "We may have a new problem with the sheriff in the hospital. We can't get into his office. At least I don't think so, and as far as we know, he doesn't have a deputy or someone to fill in. On top of that, the people that he lined up to inform him of any new Hispanics in town may stop looking with Gabe out of the picture, and even if they don't, they may not tell us. In short, the way I see it, we've lost what little control we had of the situation."

Usually quick to respond, Anne was silent for a moment. She had been looking at the man across the table from her as if he were a stranger, not someone she had worked with for two years. She was about to give him her response, or at least her assessment of the situation when Sally arrived with their breakfast. She held off.

"Here ya go. Ah'll be raht back wi' th' coffee. Ya'll enjoy." It took less than a minute for her to return and fill their cups. "Lemme know if'n ya need sumpin' else. She turned to leave.

Gary seized the opportunity. "Sally, one quick question." She stopped and turned back. "Who takes over when the sheriff is out?"

This was a question that was unexpected and totally out of Sally's realm of expertise. Her surprise was evident because she froze, and her expression went blank. After a full minute, she answered very slowly. "Well…ah reckin ah don' know. Fact is 'tain't never happened afore. Best ya ask Clyde Answel over ta th' bank. He's th' bank manager 'n' also th' mayor. Reckin he'll have ya a answer." She turned partially to look at the front window. "'Peers th' weather'll turn better after noon."

"Thank you, Sally, and thank everyone for our breakfast. It's definitely appreciated." Gary had noticed that while they were talking, locals coming in would give a nod of recognition, a wave, or a smile in their direction. This had not happened at any time prior. He started to nod back or give a slight wave. "Anne, I think we've become heroes of sorts. This may work in our favor, under the current situation."

Finally, as they finished their breakfast, she came to life. "I don't know about heroes, but at least we've developed a degree of acceptance. As to the situation, I think you're pretty much right. Perhaps the mayor, that Mr. Answel at the bank, will have the answer that we need, and things will smooth over. If not—we're hunting for one to four men in an arena that we don't know, and only a picture ID and name for one of them. Not exactly a simple scenario. You ready?"

They stood, Gary left a five on the table, and after putting on their rain-wear, they waved goodbye to Sally and departed for the bank.

CHAPTER 39

Reality

There was something to be said for small rural towns—nothing required a great deal of travel. The local bank was a diagonal walk to the west and across the street. The walk took Anne and Gary about three minutes, which included rushing for the weather. It was so close that it didn't pay to use the car. The sign at the door listed the hours as eight to eleven a.m., Tuesday through Saturday.

Once inside, Gary noted. "Last time I saw a bank like this I was watching old western movies."

The bank's interior walls were completely oak paneled. There were two teller's windows that had marble pass-through surfaces and round iron bars, spaced for both protection and visibility. One window had a curtain drawn across it. The bars had, at one time, led to those positions being referred to as teller's cages. Two small oak desks were positioned behind an oak panelled "knee-wall" and behind them what appeared to be an office, with a translucent glass insert in the upper half of the door. The glass transom above the door frame was partially opened. The floor finish was a milky-white tile, age worn in the higher traffic locations. The ceiling had a covering of hammered tin, with four inactive ceiling fans. All in all, this bank had never gotten out of the late nineteenth century

Anne walked up to the one teller's window that appeared to be active and when a woman walked over, asked to see Mr. Answel.

Without questioning the reason for Anne's request, the teller responded by turning to an old brown metal intercom and pushed a button. "Mr. Answel, there be a couple a folk here ta see ya."

Anne couldn't hear the response, but the woman told her. "Mr. Answel'll be jest a minute." The woman then returned to whatever she had been doing prior to Anne's question.

Clyde Answel opened the door of his office and took two steps out. A quick look around enabled him to easily spot the only couple that could be waiting to see him. The manner of their dress told him that they definitely weren't locals. "Good morning, folks. Come on into my office, and let's hear what you have in mind." He smiled broadly and offered a beckoning motion with his left arm.

Gary pushed open the small hinged gate in the knee-wall, and they walked to where Clyde was holding the door open, for them. Once inside, Clyde closed the office door and motioned to a couple of chairs. "Have a seat. Sorry, I'm forgetting my manners, not used to meeting with out-of-town folks." He stepped toward them, extending his right arm. "I'm Clyde Answel, bank president and town mayor. And you are?"

Gary and Anne introduced themselves and shook hands, although gingerly, with Clyde then took a seat.

"Before we get started, I'd like to personally thank you both, for your part in helping Amos get Gabe back to town. It sure helped and probably may have saved Gabe's life." Clyde re-opened his original question. "Now, how may I help you?"

Gary knew, at this point, that they couldn't maintain the façade of an ordinary couple. "We're agents of the INS, that's the Immigration and—"

Clyde stopped him. "I'm aware of the INS and what it is. Also, Gabe told me about your presence. Go on."

Gary continued. "We were working with Gabe to try and round up an illegal that we believe is headed for this town. Very recently we learned that there may be more than one of them. With the sheriff in the hospital, who handles law enforcement?"

There was a pause in the conversation before Clyde responded. "Other than an occasional fist fight or domestic dispute, we're blessed with no real criminal problems. The one time I can remember that the previous sheriff was out and we needed a hand, we called over to Sheridan, and they sent a deputy. Should I do that?"

Anne stepped in. "We don't think there is a need for that, just yet. Can we let you know if that changes?" Without waiting for an answer, she continued. "Do you have a key to the sheriff's office? He has a fax machine, and we may have to transmit or receive some updated information."

"Why yes, I do have a key, but we also have a fax machine here at the bank. You're welcome to use it at any time—during banking hours, of course.

Gary answered for both of them. "That's greatly appreciated, but if we need to send or receive and it's after or before hours, that may present a situational difficulty."

Again there was a pause while Clyde ruminated over the facts. "I suppose that I can let you borrow a key. These are the conditions, and you must adhere to them. No one but the two of you may use the key or the office, and nothing is to be removed, or otherwise disturbed. Also, the door is to be locked upon both entry and leaving. Agreed?"

"Of course, and if the need for the office ends, we'll personally return the key, to you. By the way, if you don't mind me asking. You're not from around here, are you?"

Clyde smiled softly. "I guess that was fairly evident. No, big city born, big school educated, big job and big salary, but I couldn't take the daily stress of it all. When I heard about this bank opening, I jumped at it. Four years later, they elected me mayor. I've been here going on eleven years and don't regret a single day of it."

Anne brought the feminine aspect to the conversation. "Does your wife mind living in such a small town?"

The slightly pained look on Clyde's face almost had her wishing she hadn't asked. However, he answered openly. "That's one of the reasons—maybe the biggest, why I took this job. She died of cancer, nearly twelve years ago. Got to a point that I couldn't stand to be around all of the memories, so

I guess that was the catalyst. She was a truly wonderful woman." He quickly changed the obviously still painful subject. "I believe that I have the key right here." He pulled open one of his desk's drawers and came up with a key. Gary started to reach for it, but Clyde turned toward Anne and offered it to her. "Women tend to hold on to things far better than men. If there's nothing else, and you don't mind, I have a few small items to take care of."

There's no mistaking when a meeting has been ended. Gary and Anne rose, gently shook hands with Clyde and thanked him for his assistance. As they were leaving, Clyde called after them. "Be sure and stop by if there's anything else I can help with."

When the door closed behind them, they stood on the sidewalk, silently facing each other. Both started to speak at the same time. Gary deferred to Anne and let her go on. "This is developing some troublesome twists. I think we had better get in touch with the commander and see if there's a need to change the game plan."

Gary didn't hesitate for a second. He pulled out his cell phone and dialed. As soon as he received the recorded prompt, he began entering the recognition sequence.

CHAPTER 40

Conditions

Commander Ertugal terminated a call with an agent in Iraq and had barely enough time to take a sip of the strong Turkish coffee he so loved when his phone rang again. *I wonder if I'll ever be able to finish a cup of coffee without the damn phone ringing?* He looked at the LED display to determine the caller. "Gary, have you nailed that pain-in-the-ass?" The silence after his question told him that this call was more than a "mission accomplished" check-in.

Gary started off slowly, choosing his words carefully. "There has been a sudden and unforeseen change in the procedural formula. The sheriff—"

Ertugal didn't have time for textbook oriented explanations. "Cut the academy fancy jargon and get to the point. I haven't got time to wade through a load of bull shit."

"Yes, sir. Sheriff Tanner was in a storm-related accident, last night that has him in the hospital for at least the next week. That shut down our main line of communication with the locals. As you know, these mountain folk don't open up easily to outsiders. That being the case and since all we have is one picture, this guy could be in town for a week and we'd never know it. Bottom line is this. We need a more verifiable means of identifying the target. Is the team that wrapped him up last time available for an assist? I'd hate to let him slip through, commander."

"You're damn right. There's more riding on this than just

an illegal. He could open up a nasty can of worms for the agency. I'll get back to you. Stay put." The phone in Gary's hand went dead.

Commander Ertugal placed the phone back in its cradle, pushed back his chair and walked to the window. He stood in an "at ease" position, hands clasped behind his back. He was accustomed to sudden "wrinkles" in plans. He just didn't like them, and this one had to be ironed out carefully. *This kid probably doesn't know it, but if the right interrogator got a hold on him, he's got more than enough information in his head to start a possible senate investigation. We'd more than likely come out of it unscathed. We just don't need that shit at a time like this.* He started back for his desk. He knew who he had to call. There were no other viable options. Hopefully, he would get a positive response, and they'd finally be able to put this mess to bed. He picked up the phone, pausing for a moment, *No point hesitating. That won't change a thing. The only thing procrastination does is put off the inevitable.* He pressed redial for a number from the list of recent calls.

⁊⁊⁊

The storm that had been moving northward across the Cape Fear area was heavy enough for them to miss a day of fishing. Jon had used the down time to go to a cold weapons resource that the commander used, where he purchased three new Glock nine-millimeter, semi-automatic pistols. Along with the pistols, he had purchased nine additional magazines and five fifty-round boxes of nine-millimeter, hollow-point bullets. Both Sheri and Rosita had been told that they were going to use this down-time to rearrange some items on board the *Adventure II*, to suit their methods of fishing procedure. He then picked up Carlos, and they drove to the *Adventure II*. Once on board, they went to the main cabin, put the pistols on the table, and proceeded to load all twelve magazines. That job completed, their training and experience dictated their next moves. They took each of the pistols, inserted a magazine, and pulled the slide, chambering a round. They then ejected the mags, and inserted an additional round. That had each pistol ready for use with sixteen rounds in each, and three fifteen round back-up mags. Each of the pistols along, with three mags each was hidden, a pistol and three mags, in each of the three concealed compartments that August had constructed.

Jon thought for a moment and decided that now was the perfect time to tell Carlos about a surprise that he had kept under wraps. "*Amigo,* come over here and have a seat." Jon indicated the table they had gotten up from just a few minutes ago.

"Sure, Jon. What's up?"

Jon looked straight at his closest friend and began to explain. "I'm concerned about the world we live in. It has gotten too small." The quizzical look on Carlos's face was followed by the interjection of a statement of agreement. "Let me finish before you start asking a thousand questions." A nod of agreement from Carlos and Jon went on. "I've had two close calls in the past couple of months and you, possibly, have had the same. We don't know what ghosts from our past may still be lurking out there and next time, if there is a next time, one of us may not be so lucky. This has been on my mind ever since my final encounter with El Tigre. If I am the one that gets taken out, I want you and Rosita to be able to go on comfortably. That said, do you remember the accountant that I told you about, Arthur Silverstein?"

Jon didn't wait for a response. "He got out of the corporate world, formed a partnership with an estate attorney, and opened an office in Wilmington, on Princess Street. I asked him if they could set up a form of dual ownership agreement. They could and did, back-dating it to when I was recuperating." Jon knew his friend too well and knew that he had better get to the point. "Carlos, you and I now own the *Adventure II* equally, and if either of us is taken out of the picture, the other has full and unencumbered ownership of her. We just have to meet with Arthur and put our signatures on the document." Jon paused to let Carlos absorb what he had just divulged.

Carlos said nothing for almost three minutes. He started to talk with tears glistening in his eyes. "Jon, *Madre de Dios!* Are you crazy? That's a hell of an expensive boat and gift. I mean thank you, from the bottom of my heart, but are you sure?"

Jon stood and motioned for Carlos to do the same. He then gave his partner a long and firm hug. "I've never in my life been, more sure of anyone than you, and never been more sure of what I'm doing. Now, what say we take a ride into town and get those papers signed?"

All that Carlos could do was grin, in response.

They were driving to Arthur Silverstein's office when Jon's phone rang. Without glancing at the readout, he answered. "Jon Morton speaking." A short pause, as he listened. "How are you, Commander, and why the call?" Jon's gut was screaming. *Something has to have gone terribly wrong in West Virginia.*

Ertugal was not given to beating around the bush, but he entered this conversation with a certain degree of diplomacy. "It appears that the team I sent to West Virginia has encountered an unforeseen problem. The sheriff, upon whom they were depending, met with a freak accident and is in a hospital recovering. That leaves the two of them with no dependable assistance and just a picture. Your boy Pablo could be in town, and they might never know it." Jon started to interject, but was cut off. "Before you say anything, let me give you the whole picture. If we get lucky and the kid gets taken out, then all we have to do is lose an unregistered alien's body—simple. If he gets taken by law enforcement and the wrong person or persons start to ask questions, it could open the agency and the mission that you were on, at the time, to senate scrutiny and possibly a hearing. Although I am reasonably sure we'd come away unscathed, the publicity, especially if the press got wind of it, wouldn't do any of us one bit of good. It would also hinder ongoing and future operations. Here's what I'm getting at. You and Carlos have firsthand knowledge of the target zone as well as the target, and Carlos speaks the lingo. I need the two of you to take a few days, go up there and corral this kid. We'd have him on the next one-way flight." There was no mistaking the fact that a one-way flight would be the disposition of Pablo's body in a deep ocean sector. "Jon everyone in the agency and anyone that was affiliated with the Colombia mission needs to have this kid out of the picture. What do you say?"

This request required some thought, and Jon was not about to jump right in, even though on the surface, he knew that the commander was correct. "Let me call you back in ten minutes." He could sense the intensity of his friends stare.

"Jon, what the hell was that about? I've never seen you have such a one-sided conversation with the commander and from the look on your face, it wasn't good."

As soon as a safe place was spotted, Jon pulled the car off the road. He then relayed everything that the commander had told him and, when finished, simply added, "What do you think?" He then sat back, organizing his own thoughts and waiting for Carlos to respond.

"Jon, I hate to say this, but the commander's probably right. That kid believes that there is a cache of money, some-where in Dodsonville, that he has full rights to. Sooner or later his drive to find that money will erupt into one of two things, either his death or a run-in with the law that will produce noth-ing but big trouble. We've been there and are probably reason-ably sure of where his search will take place. Our big problem is what to tell the girls."

Jon knew, in his heart, that everythin Carlos said was true. He had an idea of how to present it, so he offered his thoughts to get Carlos's opinion. "What if we tell them a part of the truth? That the sheriff who was on the lookout for the kid got injured and is in the hospital, that no one else knows what he looks like, and that an INS agent will be there to take him into custody. Now I'm sure one or both of them will want to know what makes one illegal so important. We'll tell them he's sus-pected of trying to organize a human trafficking ring between the US and South America. Also, that our government is offer-ing to pay our expenses and lost wages, with a modest bonus, to help them on this one. How does that sound?"

Carlos ruminated on Jon's proposal for a couple of minutes then answered. "Sounds okay, but if I know Rosita, she'll ask how we know this kid."

"If either of them asks, we'll say that we saw him a couple of times when we were after that turned agent, and when the local sheriff asked us for an assist in questioning him, we agreed. Next thing we heard was that the kid skipped town before Sheriff Tanner could collar him. Now, the commander called to say that, 'word is he's headed back.'"

"Sounds good to me." Carlos was satisfied with the story. "I don't think Rosita will have a problem with it."

Jon started to dial the commander. As he went through the recognition code, an idea formulated. *Let's see if we can make this one really pay.*

One ring was all it took for Ertugal to answer. "Tell me your answer is yes, and we have a go."

Jon put his plan into action. "We'd like to help on this one, but there's a problem or two that we can't get over. The first is our business—the loss of income as well as having to pay our boat crew. The second, and what may be more of a factor than the first, is Carlos's wife, Rosita, and the woman I'm dating, Sheri. We need to put their probable questions and fears to rest. The bottom line is this. We're no longer with the agency, although sometimes I have to wonder. Also, a move such as this represents a much bigger financial loss than we can handle, especially after just going through two similar situations." *This should be interesting.*

For the first time that Jon could remember, the commander did not have an immediate response. After a space of more than one minute, the answer came. "Jon, you're right, and I understand your hesitation. This one does not actually have a direct effect on you and, even if there were to be an investigation, more than likely, it would not even involve you. However, I'm asking this as a favor. I need your help on this one to make it disappear, quietly. That being said, here's what I can do. Upon completion, fifteen-thousand in cash. That should substantially cover everything you touched on. Do I have a yes?"

Jon knew that the commander's word was good and that the money would come out of one of the "blind" slush funds that were used for bribes and payoffs. "We'll do it. We should be able to hit the road in under thirty-six hours. Will that work?"

"It'll have to. Let me know when you're in the game field."

"Before you hang up, Commander. When this is put to bed, you can hand the cash to either Carlos or me. He'll be aware of everything." The phone went dead. Jon turned to Carlos and briefly filled him in on both the conversation and agreement.

With a big smile, Carlos had to ask. "What made you ask for the cash?"

"Simple, the conversation you and I just had and the fact that, no matter what happened, if we didn't get involved, it probably would have little or no effect on us. The commander knows that and needs us. I figured I'd go for it and was fairly sure we'd get a positive response. Now let's go see Arthur and his partner and get those papers signed."

CHAPTER 41

Storm Clouds

Pepe had been designated to drive the Olds. He was extremely nervous about doing anything that might cross Cholo's inflammatory nature, and so was obeying every rule of driving. They had stopped in Pine Ridge, North Carolina, just south of the Virginia border. The intent was to move quickly out of this town. The gas tank was filled, and they purchased take-out meals from a fast-food hamburger stand. Pepe was put in the driver's seat with written travel directions, and Cholo's strong admonition. "No fuckin' speeding and if you aren't sure, wake us. You created enough shit with that license plate screw-up."

Pepe was not a brave or strong person, and was without question, deathly afraid of this man. The more time he spent in his company the more he was convinced that the man was a maniac. "Don't worry—don't worry. I understand, completely." His straightforward answer appeared to mollify Cholo because nothing else was said. Inwardly, Pepe breathed a sigh of relief. *If I had a gun, I know I would kill him and feel a great relief. Now all I have to do is take eighty-one west then pick up seventy-seven north, again. I should have kept that lady's gun. Jorge will know where I can get a gun.*

༄༅

Pablo had decided to have breakfast with Salvador and

Guillermo then start for Dodsonville. He had lain awake in his sleeping bag since four a.m. worrying over the multiple problems previously not considered, but now a looming reality. Perhaps his two present benefactors would be able to offer some answers, but could he trust them? *I need to hide the truth, while presenting my dilemma.* He climbed out of the sleeping bag, rolled it up and secured the tie strings.

"*Buenos dias,* Pablo." The sudden voice startled him as it was completely unexpected at this early hour.

Pablo turned to face his greeter. "*Buenos dias,* Salvador. My movement did not wake you, did it?" He was doing his best to sound relaxed. *Now will be the best time to ask.* "I have a small problem that I would like to ask your help with. Perhaps over breakfast would be good?"

"Of course, if we can be of some help to a friend of El Tigre, it will be our pleasure. Just ask, and we will do our best."

Pablo was thrilled at the response. He had quickly become aware that playing on his association with El Tigre had opened an important door. *Now all I have to do is be careful in what I ask and what I tell them. "Muchas Gracias."*

Breakfast was simple, refried beans, slab bacon, fire-toasted bread and strong, chicory-laced coffee, inexpensive but ample and satisfying. Guillermo turned to Pablo as they ate. "So, Pablo, what is this problem that we can hopefully, help you with?"

The cards had been dealt. Pablo now had to play his hand or formulate an excuse and back down. *I've come too far and suffered too much to quit now.* "In case I did not mention it, I did not come to this country in the normal way."

"You're illegal. We know that."

"Yes, that is so, but now I need to find a way back home that will not get me arrested. Before I go, I am going to try and locate a man who owes my father a lot of money. My father told me that whatever it is this man does, it is only for cash and, therefore, I will receive cash. This money I must take home with me. So my problem is a double one. First, transportation home since I have no papers, and second how to carry my father's money without it being seen or seized by the police. Can you advise me?"

After almost five minutes, Guilermo responded. A major flaw in Pablo's query was not missed. "How do you intend to find a man you do not know and do not know where you are or where he lives? That would be like looking for an acorn in a desert."

Pablo had realized his error as soon as the words left his mouth, so he was ready. "When I know my location, I am to place a call to *La Taverna*, in Cali. The owner will get in touch with my father and call me back the next day with directions and instructions. Hopefully, I am not a great distance away."

His explanation, although flimsy, appeared to satisfy both men. "*Bueno*. Your job is not an easy one, but we will try to give you the best information and help that we can." Salvador continued, "First transportation. We know of two ships, freighters, that have regular routes between three US ports on the east coast—Richmond, Wilmington, and Miami. They depart from and return to Cartagena in northern Colombia. The first is *La Luna Media* and the second is *El Pato Gordo*. I will write down the captain's names and a cell phone for each. Either one will, for cash, transport you home, no questions. As to the money—if it can be carried in your pockets or in a jacket—" Salvador shrugged. "—no problem. If it requires more space, you must figure how much room it will take." He saw the blank expression on Pablo's face. "It is really fairly simple. US currency is all standard in size. A bill is measured in inches, which is what you will need to use in this country, six and one-eighth inches long, two and five-eighths inches wide and a stack of two-hundred bills, tightly bound and at the wrapper, is one-half inch thick. With this information, you can figure what size package or container you will need. *Entiendes?*"

Pablo sat quietly for a minute before responding. "Yes, I understand. That will make it easy for me, no matter what I have to deal with. *Muchas gracias por todo*. You have helped me, more than I could have expected." *That only helps a little since I don't know how many bills there will be, and even if I will have the time to count them.*

It was at that moment that Guillermo's cell phone rang. He glanced at the number of the caller, on the read-out, before answering. "*Hola.* You are on schedule?"

The response was crude but direct. "On schedule, and if these two assholes I'm traveling with don't fuck up, I'll meet you in Sheridan at nine a.m. You name the place, and I'll find it."

Guillermo glanced at his partner. "He's on schedule for Sheridan, nine a.m., tomorrow. Where should I set the meet?"

"My research indicated that the Red Apple Rest is a motel on the main road, west side of town. There's a large parking lot in the rear."

Guillermo spoke into his phone. "The west side of town, on the main road, there's a motel called the Red Apple Rest. The parking lot in the rear.

"Got it!" The phone went dead.

Salvador turned his attention back to Pablo. "Our client is going to be on time for our meeting, tomorrow. Therefore, it is time for us to part ways. Remember one thing. We don't exist and, if questioned, will deny ever seeing or knowing you—no matter what. You must leave now, and be especially careful as you know very little English. Good luck on your search and on getting home. Now gather your belongings and go."

Pablo collected his sleeping bag. "*Muchas gracias, señores.* You both have been more than kind and very helpful. *Vaya con Dios.*"

With his parting comment, Pablo turned away and started walking briskly back up the path to the main road. *One thing is for sure. I won't be calling Capitán Muñoz on La Luna Media.*

CHAPTER 42

Paperwork

Arthur Silverstein's new office was decorated in a warm and inviting manner. It was located in what had, at one time, been a private home. The entire neighborhood had been residential prior to having being re-zoned for business use. An attractive oriental woman, who appeared to be in her forties, looked up when Jon and Carlos walked in.

"Good morning gentlemen. May I help you?"

"Yes, thank you. My name is Jon Morton and—" He motioned toward Carlos. "—this is Carlos Montoto. We have an appointment with Mr. Silverstein."

"Just one moment, please." She pressed an intercom button on her phone. "Mr. Silverstein, Mr. Morton and Mr. Montoto are here to see you." There was a moment of quiet as she listened to the response then stood. "Follow me, please." She led the way down a hallway to a door at the rear of the building. The receptionist then knocked softly on the door.

"Come in." With that comment, the woman opened the door, and Jon and Carlos walked in. The receptionist closed the door softly, behind them.

"Jon, how are you? It's been a while since our first meeting in the barber shop. Don't think I'll ever forget it. Would you believe that I've actually returned for another haircut?"

"Proves you've got a thick skin and can laugh at yourself. That's good." Jon paused. "Arthur, meet Carlos Montoto, my business partner and best friend."

Carlos walked over to shake the accountant's hand. "It's a pleasure to meet you, Mr. Silverstein."

"Call me Arthur. I think of Jon and now you more like friends than clients. Let's get right to it. I have an appointment in," he checked his watch, "forty-five minutes." He opened the folder on his desk. "This is basically a simple form, setting forth the property in question including all legal definitions of that property. The balance of the form sets forth a statement of mutual ownership, with no encumbrances and a right of sole-survivorship agreement that automatically converts full ownership to the surviving party. Other than the legal jargon, it's just as we discussed, as well as the back-dating. Should I give you both a moment to look it over or do you want to take it with you and take your time reviewing it?"

Jon took the document and after a brief perusal offered it to Carlos. "Looks good to me. What do you think, Carlos?"

"I still think this is crazy, Jon. But, if this is what you want, then this is what we'll do. I'm thrilled and certainly don't need to read it."

Arthur pressed his intercom. "Doris, will you please come to my office and bring your stamp." He addressed Jon and Carlos. "Doris is a notary, as well as our office manager. I have prepared three copies of the paperwork. One for each of you and one I'll keep on file or give the copy to your attorney—whichever you prefer. Since my partner prepared the paperwork, I'll sign as a witness and Doris will notarize our signatures."

"Why don't you keep the third copy on file here, if that's not an imposition?"

"Don't mind at all. It's definitely not an imposition. We do it as a matter of course."

There was a knock on the door and Doris entered. Within five minutes all three sets were signed and notarized.

"That's it, Carlos." Jon handed one copy of the completed documents to Carlos then reached into his pocket. He handed Carlos a full set of keys to the *Adventure II.* "You'll need these, too."

Carlos said nothing for several moments. He was working hard at holding back his tears.

Arthur interrupted the awkward moment. "Jon, here's the other document in triplicate, you asked that we prepare."

"I almost forgot about that. Let's have it." Jon took the papers. *Looks fine to me*. Okay, let's finalize this one." He leaned over and signed in the designated places.

Arthur then witnessed them. "Doris, please notarize these." As soon as the papers were notarized, Arthur handed them to Jon.

"Carlos, here's your copy. Arthur, could you keep the third copy with the other?"

"Of course I can, Jon."

Carlos looked at the new set of papers he was handed. He was somewhat perplexed. "What is this, Jon?"

"This is a power of attorney. If I was to get hurt and couldn't manage my own affairs, this gives you the right to take over."

There was a moment of silence before Carlos responded. "Jon, this is a very big responsibility. Are you sure about this?"

"Completely, I couldn't be more completely sure of anyone else on this earth." Jon turned to Arthur. "Do you have an invoice for me? If so, I'll pay you right now.

"As a matter of fact, I do. This was a simple exercise for us, so I worked it as tightly as I could. Three hundred seventy-five dollars even. Here's your copy."

"Ordinarily, I'd pay you in cash, but for these items, we need to maintain records. I noticed that you took care of the back-dating, even on the invoice. Thanks." Jon quickly wrote the check, back-dating it to coincide with the paperwork. "Thanks for everything, Arthur, and please thank your partner. I'll see if I can direct some business your way. Please thank Doris for her assistance."

They shook hands all around. Jon and Carlos left the office and started for home.

⌒⌒

"Now to see if the girls will buy into our deception about this mess with that kid, Pablo." Carlos didn't respond. "We'll call the commander and get him to reissue the same cover IDs that we used last time."

"Good idea, Jon. At least we'll be consistent, if the need arises. I think we'll need to be careful if that sheriff is around. He's a lot smarter than he lets on."

"I'm glad you picked up on that, too."

Twenty minutes of relaxed driving and they were pulling into the driveway at Carlos's home.

"Carlos, I think it will be easier if you start the conversation. Not that it matters to me, but I have a suspicion that Rosita is starting to have her doubts about my intentions—at least when the subject of our past comes up."

"You may be right. That woman has the nose of a bloodhound and a mind that works like a computer."

CHAPTER 43

Concerns

Pablo retrieved his bicycle from its hiding place in the bushes. He then stopped to consider what his next move should be. *Is it safe for me to go back into that town? The only place to eat there knows me, and the men that put me back on La Luna Media must be working for the American Government. Why else would they take my picture and have a helicopter ready to take me, and that pero I shot, away from there? Perhaps I should return to the town where the bus let me out. I saw places to buy food, and now that I have a bike, I can buy enough food for one or two days then stay in the woods near that shed while I search for my money. Yes, that would be safest.*

☙

Cholo, too, had many venues to consider. *First thing in the morning I will meet with the men from PMP and pick up the guns I ordered. Then I have the job of locating the money, without raising the suspicions of the locals. From there, work out transportation and then kill these two ignorant sons-of-bitches.*

CHAPTER 44

Vanished

Son-of-a-bitch! They've disappeared, again." The FBI agent was more than frustrated. The last three hits on the credit card were in Rowland, North Carolina, just south of the Virginia border. The only positive information his team got from the motel was that there were three men, all Hispanic looking although the one who paid for the rooms had an Italian name. The information from the hardware store was minimal, the purchase of a disposable cell phone by a Mr. Graziano.

The waitress advised that she had given the three men directions to the Charlotte-Douglas International Airport. "They left quite a while ago…probably four or five hours. They were in early, for breakfast then drove off in an older Buick."

"Damn it!" He pulled out his phone and punched a "favorite." The moment his call was answered, he started. No formalities. "They're headed for the Charlotte Airport—probably there by now. There's three of 'em. Get some men over there and question all the ticket agents, as well as the car rental agencies. They're still in the Buick they stole. Waitress here seems reasonably sharp. Get a sketch artist over here pronto. Maybe we can get some decent likenesses on the wires."

One of these guys must be pretty smart. He's managed to keep them one jump ahead of us. Based on that and if I were in their position, I'd be ready to change cars again.

He informed the waitress about the sketch artist and then turned to the other three men on his team. "Let's get to the airport. I'm damn sure that our next lead will be located in the airport's parking lots."

CHAPTER 45

Playing Aces

Inspector Cantrell had been carefully building a net, one that, like a funnel, had a wide mouth at one end, and narrowed down to a small opening. This set-up would, when executed, force Cholo right into his hands. At the same time, he and his elite police were methodically removing the last remnants of Cholo's gang from the streets.

Alejandro sat pensively at his desk. He was mentally reviewing his plan and the trap he had carefully set. *Two more phone calls to make then it's up to the FBI in Los Estados Unidos.* He called his closest assistant. "Alonzo, cover my phone for the next hour. I need to go over to the US Embassy."

"Should I alert a team?"

"That won't be necessary. I'll take Corporal Lopez and use a regular patrol car. That will draw less attention. We've cleaned enough scum from the streets that this should be ample. I need to have a short talk with the FBI liaison, then I'll return." The two phone calls he had to make required the utmost privacy. Cantrell couldn't chance any possibility of either call being overheard.

Alonzo had been informed of the fact that Inspector Cantrell had advised the US FBI to be on the alert for Cholo. The visit to the embassy would not arouse any suspicion or questions. Nor would making this short trip, as opposed to a phone call. Phones, no matter whose, were not always private in Colombia.

The guard at the gate checked the IDs of both men although both were known on sight. Once inside, Cantrell offered a suggestion to his Corporal. "Why don't you relax in their commissary and have a snack or some coffee? We have no worries in here."

Lopez happily accepted the offer and walked toward the steps leading to the basement and the commissary. Alejandro walked down the hall straight for the door with a simple sign, *US OFFICE OF THE FBI.*

He knocked on the door and in a moment received a response. "Come in."

Alejandro opened the door and received a friendly greeting.

"Inspector Cantrell, how are you, and to what do I owe the honor of this visit?"

"I'm quite well, Sharon, and I hope you are the same. I was driving by and just wanted to check and be sure that you've got your net out in the States for that killer, Cholo."

"I'm doing fine, and, yes, we have all fifty states as well as Canada on alert."

"Great, thank you. By the way, do you happen to have a small office or conference room available for a little while? I have to make two important calls regarding an investigation and, although we have our headquarters electronically swept, once a month, you just never know."

"I understand completely. Follow me. There's a vacant office just down the hall, but it is furnished. The phone in that office is 'cold,' so you are welcome to use it with no concerns."

Inspector Cantrell settled down at the desk. The two calls were to the captains of two ocean freighters. Both of these captains were known for transporting people for under-the-table cash, as well as occasional smuggling. The first would be to Capitán Muñoz on *La Luna Media.* Cantrell was tempted to use the 'cold' phone. *Still too much of a chance.* Instead, he took out his cell phone, dialed, and waited. After three rings, his call was answered. *"Hola, Capitán Muñoz. Inspector Alejandro Cantrell aquí.* How are you today?"

Muñoz knew Cantrell well and also knew that if he was

calling, it wasn't to socialize. *"Buenos dias, Señor Inspector."* He said nothing else and waited nervously. *Whatever it is, he won't waste words.*

Cantrell was true to form and came right to the point. "I need a favor from you. You have heard, I'm sure, of the gangster Cholo. We have been ridding Colombia of his gang and have it on good information that he has fled to the United States." Muñoz started to protest that he had nothing to do with this, but Alejandro cut him short. "I have no concern about that, but I do have a concern that he will, without any doubt, return to Colombia. The safest method for him to do so would be aboard one of two ships. Yours is one of them. If yours is the one he chooses, you are to call me, once you are at sea, at this number, and give me your exact sailing schedule. For this favor, your past...let us say less-than-legal...history will disappear from our records. Should you not call, I have enough confirmed data to arrest you, have your captain's license revoked, and make you a guest of our government for at least twenty years," Alejandro continued with assured confidence. *I know I've got this Capitán Muñoz by los cojones.* He smiled as he asked his final question. "So, do we have an agreement?"

"Por seguro, Señor Inspector."

Inspector Cantrell's next call to the captain of *El Pato Gordo* was a carbon copy of the one just completed—same message, same thinly veiled threat. *That should be the last hole in my net, and now it's been shut. Just need to collect Lopez, return to headquarters, and wait.* Cantrell pushed away from the desk and stood with a satisfied smile on his face. *Think I'll join Lopez for a cup of coffee before we go.*

CHAPTER 46

Echoes

Dos hombres locos! That's what you are—after all those years of life-threatening danger. Now, finally you can live easily, and yet you choose to go back."

Rosita was not happy, and from the scowl on Sheri's face, she was in complete agreement.

"You will risk your lives for something you don't have to, for the sake of a few dollars," Rosita continued.

Carlos tried to stay calm and get his wife to calm down. "*Querida*, we are not risking our lives. We are just going to point out this trafficker to the authorities. That's all. At most, we will be away for three or four days, and, for this, we are getting paid handsomely. That's all this is." *I sure hope that's all it is.*

Jon saw both women start to soften and felt he should step in. "Sheri, Rosita, you both know we want nothing to do with our past military history, and the last two recent episodes should have made that, without any doubt, doubly certain. This is a chance to use that last experience to do some good, and we'll earn more than a week's fishing could produce— even with paying the Swedes." He paused to let his words sink in. "One of the lowest forms of life is a person that traffics in human lives and misery. You both know that, and we've seen it first hand. This is our opportunity to put one of those bastards out of business."

There was silence in the room. Sheri and Rosita cast occasional glances at each other with a form of communication that men didn't understand. Sheri broke the silence. "I don't like the idea, but, unfortunately, you may be right."

Rosita was right behind her. "Yes, for once, the two of you may have a good idea. Now that that's settled, why don't we put together some lunch?"

Jon saw an opportunity and jumped on it. "Instead of you and Sheri returning to the kitchen, why don't we run down to the diner? We can get some lunch to go and take it on board our new boat. That way the two of you can get to see the new *Adventure Two*.

"That sounds like a good idea." Rosita turned to Sheri. "What do you think?"

"I agree. Let's do it."

Both women had picked up on the fact that Jon had said "our," but neither was sure whether that was a figure of speech or had a more definitive meaning. Neither of them brought it up, but as women often will do, tucked it away for future reference.

෬෯෬

It wasn't quite noon and was also a weekday. Tables at this hour were readily available at Stavros's. This diner was one of the very few places that Jon and Carlos didn't concern themselves about sitting at a corner table.

Marie came bouncing over. "Hi, Jon, Carlos, Rosita, Sheri. What's it going to be, a late breakfast or an early lunch?"

Sheri, surprised that the waitress remembered her name, responded. "An early lunch, Marie. You don't happen to have fresh turkey today, do you?"

"No, but we do have roast fresh ham, either a plate or sandwich."

"That's perfect for me, Marie. Your uncle knows how I like it." Jon rose. "Just need to make a quick trip to the restroom."

Once in the men's room, Jon latched the door and started the dialing sequence for the commander. *Might as well get things rolling.*

"Jon, have you got a positive answer for me?"

"Yes, Commander. Let's use the same IDs as last time—Don McGill and Santos Morales. Deliver the packet to the dock master's shed. I'll inform Red that it's coming. Don't worry about security. Red's as safe as Fort Knox. He'll contact me when it arrives. Include any late pictures and all current data."

"Got it, Jon." With that, the phone went dead.

Wonder if that man will ever be able to carry on a relaxed phone conversation? Suddenly, with a mental jolt, Jon came back to the reality of the moment. *Oh shit! I forgot and evidently so did everyone else. We were going to take our food to the boat. I'd better catch Marie.* He left the men's room and caught up with Marie as she was going between tables. "Marie, I totally forgot that we had planned to eat aboard my boat. Could you please set up our order to go?"

"No problem, Jon. I'll just grab the drinks from the table, and as soon as Uncle Stavros has your order together, I'll put it all in a box to go. Oh, does anyone want any desert?"

"Don't know but I'll find out." He turned back toward the table. As soon as he arrived, he broached the subject. "We all forgot that we were going to eat on board our boat. Marie's getting everything wrapped to go. Do any of you want a dessert?"

As if on cue, Marie walked over. "For desert today we have, apple pie, peach cobbler, chocolate cake and coconut cream pie." She stopped talking and waited. Both ladies ordered peach cobbler, with Jon and Carlos each opting for Stavros's sinful chocolate cake. "I'll get it all together." With that comment, she was off.

Sheri collected another mental note. *That's the second time Jon said 'our boat.'* They collected their to-go order, Jon paid the bill, and they were off to the docks.

✁✁✁

"Wow!" Rosita couldn't help her reaction. "This one's longer and wider than the other one."

Carlos was grinning like a kid at Christmas. "Wait until you see the interior." There was a note of pride in his voice, and Rosita caught it instantly.

"All right, you two. What's going on now?"

Before Carlos could respond Jon, out of a habitual need for confirmation, looked left toward slip fourteen to verify what he was sure he had noticed, as they approached. *Definitely empty.* "Sheri, what happened with your dad's boat? Did you have it moved?"

"No. The best one of the yacht brokers whose names you got from your friend, Tony, showed it to a man from Miami. He took one look, a quick sail, and wrote a check for the full amount. A transport crew moved her out early this morning and will sail her to the man's home on Biscayne Bay. It's a relief not to look at her and dredge up all those terrible memories. Now, will one of you please answer Rosita's question?"

Jon looked at his friend. "Go ahead, Carlos. She's your wife, you tell her."

His typical broad, infectious grin had taken over Carlos's face. "Come into the main cabin, and I'll explain." He pulled out his set of keys, unlocked the cabin door, and led the way in. With everyone in, Carlos began the explanation. "Jon decided that since he has no known family or relatives, and since—" He looked at Rosita. "—we're the closest thing he has to family, he made me a full half-owner of the *Adventure Two* with papers that state, if anything were to happen to him, I would be the sole owner and, if anything were to happen to me, it would revert completely to him."

He paused, waiting for some form of explosive comment from Rosita. Instead, his wife looked as if she was in shock.

Jon started to chuckle. "This has to be the first time I can remember Rosita being speechless."

It was at that moment that Jon's cell phone started to ring. One look at the readout and the caller was evident.

"Excuse me one minute. I need to take this call." With that, he left the cabin and went out on the main deck. "Yes, Commander."

Words weren't wasted. "Your package will go out by special messenger, first thing in the morning. Advise me of your departure date." The call ended.

A slight tinge of nervous tension began to well up in Jon's gut. *This should be a simple recognition exercise, but after all this time, I'm still getting those pre-engagement tensions.* He slipped his phone back into his pocket and walked back into the main cabin. By now, it was evident that Rosita had recovered from her initial shock.

"Jon, you are crazy, this is crazy, unbelievable, impossible—but fantastic. All I can say is thank you for this offer of friendship and love. From the bottoms of our hearts, *muchas, muchas gracias*."

"Not crazy, Rosita. Carlos is closer than a brother to me, and there's not a person on this earth who's more worthy of this. Now, let's eat. I'm starving." As soon as they had begun to eat Jon remembered what he had told the commander about their IDs. "Carlos, after we finish with lunch, you give the girls the tour. I have to run over to the dock master's shed and check something with Red."

"Sure, Jon, not a problem."

"Jon, whatever you need to check can wait, can't it?"

Sheri's definitely still concerned about possible dangers or unknowns. Guess I can't blame her after what she's been through. "Just want to see if there are any additional docking charges now that we've got a bigger boat. Since we're right here, it'll only take a moment, and that's one less thing for us to think about." *I hope she buys it.*

"Okay but just that. Don't start swapping war stories."

"I promise. Shouldn't take more than ten minutes. I'll be back before you know it." With that said and Sheri satisfied, Jon finished the last half of his sandwich and his piece of chocolate cake. "Okay, be back in a flash."

Red saw Jon coming and hollered out. "Mornin', Jon. How're ya doin'?"

"Great, Red." Jon didn't respond in kind, not wanting to go through Red's standard response, which by now he had memorized. "Need a favor from you. Got a package being delivered tomorrow morning to you. I knew I'd be coming down to the boat and figured that would be easiest. No signature needed, and no money due."

"Sure, Jon. Glad ta help."

"Thanks, Red. I'm running late so I can't stop to talk. Have a good day." With that, he turned and started back toward the *Adventure II.*

"Thanks, Jon. Same to ya."

CHAPTER 47

Recovery

Sheriff Gabriel Tanner was not in a particularly good mood. He had been blindsided by a storm and now was miles from where he was needed most. On top of that, he was in a hospital bed with a broken left arm and collar bone. These injuries were coupled with a headache that rivaled the worst hangover he'd ever had, thanks to a minor concussion. The assorted cuts scrapes and bruises were meaningless and, as far as he was concerned, "Jest a part a ever'day hap'nin's." The IV drip line and vitals monitors were not "everyday."

Gabe pushed the call button on the line by his bed. Within minutes, a middle-aged woman in a white uniform with a nurse's ID appeared. "Good morning, Sheriff Tanner. How can I help?"

"Ma'am, ya kin he'p by gettin' me on th' next available transport back ta mah town, Dodsonville. Ah got a heap a trouble a brewin' there, 'n' ah got ta be there afore she starts."

"Sir, I'm very sorry, but that's not possible. Maybe you'll be able to travel in three or four days, but certainly not now."

"Ah ain't got time fer meanin' less jawin'. Ah need ta speak ta th' head a this hospital, 'n' now. If'n ya don't bring him er her ta me, ah'm gittin' up 'n' go a lookin'. Do ya git whut ah'm sayin'?"

"Yes, sir. I'll see what can be done." That said, she turned and left.

Gabe had some last words before the room door closed. "Don't be takin' all day, neither."

It was almost ten minutes before there was a polite knock on his room door.

"C'mon en."

"Good morning, Sheriff Tanner. I'm Doctor Kim Woo Sun, Director. I understand you're a bit anxious to get out."

"Pleased ta meet ya, Doc. Anxious might be yer polite way a sayin' ah need ta git out 'n' now. Any question 'bout thet?"

"No questions. Would you please explain what is so urgent that you're willing to risk your health and physical well being? You know, you were in pretty bad shape when they brought you in."

"Well, ah ain't en sech bad shape now. Here be mah point. Ah'm th' only law en mah small town. 'Nother time, ah'd stay a day er two more. Times now ain't normal. They's some bad characters headed fer mah town, 'n' ah'm th' onliest one kin point them out ta th' federal agents whut come ta arrest them. They don't git took away quiet like, some good folk er like ta git hurt, er worse. Thet's all a her en a pea pod. Now, ya gonna turn me out er do ah have ta take care a her m'self?"

Doctor Sun quietly considered what Gabe had just said for a few moments before replying. "You know your condition so you must be aware that any unnecessary physical activity could delay your healing or create complications. However, I also understand the unique and unusual situation that you're in. Therefore, against my better judgment, if you will sign a 'hold-harmless' release form and promise to return for a complete check-up after your legal business is cleared up, I'll let you go. I'll also get you a ride home. Do we understand each other?"

Gabe couldn't help a faint smile. "Betcha britches, we do. Git thet paper, 'n' let's git er goin'."

Just over one hour later, Gabe was seated in a hospital van headed west. *Hope ain't nothing' happened past three days.* "Say, driver, y'all got one a them fancy pocket phones?"

"Yes, sir, I do."

"Could ya favor me wi' a call? Ah'll give ya th' number."

"Yes, sir, be happy to. What's the number?"

Gabe passed along the number for the town information center—better known as Ethyl's.

"It's ringing. What's the message?"

"Based 'pon th' time 'n' day, Sally'll be answerin'. Jest tell er thet Gabe'll be back en town afore dinner 'n' ta let those whut needs ta know thet ah'm a comin'.'"

Thirty-five miles west, the phone rang in Ethyl's and, as usual, was answered by Sally. The phone dropped back on the base in less than a minute. Sally turned as she started for the door and hollered to the grill man. "Be raht back. Got an urgent message fer Clyde Answel over ta th' bank." With that, she was gone.

೧೩೦

Anne and Gary decided to get an early lunch, beat the crowd, and be back on the streets watching for the suspects. It didn't take Anne long to figure out that something was out of place. All it took was the grill man coming out from behind the counter to take their order.

"Where's Sally?" Anne asked. "She's okay, isn't she?"

Jeffrey was not given to conversation. "Took a message ta Clyde—be back en jest a minute. Know whut ya wantin'? Specials er on th' board."

"Give us a minute to decide and, if Sally's not back, we'll bring our order to you."

"Fair 'nough." Jeffrey turned and started back to his grill.

The moment Jeffrey was out of earshot, Gary voiced his thoughts. "I wonder what was so important that Sally had to run over to the bank? I mean why wouldn't whoever it is call or go to the bank directly. I'm sure the message wasn't from Sally herself. Just seems odd?"

Anne leaned toward him and was about to whisper a response when a familiar, bubbly voice called out.

"Hey, ya'll. Shore hope ya weren't put out by th' delay ah created." By now Sally had reached their table. "Had ta carry a message ta Clyde. Gabe's a comin' home. Fum whut I figure fum his phone message, should be jest a couple hours at most afore he walks in. Don't let on."

It didn't take higher math for Gary and Anne to figure out why the sheriff was coming back so soon. They were both relieved but were also elevated to a new level of conscious nervousness. They both quickly ordered their lunch and, as soon as Sally left to place the order, Gary brought it out. "This doesn't look good. There's only one reason a man with a broken shoulder and arm, as well as recovering from a concussion and hypothermia would come back to work after just three days. He takes his job very seriously and evidently has a very strong feeling that these Hispanics are big trouble. Fact is, from all we've learned, he's dead right, and I think we may be in for a hell-of-a lot more than we bargained for."

Their conversation was interrupted by the arrival of Sally with their lunch. "If'n ya need sumpin', jest holler." Their order delivered, she was off, headed toward another table.

Anne nodded. "Guess in a way it's good that Gabe's coming back. At least we'll know that his local 'radar' system will report in."

"I hadn't thought of that, Anne, but you're right, and that may make all the difference." The cell phone in his pocket started to vibrate. Gary pulled it out and checked the readout. "It's the commander, Anne." He pressed the response point. "Yes, sir."

"I've got a secondary response team on the way. They've had first-hand contact with the primary. They've also got extreme field experience. They're coming as Don McGill and Santos Morales, and that's all you need to know. They'll find you."

The phone went dead. The commander then made one more call, and it was one that he wasn't very happy about.

CHAPTER 48

Preparations

Cholo was reading the map, searching to shorten their trip, while Jorge drove. Pepe was doing his best to remain inconspicuous, in the rear seat. Cholo was getting angrier by the minute. *There must be a faster way. Too damn many small towns on this route.* He scoured the map, but nothing presented itself. *Probably be at least three hours until we cross into West Virginia. Looks like it'll be a lot easier and faster once that happens.*

෴

Jon and Carlos were also on the road. They didn't need a map, their route was simple. They would take I-40 west to Winston-Salem, exit on Route 52 north to connect with I-77 north in southern Virginia. They would follow I-77 until it crossed into West Virginia then pick up Route 10 a winding road that would bring them to West Hamlin. From there it was due west to first Sheridan and then Dodsonville. They had said their trip was routine, just to point out the suspect for the waiting authorities. That was what they hoped for, but each of them had his pistol, a silencer, and three loaded back-up mags in addition to the ones already in their weapons. Their "ready" state was backed up with a box of fifty, hollow-point nine-millimeter bullets.

Both men were hoping to cruise through this and return

home. But years of extreme combat experience had both of them expecting as well as prepared for the worst.

☙☙

Alejandro Cantrell wasn't travelling. He was waiting. As far as he was concerned, he had all of the possible avenues of Cholo's return covered or blocked. *Now all I can pray for is that the Americans don't get him or kill him and that I get the opportunity to make him suffer beyond the range of human endurance.* He sighed, deeply. *Even if I get the chance to do this, and as good as it will feel, it will not bring the love of my life back to me.*

☙☙

Carlos and Jon were on Route 52, northbound, when Jon's cell phone rang. One glance at the readout and he answered. "Yes, Commander." He reached over and turned off the radio then whispered to Carlos. "This can't be good."

"Jon, there's an ugly new wrinkle in our plan. We have it on solid info, from the feds, that there are three Hispanics, and they appear headed to your final. Worse is that they've left a trail of bodies behind them, including a female deputy sheriff. We also don't know if our boy is with them or if this is even related to your situation. Either way, keep a strong watch. The on-site team has been advised of your pending arrival. Also, the local sheriff is in the hospital in another town. Don't know how this is going to play out but try to keep it clean and un-complicated." The call ended.

Jon sat angry and silently, slowly digesting the command-er's call. *Will this shit ever end? Will I ever get to live a peace-ful life?*

Carlos was driving and waiting. Finally, he couldn't wait any longer. "Jon, how about filling me in?"

"Sorry, Carlos. That was not a good call." He proceeded to fill Carlos in. "One of the three may be Pablo, or this may be three strangers, and, with some degree of luck, they'll have nothing to do with our boy or Dodsonville. The other problem is the worst case scenario. That would be if they are also seeking the money, independently of Pablo. That would mean that we'll have four targets instead of one. In a town as small as Dodsonville, how the hell do we keep it quiet?"

It was now Carlos's turn for silence. When he finally spoke, it was with a degree of resignation. "I guess we can only pray for the best and prepare for the worst."

"I wish it was just that simple, *amigo*."

CHAPTER 49

First Stop

A white GMC van, with a medical insignia on both sides, drove slowly into Dodsonville and pulled up in front of Ethyl's restaurant. Sheriff Gabriel Tanner looked slowly around, seeking any signs of trouble, took a long slow breath then exhaled. He turned to the driver. "Ah shore 'preciate th' ride home. If'n y'er hungry Ethyl's here serves up th' best food fer miles around—mah treat."

"Actually, I could stand a little something to eat. I sure appreciate your offer, Sheriff."

"Least ah cud do fer th' ride." Gabe eased out of the van. Movement was awkward due to the special cast that held his arm out and bent at the elbow, as well as keeping his shoulder, immobile. *Least ways, mah best shootin' hand er free.*

The driver preceded Gabe and held the door for him. As soon as he walked in, all eyes turned to him, and the multitude of greetings was almost tumultuous. It was five-forty p.m., and there was a fair-sized dinner crowd already.

Sally took one look and let out a yell. "Yeee Haa!" With a broad grin on her face, she charged toward Gabe. His cast stopped her from grabbing him in a bear-hug. "Damn, Gabe. Shore er a blessin' ta have ya back 'n' see thet yer're gettin' healed up. Ya feelin' okay?"

"Fum whut th' doc's tole me ah reckin ah'm doin a fair sight better 'n they 'spected." He changed the subject. "Amos er thet city couple been en yet? By th' by." He pointed to the man at his side. "This fella drove me here, 'n' he be needin' sumpin' ta eat. Whut ever he fancies put er ta mah bill. Least ah kin do."

"Amos usually shows 'round six 'n' Gary 'n' Anne 'round 'bout th' same. Why 'n't ya git ta yer table 'n' ah'll git this fella whut he needs? Give me a sec, mister 'n' ah'll git ya a menu." Sally turned and flew into action.

ↄᴐↄ

Cholo's first stop was at a gas station in West Hamlin, on Route 10 in West Virginia. After filling the tank, he got directions to Sheridan and the Red Apple Rest. He hadn't told his two companions, and, as far as they knew, he was getting directions to Dodsonville.

Jorge looked up as they slowed and pulled into the parking lot of the Red Apple Rest. "What th' hell are you stopping here for?"

Cholo wasn't about to disclose his reason or motives. "We might need to stay for a night or two, and the guy in the gas station said this place is reasonable and just a few miles from Dodsonville."

This made perfect sense to Jorge, but again he had not been informed up front and feared he was losing complete control of the situation. He had to reaffirm his leadership. "We'll check it out. You wait in the car until we come out."

Cholo responded in an almost meek way. "As you wish, Jorge."

Good. He knows who the boss is. "Let's go, Pepe."

The moment the two of them entered the motel, Cholo drove around to the rear parking lot and pulled up alongside of a black van. When the driver and passenger looked his way, he opened his window and called out. *"El Cuchillo aqui."* Cholo used the street name that had become associated with him and his murderous exploits in Cali. His deadly knife usage had earned him the street name, "The Blade."

With the use of the established code, the van's passenger exited and walked quickly to the rear. He pulled open the door and withdrew a small suitcase. At the same time, Cholo climbed out of the car and went around to the rear, opening the trunk. He was completely aware that the driver of the van had now gotten out and had his hand covered by a folded newspaper, which Cholo was sure concealed a pistol. He was accustomed to this form of negotiations and had little concern.

"You have the agreed payment?"

"Of course. You have the correct order?"

"Absolutely. Two Uzi SMG nines with silencers, four fifty-round mags, and five hundred rounds of nine millimeter HP, also a Sig Sauer three-point-fifty-seven with one-hundred rounds of three-point-fifty-seven AP." He held the suitcase open for a visual verification. "Now, let's see the payment, please."

Cholo was more than pleased. *This is a good contact, especially for the armor piercing bullets.* He reached into the trunk and opened his duffel. From it, he pulled a brown paper bag and held it open to the seller. "Four thousand-five hundred, as agreed. Do you wish to count it?"

"Yes. It will take but a moment. We have a machine." In less than three minutes, the amount was confirmed. "Thank you. You have our international contact number should you have a future need."

By the time Cholo had placed the suitcase deep into the recesses of the trunk and slammed it shut, the van was already exiting the parking lot. Cholo drove back around to the front lot just in time to encounter Jorge and Pepe running toward him.

"Where th' fuck were you?"

Cholo was ready and stayed calm. "I was concerned that sitting out front might attract the wrong attention, so I drove around to the rear. It wouldn't do to have a run-in with the police, now that we're so close."

Jorge couldn't dispute that reasoning. "That's true, but you should have said something."

"I didn't think about it until you were inside." Glib lies rolled easily off his tongue. "Let's get out of here."

CHAPTER 50

Field Plans

Thanks, so much, for the dinner, Sheriff. Too bad I don't live closer. The food here is really good. I mean truly home-made. Well, guess I'd better hit the road. Be careful with that arm and shoulder and remember to get back to us for your check-up."

"Ah'll do er, fer shore. 'preciate th' ride 'n' ya take keer a goin' back." As soon as the driver left, Gabe looked around, caught Sally's attention, and beckoned her over.

"What cha needin', Gabe?"

"Ah'll take a plate a barbeque wi' fries 'n' slaw, glass a tea. Thet way, ah won't be needin' a knife er two hands. 'nother thing. Amos comes en, send him mah way."

"Shore 'nough, Gabe. Le'me git yer dinner a goin'."

Gabe was only halfway through his meal, due to the parade of well-wishers, when Amos walked over.

"Good havin' ya home, Gabe. Ya healin' okay? Shore glad thet city couple were a lookin' fer ya. Other 'n thet, she might a been too long…ya know. Fer city folk, they were right he'pful a gittin ya freed up 'n' ta th' doctor folk. Might a stressed me sore if'n ah had ta do er m'self."

That was the longest speech Gabe had ever heard from this man. "Ah'm mighty thankful fer all th' h'ep ya gave 'n' them likewise. Ah'll shore let 'em know, soon's ah see 'em. Got sumpin' ta ask ya. Kin ya set fer a bit?"

Amos took a seat and returned to his normal behavior. Just said nothing and waited.

Gabe started off slow. He knew he was on shaky ground, but had no choice. "Amos, as ah recall, they give ya a Bronze Star fer yer actions in Nam." Amos said nothing so, Gabe went on. "Was fer bravery 'n' action, 'bove 'n' beyond th' call a duty."

Again, no comment.

Gabe was also aware that he was the only man in town who knew Amos's military history. His patrol had been ambushed in Da Nang by the Viet Cong, and they were vastly outnumbered. Two of their men were killed outright, and the rest of them were pinned down, with three others wounded.

Amos told them all to fire at the enemy and keep them pinned down long enough for him to make it to the trees. They did, and he did. Amos killed eleven of the enemy that day and took three prisoners. The next day, his sergeant ordered him out on another patrol. Amos flat out told him "Ah ain't a killin' no more."

The sergeant threatened him with jail time and called him a red-neck coward. Amos walked right up to the sergeant and, with one punch, cold-cocked the man. All the men of his patrol stood up for him and, in the end, he received his medal and a "medical" discharge.

"Amos, ah'm faced wi' a raht poor situation. Good possibility thet a few nasty characters er a headin' this a way 'n' jest might be trouble fer th' town. Ah know ya know ever' man, woman, 'n' child en town, either by name er by sight. Thet's a 'portant fact. Whut ah'm askin er fer ya ta kerry yer deer rifle en yer truck, 'n' keep er loaded. Ya kin see thet ah'm not full up ta th' task, er ah wouldn't be a askin." Gabe stopped talking and waited. While he waited, he finished his meal.

Five minutes went by before Amos responded. "Gabe, ya know mah story, so ah ain't a needin' ta 'splain m'self. Ah swore, efter thet battle, thet ah'd never take th' life a 'nother man ag'in."

Gabe was not happy, but he understood and was about to

respond and let Amos off the hook. He was stopped when Amos went on.

"Ah respect ya, Gabe 'n' ah keer fer ever' one a th' folk here. Cain't be lettin' trouble makers cause ya er them eny problem er hurt. Ah'll do er fer ya 'n' hope we kin git by easy. Fair 'nuff?"

Gabe reached across the table with his good right hand to shake Amos's hand. "Fair 'nuff 'n' thank ya. Would ya keer fer some dinner long as yer settin'?"

"B'lieve so but, no offense, ah reckin' ah'll jest set en mah reg'lar spot ta th' counter."

"Ah full' understand 'n' no offense takin'"

Amos rose and walked, without hurrying to the far stool at the counter. Gabe watched as the man walked away. *Th' man's a dead shot 'n' don't fluster none. Thet shore er a relief on mah side.*

Sally saw that Gabe had finished, and Amos had moved away. When Gabe didn't get up, she hurried over. "Kin ah git ya aught?"

"B'lieve ah fancy a piece a th' peach cobbler, if'n ya got er."

"Shore do. Back en two shakes."

It was then that Gabe saw Anne and Gary walk in. He hollered to them. "Hey, Gary, Anne, y'all c'mon over 'n' set a bit."

Anne was almost effusive in her greeting. "Great to see you, Sheriff and good to have you back. You look one heck-of-a-lot better now than the last time I saw you."

Gabe couldn't help smiling. "Good ta be back, 'n' ah'm shore ah look 'n' feel a darn sight better. Got ta tell ya, ah'm raht grateful fer th' he'p ya'll gave Amos ta git me ta medical attention. Doc said ah might not a made 'er if'n ah were out en th' storm too much longer." He changed the subject Bund was back to the importance of the moment. "Why 'n't ya both set fer a bit? If'n yer wantin' ta order, feel free. Ah jest finished 'n' won't be bothered a bit. 'Sides, we're needin' ta talk 'n' git a plan set."

Gary and Anne ordered dinner and, by the time they had

eaten and shared information with Gabe, it was evident that they might expect at least three Hispanic men and, more than likely, big trouble.

Gabe filled them in on the fact that Amos was now part of their inner circle of protection, although he didn't disclose Amos's military history. "Ah've also begun ta reactivate mah local 'radar.' Th' only missin' links en mah 'radar' er th' stone trio 'n' th' gas station. Reckin ah'll catch up wi' them come mornin'."

CHAPTER 51

Checkin' In

Carlos tapped the bell on the counter three times, and they waited. The owner of Parker's High Mountain Inn came out of the back, looking as if time had frozen him in place. There wasn't one thing different about his appearance or attire.

He looked at Jon and Carlos with a quizzical expression. "Say, ain't ya th' two guys whut checked en then out, same day, jest a short bit ago?"

Jon had a non-committal response. "That's right. We got a sudden business call that couldn't wait. Now we want to take a little time and see this area."

"Shore hope ya don' git 'nother one a them calls. How long ya fixin' ta stay?"

Carlos gave their standard bland answer. "Two or three days…we're not sure. That's not a problem, is it?"

"Nope, jest so's ah kin keep a idea. Ah'll give ya cabin two, got two single beds." He handed Jon the room key. "Jest out th' door 'n' turn raht. She's near this end."

It was now after seven p.m., and they had been on the road since morning. "Think we'll get some dinner before we go to the room. That place in the center of town still open?"

"Ethyl's, yep. Ya 'member th'way?"

"Yes, we do, thank you."

They walked slowly toward Ethyl's. Carlos brought up what Jon was mulling over. "Good thing the sheriff's in the hospital. He'd take one look at us and put two and two together in a heartbeat."

"I've just been thinking about that, and, ordinarily, I would agree with you, but this isn't ordinary, and I think we may need him. Let's just offer the story that we were in the same unit as A.J. and it was one that dealt with national security so that's all we can say."

"Sounds okay to me."

They pulled open the door to Ethyl's and walked in. Sally spotted them in an instant. "Hey y'all, welcome back ta town. Rare thing fer outa towners ta be comin' back so soon. Ya jest missed Gabe. Set where ya want 'n' ah'll be wi' ya en two shakes."

They were in the field again and so chose a corner table, in the rear. Carlos whispered to Jon. "Can't hide much in a small town, can you?"

"That's exactly why our last cover won't cut it."

"Ah brought ya menus. Still got th' special—pork roast, mashed taters, gravy 'n' collards. Best collards within a hunnert miles."

They both opted for the special. Carlos went with sweet tea, and Jon ordered coffee.

Sally was back in just a few minutes. "Here ya go. Y'all enjoy. Holler if'n yer needin' sumpin." They were set, and Sally was off to another table.

They had barely begun eating when a familiar voice called out. "Y'all lost er ya seekin a ghost?"

They both turned to see Sheriff Tanner walking toward their table.

Carlos muttered under his breath. "Here we go."

Jon was a firm believer in the old adage that the best defense is a good offense. "Good evening, Sheriff. What happened to your arm?"

"Had me a run-in wi' an oak tree. Tree won. If'n yer a seekin' A.J., yer a couple a weeks late. Ya kin visit wi' him over ta th' new cemetery, outside a town." As he spoke, Gabe watched carefully for a reaction as he pulled up a chair.

"We know about A.J. Damn shame, too. We need to be

straight with you this go-round. As we said, last time, we were in the same unit as A.J. We deal with situations that involve national security issues, so we're not at liberty to discuss it. Last time we were here, we met A.J. at his burned out house. We barely got to say hello when we received a high priority call, had him jump in our truck, and rushed to meet with a helicopter pick-up at the Charleston airport. That action cost A.J. and one other man their lives."

Gabe was not ready for that response, but at least he now understood why A.J.'s truck was left on that spur road by the property. It also explained why he had left his belongings at Sally's place. Gabe now had a reasonable idea of what brought these two men back to his town. Although he wasn't pleased about it, at least these two were trained specialists and could make a hell of a positive difference if these Hispanics were to come into town bent on trouble. *Ah'll stay easy 'n' see whar she goes.* "Thet bein' th' case, whut brings ya back?"

Carlos saw, quickly, where Jon was leading and jumped in. "Do you remember that South American kid that sat at the counter over there last time we were here? It seems that he believes there is a large amount of money, hidden somewhere by drug dealers, and he's hell bent on locating it. When we were informed that you were in the hospital, we were sent to point him out to the INS agents that were sent to wait for him. They should be here, already. A man and a women acting like a married couple. Have you seen them, yet?"

"Shore have. Matter a fact, they he'ped Amos ta rescue me when thet oak fell on mah Jeep. Couldn't a missed 'em, though. When they come ta town, they stood out lahk a pig en a chicken coop." He turned toward the counter. "Hey, Amos, kin ya go 'n' fetch them city folk fer me?"

Both Carlos and Jon had to laugh. This was exactly what they were concerned about—field agents who didn't have a clue on how to "blend."

Gabe went on. "Ah don't know whut yer boss er general, er whatever he er, tole ya, but here's th' hunt as she stands. Fum th' fax sheets ah've received, we 'peer ta be facin' three, mebbe four, Hispanics headed ta mah town. Th' facts indicate thet one er more a them er out-'n'-out killers. They's a trail a bodies 'ahind them whut includes a female deputy sheriff. Folk whut don't care none 'bout life ain't much better'n a bad disease—don't care who er whut it attacks. Ah cain't have thet kinda trouble en mah town. 'Peers they's all huntin' a pile a cash thet's mebbe hid somewhere. Ah know how money 'n' greed kin change folk, but these uns 'peer ta be, out-'n'-out, jest plain rotten. Now ah'm kinda ailin' so ah reckin y'all a goin' ta have ta put yer talent enta play. Ah shore as shit don' want eny a mah good people took down by thet kinda garbage."

Carlos turned slowly to look at Jon. Both men were now sure of one thing. This wasn't going to be simple and probably wasn't going to be a quiet incident or one that just went away. They were back in the field and, unless there was a miracle, the field was going to get bloody.

Special ops training, once again, had to be resurrected. Jon put it to the sheriff, directly. "This is your town, so the first thing we need to know is this. Do you expect anything out of the daily routine, but planned for or expected, this week?"

Gabe sat quietly for a few minutes. Mentally, he was reviewing all of the possibilities in this small town. "Nope, ah don' b'lieve so." He sat silently waiting to hear what Carlos or Jon might have to say or plan when something occurred to him. "Say, ah don' know if'n this er a use. T'day's Tuesday, raht?" He paused. awaiting a confirmation. Carlos nodded affirmatively. "D'pendin' 'pon their schedule either Thursday er Friday, th' propane truck'll be a comin' ta deliver. Goes ta Ethyl's 'n' ta th' refill tank ta th' gas station. Efter thet ta Annie's Clean 'n' Carry, over ta Sheridan. Thet's a local clothes cleanin' store."

"That shouldn't be a problem. I imagine that it's usually one driver who makes his deliveries and leaves," Carlos said then pressed slightly. "Can you think of anything else? Even if it seems unimportant to you, it might prove invaluable in this type of situation."

Gabe didn't respond for several minutes. "Nope, thet's 'bout got er. Jest one bit more. If'n th' propane driver er th' reg'lar one, he works a kinda loose schedule thet'll 'low him ta stay over a day er two. Him 'n' th' widow Mulaney got kinda sweet 'pon each other." Suddenly his expression changed. "Here comes yer INS couple. Ya jest missed 'em afore. Ah sent Amos ta fetch em fum Parker's."

Anne and Gary came straight to the table at which Gabe and two strangers were seated. Gabe didn't bother to stand. "Anne, Gary, this here's Don 'n' Santos. They're fum th' government 'n' have seen yer suspect, er least ways th' one we're shore a, first hand. Why'n't ya pull up a couple a chairs 'n' set a spell?"

Jon proceeded to tell them what they already knew, but he had to act as if this was a meeting between Carlos and himself with an uninformed couple. *When the sheriff isn't with us, I can divulge some data that I don't think he needs to know.* "At this point, the sheriff has some trusted citizens on the lookout. More than likely, trouble is going to come from the direction of Sheridan, as there is nothing but country roads everywhere else around. We also have to consider that whoever it is we're seeking may attempt to enter town at night, when they're less likely to be observed. The suspect we know of is Pablo, and, as far as we know, he has no weapons. Anyone else is guesswork, but to be treated as armed and extremely dangerous. Hopefully, this other group is not headed for Dodsonville, but we just don't know. We need to be ready for all possibilities and do our damnedest to keep any actions outside of town and away from the general population. Sheriff, you have anything that I've missed or anything to add?"

"Sounds lahk ya'll 've had a bit a history, boys. Only thing else be if'n th' other group er comin' this-a-way, they're killers 'n' one a th' people they killed er a female deputy sheriff. Ah don't take kindly ta people whut kill law enforcement, if'n ya git whut ah'm a aimin' at."

Gary couldn't help his slight smile. *Sounds like this sheriff'll be happy to send those guys out of town in a box. Guess that's what they refer to as "mountain justice."*

Anne came right to the point. "How should we set up and proceed?"

There was a period of silence at the table. Gary and Anne were the lowest in order of authority, so they just waited. Jon and Carlos, although the most experienced, were not overly familiar with the town, which left the obvious respondent as the sheriff.

Gabe wasn't long in laying out the most logical procedure. "Ah've got mah key people on th' watch, so's, fer now, th' way ah see 'er, best would be if'n th' rest a ya jest roam 'roun' town like tourists. Ya spot enyone whut looks out a place, keep 'em en view till ya get a chance ta let one a us know. If'n it er thet Pablo kid, should be no problem. If'n it er them others, we have ta hope we kin git them ta move outa town afore we act." He glanced at Jon and Carlos. "Ya got eny other ideas?"

Carlos answered almost at once. "From our standpoint, Sheriff, you've got it covered for openers. We'll change plans as the situation requires."

Jon waved to Sally, which brought her over in double-time. "Ya needin' sumpin else?"

Before Jon could ask for the check, Gabe interrupted. "Girl, ya 'member whut ah tole ya 'bout lookin' out?"

She nodded affirmatively.

"Starts raht now."

Sally looked back at Jon and received her answer. "No thank you, just our check."

Gabe looked in the direction of the row of counter stools. Amos was again perched in his favorite spot. "Hey, Amos." The big man on the counter stool turned slowly. "Whut we talked about afore—starts now."

A barely perceptible nod of agreement was the only positive action that the sheriff received, and Amos turned back to the counter.

Jon paid the check, including a generous tip, then asked Gabe. "Who is he?" The question was defined by a nod of his head toward the man on the stool.

"One a mah radar. Also a 'Nam vet 'n' don't fluster none."

Gary felt he should add something positive. "Without his help, there's a chance the sheriff might not be here today. The man works completely clear-headed under high stress conditions. We know, we lived it firsthand."

"Ain't no use a settin' here 'n' jawin. Got us as set as kin be, fer now. B'lieve ah'll git me some shut-eye, whilst ah kin. Kinda amazin' how gettin' beat up a bit kin wear a body down. Ah got me a real comfortable chair over ta m' office. Thet'll do me fer now. 'Sides, ah cain't lay down comfortable lahk, wi' this mess on mah arm."

Gabe rose and started for the door. *Ah shore would like ta know who them four work fer. Shore as sunshine she ain't INS er any reg'lar part a th' gov'ment.*

Anne waited until the sheriff had reached the door. She leaned forward and whispered, "I assume you are the two men the commander said were coming?" She paused, seeking confirmation.

"Yes, we are. I'm Don McGill, and this is my partner, Santos Morales." *If they need our true names, they can ask the commander.* "You've both been here for a couple of days, so if there's anything else we need to know, now's as good a time as any. We're booked in at Parker's and understand that you are too. That'll make communication easier. Santos and I are going to go for a walk around town to get a better 'feel' for the arena."

Gary and Anne started to get up as if to go with them.

"It's best that we do it alone. It might look suspicious if we suddenly became a foursome."

The couple sat back down.

"We'll catch up with you in the morning."

CHAPTER 52

Bones

Pablo was pedaling his bike back to Sheridan. He had devised a simple plan. *I'll buy some tinned food and some boxes of crackers. That way I won't need a cook fire or pots. A day or two of cold food is worth it for such a fantastic reward.*

His route took him by the second hand shop where he had purchased the bicycle. The owner happened to be standing out front and saw him pedaling up the road. *Hope thet boy don' think ah'm 'bout ta take thet bike er eny a th' rest a th' stuff back.* Pablo just waved in the man's direction and pedaled right by without a second glance.

❧❦❧

Pepe leaned over from the rear seat and whispered to Jorge, "*Tengo muy hambre.*"

Jorge was more than hungry—he was ravenous. "Cholo, we need to stop for some food before we reach the town. We haven't eaten since early this morning."

Cholo didn't mind the discomfort of hunger, but stopping made sense. *There must be a place to eat in Dodsonville, but in a small town, there will be too many curious eyes.* "If I see a place, we'll stop. Otherwise, we'll turn around and look for a place in Sheridan. That way we won't draw attention in that small town."

The logic of Cholo's reasoning was immediately evident to Jorge. He still reacted to assert his control. "Good idea, Cholo. Why chance having the town's people wondering who we are or why we're there?" The words were barely out of his mouth when they spotted a place up ahead. A sign out front had the picture of a smiling pig with a chef's hat, and the name underneath was simply *Bones*. Jorge pointed toward the building, as they approached. "That looks like a good place. Let's check."

⌘

Pablo recognized the scenery on the road. He had just passed it two days ago. *Soon I'll be in the town. Then I can find a market.* He pedaled past a large brown building with a sign out front that made him grin. *Didn't notice that place last time I passed. Never saw a pig with a hat on. I wonder what Bones means?* He kept pedaling.

⌘

Jon and Carlos were walking the town, their years of combat experience coming back into play. What outwardly appeared to be casual was anything but.

They noted every opening, recessed doorway, low roof, and overhanging tree. It was a simple procedure, which in the past had proved life-saving. *Where can they hide, and if need be, where can we hide?*

They were compiling mental records that could be instantly recalled if and when needed. Jon suddenly had an idea that was of a completely different nature. "Carlos, stop for a sec'. Do you remember where we took Pablo down?"

"Do I remember? Of course, it's too recent to forget."

"Do you recall that large shed on A.J.'s property?"

"Absolutely."

"It was locked up like Fort Knox. That may be the target area."

"Madre de Dios, I'm sure you're right. If that's the case, it'll take the action out of town. Do you think we should take a look?"

"I do, but first let's check with the sheriff. He may know something that'll save us the trip."

"Sounds good, but I guess it'll have to wait until morning. Maybe we should turn in early and get an early start in the morning."

"My thinking exactly. Let's head back to Parker's."

⌘

"That was sure good. I'm stuffed. How about you?"

Cholo and Pepe both answered affirmatively. Pepe was effusive. "I don't think I've ever had pig's ribs done like that and everything they served with them was just wonderful."

Cholo's thoughts were back to business. "I think we should drive over to that town and take a slow ride through. Get a feel for where we're going to be. I don't think we should stay there, even if there is a place. I think we should stay at that Red Apple place, less chance of discovery."

Jorge moved to regain his edge. "That works. Then we can get breakfast there and not walk into some eating place in Dodsonville. We'd probably get too much attention in that small town. Let's go."

⌘

Sally had finished her shift at Ethyl's, and the restaurant was shut down for the night. *Ah'm done en—jest feel lahk a bit a settin' afore ah head ta home.* She settled down on one of the two benches out front. *Shore has been a powerful lot a strange goin's on of late. Fust Zeb then Zeke getting' kilt, and A.J.'s folk 'n' then A.J.* Her thought pattern shifted. *Thet were a damn shame. Thet boy shore were good en bed.* She returned to the present. *Now Gabe's tole me ta be a lookin fer Mex strangers. Wunda whut thet's about?* She heard the sound of a car approaching and looked up. *Wunda who thet cud be? Folk 'round here er usually ta home fer th' naht cum this time.* The car came slowly down the main street with only the fog lights on. It drove through to the far end of town then turned around and started back. Sally's natural curiosity, coupled with what Gabe had told her, had her staring hard. *Ah cain't be shore— daylight's too far gone—but ah b'lieve they's three men en thet car, and they 'pear ta be of Mex er Spanish type. Car 'peers ta be two dif'rent colors. Ah'd best tell Gabe, fust thing mornin' comes.*

CHAPTER 53

Sightings

Gabe walked into Ethyl's at five forty-five a.m. He was in full uniform, which was not typical of an ordinary day.

"Mornin', Gabe. Yer a fair bit earlier then usual."

"Mornin', Sally. Yep, cain't sleep too good wi' this cast. Also, damn near took me a hour ta git mah clothes on. Say, cud ya git these couple a buttons done fer me?"

"Shore 'nuff. Le'me fetch ya some coffee then ah'll git them buttons." She turned and walked quickly toward the counter area and coffee station just beyond. In a moment, she returned. "Here's yer coffee. Now face 'round 'n' ah'll git ya buttoned up proper." She completed the few buttons, quickly. "Gabe, ah got ta tell ya sumpin." His silence was an indication for her to continue. "Felt like settin' a bit, efter closin' last naht. Ah perched on th' bench ta front, 'n' were getting' comfortable when ah heerd a car. Ah recalled whut ya tole me so's ah looked 'n' watched. Car come fum th'east, real slow down th' road, jest them small front lights a burnin'. Drove through ta th' west end a town then turned 'round 'n' come back, still slow. Ah looked hard. They was three men en 'er 'n' they 'peared ta be Mex er sum kinda Spanish. Daylight were most gone so's 'tweren't easy ta be shore. Also, car 'peared ta be two dif'rent colors. Weren't enuff light ta tell whut." She stopped and waited.

Gabe was silent for a few minutes. His mind was whirling,

and his blood pressure was definitely up. He needed to remain low key—not get Sally worked up. "Shore 'preciate thet. Words been thet a number a illegals er round th' state 'n' all law offices been asked ta report eny unusual comin's. Ah'll take mah usual."

Sally left to put Gabe's breakfast order in, just as Jon and Carlos walked in. "Mornin', guys. Set where ya want 'n' ah'll be raht wi' ya."

Gabe had heard her greeting and beckoned the two men to his table. "Mornin', Don, Santos, why'nt ya join me?"

Since they were now on what might be termed the same team, they accepted Gabe's invitation. "Good morning, Sheriff."

"May not be sech a good one." He started to enlighten them on Sally's sighting. It was at that moment that Sally appeared with Gabe's breakfast. All conversation switched to everyday topics. "Sally, this here's Don 'n' Santos. They be stayin' over ta Parker's 'n' may be en town fer two er three day. They were en last night but ah'm not shore they passed their names ta ya."

Sally was her usual effervescent self. "Mornin', fellas. Whut kin ah git ya er d' ya need menus? Coffee?" She paused, looking at them quizzically. "Nope, yer raht, Gabe. Ah didn't ketch their names, last naht."

Carlos answered for both of them. "Good morning, Sally. We'll both take coffee, and a menu would be helpful."

"Be raht back." She turned and walked rapidly toward the coffee station.

"Fellas, we need ta talk, serious like."

Both men leaned slightly forward, toward Gabe.

"Best wait till efter yer food's here."

They settled back.

A quick perusal of the menus and they ordered. Both men opted for blueberry pancakes—Jon's with bacon and Carlos's with sausage. Sally refilled all three coffee cups and left to place their orders. She called back over her shoulder, "Shouldn't be more 'n' three er four minutes."

They were back to light conversation, Jon and Carlos staying circumspective and the sheriff subtly digging for information.

"Here ya er." Sally was back, sliding their ample breakfasts in front of them. "Holler if'n ya need me."

Jon and Carlos started to eat and, while they did, Gabe filled them in on Sally's observation last night. When he finished, he added his own request. "If'n they stole th' car they're drivin', could be thet one a yer people er th' FBI have a handle on th' car 'n' kin confirm whut we're seekin'."

Jon paused for a moment. "I'll see what we can find out." He dialed the commander and posed the question then put his phone back in his pocket.

"Shore a lot a numbers ta thet phone ya called."

"Yes. It goes through a switchboard and, by knowing which numbers to use, it speeds up getting to the right person. If there's anything new, we should hear back within the next fifteen minutes." Jon took another forkful of pancakes.

They had barely finished eating when the call came in. "Don McGill here. May I help you?" Jon knew it was the commander but was covering to keep the sheriff from gaining too much private information. "Okay...I see...and that was when? Okay. We'll take it from here." The phone call ended. Jon could feel the pre-battle tension starting in his gut. "Well, Sheriff, your radar works just fine. It's just about definite that these are some or all of the men we're looking for. The bad part is that one or all of them are confirmed, cold-blooded killers. The car is a 1987 Oldsmobile, four door, two-tone green. It was stolen from an airport parking lot in Charlotte, North Carolina. Couple got home last night and found their car gone. The FBI just put the pieces together."

"Ah hope thet couple fum INS er up ta dealin' wi' a mess like this. Speakin' a them, here they er." It was now just after seven a.m. "Ah'll git em ta come over."

Anne and Gary responded to the sheriff's wave with smiles and started to his table. Ever since they assisted in the rescue of Gabe, their status in town had changed from outsiders kept at a cold distance to welcome visitors. They were feeling much more comfortable, now that their acceptance level had improved. Gary smiled at Gabe. "Good morning, Sheriff. How's the arm and shoulder?" He changed directions. "Mornin', Don, Santos. You two must be early risers."

Gabe stood to leave. "Mornin', Anne, Gary. Guess ah'm healing up fine. Thank ya fer askin'. Ah'll leave th' four a ya ta talk. Ah got ta make shore th' rest a mah radar er en place— th' stone trio." He started at an awkward, but brisk pace, for the door.

Carlos addressed the new arrivals. "Why don't you join us? We need to fill you in on the latest in this situation."

As soon as they were seated, Sally came over in her usual bright, bubbly manner. "Mornin', y'all. Ah know yer wantin' coffee. D' ya need menus er are ya set?"

"Good morning, Sally. I don't know about my husband, but I'd like two eggs, over easy, bacon, some of those fantastic home-fries and a biscuit." Anne turned to Gary. "Are you ready to order?"

"Yes. Let me have the buttermilk pancakes, sausage, home-fries and..." He thought for a moment. "No, that'll do, thank you."

Sally left to place their order, and Jon took the opportunity to fill the couple in. After a brief run-down of Sally's observation, he added an important fact. "She spotted three men in that Olds. If that's all of them, it should go reasonably smoothly. However, there is the distinct possibility that the original problem is traveling independently and unaware of the other three. In that case, this'll get a little more complicated since, unless we get lucky, we may be operating on two independent fields." He paused to let the information sink in. "Do you have silencers?"

They both answered almost simultaneously. "No. Didn't think we'd need 'em."

Jon glanced briefly at Carlos. The shrug of Carlos's shoulders, coupled with the expression on his face, said it all. *No experience, limited field value.* Jon continued. "The only good thing about that is that if it comes down to shooting, they won't know where our shots are coming from."

Anne was silent. The implication of what Jon said had

slammed home. *We'd be the primary recognizable targets.*

Gary was a bit more open. "Do you think it'll come to that? I mean shooting."

Carlos answered with a slight tone of annoyance. "We hope not, for the sake of the town, but we're prepared for it if it comes down to that."

Anne started to ask something, but, at that moment, Sally arrived with their breakfasts. "Here ya er. Back en two shakes ta fill yer cups." She was back in a minute with a pot of coffee. She refilled all four cups and left to attend to other patrons.

Carlos turned to Jon. "Coffee's good but not as good as Stavros's. At least you can drink this without getting third-degree burns."

Jon just grinned and nodded. "We'll let the two of you finish your breakfast. The best thing you can do for now is stay on the streets and, if you spot any possibilities, remember the location and find us. We'll be out there, also." He stood to leave. Carlos also rose. Jon left ten dollars on the table. "That should cover our breakfast."

The moment they were out of Ethyl's, Jon turned to Carlos. "We need to catch up with the sheriff." The quizzical look on Carlos's face was expected. "What we talked about earlier. You know, that when we caught up with A.J. and this kid had shot him, we were out at A.J.'s property?" He didn't wait for an answer. "If Pablo was out there and he was told by El Tigre that A.J. had the money, then it seems to be logical that that's the first place they'll be looking for it. And if our past observation was correct, the shed will be their number one target."

"Damn, Jon. You mentioned that before, and now I'm sure you've got it pinpointed. It just makes perfect sense."

"I think so. For that reason, I want to check with the sheriff and see if the property's been sold or if anything's been done with it. Let's stop by his office, first."

Gabe looked up when his office door squeaked open. He didn't waste time on social greetings. "Thet were quick. Whut's up?"

Jon had to tread carefully now. "Just a personal curiosity. Did A.J.'s family dispose of his property? I don't remember

him ever mentioning anyone other than his mother and father."
The only safe thing now was a lie. "The reason I'm asking is
that I know a guy from the service, lives in Virginia, and is
looking to buy a small piece of land, to build a cabin and re-
tire. He mentioned that the only two places he would consider
are Tennessee and West Virginia."

Gabe sat silently for a minute, before answering. "Truth be,
A.J. left all a his property 'n' pers'nal items ta me." He enjoyed the looks of surprise on both men's faces. "Said I were
th' closest ta kin thet he had. Shore were a su'prise ta me too.
As ta sellin', ah reckin not. Gonna build me a small house on
er 'n' stay put." *Ah wunda if'n thet's th' real story?*

Jon had to continue the lie. "Wow! That's something I
wouldn't have expected. Great for you, though." He changed
the subject. "Carlos and I are going to just drive around town
and maybe a ways toward Sheridan. See if we get lucky and
spot these boys. Let me give you my cell phone number, in
case you need us quickly. While we're at it, let me have your
office number in case I need to get you."

They exchanged numbers, and Jon and Carlos left. Carlos
offered a casual parting statement. "We'll check in as soon as
we're back."

"Thet'll be jest fine, boys." *Sumpin ain't raht. Ah jest ain't
a buyin' thet story a his 'bout someun wantin' land. Ah'm
shore thet has at do wi' thet mess wi A.J., 'n' she jest don'
want ta go 'way.*

As they were crossing the street, Jon turned to Carlos. "I
don't think the sheriff bought my story."

The morning sky was almost completely covered with broken clouds, as Jon and Carlos climbed into the truck. Carlos
noted a plus factor. "At least we won't be driving directly into
the rising sun, on the way out."

CHAPTER 54

Final Preparations

Pablo was exceedingly pleased with himself. He had just filled the baskets on his bicycle with some canned goods and boxes of crackers, along with two six-packs of Pepsi-Cola. *I now have food, transportation and best of all a gun. Tonight I will sneak through the town and return to where I avenged my father. I'm sure that the money must be in that shed. Once I get it and see what I need to pack it up and take it home, I'll find a store and buy it. Maybe a back-pack or a suitcase will be all that I will need.*

〜〜〜

Jorge was happy with what he had seen. He gave Cholo his opinion. "A town that small won't have much of a police force to worry about."

Cholo was of the same opinion, but for a different reason. *Fewer police will make it simpler to kill these two mules when the time is right.* His response was totally different. "That squealing little ant said something about the man he sought having a large shed, and that was his only building. I'm of the opinion that the money must be in that shed. First, we need to find out where that shed is located. From there it should be easy." He paused for a moment to consider the possibilities. "We'll need to find out exactly where a man who is in the military, or just retired from it, lives. Military or Special Forces would be the only reason that a person would be on a mission to kill in Colombia. That is how we'll find this shed."

Pepe was listening to the conversation but had nothing he was willing to offer. He had one idea that he was afraid to mention, fearing Cholo's wrath. *This whole idea is crazy. All I can see is an impossible hunt for money, that we don't even know is real, and a shit-load of danger*. Fear was rapidly becoming the primary emotion in his life.

ဢၜၜ

Carlos and Jon drove slowly to the east end of Sheridan then continued as far east as The Red Apple Rest. They made a U-turn and as they drove back toward Dodsonville Carlos took a second look at a large brown, barn-like building. A sign on the front showed an image of a large smiling pig with a chef's hat and a single name, *Bones*. "Jon, I'll bet that's one of those country rib joints that we hear about. You know, rural and unadvertised but fantastic. We have to eat dinner somewhere so why not try it? It's not that far from town, so I don't think we'll miss anything."

Jon thought for a brief moment. He wasn't thrilled about what he now was quite sure was going to turn into a nasty confrontation. That tempered his answer. "Why not? We might as well get something enjoyable out of this mess." His thought process returned to a procedure from his operative days, trying to out-guess the enemy. *Same game—different theater. I sure as hell hope that this is the last of it.* "Carlos, if these guys have any brains, they won't stay at Parker's. My guess is that they'll go to that Red Apple Rest Motel. The other option is just to sleep in their car somewhere off the road. We might as well continue back to town and see if either the sheriff or the commander's team has received any updates."

By now, the morning clouds had dissipated leaving a cloudless, bright, cornflower blue sky. "Sun's now at our backs. Makes driving and looking for this group at the same time, a lot easier." Carlos's comments about the sun were typical for an experienced hunter or a seasoned combatant.

"You're right about that." Jon could easily read the more important meaning of Carlos's statement concerning the position of the sun.

⌘

Jorge suddenly came up with the perfect solution to Cholo's statement. "When we drove to the far end of the town, there was a gas station. In a town of this size, they must know everyone who lives here. We could ask them...say we had been in the service and were looking for a man who had been in the same unit as us."

This mule has finally come up with a decent idea. "That might just work, but only one person should ask. Three would be risky." *Now to make him feel good.* "Let's do it, but soon. I doubt they would stay open past seven at night."

Jorge was proud of himself. *I have proven that I'm as smart as Cholo.* "We should go now, when they are busiest. We would be less noticed that way. I will ask."

Cholo was in full agreement. "Very good, let's go now." *Let this fool stick his neck out. If it works, fine. If not, I won't be the one who sticks out.*

Jorge started to drive toward town. *I'm still the one in charge, and soon the vultures will feast on this madman.*

CHAPTER 55

Carlos drove straight for the sheriff's office. At the same time, Jon called Gary and told him, along with Anne, to meet them there. "At this point, a plan of action has to be formulated."

The squeak of his office door caused Gabe to look up as Gary and Anne walked in. He'd been told, numerous times, to fix that annoying hinge. Gabe liked it that way. He would simply respond, "Thet squeak's kind a like mah pers'nal warnin' device."

Anne came right to the point. "We received a call from Don to meet them here. He didn't say specifically why or what for, but he should be here in a minute or two." Anne wasn't sure if she should tell the sheriff that Don felt that a plan was needed. She'd let Don open the door to that situation.

The longer this waiting and wondering went on, the more uncomfortable Gabe was getting. Accompanying that discomfort was an air of tension, building slowly and compounded by his current disability. *'less 'n ah miss 'd sumpin, 'peers ta me we got us sum heavy hitters a comin' ta town 'n' ah got me a deep 'spicion thet these boys er 'spectin a rough time a it.* He looked hard at Gary and Anne. "Y'all shore yer givin' me th' whole story here? 'Cause ah'm a startin' ta be a th 'pinion thet they's sum 'portant pieces a missin'."

They were in the hot seat now, and neither of them had the expertise or experience to deal with it. Gary chose the easy way out. "Sheriff, we've been straight with you. If there's anything else to this situation, we aren't aware of it. Perhaps when Don and Santos arrive, you can see if they've got any other info."

"Ah reckin ah'll do jest thet."

The next eight minutes were extremely uncomfortable for Gary and Anne. They were considering going over to Ethyl's for a glass of tea when the door hinge squeaked.

∽∾∽∾

Three hundred fifty-eight miles south east, Sheri and Rosita were enjoying a seaside lunch at the Bluewater Café in Wrightsville Beach. Sheri had put it in simple terms. "If the men can go off for a few days, there's no reason I can't take you out for a relaxed lunch. You shouldn't always be in the kitchen, even though I'm acting as your assistant. Name a nice place that would be fun to go to."

They were each sipping a well-chilled rum punch, and their lunches of plump crab cakes had just been placed on the table when Rosita got serious. "Tell me, Sheri. Things look good between you and Jon. Does it look like a permanent thing?"

"Don't tell Jon, but if he asked me today, I'd jump at the chance to spend my life with him. It seems that everything between us just keeps getting better. I got the impression that once this mess in West Virginia is behind us, our engagement will quickly follow."

"That would be the best thing for Jon and, I believe, for the both of you."

"Rosita, I couldn't agree more. Let's eat—I'm starving."

CHAPTER 56

Readiness

All heads turned at the squeak, which heralded the arrival of Jon and Carlos. Jon brought up the obvious. "Sheriff, a few drops of oil would take care of that noise."

"Reckin yer raht, but thet noise tells me ah got comp'ny. Jest gonna leave 'er be. Y'all grab a couple a chairs 'n' let's git ta whut's 'portant." Gabe's attitude was simple and to the point. "Small talk 'n' business jest don't mix. Lahk ah said, let's git ta er."

It was quite evident to both Jon and Carlos that the sheriff was on edge, had strong doubts as to the identity of the two of them, and, in all likelihood, of Gary and Anne. Gabe had run out of patience with these "city folk." Jon had to both get down to the business at hand and smooth the situation over, at the same time. He didn't hesitate. "Sheriff, if you recall the last time we were in town, we encountered a young Hispanic male eating at the counter in Ethyl's." The slight positive nod of response was a positive indication to continue. "We ran into him out near A.J.'s house, or at least where it had been. We found out that he was illegal and when we left with A.J., we took this kid into custody and turned him over to the authorities in Richmond. Information that we have recently received indicates that he escaped confinement and may be coming back here. If that is factual, we'll be dealing with four Hispanic males, three of which are known to be killers, and we're not sure about the kid's abilities. Bottom line is this. They all appear to be after a supposed substantial cache of money, believed to be hidden in or around Dodsonville. That boils down to one thing—trouble." Jon paused, waiting for a response from Gabe.

Well, thet puts ta bed one a mah questions. When A.J. did leave raht quick, he were, fer shore, wi' these two fellas. Also tells me he were, fer shore, part a some undercover group 'n' these boys er shore 'nuff a part a her. "So far, thet ain't but a tech more 'n ah already knew. Mah concerns er simple. Ah ain't got a problem puttin' a bullet en someun, but ah shore as hell have a problem wi' mah town turnin' inta a shootin' war. Now ah'm shore ah cain't run ya outa town 'cause ah know y'all er federal, at some level. Ah got mah radar out, 'n' as ya kin see—she works. Thet won't stop what's a comin', jest give us a warnin'. If'n ya got eny good ideas, ah'll listen to 'em. Ah'll tell y'all this straight up. If'n ah cain't git a hold on whut yer plannin', she'll be mah way 'n' only mah way."

Jon sighed. *He's pissed off because he's temporarily disabled and, more so, because he's faced with something that never should happen in a place like this. Even though he's dead, I'm still not rid of El Tigre. He's the reason for all of this. He's still haunting me. Time to nail things down, and, at the same time, protect our identities.* "Sheriff, we have a theory and, unfortunately, it's all we have at this time."

He held up his hand to stop Gabe from responding. "Let me explain. We believe that kid is also on a hunt for this supposed money. How he got the idea or from who is anybody's guess. However, it appears that somehow he got off the ship the authorities put him on. At that point, he may have fallen in with the other three. His English, as I recall, was very limited, and they may have afforded him a temporary refuge. During that period, possibly out of gratitude, he may have told them or let slip the story about this money. However it happened, he left them and started to return here. The other three, sensing a huge dollar cache, are also on the way. They're doing it the brutal way and have left several bodies in their wake. Our objective is to take them out quickly and to leave you and your town whole and at peace. As to the money, all of the stories have enough solid evidence to indicate that it very well does exist, and possibly somewhere around where A.J. lived."

Gabe was silent for a while, digesting what Jon had just divulged.

Anne was looking at Gary, and the look on her face read "What the hell did we get into?"

Finally, Gabe replied. "Thet's th' basics, 'n' she ain't good. D' ya have a thought er a plan?"

"As a matter of fact yes…of sorts. The main way into your town is by way of Sheridan. If you have someone that you could post at that Red Apple Rest, who could just sit on the porch and could call you, quietly, if the three-man group showed up, we could stop them from even getting to town. If he had to be there more than one day, we'd pay for a room and any meals. The kid will be easy, no matter where he shows up."

Gabe suddenly felt a slight inner sense of relief. "Whut yer sayin' makes good sense. Fact be, th' manager er a tight friend a mine. We served en th' army t'gether. He'd be perfect 'n' wud call me en a heartbeat. Thet'd give us some mileage ta stop those crazies afore they git ta mah town."

"Then I say that before we do anything else, you make that call, but don't get too detailed. Keep it simple. That helps keep the average person focused."

Without a word more, Gabe rose and walked to his desk. He made the call, explained what he wanted, and other than a few simple words said nothing else. When he hung up the phone, he turned to the other four and made a simple statement. "She's done. Reynold said he'd take keer a her 'n' call right quick if'n eny Hispanics come en, er if'n he spots 'em a drivin' by."

Carlos broke his silence "Thank you, Sheriff. That should be a big help."

Jon moved quickly on. "Other than the main road through town, are there any other roads coming from Sheridan that bypass the town and come in at the west end?"

Gabe responded easily. "Been here all a mah life 'n' fer

shore they ain't a one. Less'n ya consider a deer trail. Nope, she's all heavy wooded 'n' stone outcroppings. Onliest folk go there er local hunters er them whut's gatherin' berries 'n' mushrooms."

"Good. That makes controlling the situation one hell-of-a-lot easier. Our next problem is the fact that they may try to come through town at night. At least the kid might, since he's been here before, and might be smart enough to have a fear of being recognized. With the other three—anything's possible. We also don't know one other important fact. We know they're armed. We just don't know how well or with what."

Jon's last statement created a period of uncomfortable silence. After almost three minutes, Gabe broke the quiet. "Got a man en town whut don' sleep much. Fact er, thet Anne 'n' Gary here he'p'd him when thet tree fell en me. Name's Amos. Ah pointed him out over ta Ethyl's. Strong, honest, 'n' God fearin', but he'd go ag'in' th' devil hisself ta pertect th' folk here. 'Nother thing—he er a damn good shot wi' thet muzzle-loader a his'n."

Carlos was incredulous. "Did you say a muzzle-loader? I didn't think, other than reinactments, that anyone used them anymore. Although they do have special muzzle-loader hunting seasons in some states."

"Yep! Thet's his one rifle 'n' ya don' want ta bet ag'in' him when she comes ta usin' 'er. Amos'll set his truck ta th' east end a town, 'bout half-mile out. Ah'll give him one a them pocket phones fum mah desk drawer, 'n' thet'll cover thet."

Jon was, minute by minute, gaining a lot of respect for this mountain-town sheriff. *With what he's got to work with, this man's a damn good tactician. Could have used a man like him back in ops.* "Perfect. Carlos and I will split the night into four-hour shifts. We'll need the number of the phone Amos will have. We've got yours, same as your office number."

Finally, Anne spoke up. "What do you want us to do, or where do you want us to be?"

Jon was ready for her and had anticipated that question. "I want the two of you to check into the Red Apple Rest and follow the same schedule as Carlos and me. Find an inconspicu-ous position outside and just keep your eyes peeled. That will give the sheriff's man extra eyes and cover the back door once they're in. You have my number, and I believe that you have the sheriff's." Jon turned to the sheriff. "Gabe, I think, unless you've got something else or better, that's all we can do until they show."

"Ah b'lieve thet's got 'er. 'Bout time ya got familiar. Ah reckin if'n we're a goin' ta sleep t'gether, we might's well be usin' first names, Don." Jon and Carlos both had to grin at the sheriff's last comment. Gabe had picked up on Jon's use of his first name. "Ah see ya said 'until they show.' Yer 'spectin thet ta happen?"

"Gabe, these men are greedy, desperate, and killers. That tends to drive their kind of criminal to do things you or I would never consider. So unless we get lucky or they make a major error, yes, I expect them to be encountered near or in your town."

"Ah shore as hell hope thet ain't a gonna happen."

"We're with you, Gabe. For now, Santos and I are just go-ing to drive around a bit to get a better fix on our surround-ings. After that, we plan to try that restaurant east of town called Bones. From there we'll head back to town and start our surveillance procedure. I'd ask you to join us for dinner, Gabe, but I have a strong feeling that you want to be right here. If I'm wrong, say so."

"Yer raht as rain, but ah 'preciate th' offer."

"Then we'll catch up with you later. Gary, Anne—if you want to come along that's fine, but I'd prefer that you stay in town right now. Extra manpower, if needed."

"Thanks, Don, but you're probably right. Gary and I will hang around town and grab dinner at Ethyl's. We've gotten quite fond of their good home cooking."

"Okay. All of you have our phone numbers if needed. Let's go, Santos."

That now-very-evident hinge squeaked as they opened the door. That squeak, now brought a smile to Carlos's face. The two men turned left to walk the thirty feet to Carlos's pick-up.

Once in the cab, Carlos turned to his friend. "Jon, something's wrong. You're acting differently. What's up?"

Jon didn't respond immediately, and, when he did, the response caught Carlos off guard. "Carlos, this isn't like any thing we've done in the past. We're on US soil, in a small and peaceful village in the mountains of West Virginia. The people here have never experienced the kind of hell that just might let lose, and we have to do our damnedest to protect the population, take out the crazies, and get the results out of town without raising too many suspicions. If we have to shoot, every shot has to count. Gary and Anne have range experience, yes, but I seriously doubt they've ever had to kill a person. That tells me that, in a tight spot, they can't be counted on for sure. The sheriff's good—actually, very good—and if he vouches for that man Amos, I have to believe that he's dependable.

As Jon layed out his thoughts, Carlos's face went from questioning to visibly concerned. "*Madre de Dios*, I see why you've been trying to get such a tight lock on this. We can't call on the commander because all things point to the fact that zero hour is close at hand."

ⲉⲟⲉⲟ

Gary and Anne left the sheriff's office right behind Jon and Carlos. As the door closed behind them, Gabe was deep in thought. *Thet Don, 'n' Santos also, er a whole lot more 'n they let on ta. Don looks at this en a way whut smells lahk whut ah'v heerd 'bout special forces er SEALs er sumpin more hidden. Thet musta been whut A.J. were en ta. Ah reckin thet's good. Maybe they'll keep this problem well hid 'n' low key. Wunda if'n ah'll ever git th' truth? Gary 'n' Anne, far's ah kin see, er jest whut they say.*

CHAPTER 57

Bad Timing

Carlos backed his pick-up into a parking place on the west side of Bones's parking lot, two spaces in from the front corner. "Let's hope the food is good."

Jon's mind was wrapped up with the tactical problems this unwanted mess involved. Food was not an item of importance. "As long as it's edible, I'll be satisfied."

The interior of the restaurant was barn-like, and the décor was simple. The aroma of barbeque was intoxicating. The sign at the entrance stated *seat yourself,* so they found a corner table, and in almost no time a waitress was approaching.

⋍⋍⋍

At almost the same time a two-tone green Oldsmobile passed the Bones restaurant, headed for the gas station at the west end of Dodsonville. Jorge was driving with Pepe in the front seat. Cholo was in the rear, quietly loading two ten-round mags with special 3.57AP ammunition designed to penetrate bullet-proof vests or light armor.

He snapped one mag into the Sig Sauer P-224, chambered a round, and pushed the pistol into his back pocket. The other mag went into a front pants pocket. *Being ready for anything is what keeps me alive.*

⋍⋍⋍

The two-tone Olds drove slowly by Ethyl's. Inside, Amos was getting an early supper and preparing for a night of watching. His five-ton truck was parked out front. Anne and Gary were at a nearby table, planning to eat then drive out to the Red Apple, rent a room, and begin their watch. Sally was rushing about taking care of the dinner customers. The three old men, the stone trio, that regularly occupied the bench out front had long since departed for their respective homes. Gabe was at his desk, mentally reviewing the plans they had made. The timing couldn't have been worse for the sheriff and Jon. Their in-town "radar" was completely down.

Gary was pensive for a few moments. Finally, he opened up to Anne. "I think Don's got this pretty well covered. That's a good thing. I really don't feel quite up to a running street fight. Never been in one and don't want to start now."

"You've got that right, and I agree with you one-hundred percent. As far as I'm concerned that shit needs to stay in the mid-east and Africa. I hope to never be a part of it. Frankly, the idea of that kind of scenario scares the hell out of me." She was silent for another minute then took a deep breath and broached the subject that had been eating at her for the last couple of days. "Do you remember the day we helped rescue the sheriff?" A positive nod from Gary and she continued. "I'm sure that you remember that, after it was all over, we both had a couple of hits of that powerful moonshine." Anne paused, collecting her thoughts and carefully organizing her words.

"Yes, I do. How could I forget?" There was a hint of discomfort in his reply. *Shit! I was hoping that this was history, but I'm reasonably sure that this conversation is going where I had hoped it never would.*

"Bottom line is this. We had sex that night. I don't remember it, and I don't know whether or not you remember it, but I had the proof in the morning. I just have one question and no matter what your answer is, I'll never talk about this again.

"Okay, agreed. What is it?"

"Do you have anything contagious I should know about?"

"Not a thing. I'm clean, and, no, I don't remember."

"Good and good. Just so you know, I'm on the pill, so there's nothing to worry about. Now let's forget that ever happened."

They finished eating in silence, each alone with his thoughts. Gary ordered a piece of coconut cream pie, and Anne requested the peach cobbler. These too were consumed in silence. When they had finished, Gary put a twenty with the check and broke the silence. "Guess we'd better get on up to the Red Apple Rest and get that room. I'll take the first watch, if you want."

"Fine with me."

જળજ

Carlos and Jon, seated inside the windowless barbeque restaurant, also missed the Olds when it drove by, headed for Dodsonville. Their initial warning system had been totally compromised by unanticipated bad timing.

Carlos stopped eating. "Jon, I think we're in a pretty good field location, at this restaurant. As long as everyone is in touch, why don't we just relax here until we get a call?

"That's as good an idea as any, amigo. We're off the street and out of sight. Let's try it for a while or until there's a sighting."

CHAPTER 58

Hunting

A small flat-bed truck, loaded with square hay bales, was parked at the gas pumps when the Oldsmobile drove slowly up.

Cholo cautioned Jorge. "Park off to the side, away from the windows and leave the motor running."

"I know what to do and don't need instructions from you."

Cholo let the affront go as if unnoticed and slid down low in the back seat. The sun had just slipped behind the western peaks, and full darkness was less than an hour away.

Jorge pulled off to the side, near the air hose, and put the car in park. "If I don't come out soon—maybe five minutes at most—I may need help."

He got out of the car and started for the small shop and sales office. Pepe was forced to remain in the car with the man he was in mortal fear of.

Jorge walked in and approached the man behind the service counter. "Excuse me, sir. I just arrived in town and am looking for a friend who lives here. I don't remember his name but we were in the service together, and he told me to stop by if I ever came to his town. He was about my age. Would you know who that might be or where he lives?"

The station owner had left just before Jorge drove in. It was his daughter's birthday. The clerk on duty looked the man over, judging his age and considering his request. "Ya say ya served wi' him, but ya ain't got his name?"

"We were in different units but had a few beers together. Seemed like a real nice guy. I'd like to get to know him better." A long period of silence had Jorge getting nervous. "If you can't help me, I'll leave and ask around in town."

"Matter a fact, ah mebbe kin he'p, but 'twon't do ya nary good. Onliest fella thet were en th' service recent were Albert Johnson, A.J. He got kilt jest a short piece ago. Turrible shame—real good boy. His folks got took jest a short piece afore him. 'Nother shame."

"That's a pity. I had hoped to get together with him. Where did you say he lived?"

"Didn't say. When ya leave th' lot, go ta th' raht. Go raht, ag'in at the fust road. Go up her a bit till she forks. Take th' left fork 'n' thet'll take ya direct ta th' Johnson parcel. Ain't much point, though. Th' house got burnt ta th' ground. Thet's whut took A.J.'s folks. Not much ta look at er see now."

"Thank you. Maybe I'll take a ride out in the morning. Just out of curiousity."

"If'n yer wantin' ta pay yer respects, th' whole family's buried en th' new graveyard. Eny one kin d'rect ya."

"Thank you." Jorge turned and left, walked rapidly back to the car, and got back in the driver's seat.

Cholo used a low key approach when Jorge returned. "Did you have any luck?"

Jorge saw a chance to push his leadership and took it. "Of course, I did. You need to listen to what I say. I'm still in charge."

In a flash, Cholo's hand went to the hilt of his knife then came away almost as quickly as he swallowed his fury. *I still may need these mules. Better wait until I'm sure.*

Jorge put the car in gear. "We need to get back to that motel. We can sleep in the car. It'll be dark soon, and no one will notice us if we're at the back of the parking area."

✑✑✑

It's almost dark now. No one will notice me. Pablo climbed onto his bike and started to pedal toward Dodsonville. *I know my money will be in that shed. I'll beat Cholo to it, get it, and soon be on my way back home.* Just the thought of this accomplishment had him smiling broadly as he pedaled. Headlights signaled an oncoming car. *I'll get off the road till it passes.*

∾∾∾

Amos had just backed his truck off the main road into a break in a mixed cluster of ash and oak trees, with a surrounding mix of assorted scrub bushes. He was about one-quarter mile east of the leading edge of Dodsonville. *This'll be perfik cover fer m' truck.* He reached into a box behind the passenger seat and pulled out a pair of night vision glasses. *Figger'd ah'd be a usin' 'er fer jest deer 'n' 'coons, never figgered 'pon men.* He got comfortable and started his surveillance of the main road into town. Within ten minutes, Amos picked up the sound of a truck engine. He waited and watched. *Jest th' propane truck a comin' ta make' th' weekly d'livery.* Within a minute of the truck's passing, another movement on the road caught his eye. He grabbed the night vision glasses and scanned the area of movement. *There 'tis. Fella on a bike. Don' look f'miliar 'n' cain't be shore if'n he's Mex. Best let Gabe know. Cain't be too shore.* He reached for the cell phone he had been given. *Damn! Cain't 'member whut buttons ta mash. She's on but whut button er Gabe's?* After a moment's thought, he chose. *Ah b'lieve she be this un.* He pressed number two and waited while the phone rang. The cyclist had disappeared up the road.

Sally handed the grill man the order she had just taken then reached over to answer the phone. "Ethyl's, Sally here. Kin ah he'p ya?"

"Amos here. Damn, thought ah were gittin Gabe. Kin ya scoot acrost th' way 'n' tell Gabe ah b'lieve one a th' boys he's a lookin' fer er comin' enta town 'pon a bicycle. Be quick, ah'm a comin' fum b'hind." He started his engine, pulled out from his cover, and started a slow drive toward town.

Sally dropped the phone and turned to the grill man. "Be jest a shake er two. Cover fer me. Got ta see Gabe. She er real 'portant." She headed quickly for the door, not even waiting to take the few seconds to remove her apron.

Sally's rush to get to Gabe had her running, and her path was about to put her right in front of Pablo's bicycle. The suddenness of her appearance caught him off guard, and he couldn't react in time. The collision threw Pablo off his bike and knocked Sally down, both of them having cried out in surprise and pain.

Gabe heard the commotion, came to his feet, and went quickly out to investigate the cause. Sally had gotten to her feet and so had Pablo. Close up, even in the dark, Sally recognized the person who had run into her. "Say, ain't ya th' fella whut come enta Ethyl's couple a times, few weeks back?" Her heart was pounding. *Gabe's lookin' fer this fella. How kin ah git a holt a him?*

Their yells had solved that problem. Gabe came walking slowly toward them. "Ya got a problem, Sally?" He turned to address Pablo. "Kin ah see sum identification, son?"

Pablo panicked. He didn't fully understand what the sheriff had asked, but he did see the uniform and badge. His dream was about to explode, and desperation without thought took over. Some of the dinner customers had come out of Ethyl's to see what was happening.

Gabe didn't need an audience. "Y'all go on back inside. Ah got things under control."

The onlookers returned to Ethyl's and their dinners.

Aayyy! Este no es bueno. Pablo saw only one way out. He grabbed Sally and pulled the gun from his belt. He faced Gabe and screamed. "You go. Let me go. All be okay." He was holding Sally between himself and the sheriff, as a shield.

"Ah cain't do thet, son. Turn her loose 'n' it'll be a lot easier fer ya."

Amos had just arrived in town and saw what was happening. He brought his truck to a stop in the middle of the road and climbed out, rifle in hand. He started to walk slowly and steadily toward the hostage situation. He had gotten to within fifty feet of Pablo and stopped. *Ah'll see whar Gabe takes er.*

Gabe was running short of patience but also realized that the person holding Sally might not understand his commands. Slowly he drew his gun.

Pablo saw the gun and fear took over. He grabbed Sally's hair and held her at arm's length. He pointed his gun at her head. "You go, now. Go or I shoot. Now! Go!"

Gabe tried one last attempt. "Son, put yer gun on th' ground." He leaned over to show what he meant, easing his gun toward the street's surface, but not releasing his hold on the weapon.

Pablo thought he had taken control of the situation. "Good. You go now."

Gabe slowly stood erect, the gun still in his hand. *Thet boy got 'er wrong 'n' he's actin' crazy. Ain't but one way this'll end.* Gabe raised his gun and took a bead on Pablo, still holding Sally by the hair and at arm's length. "Son ah've run outa patience. Drop th' damn gun, 'n' turn her loose."

No reaction indicating compliance was evident.

"Ah'm gonna give ya one last chance. Put yer gun down."

Amos also saw where this was headed. *Sally's 'tween Gabe 'n' thet fella. Thet leaves me ta do er.* The muzzle-loader came slowly and steadily up as Amos took a stance. He brought his gun to bear, his thumb slid over the musket's hammer spur, and pulled it back. The feel of the snap as the hammer locked into firing position told Amos all he needed to know. *Ain't no way ah'm a gonna let thet boy hurt Sally.* He leveled the rifle and sighted in on the left center of Pablo's back. Amos held position and waited a moment to see if the situation would wind down peacefully.

Gabe was trying for the same result. He tried to speak as plainly and simply as possible. "Son, shoot her 'n' ah shoot you—understand? Let her go, 'n' we kin end this wi' no one hurt."

Pablo was now mentally over the edge. Reasoning and control were beyond him. *I have to get my money. I have to get my money.* That was all that kept playing on his mind. He snapped and brought the gun to bear on Sally's head. "You go now.

You no go, I shoot lady then shoot you. Go! Go now."

Gabe could tell by the hysterical nature of Pablo's last statement that he was out of choices. Sally was almost directly in his line-of-fire and was being dragged around by her hair. The constant movement made a clear shot questionable. He held his gun at his side to stall Pablo, while he waited for the perfect moment to shoot.

Amos, too, saw that the negotiations had ended, and that left them with only one way out. His target stood still for just a couple of seconds and that was all it took. The booming report of his fifty caliber muzzle-loader froze the moment. Pablo pitched forward, his feet almost leaving the ground, when the fifty-caliber round-ball struck him in the back, shattered one rib, fractured another, then destroyed his beating heart. The now distorted ball came to a stop when it impacted the inner side of his sternum. Pablo was dead before he hit the ground, the echo of the shot still audible.

As soon as Amos had fired, habit took over. He pulled out powder, a patch, and another ball; pulled the ramrod; and, in just under ten seconds, was reloaded and primed.

Sally had rushed to Gabe, fighting back tears of relief. Amos came walking slowly over, his rifle cradled across his left arm. He stopped and glanced at the body on the street for a brief second then walked over to Gabe. "Weren't nuthin' left fer a fella t' do. Th' boy were out a control, 'n' Sally were en sore danger."

"Ya done raht, Amos. Ah were a seekin' a shot m'self. Thank ya." Gabe picked up the Taurus semi-automatic and moved to engage the safety. *Son-uv-a-bitch, th' safety were never took off. Th' boy were ignorant a how ta use er th' raht way, er jest mebbe he were a bluffin. Either way, might jest a saved Sally. Don' matter now, 'n' no one needs ta know.* He stuck the gun in his belt. "Sally, ah got but one good hand. Ah need ya ta call Orly 'n' then hand me th' phone."

The need to make that call for Gabe brought Sally swiftly back to reality. She dialed quickly and, as the phone started to ring, handed it back to Gabe.

"Thanks, girl. If'n yer up ta 'er, ya best git back ta work 'n' if'n ya git any questions, use yer best thoughts. No one's ta know 'bout this."

"Work'd be best raht now. Thank ya, Gabe 'n' Amos, too, fer shore." She did a quick straightening of her hair, turned, and started for Ethyl's.

Gabe had requested Orly to come quickly to their location with his vehicle. When he arrived, he was given explicit instructions. "Orly, ah need ya ta git this boy out a here, raht quick. Jest put him en a cooler er all, fer now. Ah'll git up wi' ya come morning' wi all a th' details. This un needs ta be kep' quiet."

"Ya, Gabe. Vill do. Amos, vill you giff me a hand?"

The two men quickly rolled Pablo's body into a black body-bag then lifted it into Orly's vehicle. Gabe collected the bicycle, picked up a few scattered grocery items, and pushed it back to his office. Sally took a little abuse about skipping out at the height of dinner and, when asked about the loud bang, had a ready answer. "Th' propane truck went by 'n' back-fahred sumpin awful."

Once in his office, Gabe dialed Jon.

Jon answered on the first ring. "Don here, Gabe. What's up?"

"Thet Hispanic boy whut were en town last time showed up t'night." Gabe proceeded to fill Jon in on the details. This was followed by, "Ya got eny ideas ta change whut we're doin? Seein' as how they's jest three now."

"Gabe, the one thing we know at this point is that they weren't together. The problem is that the other three are the ones we really have to be careful about. They've left a string of murders behind them, and there's no reason to believe that their methods will change. They have to be considered as extremely dangerous. If the kid tried to sneak through town at night, they'll probably try the same approach. By now, if any of them has half a brain, they have to realize that the law must be searching for them, and the less recognition they achieve, the better for them. Check with your friend at the Red Apple, and tell Amos to take his truck and resume the position he had used earlier. Santos and I will both stay on alert, and I'll get in touch with Gary and Anne, to update them."

"Enythin' particular yer wantin' fum me?"

"It's your town, and you know the situation. Do what's best for you and your people. We'll keep in close contact."

"Ah 'preciate thet, Don. Ya kin be shore ah will."

捌

Jorge was feelin good about himself. The motel was just up the road. His idea about how to find the shed, in which the money was thought to be, had worked perfectly. It was time to reassert his leadership. "I've thought about how to go after the money, and the best way would be at night."

Cholo was actually in agreement. "I think that would be best. The fewer people that see us, the fewer witnesses to worry about. Now that you know where this shed is, we should go. Probably should wait until after nine. Towns like this usually shut down after eight. We should be in the clear then."

"That was my thinking, exactly." Jorge was inwardly elated. *This culo de caballo finally knows who's in charge.* "We should try to get a couple hours sleep. We'll do what I said, earlier. I'll pull into that Red Apple lot and drive around to the rear. We can sleep in the car and avoid checking in."

"*Bueno, vamanos.*"

捌

Gary was on the porch at the Red Apple. He was seated in a rocking-chair, positioned back in the shadows, but near the driveway entrance. His mind was ruminating on the dinner time conversation with Anne, but with a typically male attitude. *I had a feeling we got laid. Wish I could remember if it was good or bad or even what her tits looked like or felt like. Guess that'll be one for the personal who knows column.* The sound of a car slowing jogged him back to reality. The vehicle had its left turn signal on. *It's turning in.* He stared hard as the car entered the poorly lighted parking lot. He saw the passenger in the front and got a glimpse of a person in the rear. *That makes a definite three, and the passenger up front is definitely Hispanic. Got to call Don.* He pulled out his cell phone and, at the same time, leaned over the edge of the porch to see just where the car was headed. The car passed under one of the few barely working lights in the parking area. *Oh shit! It's two-tone green.* One ring and Don answered.

"Don I'm pretty sure that our guys just pulled into the Red Apple. Three in a two-tone green, older sedan. Couldn't make out the make or model. Guy in the front passenger seat is definitely Hispanic."

Jon responded quickly. "Where did they go?"

"Just a moment. I'll take a look, and get right back to you."

"Watch your ass—these guys play for keeps. They don't give second chances."

త్రి

At the same time, Cholo cautioned Jorge. "Let me off in that dark area on the right. I saw a guy on the front porch, and he was looking at our car much too long."

Jorge slowed and stopped.

"Find a dark area and wait. Don't turn off the motor until I return and say it's clear." Cholo eased out of the car and pressed the door closed to avoid the noise of a slam. The deadly knife was immediately, actually reflexively, in his hand. He slipped into the shadows alongside of the motel and started to work his way stealthily back toward the front porch.

త్రి

Jon didn't hesitate when he hung up. He dialed quickly. "Gabe, our guys may have been spotted at the Red Apple Rest. Gary's checking—yes, I warned him. Tell your people to keep a sharp eye out. This may be it. I'll let you know."

"Shore 'nuff, Don. Ah'll git er."

Carlos had been listening, intently. "Sounds like we're on, amigo."

"Sounds like. One more call." Jon looked at the saved numbers and pressed the one he sought. "Gary may just be in over his head and doesn't know it."

"Anne here, Don. What's up?"

"Your partner may be in big trouble, and I hope we're not too late. Get outside, but whatever you do stay on the porch and yell loudly for him. Do whatever you have to to get him back inside, and let me know when it's done."

☙❧

"Oh God, no. I'm going." Her phone went dead. Anne rushed out of the front door. She wasn't about to leave the safety of the porch. She yelled as loudly as she could and did her best to sound mad, not stressed. "Gary, are you out here? Get your butt back inside. You promised me a good time when we checked in, and if you don't get back here fast, you'll be playing with yourself for the next month. Come on, dammit. I'm waiting."

Gary couldn't miss Anne's yelling at the top of her lungs. *By what she just said and the volume of her voice, I know something has to be wrong.* He answered with a covered response. "I'm coming, honey. Thought I'd left the car unlocked. No need for you to get upset." He reversed his path and headed for the porch at double-time.

☙❧

Cholo slipped his knife back in his belt. He had been within ten feet of Gary when his target turned and rushed back to the porch. *That nosey bastard just had his ass saved by a pussy. Doesn't sound like he was a threat, after all. Got to get back to the car and those fuckin' idiot mules.* When he arrived back at the car, Jorge and Pepe were standing outside, each of them smoking a cigarette. *I can't believe these assholes.*

"Between the smell of those cigarettes and the glow of the ash, it'll be a miracle if we're not spotted. Put the fuckin' cigarettes out."

Jorge instantly realized that Cholo had a strong point and turned to Pepe. "I forgot we're so close to the motel. Put it out, quickly." He dropped his to the ground and crushed it with his heel. Pepe followed Jorge's lead. Jorge quickly changed the subject. "What happened with the guy you saw watching us?"

Cholo took a soft approach. "Just some nosey guy who had nothing better to do. Wasn't a problem. What time is it?"

Jorge glanced at his watch. "Almost eight."

જીન્જી

Jon's phone rang. "Yes, Gabe."

"Reynold jest called. They's three men en th' lot ahind th' motel, standin' aside a older model sedan. He cain't tell th' make er model er color, but kin tell fer shore she be two-tone."

જીન્જી

Gary climbed the three steps of the porch and found Anne with her hand in her purse. *Got a hand on her weapon. Must be trouble. I knew for sure that she was putting on a ruse when she had yelled for me.* "What the hell's going on?" he whispered.

"Don called. He's pretty sure the guys we're after are on the motel grounds, and you out there alone in the dark."

"Hey, I'm a big boy and can certainly take care of myself."

"Bullshit! These guys are cold-blooded killers, and who knows how many bodies they've left in their wake? We've had training, yes, and been on field assignments before, but neither of us has ever taken a life or had to fight a life-and-death battle for ours."

Gary gave up his bravado. He knew Anne was right. "What do we do now?"

"I need to call Don and let him know we're secure." She made the call. "Yes, he's here with me now...got it. Will do." She shut her phone. "Don says to sit tight and wait to hear back from him. Let's grab two of those rockers. That'll let us keep on eye on that car if it pulls out."

Slightly over an hour later, Gary sighed and whispered. "Anne, I'm getting butt sore. We've been sitting in these wood rockers for better than an hour. I've got to get up and move around, a bit."

"Okay—just stay back from the driveway side. Wait! I just heard a car start. Let's get back against the wall, and duck down low."

CHAPTER 59

Showdown

Jon, we have to keep these killers from entering the town. There's just too much possibility of collateral damage. What if we were to block the road?"

"Exactly what I'm thinking. It's just a two lane road so that truck of Amos's should be enough, but we need another truck. If we have two and time it perfectly, we can box them in so they can't use their car to make a run for it. I'll call Gabe and see if he knows of another truck that we can get our hands on right now."

He punched the number.

Gabe answered before the first ring ended. "Le'me think 'pon thet fer a sec. Folk 'round here mostly have pickups er small flatbeds. Ah'll git back ta yer raht quick." He started to wrack his brain. *Don's got a raht good idea. Ah'm purty shore thet he don' plan fer these boys ta walk outa here, 'n' boxin 'em en seems ta keep this mess outa town. Whar do ah git a truck whuts got some size?* His phone rang. "What ya got, Reynold?"

"Car jest pulled out 'n' best ah kin tell, she's headed fer yer town."

⁓⁓⁓

Jon's phone rang almost simultaneously. "Yes, Gary."

"They just pulled out and turned toward town. As far as I

can recall that's the only possible destination in the direction they went. What should we do?"

☙❧

Gabe was frantically searching, mentally, for a truck. *Two pickups, nose ta nose 'd do er. Damn, cain't do thet. Thet'd put them boys en danger. Got er! If'n th' driver a th' propane truck stayed over, th' truck'll be en thet vacant patch ahind Ethyl's 'n' he allus leaves th' keys under the floor mat.* Gabe started to run, his stride made awkward by the weight and angle of the cast holding his arm and shoulder. *God, ah hope she'll be thar.* He continued his off-balance run and rounded the rear corner of Ethyl's. *Thank th' Lord, she's here. Now fer th' keys.* He stepped on the running board and pulled the truck door open. The action caused him to loose his balance forcing him to step down, or risk falling. He stepped back up and lifted the floor mat. *Keys er here.*

The truck was a "stick-shift," which, in his current state, was not even possible. He placed his phone on the truck floor and punched the number with his good hand.

After an agonizing delay, the phone was answered. "Amos here. Kin ah he'p ya?"

"Amos, Gabe here. How quick kin ya git 'roun' back a Ethyl's? An' ah mean real quick 'n' 'thout yer truck."

There was a brief pause while Amos judged himself and the distance. "Five minute er less. Thet do?"

"Yep. Git a movin."

Gabe sounds a mite stressed. Best move raht quick. Amos placed his musket in the gun rack, jumped out of his truck, and started running toward Ethyl's. He made it in four minutes, panting and sweating. "Whut ya need, Gabe?"

"Ah need ya t' drive this truck 'n' park her acrost th' road by thet spot where she pinches down a mite fum them oak trees. An' ah need ya ta do er raht now. Jest let me git inta th' other seat."

Amos didn't even pause to question Gabe's motive. He climbed into the cab, took the keys from Gabe, and started the engine. He was headed for the road through town in less than two minutes from the time he had first arrived behind the restaurant.

Gabe placed his next call. The phone was answered before the first ring finished. "Don, Gabe here. Th' truck'll have th' road blocked and be en place en less 'n three minutes, jest 'bout a hunnert foot east a Parker's. Road pinches down there due ta oak trees, so they'll be no bypassin' thet point wi' a vehicle."

"Perfect, Gabe. Why don't you hustle up there and join your buddy Amos? We're in our truck, by Bones, waiting for them to drive by. The minute they pass Amos's truck, let him block the back door. We'll be close behind them with no lights on."

"Ah'm en th' propane truck wi' Amos." *Wi a full moon out 'n' nary a cloud, ain't none a us be needin' lights.* "Soon's we git this truck en position, we'll git on up ta Amos's truck."

CHAPTER 60

The Confrontation

Don't try and speed, Jorge. From what I've seen, the people here drive like they've got nowhere to go, and don't care about tomorrow. If you speed or even drive at a normal rate, we'll be noticed by someone."

"I know what I'm doing. Don't you think I've seen the way they drive? Pepe, are you awake? You're awfully quiet."

"I feel like I'm not trusted. You have a gun in your belt, Cholo has his knife and maybe a gun, but I have nothing. Why is that?"

"We should have no need for guns in this simple town. After we get the money and get out of this area, I'll personally buy you whatever kind of gun you want. Fair enough?"

"Well…okay" *Jorge needs to know that I want a gun so I can shoot this Cholo who thinks he's so smart.*

Cholo said nothing. He smiled broadly at the comforting thought: *Only one gun between them.* "We're almost to the town. Are you sure you remember, which road to take?"

"There aren't enough roads here to make a mistake. Of course, I remember."

⁊

Jon placed a call to Gabe. "We're on the move and about two-hundred yards behind them. When Amos pulls his truck across the road, I want both of you to get behind his truck, east side, and use it as a shield. Santos and I will move on them. Just stay alert."

"Glad ta oblige, Don. Thank ya fer takin th' lead on this un." Gabe quickly gave Amos the instructions.

"Glad fer thet, Gabe. Fer shore ah had hoped mah killin' days were ahind me efter th' military. Didn't much lahk er then, 'n' fer shore, ah don' lahk er now. Ah'll stay sharp, though, till this here mess er done."

"Thanks, Amos. Ah knew ah cud fer shore 'pend 'pon ya. Git ready. Ah hear a car engine. No lights, yet.

ഗഗ

Gary strained to see what was ahead. "Anne, from what he said, we should be driving behind Don and Santos. Don said no lights, so that makes it hard to see if he's ahead. It's clear tonight and the moon's full. That should be a definite help in spotting them."

Anne reached into the glove box and brought out a pair of night-vision binoculars.

She started to scan the road ahead.

"Got 'em. They're about two-hundred yards ahead. We're just where Don wanted us to be. Maintain the same speed, Gary. We shouldn't be far from the trap location," she said as she pulled the Glock nine millimeter from her bag and snapped off the safety.

ഗഗ

Gabe had a last minute thought. "Amos, Ah b'lieve we'd be best ta git out now. Ah cain't move thet quick wi' this cast, 'n' ah don' know fer shore whuts a goin' ta happen."

Amos just gave an affirmative nod, and Gabe climbed slowly out then started to run toward where Amos's truck was hidden. Amos, in less than a few seconds, was right behind him.

ഗഗ

"Only a minute or two left, Carlos," Jon said. "Use line-of-fire procedure."

"Got it, amigo."

ଏ৩ଏ৩

"Son-of-a-bitch! Cholo, there's a truck across the road. It's one of those propane delivery trucks." Jorge's leadership instantly evaporated. "What the hell are we going to do now?"

"Get the fuck outa here. This may be a trap."

Jorge slammed on the brakes and executed a quick U-turn. He barely drove fifty feet and was faced with another truck blocking their escape.

ଏ৩ଏ৩

Almost as soon as they had gone by, Amos had driven his truck into place, and Carlos had, within seconds, blocked the remaining small space with his pickup. Amos had joined Gabe behind the east side of his truck. Jon and Carlos, pistols in hand, advanced slowly on the now-stopped Olds.

ଏ৩ଏ৩

Pepe was now completely out of control. "Oh shit, oh shit. Jorge, what should we do? What should we do?"

ଏ৩ଏ৩

Jon had begun to circle the Olds, to come at it from behind. Carlos kept a bead on the car and its occupants. Gabe and Amos, although shielded, also had their weapons trained on the car.

Jon offered the ultimatum. "We have you surrounded. We're federal agents. Get out of the vehicle, hands first, no weapons. *Now*!"

There was no movement, and Jon played the last card in the deck. "Exit your vehicle now, or we will open fire. I will count to five before we fire. One…two…three…four…"

Pepe was over the edge with fear, had pissed in his pants, and was near hysterics. "We're coming out. Don't shoot us," he screamed. He opened the passenger side door, climbed out, and cowered against the car.

Cholo's mind saw only the need to escape. *If I can make it to the trees, I can get out of here.*

Jorge realized that it was either comply or die. Then he became aware that they were within ten feet of the trees and, he too, started thinking escape. He climbed slowly out of the car, his hand on the gun in his belt.

Jon saw the gun hand. "Drop the gun, step away from it, and get on your knees."

Jorge started for the trees, pulled the gun, and got off one wild shot before Jon shot him in the head.

Pepe dove on the gun that had dropped from his dead partner's hand, grabbed it, and started to rise. Carlos shot him through the neck, a spray of crimson the result of a shattered carotid artery. His shot passed completely through to be lost in the trees.

When the shooting started, Cholo slipped from the back seat of the car, crouched low, and, with the 3.57 in hand, started a short sprint for the trees.

Jon turned quickly and fired once, hitting Cholo in the shoulder. Cholo spun and stumbled under the impact, turned back, and fired once. Jon dropped to the ground and rolled to get out of the line of fire. He was in a prone position, drawing a bead on Cholo, who had recovered enough to continue stumbling backward toward the trees. Jon was about to fire, unaware that Gabe had stepped out from his cover behind the truck. Gabe placed his arm across the truck's fender to steady his aim and fired once. His shot hit Cholo in the right side, just below the armpit. Cholo started to go down. As he fell, he managed to reflexively fire three wild shots before he succumbed.

The first shot shattered the propane truck's side door window. The second whined loudly as it ricocheted off the truck's fender, into the night. The third of those armor piercing rounds blew through the metal shell of the propane tank. The escaping stream of pressurized propane gas was instantly ignited by a combination of the heat of that round and the spark it created as it pierced the metal. In a second, there was an eight-foot jet of fire spewing from the pierced side of the tank. Jon jumped to his feet, started to run, and barely had a chance to yell "Get down," when the truck exploded. The explosive force blew him more than twenty feet through the air.

Carlos, somewhat stunned, opened his eyes and found himself partially under the front fender of Amos's truck. He pulled himself out and got groggily to his feet. *Don't think I'm hurt. Where's Jon? There he is.* He stumbled to his inert partner and dropped to his knees beside him. "Jon, Jon—talk to me, come on, talk to me." *There are no visible wounds. The blast must have knocked him out.* Training and experience took over. He pointed toward the bodies sprawled on the road. "Sheriff, check those three and give me a status."

Gabe walked quickly to each of the three inert figures, his pistol on each as he went, and did a quick check for any signs of life. He turned to Carlos. "They're dead. How's Don?"

"Alive—no visible wounds, but unconscious." *I need to make the call.* He reached into Jon's pocket and retrieved his phone. *The commander will respond quickest to Jon's number.* He dialed. The call was answered in one ring.

"Yes, Jon. Good news, I hope."

"Not Jon, Commander. It's Carlos. We have four Hispanics—all confirmed dead. No other activity. Jon appears to have been knocked out when a propane truck exploded. Will explain all in debriefing. We need a clean-up chopper and a medevac chopper, pronto. East end of the town, main road. From the air, they'll spot an old army five-ton truck. Also need a pick-up team for the Olds. It'll be at the Red Apple Rest, back lot, east of Dodsonville."

"Got it. They're dispatched." The phone went dead.

Carlos bent back over Jon. *Still out. That's not good.* "Gabe, call your coroner and have him bring that kid's body to this location. He has less than twenty minutes to get him here." He walked back toward where Jon had been when the truck blew. He was scanning the ground for Jon's pistol. *There it is.*

He bent and retrieved the weapon, unscrewed the silencer, and stuck the pistol in his belt. The silencer went in his pocket. He returned to Jon, reached into his jacket, and removed the three back-up mags. Those went into Carlos's pockets.

The propane truck was, by now, a smoldering heap of twisted metal.

Gary and Anne had just arrived when the shooting started. They had no time to engage and were, luckily, still behind Amos's truck when the propane truck exploded. They came walking slowly up to Carlos.

"Is Don okay?" Gary asked, sheepishly.

"He's alive, but that's all I know." Carlos changed the subject. "Do you two owe anyone in town money?

"I think only the Red Apple—we had checked out of Parker's."

"One of you get in your car, the other will drive the Olds. Stop at the Red Apple, park the Olds in the back, put the keys under the floor mat, and lock the car. Pay your bill then get out of there. Drive directly back to your office. Talk to no one about this. Wear nitrile gloves before getting into the Olds, so you don't leave your prints." Carlos saw the hesitation in their eyes. He had to get the scene cleared. "I'll have Amos back his truck so you can get the Olds by. Let's go—Now and I do mean now. Get moving."

Reality slammed home. "We're going."

Anne got back in their car, made a U-turn, and drove away. Gary, as soon as Amos had moved his truck, was close behind, driving the Olds.

"Sheriff, you need to keep any people from town at a real good distance until we get this site cleared and neutralized. The explosion couldn't have been missed, so use this story. Someone tried to steal the propane truck, and it blew up on the way out of town. There's no sign of the thief. He must have run off when the truck caught fire."

"Thet should work, Santos—if'n thet be yer true name." It was quite evident to Gabe by now that Jon and Carlos had been in situations like this many times before. "Amos, once they're ready here, ah need fer ya ta haul this mess ta th' side so's traffic kin come 'n' go."

Within fifteen minutes, the distinct sound of helicopters started to resonate in the night air. Gabe moved toward town. There were already about a dozen or more onlookers. "Y'all kin go on home. Had us a bad accident here, but she's under control. Ah'll post a notice 'bout 'er come mornin'."

A voice came out of the crowd. "Gabe, ah thought ah heerd three mebbe four gunshots."

"Silas, 'tweren't no gunshots. Whatever were en thet truck started a poppin', jest afore she blew. Now thet ah think 'pon 'er, she did sound a mite like gunshots. Now, go on home y'all. Ain't nuthin more ta be done here. Got insurance folk 'n' 'vestigators comin' en raht quick by helicopter."

CHAPTER 61

The Aftermath

The two helicopters landed on the road, just east of Amos's truck. The pilots remained with their craft, engines running, and ready to lift off on a moment's notice. A team of medics exited the first chopper and were directed by Gabe, who pointed to Carlos standing beside Jon.

After a brief examination, the lead medic turned to Carlos. "From what we can tell, he appears to have one hell of a concussion. That's amazing. From where you say he was when that tank blew, I'm amazed that he wasn't maimed or killed. Can't determine anything else wrong with the equipment we have. We've got to get him to a medical facility and quickly." He and his partner turned Jon on his side, pushed a stretcher in tight, eased Jon onto it, lifted him, and started for their chopper.

"Where are you taking him? I need to know."

"Our instructions were Walter Reed."

"Good. At least he'll get the best. Let me get the other team going." Carlos turned toward the other team. "Do you need any direction?"

"Looks simple enough. We bagged three, and you have one already bagged. Nothing to do now, but load and go."

"Wait one second." Carlos walked rapidly over to Gabe. "I need the pistol you collected from the first guy—evidence." Gabe relinquished the weapon without question. Carlos returned to the clean-up crew. "Here's the pistol from the guy we bagged. You should have two more from the other three."

The whine of the medical chopper lifting off halted their conversation for a minute.

"Affirmative. We also took a nasty looking knife off one of them. If we can get a little help, we'll get loaded and get out of here. We've already swept for brass. Got nine casings. Sound about right? We also sprayed down the wet spots."

Carlos thought for a moment. "That should be right on the brass." He looked around for help. *Guess I have no other choice.* "Amos, can you give us a hand?"

Amos was more than willing to get these bodies out of his town and return to his uncomplicated life.

Before the second helicopter lifted off, one of the crew handed Carlos two new body bags. "Give these to the local coroner to make up for the one he used." He climbed aboard, the chopper starting to lift before he was seated.

Orly was more than pleased, stating simply. "Der bags are expensive."

Carlos walked over to Gabe, standing with Amos. "Sheriff, I can't thank you enough for all of the assistance you gave Don and me. You're one heck of a lawman, and this town's damn lucky you're here. Amos, thank you too, for all of your help. As a private citizen, you went far above what would be expected. It was truly a pleasure meeting both of you. Unfortunately, the circumstances were not the best. You both understand that none of what happened here is to become public knowledge."

Both men nodded in agreement.

"I have to leave now. Sheriff, you probably won't get any calls about this, and it won't make the papers. Basically, this never happened."

"Santos, er who ever ya be. You 'n' Don did one hell-of-a-job en pertectin' mah town, 'n' mah people. Ah speak fer all a us when ah say thank ya. Ya kin pass thet ta Don, soon's he er better. Ah don' know fer shore who y'all work fer er whut y'all do 'n' ta be honest wi' ya, ah don' reckin ah want ta know. This ain't pers'nal, but ah hope ta never see either a y'all ag'in. But, if'n by slim chance y'all do happen ta git by this way agin, ah'd lahk ta buy ya a meal 'n' have a good drink wi' ya."

"Thank you, Gabe. That would be nice." Carlos shook hands with both men. "I've got to go now and find out about Don's condition. Hope your arm and shoulder heal okay."

Carlos turned and walked quickly back to his pick-up, started the engine, and drove east up the road. Amos had his truck hooked to the tanker and was hauling the decimated vehicle off the road before Carlos had disappeared from view.

Gabe stood in silence for a long while, his mind churning. *Them boys er fer shore perfeshnal, 'n' fum th' way this all got cleared up 'n' took away, she's jest like she were but a bad dream. Prob'ly means ah ain't never a goin' ta git th' truth 'bout A.J., nor these boys neither. Guess she's better thet a way, takes a weight off'n me fer shore.* Gabe started a slow, pensive walk back to his office. *Shore never figgered thet truck ta blow. Damn shame, fer shore. Thet Don, er who ever, be a hell-uv-a man 'n' special trained, fer shore. Ah hope he comes 'round jest fine. A blind pig cud tell, fer shore, thet him 'n' Santos bin a tight team fer a fair bit. B'lieve ah'll take me a hit off'n thet jug a 'shine ah got tucked away. Then ketch me some sleep. Cum mornin' ah'll burn thet check list ah were a workin' 'pon. Need ta ketch Sally, fust thing, 'n' tell her this ain't ta be spoke a, jest fergot. Reckin ah'll give thet cycle 'n' th' food whut were wi' her ta Emma Perkins 'n' her boy Todd. They're en sore need. Guess ah'll need ta git me a ride over ta th' hospital, next day er so, 'n' keep mah promise ta thet doc.*

❧❧

Less than six hours later, a cargo plane took off on an uncharted flight from a small private airport in Virginia. Lying in the cargo bay on a hydraulically controlled stainless steel platform were four naked bodies, all male, all Hispanic. Each body was in a coarse sisal net bag. Each body had been photographed, fingerprinted, and DNA sampled. The data collected was then placed in a secure "eyes only" file. Attached to each bag was a smaller, but similar, sisal bag. Each of those smaller bags held roughly two-hundred pounds of stone. Once the plane crossed the coastline, it dipped low, flying at under one-hundred feet above the water, to avoid radar detection.

After two hours of flying over open-ocean, the pilot made a simple announcement. "We're good to go."

The cargo door was pulled open, and a sole crewman activated the hydraulics system. The activated system first moved the platform to project the leading edge one foot out beyond the opened cargo door. The in-plane end, with the push of a button, was elevated to a forty-five degree angle, and the mesh bags, with their human contents, slid easily off and out, plummeting to the sea below. All four bags slipped immediately, and without a trace, beneath the surface. The ocean depth in this location was six-thousand, three hundred and twenty feet deep.

The skid retracted, the cargo door was pulled shut, and the pilot banked into a tight one-eighty turn, reversing their course. The plane was headed home, maintaining its low altitude position, still avoiding radar detection. By the time the sisal bags decomposed, the ocean water, crabs, microorganisms, bacteria, and any scavenger fish would have reduced the bodies to nothing but a scattering of bones.

ﻌﻌﻌ

Carlos had to tap the desk bell at Parker's High Mountain Inn three times, and not gently, in order to get a response. It was just after eleven p.m. and the owner wasn't thrilled about being disturbed. "Bad enuff ah bin shook outa bed by sum kind a 'splosion 'n' jest got back ta sleep 'n' here ya go a wakin' me agin. Whut er ya wantin'?"

"I'm sorry for disturbing you. The explosion woke us also, and since we were prepared to leave in the morning, anyway, we decided to check out now." Carlos handed him a Visa card in the name of Santos Morales. It took almost ten minutes for the owner to work out processing the card payment. Carlos signed, took his receipt, and left. The truck bed cover was locked, and Jon's belongings, as well as his, were in it. *As soon as I hit the highway, I'll call the commander and get an update on Jon's condition. Oh shit! I've got to call home and tell Rosita and Sheri. I'd better get the update first. Hopefully, it'll be good.*

Carlos was driving south on I-77. *Now's as good a time as any.* He picked up Jon's phone and pressed the redial button, for the commander. In just two rings the call was answered. "Carlos here, tell me you've got good news, Commander."

For the first time that Carlos could remember the commander was silent. Carlos's gut started to churn with an overpowering, sickening sensation. His throat tightened, and his mouth went dry as he waited for Ertugal to speak.

CHAPTER 62

Answers

Ertugal eased his way into his reply. "Jon's alive and has no evident physical injuries." He paused for a moment. *Never had a problem with bad news before. Must be getting old.*

Carlos wasn't pleased with or mollified by the commander's response, and it did little to ease his tension. He took advantage of the commander's pause. "What exactly does that mean?"

"The doctors say the concussive shock of the explosion induced a temporary coma. They couldn't find any brain damage, so it looks like a couple of days, more or less, and Jon'll be his old self again. If you stop at Reed on your way home, you can run me through what happened, and I can give you the package that I'm holding."

"That'll work. The girls don't know it's over or what happened, so that will give me the opportunity to get first-hand info, fill you in, and see Jon. I should be there in four hours or less. Do you have a room number?"

"Timing's good for me. I don't have a room, yet. The doc's wanted to run a few additional tests. I'll have you cleared at the main desk."

"Thank you, Commander. See you in a short while." *Sounds good, if that's what it is, and all it is.* His right foot pressed the accelerator down, a bit more.

სისი

Three-and-one-half hours of hard driving and Carlos parked his pickup in the main lot at Walter Reed Army Medical Hospital. It was quiet at the front desk when he walked in.

The receptionist looked up. "May I help you, sir?"

"Yes, thank you. Carlos Montoto, here to see Jon Morton. He was admitted this evening."

"May I see some identification, please?"

Carlos offered his driver's license.

"Thank you. He's in room eight-oh-nine. Use elevator bank three, turn left when you exit the elevator."

When Carlos got off the elevator and turned in the direction of Jon's room, he passed a visitor lounge on his right, and a casual glance showed Commander Ertugal seated in one of the chairs. Carlos paused, unsure whether to go to see Jon first or the commander.

At that moment, Ertugal looked up and solved his momentary dilemma. "Carlos, in here."

"Commander, any updates on Jon's condition?"

"Yes, and although it's not bad, it isn't so good either. Take a seat and listen. The specialists have a few more tests to run, but it appears that the explosion caused what they call a psychogenic coma." He held up his hand to head off Carlos's questions. "It's not very common—in fact, rather rare. What it boils down to is that the explosion may have pushed Jon over the edge, and this coma is his mind's way of hiding from past and present stress. The psychiatrists will try several tests to bring him out of it, but if the tests fail, it'll be just a matter of time, and there's no telling how long that may be. Basically, they tell me that if time becomes the issue, it's up to Jon's subconscious as to when he'll snap out of it." Ertugal went silent and waited for Carlos to absorb what he had just told him. He knew, from long first-hand experience, how close these former combatants of his were. He opened the conversation again. "Jon's not due in the room for another fifteen, or twenty minutes. Why don't you fill me in on the operation? I have my tape recorder."

Carlos was straining to remain positive and under control. "The doctors don't know Jon the way I do. He's way stronger than most. Rember how fast he recovered from that last run-in with El Tigre? A day or two, and he'll be back to normal. As to filling you in or debriefing on what went down in West Virginia—now's as good a time as any. The sooner I give it to you, the sooner it's behind me." He proceeded to fill Ertugal in on every move and detail, right up to his drive out of town. "That's got it."

"Great! This should finally put the cap on everything that had to do with the Colombia Op. Damn smart the way you boxed those bastards in." He reached down at his side. "This briefcase covers what Jon and I discussed, prior to the two of you taking on this mess in West Virginia." He pushed the case over to Carlos. "I'll continue to check on Jon, as I'm sure you will." Ertugal stood to leave. "Thanks for a well-run op. I'm sure I'll speak with Jon when he comes around."

Carlos stood, shook hands with the commander, and watched the man as he turned then walked rapidly out of the room.

"Now I've got to see Jon." Carlos picked up the briefcase, left the waiting room, turned right, and started toward room 809. As he approached the room, two orderlies were wheeling a gurney toward the same room. *Jon's just getting here. I'll let them get him organized before I walk in.* He stopped about fifteen feet short of the room door and placed the briefcase on the floor, in close contact with his right leg. *Please Lord, let him come out of this quickly and let him enjoy the kind of life he should have.*

The room door opened and the two orderlies walked out. Just as they left, a dark-skinned man in a well-tailored suit, approached, nodded to the orderlies in a familiar way, and walked in. Carlos's protective concern for his partner took over. *I don't know who he is, but I'm not taking any chances.* He picked up the briefcase, covered the short distance to the room, and hastily entered.

The man in the suit was standing over Jon when Carlos entered and turned to face him. "You must be Mr. Carlos Monto-to. I was told you would more than likely be here." His accent betrayed his Pakistani heritage. "My name is Doctor Sateesh

Patel, and I am just now completing the preliminary diagnostics. I will then implement the course of treatment for your friend."

Carlos approached the bed timidly and took a long look at his closest friend. He hadn't missed the monitoring equipment Jon was hooked up to, nor did the subtly concealed catheter drain go unnoticed. He turned to the doctor, sure that his face was mirroring the strained anxiety he felt. "He looks fine. What's wrong? Why isn't he responding?"

Dr. Patel, senior psychiatric analyst at Walter Reed Hospital, was accustomed to questions of this nature. He gave an underhand wave, indicating two chairs against the far wall. "Please, have a seat, and I will do my best to help you understand your friend's current state."

Carlos walked toward the chairs, his mind in a state of flux. On one hand, he wanted to know everything about Jon's condition. On the other, he was dreading what he might hear. *Don't have much of a choice on this one.*

Dr. Patel pulled the second chair away from the wall and turned it to face Carlos. "If anything I say is incorrect, please advise me. From what I have learned, your friend's military career involved numerous, high-stress situations. When he retired, he took up commercial fishing, in an attempt to clear his mind of the past. He may even have—or have had—PTSD, but we have no record of that. Evidently, things went well for about three years, until an incident from his past suddenly reappeared and thrust him back into a high-stress and life-threatening situation. Am I on target, so far?"

Carlos just gave an affirmative nod.

"He came very close to loosing his life in that situation," the doctor continued. "Shortly thereafter, he was again thrust into a more deadly situation, which he survived. Neither of those two situations was of his direct choosing, and he was no longer part of the military at that time. Now we have the present incident, which he undertook at the request of his former commander who, if you haven't yet figured it out, gave me Mr. Morton's background. Evidently, because of the incident just prior, he, and you as well, were the ones most capable of ending a very bad situation quickly and quietly. As in all of these situations, the unknown or unexpected can be as dangerous as the enemy. The exploding propane truck was just that."

He paused to give Carlos a chance to add to or alter anything he had said. Silence was his cue to continue. "The violent explosion of that truck, in simple terms, caused his mind to scream out 'enough, I've had enough' and threw up a mental blockade, which we refer to as a psychogenic coma. At this point, that is what our tests indicate. We do have a number more to conduct. If our conclusion is found to be accurate, we are faced with trying to locate the window into his mind to convince him that it's safe to return. He may come to that on his own, but if not, we need all of those people closest to Jon to keep talking to him about everything and anything that he can relate to in a positive manner. Absolutely nothing that would be, in any way, problematical or stressful. To accomplish this, I will need you to tell me the names and a little about the people to be involved. I also must advise you that his return could be in a very short period or may stretch out for a prolonged time. This can prove stressful to those involved, as a lack of response can make one feel that they are attempting to communicate with a statue."

Carlos sat silently and unmoving, absorbing the enormity of what the psychiatrist had just presented. His first vocal response was a question. "How long is a 'prolonged time'?"

"A true psychogenic coma is quite rare, and we have little data on which to draw. For the sake of perspective, let us say that a prolonged time would be in excess of two weeks. The one thing which I find to be almost unbelievable is that his close proximity to an explosion of such size and force didn't result in his death. Now, if you would be good enough to allow me some time alone with your friend, I wish to conduct a few more simple diagnostic tests. Perhaps I can direct you to the cafeteria, or you can relax in the lounge."

"Food is the last thing on my mind. I'll be in the lounge. Please come get me when you're through."

"Most definitely so."

Carlos dropped into the first chair in the lounge, carefully tucking the briefcase behind and in contact with, his legs. His mind was swimming. *How is this possible? Jon is so strong. The doctor said he was amazed that Jon wasn't killed by the explosion. I wonder if Hal's prayer was the reason? How am I going to tell Rosita and Sheri? Maybe he'll snap out of it very quickly, and I won't have to tell them.* His mind jumped to tomorrow. *What about the business, the boat, Sven and Bjorn. This was to be a simple op, and it's turned into a nightmare.* Lost in thought, he was unaware of the passage of time.

"Mr. Montoto, excuse me."

"Yes, Doctor." There was a tone of hope in Carlos's response.

"The human mind is a terribly complex thing, and we're just starting to get some decent understanding of how it functions. My simple diagnostics are still pointing us in the same direction. I have scheduled another MRI, and that will take place in about one hour. We will compare the results from the first MRI, when he was admitted, to the one now scheduled, and that should give us a stronger sense of what we're dealing with. You may go home or wait. Either way, I will advise you of our findings. Why don't you give me your cell phone number, and I'll give you my business card? It has all of my contacts on it."

"I'll gladly give you my number and take your card, but, if it's all the same with you, I'll wait for the new results."

"As you wish. Perhaps you should have some food. The cafeteria serves a decent breakfast, and it's almost five a.m. I will meet you here in the lounge after I have the results."

"That sounds like a good idea. Thank you, Doctor."

ﻌﻌﻌ

The cafeteria was well lighted and extremely clean. The food was better than typical hospital quality, and Carlos actually enjoyed his fried eggs and sausage. *Surprisingly, the coffee's quite good, also. Thankfully, it's not as hot as Stavros's. Now to get back to the waiting lounge, and call home. I can't see driving home then turning around to come right back. I'll soften the story, and perhaps Rosita or Sheri will make the drive here.*

Seven-thirty a.m. and Rosita's phone rang. She glanced at the read-out and answered, cheerily. "*Hola*, Carlos."

"*Buenos dias, querida.*"

"Carlos, how are you? What's happening? How's Jon?"

Here goes nothing. "I'm fine, and we've got that mess wrapped up. We ran into a problem at the end, though."

Rosita didn't respond.

"Jon and I were near a propane truck, and this nut managed to set it on fire."

Rosita still said nothing but her heart was pounding.

"Jon was closer to it than I, and the damn thing exploded."

"*Madre de Dios*! How's Jon? Are you okay, for sure?"

"I'm fine, honestly. Jon got knocked out and appears to have a concussion or something. The hospital's running—"

"Hospital? You're in a hospital? Where?"

"Rosita, please, I'm trying to explain, so let me. We're in Walter Reed Army Medical Center, and I wanted to know if the two of you wanted me to pick you up or if you'd want to make the drive here?"

"Of course, we'll come there. What is the address? You're sure you're okay?"

"Yes, I'm sure I'm fine, *por seguro*. The hospital's address is Sixty-Nine Hundred Georgia Avenue NW, Washington, DC and Jon's in room eight-oh-nine."

"*Bueno*, we'll be there in less than five hours."

The phone in his hand went dead.

Carlos sat there for a moment, staring at his now silent phone. *This op wasn't worth the fifteen thousand dollars. Not even one-thousand times that.*

CHAPTER 63

Suspended

Carlos moved from the chair to a nearby couch and stretched out. *Been up for more than twenty-four hours. I need to grab a quick nap.*

"Carlos? Carlos, get up." Rosita's insistent calling, coupled with shaking his shoulder, pulled him from a deep sleep. "We went to the room, and Jon's not there."

"Give me a second to wake up, *por favor.*" *Didn't expect to sleep that long.* "Okay now, here's what's happening. The doctor told me that they were taking Jon for an MRI so they could complete his diagnosis. They'll bring him back to the room after that and give me—us—a full update. Sheri, how are you doing?"

The answer was evident before she spoke. Her eyes were red from crying, her makeup a mess, and her cheeks were tear-streaked. "How do you think? Terrible! Ever since problems from Jon's past started to come back, this has been my worst fear, and now it has happened."

"We don't know that. Jon's strong and should bounce back quickly."

"Carlos, I hope to hell you're right because I can't take any more of these life-threatening surprises. They're tearing me apart."

The sound of the elevator door opening interrupted this uncomfortable conversation and Carlos saw his way out of it. "Let me go see if that's the doctor and Jon. I'll be right back."

He left quickly, not wanting to give his wife or Sheri the option of joining him. *If that's them, I need to have the doctor explain everything as if I know nothing about the situation. Good, the door to Jon's room is open.*

Carlos walked up to the room, knocked softly on the door jamb and whispered. "Doctor, is that you?"

"Yes. Mr. Montoto, come in, please. Sorry for the delay. They needed the equipment for an emergency accident victim."

He sounds upbeat. Hopefully, that means good news. One glance and it was evident that Jon was back in his bed, but with no evident movement. "How'd the MRI go? Before you tell me, my wife and Jon's girlfriend are in the lounge. I didn't tell them the whole story—tried to shield them—hoping for the best. So if you could explain everything to the three of us and pretend you and I never had our earlier conversation, it would sure get me off the hook."

Doctor Patel smiled broadly. "I, too, am married. I know just what you mean, and of course, I will do so. Come, let us join them in the lounge."

They entered the lounge, and Carlos introduced the doctor to the girls. "Rosita, Sheri, I have the doctor, and he will fill us in on everything about Jon's injury. Doctor Sateesh Patel, my wife Rosita and Sheri Kreitzer, Jon's girlfriend."

"It is so very nice to meet you ladies. Now, if we can all be seated, I will do my best to explain exactly what has happened to Mr. Morton."

Half an hour later, and with Sheri and Rosita in tears, and Carlos fighting back tears, but highly distraught, Doctor Patel summarized. "All of out tests, and everything we know presently, points to a psychogenic coma. Basically, this amounts to a person's brain calling a timeout, so-to-say. The brain is saying 'I've had too much and do not want one bit more' and so the conscious level shuts down. We believe that he can still hear you when you talk but will offer no response. The best medicine is for those close to him to constantly interact with him in the most positive manner—talk, joke, even play music that he likes. The objective is to convince his subconscious that it's safe to come out, to wake up. The one thing that I and no one else can do is give you a time frame for his recovery. It could be days, maybe weeks, or possibly more. Sadly, this is the unknown we have to deal with."

The three of them sat in numbed disbelief. Finally, Sheri broke the silence. "Can I see Jon, Doctor?"

"Why yes, of course. Let me take you."

Carlos started to rise but was stopped cold by Rosita. "She needs to be alone with him, right now."

They left the hospital three hours later, mentally drained and numb. Sheri made arrangements to get a hotel room, near-by. Carlos and Rosita would return tomorrow afternoon after Carlos got some sleep and set up some form of work schedule with Sven and Bjorn. They were told that Jon had been in an accident that left him in a temporary coma. The three of them decided they would try to run the boat themselves, for what, all hoped, would be a short period.

∾჻∾

Between the doctors, nurses, physical therapists, and them-selves, everything was tried and everything failed. The only difference between Jon and a corpse was the fact that he was warm and the monitors said alive and stable. A few days be-came a few weeks and then started to become months. Carlos decided that he had to do what would be best for Jon as well as Sheri, Rosita, and himself.

Carlos, after talking it over with Rosita, called the com-mander. "I have a request to make."

"What is it, Carlos? Any change in Jon's condition?"

"No change and frustrating as hell. The doctors and all in attendance say that Jon is completely stable. He doesn't need life support equipment and would just require a trained nurse for the IV and the catheter. He will also need a physical thera-pist. That being said, I would like to have him moved to my house. Our third bedroom is never used and is large enough to accommodate any of his needs. Also, being in a familiar home amongst family might jog him back to us. So—the bottom line is this. Could you make that happen and pick up the expenses as you have been?" *Okay, I said what I had to. Now we'll see.*

Ertugal was quiet for almost a minute before responding. "You may have hit on a plan, Carlos. I'll get on it and make it happen. Will let you know when it goes into action."

The phone went dead.

Gracias a Dios. I will bring my brother home and then bring him back to us.

The transfer from the hospital went smoothly. Carlos and Rosita's guest room was outfitted as well as the finest hospital. The necessary nurses and therapists came on a daily basis. That transfer took place after Jon's third month in a coma.

∽∾∽

Month four and then month five came and went. Early in month four, a change took place. Not with Jon, but with Sheri. Her visits went from daily to four times a week, then to every couple of days. Jon's coma was taking its toll on all of them.

CHAPTER 64

Final Echoes

In Cali, Colombia, Inspector Alejandro Cantrell received a diplomatic envelope routed through secure channels in the American CIA. The contents were minimal but definite. A short message informed him that the Colombian gangster Cholo had been shot dead. There were three pictures of the corpse enclosed, each from a different angle. There was no mistake as to the identity. Cantrell leaned back in his chair, took a deep breath, and exhaled slowly. *I'm not one bit happy that they got to kill that son-of-a-bitch. I so wanted that pleasure for myself—to inflict on him the kind of pain that would make him beg to die. Que lastima. Pues, asi es la vida.*

༺✦༻

Two months had passed since that deadly incident in town. Gabe's activity-inhibiting cast had been removed. He closely followed the regimen of exercises the therapist had taught him and had returned the muscles in his now-healed arm to almost their full strength.

He walked into Ethyl's at six a.m., ready to start a day with a different aspect. "Mornin', Sally. 'Peers we're gonna git us a hot one t'day."

"Mornin', Gabe. Shore looks lahk thet. Coffee 'n' yer usual? Yer a tad earlier than reg'lar. Sumpin special?"

"Yep, ta th' usual. Drivin' out ta the Johnson land, ta meet wi' a man whut kin draw me up a plan fer a house. Figger'd ah'd git out a bit ahead 'n' jest wander about."

"Jest don' be a tanglin' wi' no oak trees." She laughed at her quip.

"Don' ya worry none. Once were more 'n a plenty."

൘

This here's a raht fine location. Ah still cain't b'lieve thet A.J. left her all ta me. Reckin ah'll have me a good look at all whut's en thet shed. Good ah put mah own lock on 'er.

Gabe released the lock, removed the chain and bar, then walked slowly in, and began a casual walk around. *Shore er clean 'n' neat. Ed Johnson 'n' A.J. kep' their tools 'n' sech jest raht.*

He continued to walk and survey the interior as well as the tools and equipment. A different sound as he walked caught Gabe's attention, and he stopped, backed up a few steps, then started again. *Strange, this here piece a floor got a diff'rent sound fum th' rest.* He walked around the shed again then returned to the rear and walked the area that had caught his attention. *Yep, fer shore she's diff'rent. Don' make sense. Johnson were fer shore a first rate carpenter. Cain't figger whut'd be diff'rent 'bout this one spot. Cain't be rot. Reckin ah'll jest lift a board er two 'n' give 'er a look.*

The honk of a vehicle horn interrupted his search for the tools he needed. *Plannin' fella must be early. B'lieve checkin' th' floor'll have ta wait fer 'nother time. Don't much matter time wise. She fer shore ain't a goin' nowhere.*

CHAPTER 65

Full Circle

A dignified and strikingly attractive middle-aged woman sat quietly at her desk in a small, but well-appointed office. Nothing was unusual about this, except her office's location. It was on the ground floor of an eighteen-room Victorian mansion. The opulent home was situated on West Shore Drive in the affluent community of Smoke Rise, New Jersey. The small clock on the desk read two forty-eight p.m. She had been waiting for more than seven months for the call that was due to come in at three.

Her initial call, made eight months ago, from a disposable cell phone, was to another cell phone in Washington, DC. When her call was answered, there was little social interaction. "Sam, this is Sarah. I need a big favor. A very good investigator—actually, the best there is. These are my requirements—thorough, low-key, discreet, and one-hundred-percent trustworthy. Do you know someone?"

There was silence on the other end, for about one minute.

"Nice to hear from you, too, Sarah. I believe that I've got the perfect person—left the Marines about two years ago. Works independently and will travel wherever the job requires. His lips are tighter than a flea's asshole. Nothing slips out. One thing more, he's not cheap, but I know that's not a problem."

"Sounds perfect. Fax me the data. I owe you a bottle of fine Bourbon."

With that last statement, the call had been ended.

Now eight months later, she had received a new fax. It arrived just two days ago. The message was simple. *This coming Wednesday, your phone, at three p.m.*

There was no signature. None was needed. She used a secured fax when privacy was of primary importance. Sam had once informed her that, due to the difficulty of tracing, they were less likely to be tracked. It was now two fifty-seven. She was suddenly aware that her pulse rate had elevated.

The tone of her cell phone tone startled her. She glanced reflexively at the desk clock. *Three o'clock. Can't ask for a more punctual person.* She let the tone sound two more times, letting her nerves settle, then answered. "Yes?"

A male voice responded. "Tomorrow, at the park off Cove Lane by the lake. Parking lot, third space from the north end. The one nearest the large oak tree. Seven a.m."

The call ended.

Eight months and forty-five thousand dollars. The answer will come tomorrow morning, and the final payment of thirty thousand dollars will be due. Sarah was both elated and nervous at the same time. It was not about the money—that was insignificant. She had instigated this improbable search for someone she had put out of her life thirty-two years ago. And now she finally felt secure enough to put closure to one of the most difficult decisions she had ever made. She was nineteen at the time, single, living and working in Manhattan. There she made a classic, youthful mistake—she mistook lust for love. Pregnant and scared, she sought out a midwife and gave birth in a small, uptown hotel. Two days later, in the bitter cold of a February night, she bundled the infant as warmly as possible and placed him in a large cardboard box. She had removed all tags and labels from the baby's clothes and blanket. Sarah left him along with a simple note on the receiving platform of the Mount Sinai Hospital. Sarah abandoned her baby and returned to her parent's home, determined to pick up the pieces and start her life over.

But a nagging sensation had started to eat at her more than ten years ago. She couldn't pin it down, at first, but year after year it became stronger until one day the reason became evident. A frigid January night in Manhattan, her anguished desperation, the need for secrecy—all of it flashed through her mind as if it were yesterday. *I have to find out what became of my baby.* Tomorrow she should have her answer.

∽∾∿

The parking lot was completely empty. It was a chilly fall morning and other than a scattering of fallen leaves, an empty six-pack, and an indiscreetly discarded used condom the entire area was devoid of anything resembling human activity. It was six-fifty when Sarah pulled in, drove through the lot, and parked in the third spot near the north end. The huge oak tree, just adjacent to her spot, was an eye-catching blaze of autumn red leaves. On the car seat, to her right, were her handbag and a plain white bakery bag. In that bag, neatly bundled, was thirty-thousand dollars in cash.

Seven-oh-two. He's always been spot-on punctual. She looked around and saw a car approaching slowly from the far end of the parking lot. *That must be him.* As the car drew closer, very recognizable details proved her wrong. *Shit! It's the police. I doubt he'll show right now.*

The patrol car pulled alongside, and the officer opened his window. "You okay, ma'am?"

"Yes, thank you. I just needed a quiet place to sit and think for a while."

"If you don't mind, I'll just take a look." *Could be someone down low on the front or rear seat.* He put his car in "park" and climbed out. As he did, he released the strap that secured his pistol in his holster. He approached the silver Mercedes from the rear on the passenger's side. He took his job very seriously. *If someone's hiding, they'll expect me on the driver's side.* "Ma'am, please open the rear windows." *Wish they'd outlaw that damn tint-darkened glass.*

She pressed the buttons to open the rear windows then enquired, "I'm not doing something wrong by parking here, am I, Officer?"

He had completed his check. "No, you're not. It's just that we can't be too careful in this crazy world."

"I fully understand and appreciate your precautions, Officer. Thank you." She watched as he got back in his patrol car and drove off in the direction from which he had come. The clock on the dash now showed seven-eighteen. *I'll give him until seven-thirty then try the contact number.*

Sarah's eyes were now focused on the drive at the end of the parking area, the spot where the patrol car had disappeared. *Come on—come on! Where are you?* Subconsciously, she was attempting, mentally, to will him to appear. A sharp tap on her window startled her, and she turned abruptly toward the intruding sound.

A man dressed in clean, casual attire with a military style haircut backed away a few steps. He appeared to be in his mid thirties. With a circular hand motion, he indicated that she should open the car window. "I thought that cop would stay forever. He's good, though, quite thorough and very professional. I was behind the oak and observing, but enough about him. Let's get to our business." He raised his left hand high enough above the base of the car window, enough for her to see a large manila envelope. It was devoid of markings, but she knew it would contain her answers. "Why don't you slide over? I'll drive, and you can concentrate on the data. I'll answer any of your questions and explain, as needed."

There was no question about the logic of his suggestion. Sarah knew that his primary reason was to avoid sitting in one place for too long a period. She exited the car and walked around. It was definitely more dignified than the acrobatics it would have required for her to climb over the center console.

He slid into the driver's seat and started the engine. As he put the car in drive, he offered a quick introduction. "Name's Gerald, and the envelope contains everything that you requested, and more."

Sarah took a deep breath, paused for a moment, then opened the envelope. She slid the contents out and slowly fanned the enclosed sheaf of papers, scanning as she went. *My God! This is unbelievable. He's got copies of every document from his admission in Mount Sinai's ER, to the registration of the baby into The Sisters of Mercy Orphanage, to his high school diploma and his Marine induction papers. A few of these are supposed to be "sealed." How did—*

She let that thought go. Sam said he was the best, and this certainly was proof enough. How he obtained the documents was irrelevant. Sarah looked first at the copy of the birth certificate. *They listened to my request and named him Jon.* That brought a soft smile to her lips. Her eyes misted. A smaller envelope, enclosed with the documents, yielded a number of photographs. They were sequentially ordered, starting with the ER photos in the hospital and progressing to one of Jon in full dress Marine uniform. *He's even more handsome than his father was.* "Gerald—What about the present? Is he well? Where is he living, and is he married? Does he have children, and what does he do for a living?"

Her final barrage of questions had been anticipated, well in advance. "The answers to all of the questions you just posed are in this one." He reached into the breast pocket of his jacket and withdrew another envelope—not quite as large as the first. He placed the second envelope in Sarah's outstretched hand. He was still driving at a casual rate of speed, without specific direction, through the peaceful suburban streets.

Sarah wasn't sure why, but a hint of nervousness had taken hold. *Probably the fact that three-plus decades of unknowns are about to become, for better or worse, the known. Oh, well, here goes nothing.*

The envelope contained a slim, spiral-bound notebook, somewhat like what a person would use as a personal journal. The front or starting point was quite evident. She turned back the cover and was greeted with a photo of a brick ranch house that appeared to have been built in the late nineteen-fifties or early sixties. A simple caption noted *subject's home.* Below the caption was the physical address, zip code, and phone number. The next page contained another picture: *subject's business.* It was a commercial fishing boat. The name *Adventure II* was painted on the prow. When the page was turned, the explanation was there. *The subject lives in Kure Beach, in southeastern North Carolina. When he retired from the Marines, he took up commercial fishing and has been at it for just over four years.* This was followed by several pages of pictures of Jon, one holding hands with a very attractive blonde. Sarah couldn't help her happy thoughts. *She's quite pretty, and they appear to be quite fond of each other.*

The next page destroyed the happiness. *The subject was involved in an off-the-record altercation with a number of South American nationals. During that action, a propane tank explosion left the subject physically uninjured but in a deep coma. He has been in that comotose condition for more than six months. The current prognosis is vague. The doctors have stated that he could awake at any moment or remain in a comatose state until death. He no longer requires hospitalization and has been moved to the home of his closest friend, one Carlos Montoto, wife, Rosita. They live in Carolina Beach, on the same island. The address is 29 Quince Court. A nurse and a physical therapist visit once a day. The girlfriend had been coming daily, but that is tapering off.* Sarah closed the journal and sat silently, alone with a whirlwind of thoughts.

"Ma'am, we're here." Sarah looked up. They were back in the parking lot, same space, by the oak tree. "Do you have any questions, and have I fulfilled the assignment to your satisfaction?"

Sarah could think of nothing that had been missed and, after a moment responded, "No questions, Gerald. You've more than covered the assignment." She handed him the plain white bakery bag. "I believe this covers our agreement."

He glanced quickly into the bag then stepped out of the car. Gerald turned back to face her. "It's a damn shame. He was the finest team leader I ever had the pleasure of serving with."

After Gerald's last remark, he turned and jogged into the brush next to the oak tree. He didn't wait for her response to his statement.

His last statement slammed home with an impact, coupled with an audible gasp. *My God! He knew Jon, personally.* She looked, hopefully, toward the bushes, but he had completely disappeared. She was about to call after him but changed her mind. *I'm sure I'd just be yelling at air. I have his contact number if I need more answers.* Her mind was now running at a breakneck pace. Myriad thoughts, regrets, hopes, and scenarios were racing around in her head. The car was idling, the driver's door still open as Gerald had left it, assuming she would immediately change her position. She was aware of none of this, being totally consumed by the facts just delivered.

"Ma'am, are you sure you're okay?" It was the same police officer who had checked on her when she had first arrived. He was leaning in through the still opened driver's door.

The sound of his voice snapped her train of thought and brought her back to reality. "Yes, I'm quite sure." She fabricated a quick excuse. "I changed seats in order to stretch out for a bit and must have dozed off. Honestly, I'm really okay." She glanced at the dashboard clock. *Eight thirty-seven.* "I really should get home."

"Yes, ma'am. You need to be careful about leaving the engine running. Carbon monoxide, you know. If it's all the same with you, I'll just follow and make sure you get home okay. What's your address?"

Sarah gave him the street number on West Shore Drive, thanked him for his concern, and started for home. A quick glance in the rearview mirror showed the officer's vehicle just a car length's distance behind. In the short amount of time it took her to get home, she had made what amounted to a life-changing decision and a firm commitment. *I've got to get to Carolina Beach, and finally meet my son.*

CHAPTER 66

At Last

The flight from the Newark, New Jersey, Liberty International Airport to Wilmington, North Carolina's ILM Airport, arrived five minutes early. *I guess that's the advantage of flying into a small airport.*

The baggage claim area was a right turn and a short walk after exiting the gate area. She stood and waited by the carousel for her one bag. In less than ten minutes, suitcase in hand, Sarah was on her way to the car rentals area, and rented a mid-size Dodge sedan. Now armed with directions, coupled with a route-marked map offered by the rental agent, she was on her way to 29 Quince Court, Carolina Beach.

It was Friday at five p.m. The sky was a brushstroke canvas of multiple colors, one of the Cape Fear region's exquisite sunsets. The weather was quite mild for an early November evening when Sarah drove slowly down Quince Court. Both sides of the road were lined with simple brick ranch style homes, common construction from the late fifties to the mid-eighties. Number 29 was at the end of the cul-de-sac.

Sarah parked on the street, took a couple of deep breaths to relax, walked to the door, and rang the bell. An attractive Hispanic woman answered the door. Sarah asked a simple but direct question, "*Este es la casa Montoto?*"

Rosita Montoto responded to the obviously American-accented Spanish cautiously. "*Si, corecto. Hablemos Inglés si tu quieres.*"

She said nothing else and waited for the stranger to state the reason for her visit.

Sarah was relieved that she didn't have to strain her way through Spanish. "My name is Sarah Taylor, and I live in New Jersey. If my information is correct, you have a house guest by the name of Jon Morton. Is that so?"

Rosita was not at all prepared for that question from a total stranger and was immediately on guard. She stepped out of the doorway and quickly closed the house door behind her. She responded brusquely. "What makes you think that, and why do you ask?"

As Sarah was about to begin what would seem an almost impossible explanation, a pickup truck came down the street and pulled into the driveway, parking on a concrete pad adjacent to the garage. Rosita was instantly relieved and, as soon as the driver stepped out of the pickup, she called out, "Carlos, *venga aqui, rapidamente.*"

Carlos caught the tone of his wife's urgent request and walked quickly toward the two women. "What's up, *querida?*"

"This lady says that someone told her that Jon Morton is staying here."

Carlos reverted, instantly, to the past. *What kind of trouble do we have now? Sure wish my Glock was on my belt and not inside in my desk.* There had been too many wild events over the past year, and the last of them had left Jon in a coma, now nearing the end of its sixth month. Carlos was less than polite. "Who told you that, and why do you care whether he is or isn't here?"

At this point, it was immediately evident to Sarah that she had touched a very sensitive nerve. It was also quite apparent that Jon was in this house. There was no point in trying to be subtle. That would get her nowhere. "Let me explain by showing you something. Please give me a moment." She turned and walked briskly back to her car. It took less than two minutes for her to retrieve what she was after and return to Carlos and Rosita. "I want you to look at the contents of these two envelopes, starting with the larger. I'll wait." She handed over the results of Gerald's extensive investigation, walked slowly to a nearby porch swing, and took a seat.

Carlos opened the larger envelope and, together with Rosita, started thumbing through the pictures and documents. Now and then they would stop to read or go back to check. Their conversation was all in Spanish and much too low for Sarah to pick up. The now-reviewed contents of the larger packet were returned to the envelope, and the couple proceeded to the smaller one. It was evident by their actions and posture that their attitude had changed dramatically. When they had finished with the second envelope, they both looked as if they were in shock, standing quietly and deep in thought.

Sarah arose and walked slowly back to the couple. "Carlos, I know that you and Jon were in the Marines, together. The investigator who conducted this search for me was also in the Corps, and served with you. His name is Gerald. Does that ring a bell?"

Carlos didn't respond at first. The name was familiar but from where? Suddenly came the moment of recognition. *Madre de Dios! The Colombia mission.* "Please, Ms. Taylor, our sincere apologies. We're being rude. Won't you come in and have coffee, perhaps stay for dinner?"

"Of course, I will, and please don't apologize. I fully understand your situation and the need to protect Jon's privacy."

One hour later, after a rather casual but intense session of questions and answers between the three of them, one fact became glaringly evident. Sarah was truly Jon's birth mother. There was a short period of silence while each of them adjusted to this monumental revelation.

Carlos broke the silence. "I have to tell you the truth. Jon spent a lot of time searching for his parents, and, when he found no one, gave up and moved on." He was quiet again, but after just a minute broached the subject that was now looming over them. "I suppose that, after all you've done to find Jon, you'd like to see him." He waited for a response.

Sarah was silent, at first. Her thoughts were coming at breakneck speed. Her nerves were at a level of tension, never before experienced. Finally, she answered. "I would very much like to see Jon, but I need to calm down. I think if I were to see him now, I'd break down or collapse. If it's all right with both of you, I would prefer to return in the morning, when I'm rested and have had time to sort out my emotions."

Rosita seized the moment. "But, of course, we fully understand." She changed the subject to reduce the tension. "Would you care to stay for dinner? Please. It would be our pleasure."

Sarah thought about the offer for a moment then accepted. "It would be my pleasure to have dinner with you." She knew inwardly that this would also reduce everyone's tension and make tomorrow's meeting much smoother. "May I help in any way?"

"Absolutely not." Rosita was resolute. "You are our guest. Perhaps a glass of wine or a cocktail?"

"Do you happen to have any scotch?"

"We do. Neither Carlos nor I drink it, but we keep a bottle of Jon's favorite on hand for him. It's called Laphroaig."

"Sounds like a single-malt. That'll be perfect. Just in a glass, no ice or water."

Carlos was shaking his head slowly, in amazement. "That's just how Jon drinks it. He likes it in a brandy snifter—says it enhances the flavor and aroma."

"Well, if you have a snifter, I'll try it that way."

❦

Dinner was excellent. Rosita prepared a cubed pork shoulder, slow baked in *salsa verde*, served over rice, and accompanied by fried plantains. During dinner, almost all conversation revolved around Jon, his relationship with Carlos and Rosita, and of course, what had brought Sarah to this point.

Sarah glanced at her watch. "Oh dear, it's after nine. I apologize for disrupting your evening and staying so late. You've both been wonderful to me, and I can easily see why Jon has you as friends. I should really be going. How early may I return tomorrow?"

Rosita answered immediately. "The morning nurse comes at seven and is usually here for about one hour. Any time after eight will be fine. It has truly been a surprise and pleasure to meet you. I only wish the circumstances were better."

A slow nod of agreement was Sarah's reply to Rosita's last statement. "That sounds perfect. I look forward to seeing you, tomorrow, at eight."

Carlos stood in the doorway, Rosita at his side, watching Sarah walk to her car. "*Madre de Dios*. This is amazing. Maybe even a miracle. Let us pray that Jon recovers and can meet this woman, his mother."

Rosita offered a simple response, "*Si, querido*." She turned back into the house as Carlos slowly pulled the door shut.

CHAPTER 67

The Meeting

There was a white medical van in the driveway when Sarah arrived, the next morning. It was ten after eight. *I guess the nurse must be running behind schedule, to-day.* Sarah parked the rental car on the side of the road and walked to the door. She was about to ring the bell when Carlos opened the door.

"*Buenos dias*, Ms. Taylor."

"*Buenos dias*, Carlos. Was the nurse late, today or is there a problem?"

"No problem. Today is one of the days that Jon gets a bath so that takes a little more time. It should just be a few minutes more. Come in and have coffee with us. Rosita has some fresh pastry—please."

"Thank you, Carlos. That sounds excellent."

The aroma of fresh brewed coffee filled the air as they walked to the dining room. There were three settings at the table, and a large platter of assorted pastry was accompanied by a bowl of fresh fruit.

There's something positive to be said for Spanish hospitality. "This looks delicious, Carlos. I would have been happy with just coffee."

"*Buenos dias*, Sarah." Rosita's voice carried from the kitchen. "Just coffee is no way to treat a special guest. Please have a seat. I'll be right there."

In spite of the warm welcome, Sarah was aware that her

nerves were on edge, and she was experiencing a heightened sense of excitement, coupled with an overriding state of anxiety. *Thirty-two years is a long gap in time to meet a total stranger who is your only son.*

Rosita walked into the room, breaking into Sarah's thoughts. "*Vamos a comer.* Sarah, please help yourself, while I pour the coffee."

Their casual breakfast was interrupted by a soft male voice. "Excuse me, Mr. and Mrs. Montoto. I'm all set." An Oriental man, in a white uniform, was standing at the dining room entrance.

Carlos asked one simple question, which had become routine. "Any change?"

"As a matter of fact, yes, his blood pressure has come up a few points, his skin color has improved slightly, and his output is not as dark. These are all positive signs, but don't get too hopeful. They could easily go the other way. We need to remain hopeful and see if this becomes a pattern of positive progression. Enjoy your breakfast. I'll let myself out and will see you on Monday." The nurse turned and started for the door.

Carlos was smiling, broadly. "Positive signs. Hopefully, that means he's coming back to us." His statement was directed to Rosita, as he had not yet fully accepted Sarah's position.

Sarah asked Rosita, politely. "Was that man the nurse?"

"Yes. He's very good, efficient, and extremely professional. He's been taking care of Jon for just over five months and has never missed a day."

Sarah was not ignorant of the kind of expense those nursing visits represented. "That must be a very expensive form of care." She was trying to politely avoid the evident kind of strain that in-house nursing could place on an obviously middle-class household. She also was not a total stranger to the personal pride of Hispanics.

"Yes, I'm sure that it is very expensive, but we have no idea of the amount. Jon's former military commander made all of the arrangements, and it has not cost us a single penny. We have a few minor additional expenses, yet these are no different than what we would incur for a house-guest, under normal circumstances."

Rosita's statement gave Sarah one more bit of information. *Whatever Jon did when he was in the Marines, it had to be of a very sensitive nature. That's the only way the military would pick up these expenses.* "May I see Jon, now, Rosita?"

"Now would be good. He always seems at his best after Lee's visits. You can talk to him. Of course, he won't answer, but the specialist said that people in this state can hear what you say, and sometimes it helps to connect their brain back to the conscious world. The doctors have told us that the form of coma Jon is experiencing is called psychogenic. It's as if his mind has found a secure hiding place. Let's go."

CHAPTER 68

The Reunion

Rosita led the way down the hall and stopped at a partially closed room door. "Let me make a quick check, before you go in." She stepped into the room and pushed the door back to its partially closed position. "Good morning, Jon." Her voice was bright and cheery. "How are you today? Did you have a good night? I have a surprise for you this morning. You have a visitor."

Sarah's heart was pounding as she listened to Rosita talking to Jon. *This couple and Jon must have an extraordinary relationship. She sounds so positive and upbeat, even more so than a family member would be.*

"Sarah, you can come in now. Jon is definitely ready for some new company."

The door she was about to push open was not just to a room, but to a piece of her life that she had mentally closed the door on approximately thirty-two years ago. She hesitated for a moment. The questions, doubts, and fears all started to rear up. *At this point, it doesn't matter. I can't change the past. I can't alter the present and can only hope that maybe—just maybe I can change the future, hopefully, for Jon, and possibly for me.* She stepped softly into the room, as if treading on dangerous footing.

"Jon, I want you to meet your new visitor, Sarah Taylor. She has come a long way to meet you."

Sarah walked hesitantly to the bedside. A rapid visual

search of the immediate area in and around the bed showed the IV unit and line. She didn't miss the auxiliary oxygen tank and the partially hidden catheter drain. All of these she put out of her mind and concentrated only on the inert man, her son, in the bed. "Good morning, Jon. Yes, I've come a long way to meet and visit with you—a very long way." She looked back at Rosita, an unspoken question on her face.

"I will leave the two of you alone for a while, to allow you to visit privately." Rosita departed and again pulled the door to a nearly closed position.

Sarah turned back to Jon, staring hard at his evident good looks. Without warning, thirty-two years of suppressed emotions, the mental protection that came with the total abandonment of this man, when just a two-days-old infant, came flooding to the surface. Her strength dissolved into gut-wrenching sobs and tears, at an uncontrollable level.

Almost five minutes passed before Sarah was able to regain control of her emotions. The door to the room opened slowly. "Sarah, perhaps you should take a short break." Rosita had been standing outside of the door all the time that Sarah was alone with Jon.

"I think that's a good idea. Do you have any more coffee?"

"But, of course." Rosita turned toward the bed. "Jon, your visitor is a little tired from her journey. I'll give her some coffee and have her back, soon."

Sarah made a hurried exit, and Rosita followed, pulling the door shut behind her. When they reached the dining room, Carlos caught the "look" from Rosita and excused himself. "I need to get a few things organized in the garage."

Rosita poured two cups of coffee. "Let's sit in the living room. It's more relaxed."

"That should help. My nerves are wound up tighter than an eight-day clock."

They sat for almost ten minutes—saying nothing, just sipping their coffee. Finally, Rosita had to break the silence. "Do you think you should tell him who you are? I think it might give him a push toward recovery. You know—a chance to meet a person he's been seeking for his entire life."

"What if he never recovers?" Sarah choked on a sob.

"Then at least you will have had the opportunity to tell him who you are, and if you wish, why you left." Rosita had said what she felt must be said. Now she waited for a response.

Fifteen minutes of silence then Sarah answered. "Rosita, you're right. Thank you." This was followed by another short period of silence. "One thing more, I was married to a wonderful man. Unfortunately, I lost him to cancer." She held up a hand to stop Rosita from interjecting. "He left me very wealthy. I would need three lifetimes to spend what I have. If you and Carlos need anything, for Jon or yourselves, just let me know. I'll leave you my card. It has my address and all of my contacts. I also want you to have this." She stood, walked over to Rosita, and handed her a small envelope along with her personal card. "Now I'm ready to make my peace with my son," she declared as she rose and started for the guest bedroom.

Rosita placed the card and the envelope on a side table, poured some more coffee, and waited. Her wait was almost two hours. Carlos had come back in and was sitting with her, talking quietly, until Sarah reappeared.

One look and it was evident that a lot more tears had been shed.

"I can't thank you enough for taking care of Jon and for affording me the opportunity to see him and have some very special alone time with him. Words can't express what this has meant to me."

"Won't you stay for dinner?"

"As much as I would love to, any more time under these circumstances would tear my heart out. No, it's best that I go now and pray that Jon will come back and give me the opportunity to truly meet him. Thank you, both of you, so, so much. Now I must go. Rosita, remember what I said. Promise me that you'll do that."

"*Si*, Sarah, I promise."

The three of them walked to the door. Sarah hugged each of them, tightly, stepped outside, and walked without any hesitation to her car.

Carlos and Rosita watched and waved as Sarah drove away. "Rosita, I need to look in on Jon before the day nurse arrives. Maybe Sarah's visit made a change."

"*Bueno*. Also, I forgot, Sarah gave me her address and phone number, but she also gave me a small envelope, which I neglected to open." The two of them turned back, Carlos in the direction of the guest bedroom and Rosita toward the living room.

Carlos returned to the living room in just a few moments, a look of sadness on his face. "No change or at least none that I can see." It was then that he noticed his wife and the expression of amazement on her face. "What is it?"

"When I picked up the envelope, I noticed that something was written on the outside. It says simply, 'To be used as needed.' I opened the envelope and this was inside." She handed Carlos a check in the amount of twenty-five thousand dollars, made out to Mr. and Mrs. Carlos Montoto. On the reference line it stated *care for Jon Morton*.' "She told me that she was very wealthy and to contact her if more or anything else was needed."

Carlos was staring, open-mouthed, at the check when the doorbell rang. "That must be the day nurse."

CHAPTER 69

Surprises

Carlos rushed to open the door. "Sheri! Come in. We thought it was the nurse. Would you care for some coffee? You won't believe what just happened. Come into the living room. Rosita is there."

Together they filled Sheri in on the totally unexpected appearance of Jon's mother and how she had located them. The only reaction from Sheri was a faint and fleeting smile.

The dramatic change in Sheri's demeanor was noticed instantly by Rosita. "Sheri, what's wrong? Is your mother okay? Has something happened?"

Sheri's face took on a pained look. "Mom's fine. It's me. I have a problem."

"You're not sick, are you?"

"No, and yes—heartsick is what it is. You both know how deeply I love Jon, and how I was prepared to spend the rest of my life with him." She held up her hand to stop Rosita from commenting. "Please let me continue, uninterrupted. Whatever Jon's job or position was, when in the Marine's, I have figured out that it wasn't ordinary military duty—maybe even what they refer to as black operations. Whatever it was, his past keeps coming back and, on three occasions, has nearly gotten him killed. This last time has left him in a coma, and no one knows when or if he'll ever come out of it. The bottom line is this. I can't go on like this. I can't live from day to day, wondering if he'll ever get better or, if he does, when the next life-

and-death event will occur. I'm here to say goodbye." Tears began to well up in her eyes, her voice choked. She took a deep breath to regain her composure and continued. "My hopes and dreams have been shattered, and I need to rebuild myself. The two of you are some of the most wonderful people I know, but I can't continue with our relationship without some aspect of Jon always being there. I am here to say good-bye—to him, to you. I will leave him a sealed letter of explanation, and I ask that it remain sealed, only to be read by him, if he recovers." Then she rose and walked stoically back to the guest bedroom.

Rosita sat with tears streaming down her cheeks. Carlos looked as if he'd been struck by lightning.

Sheri pushed open the guest room door, entered, and closed the door behind her. She took a deep breath, steeled her resolve, and began her goodbye. When she had said all she had to and could, she placed a sealed letter on the dresser, walked back to the bed, leaned over, and gave Jon a soft kiss on the forehead. "Goodbye, my love. *Vaya con Dios.*" She turned away from Jon's bed, and, without a single glance back, walked quickly out of the room.

Rosita and Carlos both stood as she came into the living room. Tears were still running down Rosita's cheeks. Sheri held her index finger to her lips and gave an almost imperceptible, negative shake of her head. She was emotionally unable to talk and, by her actions indicated that they, likewise, should say nothing. She gathered the two of them tightly in her arms for a long and emotion-filled hug. When she released her hold, she stepped back and smiled thinly at both of them. "*A Dios, mis amigos.*"

Sheri turned without another word, walked out of the room, out through the front door, and out of their lives.

The guest room was occupied only by Jon after Sheri departed. If someone had walked into Jon's room, immediately after Sheri walked out, and if they had looked at Jon very carefully, it was possible they might have spotted it. A tear, perhaps two, had welled up and slipped out from the corner of one of his closed eyes. The watery emotion trickled slowly down his cheek, without witness, without a record, and without a sound. The tiny rivulet of liquid anguish was immediately absorbed, disappearing forever into the soft cotton fabric of the pillow case.

About the Author

J J Burke was born in Brooklyn NY and, through subsequent moves, spent the majority of his formative years in New Rochelle, NY (Westchester County). He attended the Philadelphia Textile Institute and has been a prolific reader all of his life. He was first introduced to the joy of writing, and encouraged to pursue it, by his college English Professor. He wrote for his college newspaper and prepared business advertising copy for local and national printed media. His first exercise in fiction was demonstrative writing for his older son. Burke was more than pleased with the results and was "hooked," but never went any further with writing as a serious pursuit, until now.

Burke's business career started in the textile industry, which was where his international travels began. These travels covered Canada, northern South America, some areas of Central America, Europe, and a number of Caribbean islands—Cuba being the primary one. He and his wife of twenty-nine years live in southeastern North Carolina. He is self employed as a residential appraiser.

His first novel, *The Lethal Fisherman*, employs some of what he experienced on a firsthand basis, and some from acquaintances, as well as the use of his current location as a geographical background. This is the first novel of a trilogy. The idea to write this novel came to him when walking his dog at four-thirty a.m. It was unusually dark that morning and he muttered, "God it's dark." He walked a few steps farther and decided that would be a good line in a story. After just a few days of thought, he sat down and began.

Burke enjoys woodworking, cooking (he cooked professionally for ten years), and when time permits, fishing and travel. A favorite enjoyment of his is dining out and experiencing new restaurants and cuisines.